HALC

HALO

BROKEN CIRCLE

JOHN SHIRLEY

BASED ON THE BESTSELLING VIDEO GAME FOR XBOX

G

GALLERY BOOKS

New York | London | Toronto | Sydney | New Delhi

G

Gallery Books
A Division of Simon & Schuster, Inc.
1230 Avenue of the Americas
New York, NY 10020

First Gallery Books trade paperback edition November 2014

GALLERY BOOKS and colophon are registered trademarks of Simon & Schuster, Inc.

For information about special discounts for bulk purchases, please contact Simon & Schuster Special Sales at 1-866-506-1949 or business@simonandschuster.com.

The Simon & Schuster Speakers Bureau can bring authors to your live event. For more information or to book an event, contact the Simon & Schuster Speakers Bureau at 1-866-248-3049 or visit our website at www.simonspeakers.com.

Interior design by Leydiana Rodríguez-Ovalles
Jacket art by John Liberto

Manufactured in the United States of America

10   9   8   7   6   5

Library of Congress Cataloging-in-Publication Data is available.

ISBN 978-1-4767-8359-8
ISBN 978-1-4767-8360-4 (ebook)

To all the fans of the Halo universe,
be they in this solar system
or elsewhere in the galaxy.

PROLOGUE

San'Shyuum-Sangheili War
Skirmish of the Planet of Blue and Red
Circa 860 BCE
The First Age of Conflict

Mken 'Scre'ah'ben, a San'Shyuum High Lord of Sacred Relics, floated toward the open hatchway. He paused his antigrav chair at the door and listened, fascinated by the discordant singing of an alien world: the screeching of the planet's endlessly churning winds.

"The enemy is just beyond the ridge, High Lord," warned the Steward, his military advisor and—theoretically—his bodyguard. "There is no need to leave the pod. It would be wiser to observe from orbit, using the Eyes. The Sangheili are fierce and cunning."

High Lord Mken gave a dismissive gesture. "I have never been here before, and I will see this world firsthand. I am not without experience in combat. But if you are anxious, Steward, I shall be wary. My chair is weaponized—and I have you at hand. Stay close, but do not distract me."

"Your orders are a joy to fulfill." The Steward held back, adjusting his antigrav belt and noisily checking his pulse rifle. He seemed a trifle annoyed about being put in his place. The Steward was no doubt aware that, with his chair, Mken was better suited to protect the Steward than the reverse.

Still, Mken was indeed wary of this world, in spite of his bland bravado. He was not terribly comforted by the emplaced force field projectors set up near the pod—they moderated the wind, but would they protect him from attack? He scanned the sky for Sangheili fighter craft as he drifted his chair out the drop pod's air lock. Here he paused, his chair hovering over the blast-scarred stone the pod had landed on, and swayed his long, gold-skinned neck with sinuous aplomb as he gazed curiously about, taking in the striking color contrasts, gust-flailed dunes, and rocky outcroppings of the planet's principal continent.

The constantly shifting, shrieking winds were partly a product of the celestial objects that also gave this world its dual coloration: the blue dwarf star hanging in the sky to Mken's left, the much larger red-giant sun to his right, both just forty-five degrees above opposite horizons. As per the High Lord's orders, the pod had set down right on the Purple Line so he could appreciate the contrasting views. Hierarch J'nellin had been right to note in his monograph on the Planet of Red and Blue that the remarkable duality of hue, along either side of the Purple Line, was one of the wonders of the galaxy. On the left, the outcroppings and dunes were all gradations of blue, the sand lighter blue, the rocks darker; on the right, rugged landscape was entirely red, muted or emphatic, but all the way to the horizon. Only the relatively narrow Purple Line mixed the colors. The two suns in the binary-star system, one closer than the other, were always at the same angle, with respect to this motionless world, for there was no night on this side; the planet was prevented from spinning by the interlocking gravitational fields of the two stars. They played an eternal game of push-and-pull that would someday rip the planet apart. But until then, millennia from now, this world's placement in the galaxy made it of strategic importance to the war effort; perhaps more important, there were Forerunner relics here in this area, and more buried in other parts of the planet—the Luminary had confirmed it. The necessity of investigating Forerunner relics was the only reason the San'Shyuum had descended from high orbit to the surface of this world, risking certain confrontation with the armed and dangerous Sangheili.

The shaped stones near the pod were the remnants of an ancient city belonging to an extinct species, an unknown biped . . . but on the jutting stones were carvings that suggested they had a knowledge of the Forerunners, who had been here even earlier than the stone carvers.

The densely compact blue sun was in the east; the bigger, sprawling, more diffuse red sun bulked in the west; the planet's winds, urged by the opposed gravity that flexed back and forth, slashed first one way and then another, constantly eroding the stones with a kind of relentless brushing, turning them gradually into dunes that gave off ghostly plumes of dust and sand, plumes that shifted with the winds, as if doing a primitive dance. The red dancers flitted on one side, the blue on the other.

"It truly is a marvel," sighed Mken, absently adjusting his robes. A commander's ornately sewn ceremonial robes were impressive but not pragmatic; under them, he was fitted with clinging body armor. "It is worth the risk."

His Steward grunted noncommittally, then, remembering himself, muttered, "Your insights shine like the hub of the galaxy, High Lord."

The Steward's tendency to engage in superfluous, honorific courtesies was a mild source of annoyance to Mken. There was a subtle touch of mockery in the old-fashioned usages, which might reflect the Steward's awareness that he was chronologically elder to Mken, but having come from a lower-caste brood, was forever obliged to serve as a subordinate.

Gazing at the eerily beautiful landscape, Mken knew he was indulging his connoisseur side overmuch. He had once dreamed of being merely a relic historian, and had spent many glorious cycles studying the niceties of Forerunner design and ancient holographic renderings of the San'Shyuum homeworld, Janjur Qom.

Thinking of their homeworld, even looking at the holographs, always made him melancholy. Mken's branch of the San'Shyuum had been forced to renounce the cradle of their civilization, their planet of origin, in the aftermath of the Stoic-Reformist conflict. Mken and his peers came from the Reformist line, which had fled the homeworld in the Dreadnought—the Forerunner keyship that had been the focus of the civil war between Stoics and Reformists. And the Reformists had set about searching for sacred Forerunner relics throughout the galaxy . . . until nearly eighty cycles ago, when they had come upon the Sangheili squatting in the shadow of numerous Forerunner artifacts. The war-mad saurian race had worshipped Forerunner vestiges without regard to their true utility. Worse, they had refused to allow the San'Shyuum access. The Sangheili in turn were horrified to see that the San'Shyuum actually used some Forerunner relics for practical purposes. To the Sangheili it was desecration, heresy.

Mken's people tried conciliating the Sangheili, sending a delegation that explained that the San'Shyuum, under the direction of their Prophets, also worshipped the Forerunners . . . but to no avail. The delegates had been butchered, summarily slaughtered by the Sangheili. An all-out war had begun—and continued ever since.

"Ah well," said Mken, rippling the three long fingers of his right hand in the ancient gesture of regret—a sign that said *All things flow away.* "Let us get to work. Summon the Field Oversight surveillance officer. I shall consult the Eyes."

He tapped the armrest controls that summoned Eye Seven, then climbed out of the chair, stretching—he was expected to use an antigrav chair due to his high caste, but here his gravitational mod belt was enough, even in the substantial and eccentric gravity of the Planet of Blue and Red.

"High Lord," the Steward tautly remarked, "you make all too good a target by stepping out of your chair."

"We are well protected here," Mken replied. He watched as Eye Seven flew into sight, looking red itself in the western vista.

Roughly diamond-shaped, the glassy device drifted near and came to a stop. It hovered expectantly as Mken said, "Report enemy movements."

"Main enemy phalanx is northeast," the Eye responded. "They encamp beyond Ridge Fifteen, at Site Two. They are present with considerable defenses, but probability estimates suggest they plan to assault our Forerunner reliquary excavation at Site One."

"Not unexpected," Mken said thoughtfully. "Show me the key enemy positions."

The Eye projected a whirling beam of multicolored light that quickly built up a three-dimensional image of the Sangheili positions, seen from above and to the west, as per its long-distance observation. Mken stepped closer to the hologram, looking it over critically as his Steward walked around between the High Lord and the wilderness of stone and sand, nervously peering at the angling thrusts of rock formations.

In the image, Sangheili troops gathered protectively around a half-buried and tilted tower, the enormous Forerunner structure at Site Two, an imposing transmitter of some kind, sleek and efficient, showing little wear. Most of its immensity was hidden underground. Its sharp edges and polished surfaces contrasted with the red, dulled stone at the outskirts of the site. The entire scene was bathed red and red-brown in the elongated shadows.

The Sangheili were organized into roughly curving rows around the relic, facing toward the tentative San'Shyuum lines—tentative, because the San'Shyuum had no plans or forces for extensive ground combat. The San'Shyuum were simply outnumbered, and not physically capable of meeting the Sangheili at close quarters. The San'Shyuum defensive lines were here purely to protect relic hunters and retroengineering specialists. But the San'Shyuum's ground force did have the Sentinels: flying self-controlled assault constructs, shaped like squat, gray-and-white, one-eyed insects, with grapplers and antigrav undercarriages, their single "eye" a heat-beam projector. Although still something of a mystery, the Sentinels appeared to have been used by the Forerunners to defend specific installations and assets—but the San'Shyuum had adapted the Sentinels for their own purposes. The Sentinels and another, even more lethal Forerunner technology gave the San'Shyuum the edge. At least, Mken hoped it was so.

Looking closer at the hologram, Mken spotted the bunkers around Site Two—they had been reported to him before he'd come down to the surface. Beneath those bunkers were underground quarters. A great many of the Sangheili could retreat into them, if the Dreadnought was brought into play—a safe haven for the enemy, since the Dreadnought could not be used at full power where Forerunner artifacts might be damaged. Its most destructive energies were reserved for hit-and-run attacks in open space on Sangheili fleets, and had already been used with devastating results.

Before even the moderated energy of the Dreadnought could be used on Site One, San'Shyuum personnel needed to be evacuated first—when the time was right.

The San'Shyuum on this side of the ridge had been working at the Site One excavation for some time; plans had been made to excavate Site Two, but then the Sangheili assault force had descended, arraying itself around that tilted, half-buried tower.

No matter. The San'Shyuum scientists and those who protected them were ready to leave the combat zone at a moment's notice. Their drop pods were pulsing with energy, prepared for a quick jump to orbit. For now, though, it was useful to keep the Sangheili focused.

Mken noted enemy plasma cannons set up in advance of the Sangheili lines, angled to point up the slope leading to the ridge top. Near the center cannon, an imposing Sangheili officer in silver armor stood gesturing broadly, giving instructions to a group of underlings. This officer had the aura of authority and sharp awareness that Mken instinctively knew made him both interesting and dangerous.

He pointed at the silver-armored figure, his finger activating a spotlight on the Eye image of the Sangheili. "Is that Sangheili identifiable? Any information on him?"

"Sangheili identified as Ussa 'Xellus. Designation is Significant Field Commander, relatively young. Strong, quick, experienced. He came to this colony not long ago, and has completely reorganized its defenses. Surveillance shows him in almost constant activity. He is estimated as a high-innovation individual."

Mken stroked the furred wattles dangling from his jaws, tilting his oblong head thoughtfully. "Mark him for assassination, to be carried out as soon as the skirmish commences. Assign a squad of Sentinels."

"Marked for assassination," the Eye dutifully said.

Mken regretted the necessity. He'd have preferred to capture and interrogate the officer. He would like to know much more about the Sangheili, and this one might provide answers, perhaps even potentially act as liaison for the submission of the entire

Sangheili race. The San'Shyuum were aware of the need for ground troops—they could not use the Dreadnought everywhere at once, and they were sure to encounter more opposition on the Path to the Great Journey. The warlike, courageous Sangheili would make ideal allies, if they could be placed under San'Shyuum authority. To do that, they would have to be taught a lesson . . . would have to be shown that the San'Shyuum were their masters. If that Sangheili commander could be brought to heel . . .

"Belay that assassination order," Mken said after pondering a moment. "Perhaps that especially clever Sangheili can be useful . . . at some point."

"High Lord, I have a relayed report," the Eye said, its tip light flashing. "Eye Thirteen informs us that an incursion party of Sangheili is advancing toward our lines."

"You'd best go into the pod and handle this from orbit, High Lord," the Steward said anxiously.

"All in good time," Mken said. It was so tedious staying on the ship. He felt more alive here, on the edge of a battle. But it would be short, abortive—really, their defense would be a kind of feint, to draw the enemy into maximum concentration. The Sangheili, when dispersed, were difficult to annihilate. They were prone to organizing themselves into effective bands of transgressors.

The Eye relayed the image from Thirteen, reproducing it in front of Mken. He could now see about two hundred Sangheili advancing on foot toward the ridge and, beyond that, Forerunner Site One; the infantry was protectively flanked by hulking armored vehicles awkwardly floating on electromagnetic fields, sparking blue in the backdrop of red light. A sizable force remained behind to guard Forerunner Site Two.

How would the Forerunners feel, Mken wondered, knowing that two races who worshipped their memory were fighting to the death over control of their ancient sites? Mken suspected they would be appalled.

But he had his duty to perform.

"Deploy the Sentinels," he told the Eye. "See that they are not *too* effective. We do not wish the attack entirely stemmed—the Sangheili may retreat too soon. We will draw them into a better firing position." The Sangheili could conceal themselves in the bunkers around Site Two; the more who were trapped in the open, the better.

"From what I've heard," the Steward said quietly, "the Sangheili retreat only rarely. But the High Lord, imbued with inspiration, knows best . . ."

Mken ignored him and continued to watch the Sangheili advance—and noted there were now three columns of attack. The main force was heading straight up and over the ridge; two of the tanklike vehicles accompanied it. Two other tanks had joined a smaller force.

All were headed toward his position—Mken's own drop pod.

The third phalanx was behind the first wave, holding back but still advancing, and Mken suspected them of having a secondary objective. Because in their midst was Ussa, carrying a directed-energy rifle as he trudged up the steep incline.

Four Sentinels lifted from Site One and drifted horizontally, almost casually, over the ground toward the ridge. The Sangheili were just coming over the ridge's crest, weapons glinting faintly in the red tint. They immediately opened fire on the Sentinels, making the defensive fields on the machines flare. The Sentinels returned the assault, laserlike orange-yellow beams of murderous energy searing the Sangheili ranks. Some were struck repeatedly, charred and dead—but in accordance with orders, the Sentinels drew back and fired only sporadically.

Where was the Sangheili commander? Where was Ussa 'Xellus? Mken redirected the Eyes, and found Ussa and his smaller force taking to a small rift, a ravine slanting roughly toward Site One. They were coming at the site quickly, in a flanking maneuver, while the San'Shyuum were occupied with the main assault.

"We will have to cut off Ussa's flanking assault at—"

Mken didn't finish the order. A flash of sickly yellow light stunned his eyesight, and the ground pitched under him.

"They've knocked out the force fields!" the Steward shouted as he backed toward the drop pod, firing at something Mken couldn't see. "They've hit them from below! There's a tunnel in the—"

A lance of yellow energy struck upward from the collapsing ground—from an artificial sinkhole that now revealed the Sangheili assassins who'd detonated the tunnels under the force field generators.

The Steward shrieked, burned by the vicious energy beam, the eyes melting from his head. Mken choked at the smell of the Steward's burned flesh.

"Cunning," Mken muttered in admiration, hurrying back to the air lock even as two more searing bolts from the exposed tunnel struck the Eye, detonating it, and a third slashed through the air where Mken had stood only a moment before.

But Mken was in the air lock now, shouting for a seal and emergency liftoff. His gravitational mod belt kept him from being flung helplessly about as the pod lurched into the air.

"Strike forces, here are my orders!" Mken shouted as he floated into the pod's command seat. "Abandon Site One! Lift off and navigate clear of Dreadnought bombardment!"

"He's gotten away," observed Ussa 'Xellus, his head tilted back as he watched the pod rise toward orbit. "And he will be giving orders right about now." A couple of errant blasts from his assassins flicked after the pod, but it was already out of effective range.

His second-in-command, a large Sangheili colloquially hailed as Ernicka the Scar-Maker, was firing at the other pods already lifting off from the excavation known to the San'Shyuum as Site One. His rifle's energy bolt struck one of them, but to little effect. His multiple, clashing jaws quivered in angry frustration, their rows of teeth clacking.

"They were ready to go," Ussa mused. "All too ready. And those flying attack machines seemed curiously restrained. I suspect . . . they will fire their orbital weapon."

"They cannot fire on the excavation without damaging the Sacred Dome," Ernicka said. "Even they would not dare such blasphemy!"

"So I assumed," Ussa said. "Now I am not so sure. The dome is of Forerunner hardened energy and holy metals—it would depend on the magnitude of . . . yes!" His clawed four-fingered hand closed into a fist with which he struck his silvery armored chest, as if smiting himself in rebuke. "I've been a fool. Quickly—into the air chutes!"

"If we go down that way, we won't get back up for—"

"I said quickly! Tell the strike force to retreat, and to those we brought in the site—order them down into the chutes, now! There's not a second to waste!"

Equipped with a new chair, Mken sped into the orbiting shuttle's control room, shouting for the communications officer. "Signal the Dreadnought! I want the modulated cleansing beam on Site One! Hurry!"

"My Precious High Lord," the communications officer said, "it is a privilege to—"

"Just be quiet and do it!"

There was a moment as the officer conveyed the order and another as the Dreadnought's attack array—weapons the San'Shyuum had added to the ancient Forerunner keyship—powered up to firing capacity, drawing on energies the Forerunners had intended for other purposes, some of those unknown.

"Modulated beam prepared and focused, High Lord."

"Discharge!"

Mken could see the Dreadnought on a viewscreen, in orbit over the Purple Line, well above the churning atmosphere of the Planet of Blue and Red; the convergence of the Forerunner craft's armament was now pulsing with bright blue energy. Like a blade of fire, the energy suddenly stabbed down into the atmosphere. The viewscreen split to show its impact on Site One.

Mken silently prayed to the Prophets that the beam was modulated properly—their computational systems had assured him that the cleansing bolt would not harm the hardened Holy Dome exposed by the excavation. But it should destroy any living thing at the site.

The surface glowed with the Dreadnought's destructive power—but to Mken's relief, the Holy Dome appeared to be undamaged.

"We're getting a number of organic incineration indicators," the communications officer said.

"How many?" Mken demanded.

"Six, seven . . . no more."

Mken sighed. "Fire at Site Two! Destroy all troops there!"

"Some of them are already retreating into bunkers—"

"Then burn the ones you can! Quickly!"

"It is my privilege to obey."

Mken touched the control arm of his floating chair. "Kucknoi, have you docked?"

"We are here on the shuttle, High Lord," confirmed the head researcher from Site One. His voice carried a hint of accusation as he went on: "Do I understand that you are *attacking* the excavation?"

"It is not being harmed, merely cauterized. We have modulated the beam to be certain of that. Kucknoi, there were *tunnels* under my drop pod. You were aware of them?"

"Not until they were breached. There is a great deal under the surface we have not yet charted, High Lord."

"And under Site One?"

"There is a subterranean chamber, noted by our subsurface resonator. We believe it could be a major reliquary. We had just found an entrance and were hoping to open it, when this untimely interruption wrenched us from our work . . ."

"Had we not interrupted you, I can assure you the Sangheili would have. They would have cut you all to pieces. Is there a way Sangheili can penetrate the subterranean chamber, from above, without major excavation?"

"There are air shafts that one Sangheili at a time could use, I suppose. We did not choose to utilize them . . . They are not suitable for our chairs or antigrav belts."

Mken grunted. "No doubt. And no doubt Ussa 'Xellus knew about them. They are nimble creatures, capable of going exactly where we cannot. We'll have to send the Sentinels in and clear those Sangheili out."

But by then, Mken knew, Ussa would have probably moved on. He'd have found his way out of the hoary Forerunner structure, and would make ready to strike again at the San'Shyuum.

Mken was surprised at his own feelings—he was inwardly glad Ussa had escaped, though he'd have destroyed the Sangheili, rather than allow the saurian commander to further interrupt their excavations.

Yes, there was potential in this Ussa 'Xellus. Mken was aware that to other San'Shyuum, the Sangheili were just impediments—but Mken was also a San'Shyuum of vision.

If the Sangheili were not entirely exterminated, then perhaps, on some faraway day . . .

And as for the Sangheili known as Ussa . . .

If this Ussa is not annihilated, he and I will meet again.

I can feel it . . .

PART ONE

A Place of Refuge

CHAPTER 1

Dreadnought Keyship
Conference Deck
The Age of Reconciliation

Despite his current status as Minister of Relic Safety, High Lord Mken 'Scre'ah'ben—the Prophet of Inner Conviction—was always a bit intimidated by the Chamber of Decision. Those he was expected to worship had presumably sat here, at this long, sweeping translucent table within the Dreadnought. The San'Shyuum used their own chairs, but the rest of the room remained just as the Forerunners had left it. The table itself seemed imbued with fractals, animated nesting scrolls that moved into and out of larger forms: three-dimensional, then two-dimensional, then three again. The area faced not a window so much as simply a transparent wall. The hub of the spiral galaxy itself glowed effulgently blue, in places streamed with scarlet and purple nebulae, wheeling with unspeakable immensity, ever transforming, chaotic yet appearing to be an eternal fixed shape.

Who were the San'Shyuum to be here in this vessel, Mken wondered, who were the San'Shyuum to roost here like a flock of the bony-winged *rakscraja* that dwelled in the vine-choked trees of ancient Janjur Qom?

But here they were, full of officious self-importance, as they awaited the Sangheili treaty commission.

With Mken at the table were Qurlom, the San'Shyuum Minister of Relative Reconciliation, and GuJo'n, the Minister of Kindly Subjection. War had given GuJo'n, the chief diplomat, little to do until recently—his job had been only a sinecure, purely theoretical. Now as he unconsciously braided the tufts on one of his wattles, he seemed puffed with an exaggerated sense of his renewed status. His new scarlet robe was splendidly sewn in golden thread to represent interlinked star systems. Rather a pretentious garment, in Mken's opinion. But he rippled his three-fingered hand in the traditional sign of *Esteemed colleagues, let us begin*, and GuJo'n returned the gesture with a magisterial accent.

Qurlom, the elderly former Hierarch, was more pragmatic, and simply began with "The inscription on the Writ of Union is not quite dry, and already the naysayers, the doubters, the heretics begin to arise." Qurlom was quite serious about the Great Journey; indeed, he was such a true believer that he didn't waste effort on any ritual, like the social sort, that wasn't religious in nature. He always launched into the work at hand. "Something must be done." Qurlom wore a white robe with a platinum five-spiked fluted mantle; his robe bore a simple design: seven circles interlinked in circular chain—the seven Holy Rings.

"I've heard such rumors of sedition," Mken admitted. "There are Sangheili who resist our new Covenant. But it is predictable—a flutter here and there, soon gone in all probability . . . once we make a few examples."

"No!" Qurlom writhed his long, wrinkled neck for emphasis.

His wattles shook angrily and his antigrav chair wobbled. "Do not make light of this heresy, Inner Conviction!"

"I would certainly never make light of heresy," Mken said calmly.

"Perhaps these doubters among the Sangheili do not regard it as a religious matter, but as a cultural one," suggested GuJo'n smoothly, making an elaborate gesture that meant *I do not contradict you.*

Qurlom snorted. "Ah, but you *do* contradict me, GuJo'n. There is no doubt they are heretics."

"My understanding," said GuJo'n, "is that the Sangheili object to surrender of *any* sort—that it is counter to their ethos to ally themselves with their conquerors. They object to subjugation . . . but they can adapt to it, in time."

"And you truly believe this? I have documentation suggesting that the leader of these heretics, this Ussa 'Xellus, does not just *object* to the Writ of Union. He *acts*!"

Mken remembered the Planet of Blue and Red from several solar cycles earlier, when he had been a mere High Lord. Ussa 'Xellus had escaped the planet and gone on to fight, with characteristic craftiness, in many ensuing battles against the San'Shyuum, on other worlds.

His voice almost a growl, Qurlom went on. "This Ussa 'Xellus declares, and I quote . . ." He touched the arm of his chair, summoning a holoscreen that flickered into definition in the air over the table, and read out the text unscrolling there. " 'This Great Journey—what is it? Just another surrender, from what I can tell! Did the Forerunners truly summon us to sublimation, in the shadow of these Rings? Or is that an excuse on the part of the San'Shyuum to exterminate us? It is a murky pond in which no Sangheili would dare bathe!' "

"Very inflammatory indeed," GuJo'n allowed. "Who provided this quote? Perhaps some profiteer?"

"Again you rebuke me, GuJo'n," Qurlom snapped. "You imply my information is fallacious."

"I am merely curious as to intelligence sources."

"And I would like to know as well, Qurlom," Mken put in gently.

"My intelligence source is the Sangheili themselves," Qurlom replied. "Those who committed to the Writ of Union have no notion of being made fools of—they are quietly providing surveillance of all dissenters for us."

Mken gave a hand sign of approval. "You've been thorough, Qurlom—I am happy to see it."

"So then, Prophet of Inner Conviction"—Qurlom gave Mken's spiritual title a fillip of irony—"what shall we do about it?"

"Ideally, it should be something taken care of by the Sangheili," said GuJo'n.

"Yes," Mken agreed. "Then let us have the Commission here . . . and I see they have just arrived. We will bring this up with them."

By the time the Commission arrived, the keyship had turned in space, the enormous, towering Dreadnought structure ever so slowly rotating as it coursed its orbit. And now as the Sangheili filed in, Mken could see the skeleton of new construction through the viewing wall. Destined to become a kind of shell around the former Dreadnought, the mobile capital city dubbed High Charity was being manufactured by robotic and Covenant workers, all toiling on the rocky base, long ago ripped from the homeworld of Janjur Qom. A force field kept in the atmosphere needed by the workers, and held the void and detritus of space at bay. It was already a habitat. Someday it would be far more.

In time, High Charity itself would become an interstellar vessel, as well as the new, traveling center of San'Shyuum power. Thus far High Charity was only a living sketch of its potential, the semiglobular shape catching the starlight as the city gradually accreted. Fairly soon, the former Dreadnought would complete its decommissioning as a weapon and fulfill the terms of the Writ of Union; it would be set upon an anointed altar in High Charity, permanently attached. It had once been the most dreaded weapon in the known galaxy—now it was a symbol of disarmament, at least among the members of the Covenant.

And yet the Covenant still had teeth.

Mken looked over the visiting Commission. They consisted of two Sangheili, Commanders Viyo 'Griot and Loro 'Onkiyo. Behind them were two Honor Guards—the San'Shyuum referred to the Sangheili as "Elites," in part to acquiesce to their appetite for honorifics, but also to adequately express the Sangheili's uncategorical expertise in combat. In turn, the Elites generally noted the San'Shyuum as "Prophets," though only a few actually held such formal stations.

The Honor Guard stood in the background, heads bowed respectfully; the commission stood, too—only because they were not being offered seats, as that would imply equality with the San'Shyuum. They would remain standing for hours at a time, like mere petitioners. Mken could barely tell them apart—they both had the mandible-like, four-part jaws that clapped together as arthropodic mouth parts; the multiple rows of sharp teeth; the gray, saurian skin and serpentine eyes. Their massive arms and thighs were thick with fighting muscle, and these two wore gleaming silver cuirasses and helmets, adding to their bulk—but it was Mken's understanding that they were what passed for diplomatic corps types among their species. He noted that Viyo, on his right, was a little taller, and his helmet, itself with three fins on it as if echoing Sangheili jaws, sported blue panels alternating with silver.

Viyo flexed his clawed, four-fingered hands as if looking for a weapon that wasn't there, glancing around uneasily. Mken doubted if the Sangheili had employed any true diplomats at all until the Writ of Union had been executed, and these two were clearly uncomfortable in their assigned roles.

Having concluded formalities, Mken asked, "Commissioner Viyo—what of the deployments? Are your troops en route?"

Mken hoped his chair's translation device was up-to-date— over time they'd obtained a more comprehensive understanding of the Sangheili language mostly through interrogating prisoners, and cooperation had been predicated on rather vicious torture, which was perhaps not the best way to learn a new tongue.

"The troops are en route, Great Prophet," Viyo replied. "The vessels are doubly crowded with soldiers of many specialties. They will soon be arrayed in advance of all San'Shyuum expeditions— all discoveries of Forerunner artifacts from this time forward will be fiercely protected."

"Just as it should be," said Mken.

"But heed me," Qurlom put in. "You speak glibly of Forerunner artifacts. These troops of yours—are they truly committed to protecting them? We must know: are they fully devoted to the Great Journey?"

"Indeed they are, Minister!" said Loro 'Onokiyo, with something that might be the genuine enthusiasm of a recent convert.

"The Great Journey is not merely a matter of being ready militarily," Qurlom portentously asserted, "though that is of importance. But truly, those who seek the light of the seven Rings must be purified within, utterly convinced of the truth of the Prophets, to the last vestige of their being, and willing to die for the cause without hesitation."

"It is so, Minister. We are all ready to die for the Great Journey. Always have the Sangheili revered the Forerunners—and now we know at last just how to clearly hear the true word of the Forerunners and obey it. We are purified in the light of the Rings!"

Mken wondered, as he did every day, if he himself was purified within, if he himself was utterly convinced. He was the Prophet of Inner Conviction, because of the intrinsic purity he had once preached—he was hearing his own sermonizing echoed back. But increasingly, as he studied what could be gleaned from Forerunner machines and records, he wondered if the true purpose of the Halos was indeed a mass propulsion into a higher plane, a Great Journey to the paradise foreseen by the Prophets. It was true that the Rings seemed associated with a purification process—but what exactly had they purified, and how?

But he cut these heretical thoughts short. *Blasphemy. Prophet of Inner Conviction, indeed—what irony. Find your own Inner Conviction!*

GuJo'n meanwhile signified satisfaction with the data on troop movements, using a gesture the Sangheili probably could not read, and added, "Very good—but what of this tale of sedition that's come to us? I speak of the one called Ussa 'Xellus. He and his followers have been cited in accounts from your own spies."

"Ussa 'Xellus? That crawling fur grub cannot be called a true Sangheili!" retorted Viyo 'Griot.

"Yet he is a highly effective military strategist," Mken remarked. "One who should not be underestimated. I have seen it myself, long ago, on the Planet of Blue and Red."

"Once he served Sanghelios, it is true," Viyo admitted. "But no more. He rejects the Writ of Union—he claims it is shameful to join our strength with your own! Even to negotiate peace with the San'Shyuum is tantamount to surrender. When his sedition was first accounted, we entreated him and his people, as he was once a warrior like us. But he refused to listen to reason, and brought war to Sanghelios. Our own keeps responded with . . . less subtle means, subjecting the entire state of 'Xellus to incredible firepower. We intended to cut off the root of treason at the source, but apparently many of his people survived. We suspect he now hides like a coward somewhere in the barrens near the south pole of Sanghelios. A little-known region called Nwari. We have not heard from our spies for some days—it may be that they have been compromised. But we have our assassins looking for Ussa 'Xellus now. When they do find him, be assured, they will choose their moment . . . and they will kill him. His followers are drugged into madness by his word. It seems likely that with him gone, their cult will dissolve."

"*Will* it dissolve?" Mken wondered aloud. "Have you never heard of martyrdom?"

A Sangheili Mining Colony on the Planet Creck
The Age of Reconciliation

The mission was a failure.

Ussa 'Xellus and his mate, Sooln, had traveled to the Creck colony, to recruit new followers into the resistance. Creck, named after 'Crecka, the Sangheili who'd discovered it a generation earlier, was in the Baelion system—the seventy-sixth of designated worlds explored by Sangheili. It was now a Covenant mining colony, operated, largely underground, by Sangheili. A few translucent meteorite-scarred colony domes rose above the rugged, methane-choked surface of the planet. They were the tips of the colony's iceberg. On the other side of the mountains that brooded over the domes was a great sea of half-frozen hydrogen cyanide; there were said to be simple lifeforms, like great swimming worms, surfacing from time to time in that opaque ocean of toxin.

But the Sangheili were here for the minerals and metals—the minerals to power their ships and the metals to sheath the hulls of those vessels. They delved deep into Creck, following mammoth crystalline veins down, with other shafts running to magma used to provide the base energy of their colony.

Ussa and Sooln were riding a lift up a shaft from one of those scorching power plants. They'd spent some time there, traveling in the guise of engineers pretending to check for heat-fatigued walls, and talking as discreetly as possible to those who toiled over the generators. A defector from Creck had told Ussa there was discontent here. Who wouldn't feel ill used, working in the geological energy plant? The structure couldn't be climate controlled efficiently—and the heat was unbearable.

But his primary contact, Muskem, had perished the day before Ussa arrived. Muskem had inexplicably fallen into a throbbing pit of magma, where he was instantly incinerated. Ussa had a strong intuition, after speaking with a supervising officer, that someone had arranged the unfortunate accident.

Ussa almost hadn't come to Creck at all. It seemed foolishly risky. But there was another, too, who'd contacted Ussa. A Sangheili who called himself 'Quillick, which was an ancient word, from Sanghelios, for "small hunter," a little animal known to catch mammals for farmers. Clearly it was this Sangheili's code name. 'Quillick's communication was folded in with Muskem's: *There is a place where much can be found to help you. It is a world no one knows. But I know . . . I fought beside your uncle at Tarjak, under the stone trees . . .*

What could this mean? Was this the fantasy of some eccentric? But the remark about Tarjak and the stone trees referred to a story his uncle had told him—one his uncle was reluctant to tell. Covenant agents were unlikely to know about Tarjak and the stone trees—the gallery built of petrifactions, a long-extinct forest. There a small but vicious battle, clan against clan, had gone on for several bloody cycles.

The note had promised *a place where much can be found to help you. It is a world no one knows.* Ussa had been intrigued enough to take the risk of visiting the colony at Creck.

He had little hope in finding this 'Quillick now, and it was difficult to know who else to contact here. No sane Sangheili would talk openly of joining the resistance to the Covenant—and few would talk even secretly. *The Writ of Union is written*, was the phrase Ussa had heard so many times that he wanted to scream when it was repeated to him. *It cannot be unwritten.*

Now Ussa repeated the trite point to his mate, but his voice was bitter. "The Writ of Union is written—it cannot be unwritten. This was said over and over. Someone has gotten to these Sangheili."

"How can you be so certain?"

"To hear them all repeating the same declaration—they have been told to do so. And every Sangheili I spoke with appeared miserable. They *knew* they were being dishonorable cowards."

Sooln tapped one of her mandibles thoughtfully. "What else can they do? It's not as if there is some clear enemy of Sanghelios left to fight. If that were the case, they would be there in the heart of battle. But this is the Council of City States—it is Sanghelios itself, threatening them. Yet they know we should not be surrendering to the San'Shyuum."

"And Muskem was our contact for finding 'Quillick. Our visit here could be a waste of time."

The lift hummed on for a few moments, getting cooler almost by the second as it left the zone of active volcanism. Then Ussa looked fondly at Sooln—compact, perhaps a bit uppity and bold for a female Sangheili, but also delicate and petite . . . or so it seemed to Ussa. Her mind was quicker and more analytical than his, he knew; she had a genius for science that he lacked. "Sooln, perhaps you're speaking this way about the Writ of Union to please me. Perhaps you wish, for the sake of our lives together, that I would accept the Covenant . . ."

She clamped her mandibles in amusement. "I believe as you do. I do not trust the San'Shyuum. Their vision of a Great Journey is fantasy."

"I fear that I should not have brought you. Do you believe anyone has detected us? The death of our contact concerns me . . ."

"I haven't noticed any drones following us; I haven't seen any spies lurking about watching us. There was that elder Sangheili yesterday, but—he never spoke to us . . ."

"What elder Sangheili?"

"You failed to notice him? He followed us from the mines, back toward the spaceport. But he was slow, weary, scarred . . . He could not keep up. I thought perhaps he wanted to join us, but when I looked back again, he was gone. He seemed too feeble to be a Covenant operative."

Ussa growled softly to himself. "We shall soon know, one way or the other. Because—"

But he broke off then, as they'd reached the colony's residence level. The lift doors opened and the two stepped onto the darkened street, between the stubby, utilitarian buildings, and walked together toward the spaceport, where their ship waited. Ussa was careful not to hurry as they walked by two sharp-eyed guards on patrol, though he'd have liked nothing more than to pick up his stride. He wondered if Ernicka the Scar-Maker was keeping order in the caverns back on Sanghelios. Perhaps they had already been found, and routed. But surely he would have received a communiqué if there had been an attack . . .

He wondered, too, if he and Sooln were still safe in this place. He'd brought his mate because she had access to engineer's documentation—she was able to create a suitable cover identity for them. She knew the proper terminology on visits to the mines and power plants. But suppose their disguise had been penetrated? He might very well have led her to a tragic end here.

Still, they crossed the square without incident. The two edged through a crowd of sullen-looking Sangheili, dusty miners coming off work shifts, and then scurried between two processing structures to the port.

They were permitted past the gate guards, a young Sangheili scarcely glancing up at them from his talkscreen, and headed to their spacecraft.

The *Clan's Blade*, a blue-and-red vessel shaped like a dart and just large enough for a handful of travelers, was fueled and prepped for departure. Ussa 'Xellus confirmed this remotely through his wrist interface. But as he approached the hatch, he noted someone step out of the shadows.

It was an ancient Sangheili in a much-repaired subcommander's uniform. Most of the teeth were missing from his jaws, and one of his eyes had long ago been scarred over.

"You . . . This is the one who was following us yesterday!" Sooln exclaimed.

Ussa reached for his pistol, and then saw the old warrior raise his arms in the air. His left hand was missing.

"Do not fire on me, brethren, until you have at least spoken to me," he croaked. "I have no weapon."

This one makes Ernicka look young, Ussa thought.

"Who are you, old warrior?"

"I am 'Crecka," said the elder Sangheili simply.

Ussa snorted. "Nonsense."

"I am he. I may also be known to you by another name: 'Quillick."

"*You* are 'Quillick?"

"Yes—and I need to speak to you alone. Inside."

"And how do we know you're not just some cunning old assassin?"

"You would have been under arrest by now, if they were aware of your identity here—not targeted by an assassin. You are too important to simply assassinate, Ussa 'Xellus. Please, you may search me for arms and then permit me into your ship, if you choose, and I will tell you why I am here."

Ussa grunted. But he did search the old one for hidden weapons and found nothing. And, too, there was something inexplicably trustworthy in this Sangheili. "Come in, if you must. But we are leaving the planet very shortly. It will not take us long to get proper clearance. I will only give you a few moments."

The three were soon in the tiny bridge of the craft, Ussa in his pilot's seat, Sooln checking systems beside him. But Ussa had his seat turned toward the old warrior, who stood on the deck behind the control panel, his maimed arms folded over his chest.

"Make it quick," Ussa told him. His hand was not far from that pistol as he spoke.

"I am who I said I was. I have been watching for you—Muskem and I expected you. But I wasn't sure if you yourself were being watched. I was reluctant to speak."

"Speak now. We are alone."

The old warrior rubbed thoughtfully at his scarred eye socket. "Many cycles ago, I was the last survivor of a vessel brought down by hostiles—we never knew what race it was. They did not speak a civilized tongue. All this was on the far side of the galaxy from here, in the System of Miasmic Giants. I managed to escape, piloting the ship through slipspace to another system—one chosen almost at random. It was the farthest I could reach. There I saw something most peculiar . . . a world made out of an alloy I've never seen."

"You mean a space station of some kind."

"No. A small planet. But encased entirely in metal. I had never seen the like. An artifact so large—it was beyond belief."

"It is difficult for me to believe as well."

"No doubt," said 'Crecka. "I had to see for myself. I landed on the outer hull, in a place that looked like it might have an entry point—and found a portal. I descended into the metal skin—and on a lower deck, a machine came floating out to greet me. It was a machine intelligence, built by the ancients! It had already sorted through my ship's computer, with some kind of scanning device. I believe that's how it was able to speak our language. It told me a few things; but it refused to divulge its origin. It had a name—Enduring Bias, it called itself. It had been left to oversee the planet—the 'shield world,' in truth is what it called this place—until its creators should return. It ordered that I should provide it with information about the Sangheili and make myself available for study. But I escaped. It was . . . confused; many of its systems no longer worked and it was not so difficult to get away. I managed to get into slipspace . . . and ended up here, near what is now called Creck. A scan told me there were valuable minerals here. I reported this world—but not the other. The other was full of relics, of things from the ancients. The Forerunners. I was afraid that Enduring Bias would kill anyone I sent. For so it had threatened, should I depart . . ."

"And you kept the secret of that place until now . . . with all those relics there?"

"I did. I was a warrior, not a scientist. I fought and was maimed in sixteen of the great Clan Battles on Sanghelios. The eye I lost fighting beside your uncle under the stone trees!"

Ussa nodded. "He mentioned someone called 'Quillick—because he would scout out the enemy for them, the way a 'Quillick would slink silently through the shadows."

"It was I! But it is not my friendship for your uncle that brings me here. I know your cause. It is my cause, too. This world can be a refuge and a resource for your people—for *our* people. Away from the Covenant."

Ussa pondered this. If the elderly warrior—who had fought beside Ussa's own uncle—could be trusted, then he might be offering a key to something that could truly empower the rebellion against the Covenant. Again he wondered if this could be some kind of trick or trap—but then why go to these lengths? Old 'Crecka was right: they could simply have arrested him. And few could know the tale of 'Quillick and the stone trees.

Ussa's hearts thudded with excitement as the possibilities glimmered in his imagination. But it *could* all be a trap—without 'Crecka knowing. If the Covenant knew of the planetoid.

"Think back: you must have told *someone* about this metal planet. Someone—somewhere."

"No! I was afraid I would be executed if I spoke of what I had seen. What I learned on the shield world—ah, I might well have been put to death for having entered the planetoid and communicating with the machine, which was heresy back then. That is no honorable way to die. But then . . . when you were in the mines, I was conversing with my son. He is an engineer here. And I overheard you speak, railing against the Covenant. I have heard something of Ussa 'Xellus, and his mate. You fit the description. So I came here to help—because I have a wish to return to that world—and I believe it will offer a refuge for you and those who follow you. You and I . . . are of a like mind. We should never have surrendered to the San'Shyuum."

The old warrior paused to cough into a mangled hand, and Ussa pondered again in silence. Could 'Crecka simply be senile, addled by war, imagining things? But the ancient Sangheili had a character that rang true, like the well-seasoned metal of a sword forged on Qikost. And he truly had fought beside his uncle. Ussa could not help but believe the tale, as fantastic as it was.

Sooln spoke up then. "Such a place, a world that is one great Forerunner relic—it should not fall into the hands of the Covenant. We should at least see if it is real, Ussa. What have we to lose? He is right—it could be our chance! Think of the potential of such a place!"

"You believe it is real, then?"

"We have to see for ourselves. We must take the chance. We have so few prospects for the cause . . ."

Ussa paced the deck, and at last said, "It would be difficult to imagine the spies of Sanghelios contriving such a tale." He turned to 'Crecka. "Can you show us this world covered in metal—immediately?"

"I have the waymarkers. I'm ready to take you there. It will probably be my last journey anywhere. I'm dying, you see. But—I want to see those marvels again, one last time, and I want to help you. You are right: the Covenant is wrong. It is that simple."

Their disguises had held up: departure from the spaceport was granted. Within a few minutes they were in orbit, burning their way into the slipspace aperture that was like a glowing wound in space-time.

They passed through and into slipspace, where time is not easily reckoned. There was opportunity to rest, eat, and hear stories from 'Crecka about the Clan Battles of Sanghelios. By degrees, Ussa increasingly came to trust the old fellow.

But still—he could be on a fool's mission. He had failed to recruit more converts, unless old 'Quillick could be counted as such.

Perhaps this voyage was just a desperate stab in the darkness of space.

An Uncharted World
851 BCE
The Age of Reconciliation

They were in orbit over something extraordinary.

Ussa waited, his fingers hovering over the controls, ready to begin high-acceleration evasion maneuvers. He half expected defensive measures of some kind to be fired at them from the colossal sphere of silvery-gray alloy. But though there was a regular pulse of internal energy signatures from the shield world, as 'Crecka called it, no attack was forthcoming.

"Come, let me show you the portal," 'Crecka told him. "It's on the farther side . . . the only one I know of."

They accelerated into a faster orbit and homed in on the coordinates. They descended, spiraling down carefully, Ussa still wondering the whole time if this was some kind of trap—but he was far too intrigued, too caught up in a sense of inexorable destiny to turn back now.

The metallic hide of the planet loomed, details defining through thin mists of a pseudo atmosphere. Seams showed; here and there curiously shaped antennas sprouted.

Ussa 'Xellus shivered as the *Clan's Blade* approached the rectangular object, almost flush with the curved surface, which 'Crecka identified as the portal. Ussa felt a superstitious fear as he settled the ship into the rectangle. Its outlines seemed to grow within themselves, walls rising up around the spacecraft, rather than from inside the planet.

In a few moments, a ceiling had formed over them—and the ship's instruments soon showed pressurization and breathable air. There were no indications of dangerous microorganisms.

"Come along," said 'Crecka, looking almost excited. "Bring weapons—the intelligence has access to them. It may be annoyed with me. But it also may have been bluffing."

"If it is still operating at all," said Sooln.

"I may be along in my cycles, but not by that much," said 'Crecka. "I was not quite young when I found this place. But it is unbelievably ancient. You will see. How many times I have wanted to return. But I felt it unwise to come alone—and until now there was no one I trusted. And no great need. It is the cause—that is the need now . . ."

"Wisdom is the fruit of age," Ussa said, quoting a Sangheili homily and briefly placing a hand on the elderly warrior's shoulder.

Ussa and Sooln carried plasma rifles, 'Crecka a pistol Ussa had given him. Together they emerged from the ship's hatchway and descended the ramp to a flooring that was more than mere metal.

A door opened, as if beckoning to them. They passed through it, finding their way down a series of gently descending corridors, to a platform that overlooked an awe-inspiring sight: a world enclosed within a shell, like the tank that scientists sometimes kept small animals in, back on Sanghelios. But this "tank" was on an unthinkably gigantic scale—it could house a planetoid itself. Light shone from shafts in the ground below, and from panes in inverted structures projecting from the convex artificial ceiling; they were tapered formations like giant artificial stalactites.

Below the craggy remnants of some ancient planetoid, it bristled with plant life, gleamed with streams and waterfalls. Flying creatures he couldn't clearly distinguish flapped through roseate mists, which thickened at the distant horizon. A mechanized transport flew past, just a sort of aeronautic wagon with what looked like pieces of machinery piled in the back. A freight mover of some kind. It was there, and suddenly gone.

The air smelled like exotic plants, and water, and minerals, and there was a smell of ozone somewhere, too, carried on the artificial breeze.

Suddenly the platform they were on detached itself, startling Ussa and Sooln, before descending, slowly, to the ground. They were in an area that looked too haphazard to be a cultivated garden, but too orderly to be wilderness.

Ussa walked to the stream flowing nearby. Its perfectly transparent water showed no algae—but something swam by, and was gone.

"This place is so . . . intact!" Sooln whispered, in awe.

"Yes," said 'Crecka. "The machine told me it has been here for many, many millennia. He called it the 'eco level.' It is built to last. And it is safe for us to live in—for your people to live in."

A shadow passed over them—Ussa glanced up, hearing a soft male-inflected voice, speaking the language of Sangheili.

"I welcome you to Shield World 0673. I am Enduring Bias."

A floating, roughly hexagonal mechanism, with three lenses glinting on its nearer side, moved easily about in the air, bobbing, shifting to get a better view of them. It was about the size of a Sangheili's chest, in some parts intricately surfaced, in others elegantly simple.

"I am Ussa 'Xellus." There seemed no point in trying to maintain an alias. "And this is my mate, Sooln. You know 'Crecka, I believe."

"Yes. I might have prevented his escape, but I'm afraid a sort of existential fatigue slowed me—a desire for company, really. My original bias, my general programming intent, is fogged by the ages, and, to the extent I'm aware of it, apparently irrelevant now. I perceive that you are genetically related to one of the races reseeded by the Librarian . . . and so it is not inappropriate for me to permit you shelter here. Now . . . you will inform me of your intentions."

Sanghelios
Southern Nwari
851 BCE
The Age of Reconciliation

Young and strong but without a mature Sangheili's musculature, Tersa 'Gunok had difficulty keeping up with Ernicka the Scar-Maker, but he was thrilled to be allowed to be of service to so great a warrior.

They were carrying crates of dried food from the drays into the vessels perched on the rocky floor of the volcanic crater. Snow skirled down from time to time, blown from the edges of the crater by the frigid winds of Sanghelios's south pole, and Tersa's lungs ached with the cold; his knuckles burned with it.

But he hurried after Ernicka and into the ship, proudly stepping onto a lift beside the Scar-Maker. Usually silent though he was, Ernicka emanated respect for everyone who did their tasks. They were all united, after all, in the blood oath of Final Decision: *We are prepared to die fighting beside Ussa 'Xellus, in the struggle against the Covenant. This is honor, and honor is meaning.*

Every one of them had spoken that oath—and every one of them had heard it spoken.

The lift stopped and Tersa, arms aching, carried the crate to the hold and placed it with the others.

"Commander," came a voice from the grid on the bulkhead. "We have news of Ussa 'Xellus. He returns with important information. Come to the bridge for a full briefing . . ."

Both of Tersa's hearts beat in pattering tandem. This hiding in the caverns would soon be over. Ussa would take them from shadows and into the bright solar glare of renewed honor.

Perhaps it was foolish to make Ussa 'Xellus his hero—his mother had warned him not to follow Ussa. But she had been back home in their own keep; she had not seen what Tersa had witnessed . . .

The memory was still sharp, burned into his mind.

Tersa had been training in Ussa's keep because his small clan had an ancient pact with the 'Xellus family. And there Tersa had seen what happened to those who did not hold with the Covenant.

He had heard, the cycle before, Ussa speaking to a crowd in

the flagstone plaza of the keep: "If you wish to follow the Covenant, then leave here now! For myself—I will not surrender to the San'Shyuum! Nor will anyone loyal to my clan! And do not be deceived—the tale that this is alliance and not meek surrender is a lie! What is a Sangheili but his honor? His honor is equal to his soul, and his soul to his honor! We cannot submit to the Covenant. It is better to die than to live without dignity."

Deeply moved, Tersa had joined those shouting in agreement and hailing Ussa.

But he saw some others walk away from the plaza that day. He spied two of them setting out in flyers for distant places.

Perhaps it was they who precipitated what happened next. Who spoke out against Ussa, doubtless to curry favor with the Covenant.

Tersa was on the wall, overlooking the plaza on one side and the rolling, austere hills outside 'Xellus Keep on the other, when the attack came. He was carrying out an exercise with two friends, with distance glasses. As he raised the glasses to his eyes, he saw the black specks swarming the horizon. In the scope, the specks became nine low-level attack fighters, roughly shaped like the flying, leatherwinged predators called 'sKelln.

"Shout the alarm!" Tersa yelled.

"Yes, alarm and so on," his cheerful friend N'oraq called back, yawning.

Tersa realized N'oraq thought this was only an exercise—that Tersa was just fooling about. He hadn't seen the attackers. "Look, there!" Tersa said, handing him the glasses. *"Look!"*

Tersa himself shouted an alarm, and startled faces turned toward him. Some scowled, thinking he was but a panicked youngling. But a moment later they knew who was mistaken, as the matte-black fighters dove in and loosed explosive charges on the plaza. Projectiles strafed, one of them tearing N'oraq in half.

Then pillars of fire rose; dark blue blood gouted up in fountains. Sangheili shrieked as they were tossed, broken, through the air, and others ran helter-skelter, looking for surface-to-air weapons.

Five sweeps the enemy made over the keep, and only one of the nine attack flyers went down, shot by Ussa 'Xellus himself with a fire-wand launcher.

The keep burned . . . and hundreds died. The flyers simply departed without further incident. But everyone had seen the Sacred Rings sign of the Covenant on the wings.

Tersa spent a long day helping to cope with the dead and dying.

And from that day forward, Tersa vowed he would do nothing for the Covenant. Nor would he give them quarter.

Then the war widened, became a civil war on Sanghelios that in some places was of magnitude enough to damage Forerunner relics, sacred machinery kept underground. Ussa took his followers to Nwari, where they might seek cover. And it was there that the ships waited. Ussa had used most of the fortune of the 'Xellus clan to pay for those vessels, to have them brought to the sleeping volcano.

Now, as he worked in the cavern, Tersa sighed. He had taken an irrevocable course that day. *Follow a clan's hero to battle*, his mother had said, *and you have a chance to fight honorably and return. Follow a rebel and you will be overwhelmed, shot down without a chance to return fire . . . or executed.*

Would he see his mother again? Was she safe from the Covenant? He did not know, and he ached to realize he might never find out.

He mustn't think of that. Especially not with Ernicka glowering down at him. "You, youngling—go back and help organize the weapons. I'll bring you the news soon enough."

"Yes, Commander."

Tersa hurried off, slightly annoyed to be called a youngling, and wondering if Ussa had recruited the soldiers they needed for the revolt . . . or if he had some other plan entirely.

With Ussa, one never knew what was coming until it had already been decided.

The hills of Nwari were desolate, forbidding. But many of the caverns hidden beneath them were warm, bubbling with volcanically heated springs. Warmth, Ussa knew, was not enough.

He stood on a natural balcony of stone, overlooking the Sangheili clans as they milled below, his followers doing tasks he had given out mostly just to keep them busy. There was a pervasive restlessness among them, and many times the clansfolk glanced up at him, as if wondering if he'd brought them here only to meet some ghastly end.

The Sangheili had evolved in tropical wetlands, and their instincts rebelled against extended stays in these dark, natural amphitheaters. The coldly reverberant spaces, the clamminess whenever one strayed from the bubbling pools, the shadowy reaches of the place that seemed resistant to their lamps—perhaps resistant because of the thick mist from the sulfurous springs—all this made any normal Sangheili look about the encampment with distaste and mistrust. But Ussa had led his people here, remembering that in ancient times the clans had often taken shelter in deep places under the mountains of Sanghelios.

Having retreated here, Ussa had ordered the subterranean approach from the north closed with plasma beams—melting the rock to seal it off as quietly as possible. The caverns were vast and labyrinthine, but Ussa knew that the Covenant author-ities might well have guessed his general whereabouts; if they chanced upon the southern entrance within the dead volcano, all would be lost.

Ernicka the Scar-Maker approached Ussa, grimly gnashing his teeth—which indicated that the news was not good.

"Great Leader," Ernicka rumbled, "the listeners have detected new perturbations. The searchers are probing the sealed passages. They seem to know where we are."

"It is soon for them to know that," Ussa observed, watching the silvery mist undulate, a low, hot fog churning in the lamplight over the milling clans. "What does that suggest to you?"

"Perhaps we were not as careful in our relocation as we had hoped?"

"That is a possibility. Another is . . ." He looked about them—no one was nearby. But he gestured for Ernicka to follow him to one side, close against the wall. There was a good deal of noise from the clans, and the sounds of springs; now that they had moved away from the ramp, no one should be able to overhear them. But even so, Ussa lowered his voice and Ernicka could just barely catch his words. "Another possibility is there are spies among us, with some means of transmitting messages."

"How shall we deal with this?" Ernicka whispered urgently.

"I'm pondering that."

"It would be a hard thing to interrogate our clansmen . . ."

"Yes—and which ones would we interrogate? Where are the suspects? Everyone? We have no time for such matters. And I would not lose the loyalty of innocents by torturing them—or their clanfellows."

"Then what are we to do?"

Ussa paused for a moment, thinking, and then asked, "How close are we to having the transports loaded and fueled?"

Ernicka scratched thoughtfully at a battle scar on his chest. "All three are nearly prepared—indeed we could go now, leaving some supplies behind. But—we cannot go with spies aboard."

"We might be able to bring at least one of our hypothetical spies out into the open. Perhaps there is only one, after all. That's more than enough. Ernicka, if we leave quickly, taking everyone with us, we can see to it that no one reveals where we're headed. Only three of us know the route. The San'Shyuum aren't aware of it; those loyal to the Covenant among the Sangheili also do not know of it. The spies will not be given a chance to transmit from our destination . . . if any of them survive what I plan now."

"And what is the plan, Ussa?"

He leaned close to Ernicka and whispered something. Then he added, "Stay within a few paces of me. Defend my back."

Then Ussa turned to the crowds below the natural stone balcony and held up his arms, calling out in a carrying, resonant voice, "Clansfolk! I speak to all!" His words echoed from the stalactites jutting from the curved ceiling; below, mist-blurred faces turned toward him, their murmuring now silenced, all listening raptly as he went on. "Males! Gather up the armaments and convey them to the transports! Females! Those of you brooding eggs, take them up in your arms and do likewise!

"We will go quickly! I have a means with which to strike at those loyal to the Covenant! I will strike at the high clans who would force us to crawl for the San'Shyuum! Then we will take to the skies; we will conceal ourselves in the dark places of the galaxy, and we will create a new Sanghelios! We will restore the pride of our people! We alone will embody its pride! We alone will fight for its pride! Clansfolk—do your hearts beat with mine?"

The final invocation had a ritual response, as ancient as sunlight warming eggs.

And the response was given.

"With your hearts do ours thunder!" they cried out, in ragged but deeply felt unison. For Sangheili, with their binary vascular systems, each had two hearts working in tandem.

"Then I come to walk among you, and I will help you prepare for the journey! I will use my own hands to work beside you!"

Cries of joy and mutters of trepidation arose then, but already Ussa 'Xellus was descending the ramp of stone from the balcony to the floor of the cavern. He smelled the happy reek of small offspring running about their brooders; he heard more cries of "With your hearts do our hearts thunder!" He heard exclamations of awe as he strode into the crowd—for some ironically regarded him as a kind of prophet as well, a divine being.

The throng parted for Ussa; he was aware of Ernicka, as per orders, a few steps behind him, watching warily.

Ussa stopped at a warmer for brood eggs, lifted an egg up himself, and placed it gently in a carrier—though this was normally a female's work, a great leader sometimes did it as a sign of love for his people. A general murmur of approbation followed. The applause of clashing jaws followed, and he walked on, patting the unhelmeted, scaly head of a Sangheili childling; stopping to closely examine a plasma launcher being prepped for transport; lifting a crate of dried meat onto an autodray. All around him, not to be outdone by their leader, his adherents busied themselves, frantically packing up.

"Great Leader!" called a lanky, helmetless male, carefully

setting a box filled with burnblades on another dirty, scarred old autodray. The Sangheili kept one hand on the open box of swords as he turned to Ussa, ducking his head in respect. "May I inquire . . . ?"

Ussa recognized him: a known weapons dealer. "Yes, Vertikus, anyone may inquire of me. What do you wish to know?"

"On the world to which we go . . . how will we bring new weapons there? We have some here—these are genuine Qikost swords. Their blades are ever fine and true. But can we learn to make such in this new world? Is it so far that we cannot find a way to send a secret delegation from there to Qikost?"

"You wish to know if it is near or far from Sanghelios?" Ussa asked, glancing at the box of murderous burnblades. They were forged of metal, heated from within for extra destructive power. "It is indeed far—but I will not tell you, or anyone, where it lies. I will guide us all there. I will say only that we must go there immediately, for I take an action that cannot be reversed. This cannot wait."

Vertikus made a resigned hissing sound, the equivalent of a Sangheili sigh, and then blurrily fast, he snatched a sword from the crate. Slashing viciously at Ussa's throat, he snarled, "Truly *this* cannot wait!"

But Ernicka the Scar-Maker was suddenly there, leaping in front of Ussa, his own burnblade intersecting Vertikus's weapon, so that red sparks spat at the contact. Ernicka's weapon stopped the would-be assassin's sword the width of a childling's tooth from Ussa's exposed throat; Ussa could actually feel the heat of Vertikus's burnblade lightly scorching his flesh.

Larger and vastly more experienced, Ernicka forced Vertikus back with a single powerful thrust, so that the would-be assassin staggered and fell to the ground.

Other Sangheili rushed in, tearing the sword hilt from the traitor's grasp.

"Fools!" Vertikus shouted, scrambling to his feet. "Ussa will lead you into damnation! The Covenant is our only hope for redemption!"

He tried to run, but the crowd closed in around him.

"Wait!" Ussa called. "We need to interrogate him! He might have knowledge of—"

Jaws flashed, talons slashed, purple Sangheili blood spurted, and Vertikus—attacked by ten at once—was already torn to gouting shreds.

"It is too late, Ussa," Ernicka said, sheathing his sword. "But you cannot blame them."

"No, I cannot. So be it. Have the traitor's body disposed. Load up the transports. We will depart before the Covenant knows we are gone."

"You spoke of an action to be taken? Do you intend to strike before we go, or . . . ?"

Ussa made a rachitic sound that expressed dry irony. "No. That was merely to draw out the spy."

"You took a terrible chance, Ussa, walking among them all so boldly."

"I have great trust in you, Scar-Maker. I knew you would protect me."

"I wish, Ussa, that we could strike at the Covenant's slaves before we go—I am ready if you order it."

"In a way, we already strike at those fools. We have escaped them—and when they learn of our escape, that will strike hard at their confidence. We go to the shield world that 'Crecka found. In time we'll use that world as a base to prepare a return to Sanghelios, rearmed and fortified by a new generation. It may be that the Covenant will find us in time. But if they do, they will lose us again. We will grow, we will build a new population, and with it a new army. And one day we will destroy the Covenant. So it shall be, Ernicka. Now . . . let us inspect the transports. It is almost time to leave Sanghelios."

"To leave our home forever—it makes me ache inside, Ussa."

"We may return someday, or our children will. For now, Sanghelios is wherever we go, Ernicka. We are its true soul."

Then, together, they went through the stone passages to the transports that lay a short distance away, waiting on the rocky floor within the cone of an extinct volcano.

From here, gazing up, one could see the sky—Ussa saw the moons of Sanghelios, and a cluster of stars beyond the volcanic mouth.

And somewhere up there, Ussa and his clansfolk would build a new world.

It was nameless, so far. And yet Ussa 'Xellus had seen it, and he knew it would come cracking into being as surely as an egg hatched in the sun. The shell must break for new life to appear . . .

CHAPTER 2

O ur assassin has failed. We suspect our spy was caught and executed. And it seems that Ussa 'Xellus lives."

Mken, the Prophet of Inner Conviction, could not discern if the Sangheili commander had an apologetic tone in his voice—the translation being maddeningly indeterminate at times—but his body language seemed to suggest it. He stood there with his long, split-jawed head bowed.

"So, where is he, then?" Mken said, and Qurlom beside him grunted acknowledgment.

Commander Viyo 'Griot shifted his metal-sheathed boots, which clanked softly on the deck as if to proclaim his discomfort. "We have confirmed only that Ussa 'Xellus has departed Sanghelios. A handful of his adherents, just six, lost heart and remained behind—they'd planned to follow him, but lost their nerve. They watched the ships depart and insisted that Ussa's intention of leaving the planet was clear. These disheartened ones came crawling to us, full of remorse . . . which will of course do the traitors no good."

"It's surprising that Ussa allowed them to stay behind alive," Qurlom rumbled thoughtfully as he tapped the arm of his antigrav chair to produce a pungent tea. He inhaled the fragrant steam before sipping it—at Qurlom's age, his use of traditional medicines was intensive.

"Perhaps not so surprising," Viyo remarked. "Ussa is unusual and paradoxical. On the one hand, he can be merciful, more than we are accustomed to; on the other, he insists on the traditional ethos: *strength is character*, as we say, and of course . . ." He seemed to hesitate, perhaps not wanting to be impolitic.

"Yes?" Mken prompted.

"And of course—*never surrender*."

Viyo looked away, jaws spread grimacingly wide.

Mken was mildly amused. The San'Shyuum, and the Writ of Union itself, politely insisted that the Sangheili hadn't surrendered—they had, instead, *joyfully* chosen to throw in their lot with the San'Shyuum, had wisely chosen to set out on the Path that led to the Great Journey; they had experienced a species-wide spiritual epiphany, realizing that the Prophets of the San'Shyuum were correct all along.

But Mken knew that many Sangheili nursed a secret shame, the unspoken belief that it had been surrender, after all.

Qurlom slurped down the last of his tea, then asked, "So those who stayed behind were clear on Ussa's intention. What determines their clarity? What *is* his intention?"

"They claim he has found a world on which are many Forerunner relics—an uncharted world, Minister. Only he, his mate, and his second-in-command know of its whereabouts, or anything more of its nature."

"And no one else knows where this world lies?" Mken asked. "I find that preposterous."

"Yet it would seem that way. So far—no one else," 'Griot confirmed. "Nor do we know what course they plotted. This was kept a secret. Ussa must have surmised that his clans were infiltrated."

"They entered slipspace . . . and after that?"

"They seem to have changed course many times, and we were not able to trace them."

"Still, we must continue to search," Qurlom said. "This Ussa 'Xellus is a vile and perfidious heretic. He must not be allowed to spread his poison."

"I assure you, we will find him," Commander 'Griot said fervently. "He has blighted all Sangheili. He has called us . . ." Again, 'Griot hesitated. "*Cowards.* The greatest insult known to our people. Unimaginable."

"It is he who is the coward," soothed Mken. "He has fled with his retinue, has left his homeworld and hidden himself away! There is nothing heroic about those deeds."

But privately Mken suspected that this was no act of cowardice. Ussa 'Xellus was, as 'Griot had said, unusual. His motives were all but inscrutable. But cowardice? No.

In all probability, the traitorous Sangheili had some grand scheme in mind.

And at this moment, the Prophet of Inner Conviction was inwardly convinced of only one thing: that when they all learned of the true purpose of this endgame, it would be a dreadful knowledge indeed.

An Uncharted Forerunner Shield World
850 BCE
The Age of Reconciliation

"Great Ussa 'Xellus, I do not challenge your leadership! The clans have accepted you. Who am I to challenge a kaidon?"

Ussa said wryly, "You are 'Crolon. You have always been 'Crolon, and you will be what you have always been. A pain in my side."

Salus 'Crolon closed his jaws firmly—the Sangheili variant of a smile. But he didn't keep them shut for long. "As the ancient saying goes, *Only a coward is always soothing.* But Great Ussa . . . where are we now? We have come to a stranger place than all strange places. At least the caverns you led us into were on Sanghelios. But this is far from our world."

Ernicka the Scar-Maker shot a dark look of suspicion at 'Crolon.

Ussa murmured aside to Ernicka, "Do not jump to conclusions about him. No need to mistake an annoying personality for a treasonous one."

Ussa had seen many good warriors killed alongside the genuine traitors back on Sanghelios. The average kaidon had a short way with those who were disloyal, typically by separating their heads from their necks. But sometimes there was more impulse than judgment in an execution. To slay a true enemy—now, *that* was honorable. Technically, 'Crolon was a warrior, like all male Sangheili. To destroy a soldier out of pique was wasteful.

So Ussa remained calm, and glanced around at their environment. "Yes, 'Crolon, it's true, this place is strange to the Sangheili. And yet I believe it was intended for us—or for those who feel as we do."

They were deep underground, but not in a cavern—they were under the outer shell of the shield world his followers now called the Refuge.

Nearby was the Tomb of 'Crecka, a simple half dome of metal, inscribed with the late warrior's name. The elder had passed on within a short period of arriving for the second and last time on the shield world. He had been walking in the natural garden of the eco level, and had lain down . . . and simply not awakened. Ussa intended a grander monument for the old Sangheili one day, for it was he who had made this refuge possible for Ussa's adherents.

But perhaps the entire shield world was truly his monument. The artificial world was sheathed in metal, like 'Crecka's tomb— or rather it was sheathed in what appeared to be a spherical, all-metal exterior. What it was truly composed of, what the Forerunners had forged, remained a mystery. Within the shell was a hollowed-out planetoid, the rocky surface lifeseeded to create a tolerable habitation for occupation, complete with plant life, hills and valleys and streams, edifices of unknown purpose that could be used for habitation, and most important, a breathable atmosphere. Artificial sunlight beamed down from the concave shell that surrounded the world—in the distance, giant stalactite-like formations projected downward, like inversions of the towering city constructs of Sanghelios. Some of these structures seemed to be related to the shield world's power distribution.

Below the inner crust of stone, soil, and water was another layer of artificial world, housing the inner workings of this ancient sanctuary: atmosphere generation, power conduits, maintenance. Parts of it seemed unfinished—and indeed Ussa was convinced that this shield world had not been completed by the Forerunners. He had a strong suspicion it was a new model, with new capabilities—and never quite tested. He intended to test those capabilities, if it was possible, when the time came.

It would be dangerous. The results would either destroy all his people—or save them. He reckoned the chances for either outcome were just about even.

"Know that this world is a Forerunner creation," Ussa went on. "And thus it is sacred. But it was intended by the Forerunners as a refuge, and we will use it exactly in that manner. We have enormous tasks to carry out. It will take a long time—many cycles—and it will demand tireless efforts from all of us. We will live here upon this surface. But most of the work will take place below, on the inner shells, in the artificial galleries below."

"But Great Ussa," 'Crolon said, keeping his tone respectful and mild, but his words insistent. "We are woefully unprepared to function as part of . . . this great machine you have brought us to. We do not know what we're doing here! These Forerunner artifacts, much of the apparatus we see—it is a mystery to us. We have known Forerunner works—we have discerned the function of some of them." Sangheili had taken up retroengineering the Forerunner technology in earnest in the latter part of the war with the San'Shyuum. "But this . . ."

"Your attitude, 'Crolon," Ussa sharply replied, "is what kept us in the dark shadow of the San'Shyuum to begin with. It was Sangheili like you who were reluctant to delve more deeply into the meaning of the Forerunner devices. But we learned that what is sacred can be also useful—and perhaps even more sacred as a result. We nearly fought the San'Shyuum to a standstill, using what we'd learned. If not for the cowardice of those who surrendered to the Covenant . . . But that is why we are here."

"Yes, Kaidon," 'Crolon said, almost whining, ducking his head in superficial submission. "Your will is law. Still, as this world's mechanisms are entirely new to us, there could be great danger in meddling with them. Dare we—"

" 'Crolon!" Ernicka growled. "Ussa is one who sees the world from the sky!" Ernicka was invoking an ancient Sangheili expression referring to a being capable of mastering many arts, a person of genius and vision. "He studied this place with Sooln 'Xellus, long before we came here! This is not his first visit! He knows all the apparatus well!"

That, of course, Ussa reflected, was not really true. He understood some of the Forerunners' great creation, but there was a great deal more to learn, along with his loyal adherents. It could take an epoch to puzzle it all out, if ever. But he had also found the artificial intelligence, Enduring Bias, which was able to explain what he needed to know most—once it had decided that explanations, at least some of them, somehow connected to its own purposes.

Sooln had a particular fascination with Enduring Bias, and engaged the Flying Voice, as some Sangheili called it, in long interrogatory conversations. Most of the Sangheili here respected Sooln, but being female, she did not evoke full confidence; the Sangheili patriarchy was naturally unwilling to trust a female with the most critical leadership matters. But Sooln had undeniable technical gifts and Ussa had learned to defer to her.

Before 'Crolon could grumble about Sooln not knowing her place, Ussa spoke up, making his voice boom over the crowd. "Clansfolk! You have trusted me thus far! I have taken you from one world to another! You must trust me here—we have crossed the Great Torrent!" The Great Torrent was a mythical fiercely rushing river that once crossed could never be passed through again. "We cannot turn back! I believe we are safe here—the Covenant does not know of this world! It is an uncharted place and they are not likely to find it! If they approach, we will have ample warning. We will survive! We have food, water, air, and most of all, hope! Rejoice with me in this . . . and remember that true Sangheili are always prepared for self-sacrifice! This is our *keep* now! Our home! Yes—and it is Sanghelios! Because wherever we go . . . *there* also is Sanghelios!"

And his followers raised their arms in the air, clacked their mandibles, and roared in response.

High Charity

850 BCE

The Age of Reconciliation

"I must tell you that High Charity now has a new Ministry, Mken," Qurlom was saying, his voice low. "And a new Minister to go with it."

"Not another one . . ."

"Oh yes! And it's one to take special note of."

They were descending on a purple-violet antigravity beam, their chairs side by side. In a short time they'd reach the Compartments of Comfort, the residential facilities used by High Lord Prophets.

Down they went, Mken gazing fixedly upward. Though Mken had long ago grown accustomed to the gravity lifts, he had always been a trifle uncomfortable with heights, and chose never to look down while using the device—since there was nothing under his feet but light and the long, long tube enclosing the lift area.

A new Ministry . . .

Mken glanced at Qurlom. The elderly San'Shyuum was hunched, gazing boldly down into the misty depths. "Ministries seem to proliferate," Mken said. "Certainly faster than San'Shyuum.

Soon there will be more Ministries than there are members of our species."

"You are pleased to be facetious, Mken, a bad habit of yours, but this is no matter for amusement. The Hierarchs have created the Ministry of Anticipatory Security. And the Minister . . . is your old friend R'Noh." He made the gesture of irony to go with the word *friend.*

"No, truly? They chose R'Noh Custo?"

"Yes, it is he. You two have been at odds many and many a time. I thought you probably had not been told yet—and you should be warned."

They reached the residence level, and drifted their chairs off the lift, heading down a translucent passage to the transverse corridor.

Impulsively, when they got to the place where they would part, Mken murmured, "Qurlom, thank you for letting me know. About the Ministry, I mean."

Qurlom glanced around to see that they were alone, and tugged meditatively at one of his wattles. "I have myself been a Hierarch, as you know. The reason I stepped down was not as much a question of my health as I'd let on. Not health in that sense."

Mken was surprised at this. "Then—what was it?"

"I felt something festering there, among the Hierarchs. Some . . . I do not say who . . . are more concerned with their ambition than with the Path to the Great Journey. You at least seem to have the Inner Conviction that led to your cognomen. I am happy to be able to give you a warning—but do not look to me for help with R'Noh. Just consider what this term 'Anticipatory Security' might really mean . . ."

Qurlom gave the gesture of *Be well and be discreet,* and turned his chair to float off toward his living quarters.

Mken gazed after him, musing, *Yes, the phrase "Anticipatory Security" is quite unsettling.*

The new Ministry could be a danger to High Charity if it were working not for the benefit of all San'Shyuum, but for one of the Hierarchs. In all likelihood the Hierarch behind the new Ministry was the simpering Prophet of Excellent Redolence—he humbly preferred to be called merely Excellent. He had chosen Prophet of Excellent Redolence as his regnal title, but Mken had known him as Quidd Klesto before his ascendance. Excellent was the master of subtle aggression, a great hinter of threats, of dire outcomes for those who crossed him. The threats, in good time, usually bore their poisonous fruit.

And yes, Mken had once crossed Excellent, had gone to the other two Hierarchs to have him overruled, in that regrettable matter of the plan to kidnap females from Janjur Qom.

Excellent had pretended to shrug the matter off, but he wasn't likely to forgive Mken—not ever.

Mken turned away, eager to put these concerns behind him. He badly wanted to be alone with his spouse, the graceful Cresanda . . . to feel her long neck twined around his, to savor her soft nuzzling of his wattles, her prehensile lips gently tugging at their fur.

His desire for such intimacies seemed increased lately, and he wondered if there were certain, quite specific hormones involved. Could it be . . . ?

Mken drifted to his residence's front door, sent the code from his chair to the door to unlock it, and passed into the understatedly incense-scented rooms. He felt a wave of relief when the door hissed shut behind him. Here, he could be himself.

The San'Shyuum Reformists, who'd stormed the Dreadnought, occupying it in preparation for using it as a method of escape, had made secret forays to stock it with plants, wood, seeds, and other goods from Janjur Qom. After the Dreadnought took to the stars, an entire deck was adapted with special lights to grow stunted trees and plants for herbal teas and fresh food. The intricately carved screens that covered most of the walls in Mken's residence had been sculpted from wood grown on board. The stone fountain in one corner, tinkling softly to itself, was made of pieces of the rock drawn along behind the Dreadnought when it had lifted off from the homeworld. The green shaded lighting was an attempt to replicate the tint coming through high canopies of plants in the dense forests found in the lowlands of Janjur Qom.

Looking around with satisfaction, Mken eased out of his chair—he kept his relative physical firmness a secret from all San'Shyuum apart from Cresanda. He didn't need the antigrav chair, at least on High Charity, as much as the others did. He had been careless about it, several solar cycles ago with his Steward, and it had been one of the sources of the fellow's resentment. Unfortunately, or perhaps fortunately, the Steward had been killed on the Planet of Blue and Red.

Mken often left his chair bobbing in the corner of his residence's front room. He enjoyed the use of his muscles. Cresanda, too, moved about the apartment without her chair, and now she glided toward him, her sinuous neck moving with graceful pleasure on seeing her spouse.

"Beloved Mken, axis of my life, here you are already!"

"We left our conferencing a bit early today, my dear. Qurlom was fatigued and the others occupied." He added teasingly, "Am I intrusive? Should I go to the herbal steaming-station and gossip with the attendants?"

"Don't you dare! You stay right here! I have a lovely herbal tea for you. Seat yourself."

"I prefer to stand for a time. I've been in that chair all day."

She had come closer and he could not keep from twining his neck with hers, nipping at the feminine hump on her back, just under her long neck.

"Oh you scamper-sneak!" she chided, returning tease for teasing.

"There is something, lately, that has me . . . yearn for you. Of course I always feel that way. But lately . . . to be close to you . . . is all I can think of!"

"You? You're not one who thinks of such things at length. You're more likely pondering classic art or planning the great doings of the species. You don't fool me a bit, Mken. Still, there might be a reason . . . perhaps."

He drew back and, so breathless he could scarcely speak, looked into her large green-brown eyes. "And that is . . . ?"

"Yes—" Her eyes glittered with inner excitement. "The time of Reproductive Yielding."

"Truly?"

"Truly. It is upon me! And, as you and I are not on the Roll of Celibates, and as our people are in tragic need of offspring, of continuation . . . I suggest that when the mood strikes us this evening, we look to the possibility of generating a new San'Shyuum life . . ." She looked away shyly. "But perhaps that convergence is not of interest to you. And we can wait many cycles for another such opportunity. And perhaps I will quietly prepare your tea, your protein mashes, and we will speak of the progress of High Charity's construction, or perhaps a new color gloss on the throne of ease . . ."

"Don't tantalize me!" He twined Cresanda again, his neck snaking half about hers. "And don't mock me either. You know that I want nothing more than making a child with you. Still . . ."

She drew back and looked at him gravely. "Still . . . what?"

"There are . . . considerations." He lowered his voice, though he regularly made sure that no surveillance mechanisms had been planted in his home. "You know that there were . . . were issues, with respect to my clearance from the Roll of Celibates."

"And?" Cresanda signed: *What of it?* "You took care of that long ago."

"Yes. I saw to it I was not disapproved—it would have been unfair." There were so few San'Shyuum—at least in space—and because there was a tendency to genetic blight among them, it was difficult to stay off the Roll of Celibates, the list designating those who were not approved for reproduction. "But there were questions, and I was nearly on the Roll. And R'Noh Custo is aware of this. *And* . . . there is a new Ministry."

"Pfft! It seems as if there's always a new one."

"So I remarked to old Qurlom. But the latest addition is called the Ministry of Anticipatory Security. And R'Noh is now its appointed Minister."

"Anticipatory Security—what does it *do*?"

Mken snorted. "I suspect it deals with security matters by anticipating them. That way, R'Noh and perhaps his sponsor, Excellent Redolence, can condemn whoever they like . . . because they *anticipate* that person will be a danger to High Charity."

"What? Such a Ministry could not long remain. It's madly unjust! People won't stand for it!"

"I suspect you're right—in time it will be undone. But in the *meantime* . . . we could run a risk by openly reproducing. R'Noh is not friendly to me. If he finds out about a pregnancy . . . and he inevitably will . . . it could lead to some dark treachery on his part. Used against both of us."

Cresanda looked at the floor. "I see. Then . . . we will speak only of construction and color glosses. And nothing more."

He clasped her hands in his. "Cresanda! Please do not mistake me! I could not keep from you. But . . . I just wanted you to know. That there *is* risk. I wanted to be fair to you . . . and—"

She put a hand on his lips. "Mken, it's always a risk to start a family. Everything joyous is a risk. Only in fear is complete safety. And then one lives in its jaws forevermore. You and I will not live that way."

And then she came closer, and entwined with Cresanda, Mken felt he had truly come home.

CHAPTER 3

The Refuge: An Uncharted Forerunner Shield World
850 BCE
The Age of Reconciliation

There are two choices only, in fact," said Salus 'Crolon, adjusting a dial on his scancam. "That is what I believe. Either Ussa is the true prophet of us all, the leader who will take us across a great wilderness to the promised land, or—he is simply wrong, and he has led us from our home to an alien world . . . for no real purpose. Of course, I would never espouse the second interpretation of the facts. No! I would not have the nerve to question our leader, our kaidon! But . . . some would say . . ."

Tersa 'Gunok was feeling very uncomfortable, listening to 'Crolon spout what could well be sedition. The older Sangheili's rhetoric walked along the edge, never quite slipping over the border into outright treason. But it would be enough for many kaidon to behead him, and then dismember the body.

Still, Tersa had been assigned to work with 'Crolon, and he could not properly snub his work partner, especially as 'Crolon was senior to Tersa. Together they were surveying the south side of the uncompleted Forerunner devices in the Storage Chamber under the secondary inner shell of the Refuge. Other Sangheili, thankfully out of earshot, surveyed the farther fringes of the four-acre collection of slightly wobbling tiers filled with mysterious objects. The vast chamber, with its arching metallic ceiling, contained thousands of Forerunner artifacts, relics, pieces of sacred devices, all stacked in blue stasis fields, devices that few but Ussa 'Xellus and Sooln possibly understood. And it was doubtful, according to 'Crolon, that even the kaidon and his mate would ever really be able to harness the secrets of all these mechanisms.

Pondering Salus 'Crolon's mutterings, Tersa used the scancam to take a three-dimensional image of a cylindrical object that spun slowly in place in its stasis field, the whorl marks on its white, shiny skin seeming to react when Tersa came close, as if it were scanning Tersa even as he did likewise. And that was possible. Was this not a creation of the Forerunners? Would it not be mystically infused with their intelligence, their essence?

What secrets vibrated within these relics?

For ages, the Sangheili had believed that the Forerunner relics must be held in reverence, and not interfered with. Sangheili with a scientific bent, who covertly probed into them well past the point permitted, were inevitably put to death when their blasphemous inquiries came to light. But there were those who secretly studied the relics in hidden laboratories, delving into the cryptic interiors of the artifacts. Those few heretics had kept secret records, had shared their data in a kind of scientific underground, using codes, cryptograms.

Then the San'Shyuum had come—had driven the Sangheili from their interstellar colonies, appropriating Forerunner relics, openly and blasphemously utilizing the artifacts for their own foul purposes, expunging many clansfolk, sending others scurrying like a squealing pack of fur grubs. There was no honor for the Sangheili in being driven back and further back—and the San'Shyuum were looming ever closer to Sanghelios.

It was impossible to effectively fight the Dreadnought and the gut-boiling weaponry of the San'Shyuum's Sentinels, so the underground movement of Sangheili scientists had emerged, confessing their sins, and declaring that the secret lore of the Forerunners was the only hope for the Sangheili. If they did not utilize at least some of these discoveries to create weapons, to build new and better and faster attack fleets, they would lose the war, and the San'Shyuum would locate Sanghelios, would overrun it, loot it, and then, doubtlessly, commit an act of genocide, destroying all Sangheili on the homeworld. Warriors would die without honor, executed with remotely fired weapons, never having the opportunity to face their adversaries in battle; females and even childlings, fresh from eggs, would be burned away by the Dreadnought like troublesome microorganisms.

The Sangheili were desperate—and the underground of Sangheili scientists were allowed to live; their secrets were put to use. A great interstellar war, with attacks on the Dreadnought and its array of lesser vessels, rolled explosively across the galaxy. But though they succeeded in holding the line, the Sangheili fleet could not triumph—the Forerunner keyship was too powerful.

Yet the Sangheili sometimes gained ground, and hemmed the San'Shyuum in with a cunning use of slipspace and hit-and-run tactics—they kept the ancient Dreadnought from effectively deploying its full arsenal.

And so something akin to a stalemate was reached, though the San'Shyuum still had the edge with the keyship, the gigantic tripod in space pulsing with power.

The Dreadnought couldn't be everywhere at once. The San'Shyuum, its numbers few, needed an army. So Ussa 'Xellus had explained it. And so they turned to the Sangheili, and negotiated the Writ of Union. *And why?* Ussa demanded, when he'd first fomented his rebellion. *So that we might do the San'Shyuum's bidding! So that we might be the serpent-necks' enforcers! We now become lowly caste!*

But only a few of the clans listened to Ussa. The rest, fearful lest Sanghelios itself be utterly destroyed, had submitted to the Writ of Union.

Ussa, seeking a new homeworld for his followers in the wake of his own country's destruction at the hands of the Covenant, had since found the uncharted shield world and led them all in delving into the secrets of the Forerunners, hidden technologies that they would use to escape the predation of those who had sold out to the Covenant, which would one day make possible a restoration of true Sangheili honor.

That was how Tersa understood it, how he had fervently believed. But here was 'Crolon, chattering on, casually sowing doubt. Salus 'Crolon no longer voiced these doubts within the hearing of Ussa or Sooln or Ernicka the Scar-Maker. But on the outskirts of their new, small colony, 'Crolon relentlessly asked his corrosive questions.

"I merely mean, we can *wonder* at these conundrums," 'Crolon was saying lightly, as he turned his scancam to a new artifact, a floating pyramid as high as two Sangheili, intricately figured on each of its faces. The scanning camera hummed, and the holographic image of the interior and exterior of the pyramid was projected in blue and green light overhead for a moment, confirming its scan. "Either Ussa is right—or we are all lost. There is no middle ground." 'Crolon now glanced around to see if anyone else was listening. He clearly knew he was treading dangerous ground. "And suppose he is wrong? Will we not perish here, away from our homeworld, in a place we can never understand? Perhaps this world is a Forerunner temple! Perhaps we are defiling it by our very presence here!"

Tersa squirmed inwardly upon hearing this. He was a youth, and he knew his place; he was expected to give 'Crolon respect. But it was all he could do to refrain from a shouting argument. He took a deep breath, clasped his lateral jaws together firmly for a moment, to show smiling patience, and murmured, " 'Crolon . . . it is as Ussa said, we have crossed the Great Torrent. There is no turning back. We are committed. I believe we are *rightly* committed. There is nothing but shame in submitting to the Covenant. And truly that *is* our only other choice. What do you think would happen to us if we returned to Sanghelios? We'd be put to death for siding against the Writ of Union."

"Oh, I am just speculating on all this for the sake of discussion," 'Crolon replied mildly. "Though—there might be another way. A deal could be struck, perhaps . . ."

"With whom? That sounds like treachery . . . !"

"Keep your voice down, fool of a childling—you'll have Ernicka after us both! I did not mean it that way. I am one who thinks logically and methodically, who looks at all sides of a dilemma."

"I see no dilemma here. I see only the path we've taken. Of all Sangheili, only *we* are honorable now."

"Oh certainly, but . . . well, it was just a thought or two, nothing more. I hope I can count on you for discretion, my boy." He cleared his throat and spoke more loudly. "Ah! Here comes the Scar-Maker! Greetings, Ernicka!"

"You two," Ernicka the Scar-Maker rumbled as he went

striding by, "are doing far more chattering than scanning. Ussa and Sooln must decipher these devices—we will need them! Set to work!" As if for emphasis, he had one hand on the hilt of a burn-blade, sheathed on his hip.

"You are shiningly correct as always, Ernicka," 'Crolon said, exuding humility as he turned to the work at hand.

Tersa kept his head down and said nothing. He went back to his task, thinking that with any luck he would not be appointed to work with 'Crolon tomorrow. But Tersa felt as if in listening to 'Crolon he'd ingested a subtle poison. What if they *were* sullying this sacred place? What if Ussa 'Xellus was simply a misguided fanatic who'd led them into the hollow heart of an enigmatic world where they would wither away, where they would die blighted with Ussa's growing insanity?

By the Forerunners and all that was holy—what if Salus 'Crolon was right?

High Charity
850 BCE
The Age of Reconciliation

Mken was in his private study, hunched over grainy holograms of ancient Forerunner sculpture. Some of the artifacts were not true sculpture, perhaps, but devices that only looked like works of art. It was often hard to tell.

He caused the image to rotate, taking in its curves and hollows, its sweeping volutes. The shape seemed to suggest evolution, galactic spirals, a tower of swirling shapes all writhing together . . .

His understanding of the Forerunners identified them as

beings who had maintained, for a time, organic, material form; they became somehow channelers of a divine inspiration that transformed them and made them suitable for the Great Journey to a higher realm, through the agency of the seven Rings. The Rings, set about the galaxy in spiritually significant positions, had been designed to summon sublime spiritual energies that burned away falsehood and freed the soul to speed rapidly to the heart of the godhead.

The San'Shyuum believed the Forerunners had deliberately left their traces across the galaxy as signposts, pieces of a holy conundrum that once solved would allow other races with enough faith to walk the path of the Great Journey, eventually joining the Forerunners.

But if the Forerunners were like avatars of God—then who ultimately was that God? Was there not some *over*-God, that all must submit to?

There must be. And perhaps the end of the Great Journey was a glorious encounter with that ultimate deity.

But again Mken was peppered by doubts about the Great Journey and the purpose of the Halo array, which the Forerunners had created. Did the description of the effect not sound like weapons? Were there not references—if they were translated correctly—that suggested that the energies were capable of great displays of power?

But of course those references were murky at best. Probably mistranslated. And he'd never dared share them with other Prophets. Strictly speaking, he should have worked till he found nonheretical interpretations.

The Holy Rings were most certainly real, though they had generated a mythos of their own among the San'Shyuum. Mken wondered if they still existed at all—if they were still out there in the galaxy, and somehow had remained intact?

Could the San'Shyuum find them—and discover the true purpose of the Great Journey?

And who am I to question the Great Journey? Am I a heretic to even wonder at it? I am but one small being, a speck in the universe. The Forerunners were at one with the purpose of the universe itself, were demigods whose powers of invention crossed from the realm of the natural into the supernatural—or so it appears. Who am I to question? And who am I at all? Am I the Prophet of Inner Conviction? Or am I just the San'Shyuum who once did the childish ripple dance with the others?

"Prophet of Inner Conviction—are you there?"

Mken sat up straight, startled, making his antigrav chair bobble slightly on its field.

He looked up to see the screen above his work space blinking with an indicator of an incoming visual call, a verbal message resonating in the air.

He flicked his fingers over the glowing holoswitches, summoning a response with the precision of ingrained habit, and the holographic image of R'Noh appeared before him. R'Noh wore a silver filigreed robe and a high, branching copper-colored collar that was not like a Hierarch's, but seemed suggestive of one, like a child's mockup of a Hierarch's headdress.

R'Noh's large dark eyes glittered with menace; his nostrils flared as if he were some distant, primitive San'Shyuum ancestor on a hunt and scenting his prey.

"Ah! There you are, Inner Conviction!"

"Yes, R'Noh, here I am. And here you are. Do please state your purpose. I'm engaged in study. Sacred study."

"But perhaps you can *spare* a minute or two?" Just a mild flavor of mockery in his words.

Mken considered refusing. But why court trouble? There was R'Noh's fresh posting to head an absurd, newly minted Ministry to consider. *Anticipatory Security.*

"Certainly, R'Noh."

"Oh thank you, Inner Conviction. This will not take much of your time. There are a few matters—and it may be that one will be the solution to the problem presented by the other."

"And what problem would you bring to *me*, R'Noh?"

"Ah, should I not be bringing them to you? You speak as if you imagine my status is the same as when we last met."

"No, no—Anticipatory Security. I heard that you were now a Minister. I should have conveyed congratulations before now. I only just heard. Felicitations. Now—what can I help you with?"

Mken so badly wanted to flick R'Noh's face away with a thumb stab at his holoswitch. As if crushing some insignificant chitinous crawler. The vile memories . . .

But he gestured *Happy to be of service.*

"Thank you, Inner Conviction—I will get right to it, then. You know how difficult, how time-consuming, how tiresome and embarrassing a genetic sorting can be. We don't wish to impose one upon you. But we are automatically informed when anyone's medical interface is consulted about pregnancy."

Mken blinked. "Indeed? And how long has that been the case?"

"Oh it's a recent . . . arrangement. A little while ago it was decided that the new Ministry was a good idea and at that point . . . the anticipatory information was approved."

"Anticipatory. As in looking ahead. I see. Someone has been checking to see if they are pregnant—and this is of concern to me because . . . ?"

"Because it was your mate."

Mken struggled to keep his equanimity. *Do not lose your temper.* "And what of it? We are not on the Roll of Celibates."

"Yes—about that. It seems to some of us who have looked into this matter that you might well have been on the Roll—except for some nudging here and there, perhaps."

"You are alleging corruption? You have not been Minister long—I did not expect you to go mad with power so quickly, R'Noh. Has it not occurred to you that you are making a very severe accusation?"

"I am accusing no one of anything, Inner Conviction. But only consider what the nature of the new Ministry is. We must try to halt problems before they take root and grow. This means we must cast around for those problems. And casting around can include parsing rumors. Including rumors about you."

"And yet you claim you are not accusing me of anything?"

"We are just . . . inquiring. Perhaps there is a shadow of suspicion. Perhaps not. But . . ."

"I assert again—I am not on the Roll of Celibates. So no wrongdoing has been committed here. We are permitted to have offspring. It is no concern of yours if my mate looks into the possibility of pregnancy."

R'Noh made the gesture of *One is but thinking aloud.* "Ah, but one can, if there is sufficient reason for suspicion, be *added* to the Roll of Celibates at any time, Inner Conviction."

"And is that why you've reached out to me? Because I can expect you to advocate for this . . . this blight on my reputation?"

Mken was working very hard to keep himself calm and motionless. He would not let this wretch see him with his wattles waggling with anger.

"Why, Inner Conviction, no one has decided to advocate for any such thing. Certainly, information would have to be gathered.

Interrogations made. Who knows how far it could take us? Even if nothing was found, the inquiry alone is a blot on one's reputation. You know what our brethren are, so prone to jumping at assumptions. Rumors would redouble and would themselves reproduce and multiply." R'Noh seemed quite pleased with his witticism.

"All this is pressure, held over my head. There is something you want of me. State your true business. I have work to conduct."

"You are perceptive—I say that without confirming or denying your supposition. But, Inner Conviction, coincidentally there *is* something we want you to do for us."

"We?"

"Yes. In fact, the plan issues from his eminence, Excellent Redolence, and myself, in a humbler way."

"The Hierarch. The High Prophet of Excellent Redolence. He approves this . . . this blackmail? This extortion?"

"What? Am I hearing correctly? You would accuse Excellent of extortion? Surely not, Inner Conviction!"

Mken grated his teeth. He wanted to say *Direct extortion would take courage, so perhaps it would in truth be unlikely since Excellent is craven, is one who jockeys for power when others have their backs turned . . .*

Instead, Mken merely asked, "What is this 'something' you want of me?"

"We merely want you to lead a covert team to Janjur Qom. Where you will obtain a certain object . . . and genetically healthy females for breeding purposes."

Mken was stunned. "You cannot be serious. I told you what I thought of that heinous plan when you first proposed it!"

"Yes. I recall it clearly. You quite humiliated me in front of the Hierarchs."

"Oh. I see. And now this is repayment, revenge for that embarrassment?"

"Perhaps there *is* an element of, as you say, repayment." R'Noh's nostrils flared again. His eyes narrowed. "But—I will tell you that plans of forced abduction have been discarded. It has been decided we will take only those females who will freely come to High Charity. We have sent Eyes to the homeworld, and we have found a settlement where we believe we will obtain willing prospects. A place called Crellum. A holographic message was shown to certain females. And there is something else— nearby is a place called the grotto of the Great Transition, in which we may find the Purifying Vision of the Holy Path itself. And with it—a Luminary."

Mken snorted. "There is no proof that the Purifying Vision actually exists. There are many tales of such a holy artifact—but none has been found."

"Nonetheless, the records of those who served on the Dreadnought before it departed mention the possibility of the relic in a certain place on Janjur Qom—they apparently received a sacred sign through the ship's Luminary. If the relic is indeed there, it will provide additional gravitas—holy affirmation much needed in this time of spiritual turmoil so soon after the Writ of Union."

Doubtless much of that speech about the time of turmoil was R'Noh paraphrasing Excellent Redolence. R'Noh spent no appreciable moments contemplating anything spiritual.

"Very well, send your expedition. But there's no need to involve me."

"Oh, but there is—there are actually two reasons. First we have need of your learning with respect to the homeworld."

"I am unlikely to have practical information about anything that could apply to such an expedition—"

"But you *do* have what we need!" R'Noh's interruption was an outrageous breach of protocol. He went on blandly. "You have studied the area in question, O Prophet of Inner Conviction. You know a good deal about the southeastern edge of Reskolah."

"Reskolah?" Mken's heart thudded at the storied name. An area rumored to contain many undiscovered relics. It was almost tempting. But absurd. "I've studied topographical maps—the most recent data I could unearth. But . . . there is much I do not know."

"You are still best suited—and the one chosen by Excellent Redolence—to lead the Appropriation Party."

"So that is what you call it? What a clumsy euphemism for raiding. We may have to kill San'Shyuum to make good our seizing of relics and this supposed recruitment . . ."

"Kill *San'Shyuum*, Inner Conviction? Why, those are *Stoics* you are referring to! Heretics! They're fortunate to be losing only a few of their females and a relic—and we simply must reproduce. The Roll of Celibates, the rarity of fertility cycles—our population shrinks. If the Sangheili were to take note of our low population count, it might embolden them to rethink their loyalty."

"Then why not simply relax the Roll of Celibates?"

"It was created for a reason. It is necessary to keep our genetics from drifting into degenerency, Inner Conviction. We have reason to believe the Stoics, at least, are genetically sound. They are more numerous—not likely to be challenged with inbreeding. And again, the Purifying Vision of the Holy Path is valuable beyond calculation. We need to make sure the Sangheili are truly loyal, truly converted—the shine of such a holy relic will erase all doubt and inevitably unite them behind us!"

"And if I am killed? Do you suppose, R'Noh, that the Stoic San'Shyuum of our homeworld will not detect us? Will stand cheerfully by while we snatch up their females and make off with them?"

"I suppose nothing of the sort. We hope to avoid battle—to avoid detection entirely. But . . . we cannot be sure of it. You have studied Janjur Qom, at a remove. And you are not without military experience. You will go in clandestinely and escape with equal stealth. You will *probably* not be killed. If you are, I doubt if his eminence the Prophet of Excellent Redolence will be greatly saddened."

"I'm touched," said Mken dryly.

". . . And he will then find someone else to send. The plan *will* move forward, however. Now, Prophet of Inner Conviction, you should prepare yourself to leave for Janjur Qom with all speed . . ."

CHAPTER 4

The Refuge: An Uncharted Forerunner Shield World
850 BCE
The Age of Reconciliation

ooln, you look concerned. Unhappy. What has the Flying Voice told you?"

"I am not unhappy, but perhaps I'm a bit disturbed by something Enduring Bias said—the way boiling blood is disturbed in a cauldron."

Ussa closed his jaws in a Sangheili smile. He liked the way Sooln expressed herself. Always a touch of the poetic. It was one of the qualities that endeared her to him. "Tell me what has your cauldron bubbling, then."

They were walking in a place that Sooln called Ussa's Garden. It was an arboreal, rugged setting on the secondary shell of the shield world, far beneath the metallic sky, the high, curved protective surface, concave from this vantage beneath it. Enduring Bias had imparted to them that the Forerunners built the sheathing to protect this world from more than one sort of danger—and it had more than one sort of protection.

There were variously shaped plants here—some twisted, some like frozen bomb-bursts—and there was an artificial breeze sighing from outcroppings of gray and gold stone. Ussa felt a great comfort in walking with Sooln in such a place. Somehow it felt like traveling with her through the landscape of their life together. After all, she was his mate, the layer of eggs—though his son, Ossis, who had been killed in battle, was the only product so far of that laying—and even when Ussa had to go into battle, she was never far from his thoughts.

At last Sooln said, "Enduring Bias, Ussa, has told me that this world indeed has hidden possibilities. This is the last of many shield worlds created, an effort that apparently ended prematurely. It had a fail-safe setting, a possibility of surviving even if it broke apart. This was not something the others had. But this one was special. Only, the necessity of firing the great Rings came before it could be completed . . ."

"So—it is as we guessed? As in meta analysis?"

"Yes. Enduring Bias claims that properly triggered, this world can disassemble itself—and its disparate parts can survive."

"Would you care for a visualization?" asked the intelligence in a gentle voice, dropping down from above. The flying machine hummed lower, situating itself in front of them, as if wishing to be companionable, its three lenses flickering.

Ussa growled within himself and demanded, "You were *watching* us, up there? Following us?"

"Of course, Ussa 'Xellus! I am here to oversee this world, after all," Enduring Bias replied. There was a casual whimsicality in its tone that always annoyed Ussa.

Ussa knew a good deal about Covenant beliefs—he had not discarded their teaching lightly. He had heard, monitoring High Charity transmissions, that the San'Shyuum had a damaged distributed intelligence, rather like this, a thinking device they called the Oracle. It was rumored to be mostly mute, only on occasion relinquishing sacred clues. But Enduring Bias, though capable of fantastic feats of intellectual calculus, seemed without gravitas, to Ussa—without real dignity and certainly without the power of divination. All of which was more proof that the Covenant was wrong.

"It's all right, husband. Enduring Bias has chosen to work with us now," Sooln said, touching Ussa's arm. "He has assured me so—and I believe him."

"He?"

"The voice sounds male to me. Yes, Enduring, please do provide visualization. Unless—is he allowed to show the image here, Ussa?"

Ussa glanced around. They seemed to be quite alone. "Yes."

Instantly a beam of blue light lanced down to sketch in a holographic image in front of them: a globe in lambent three dimensions. It was this very shield world—the Refuge, as his followers called it—as it would look from space.

"Here you see Shield 0673, which you now inhabit," intoned Enduring Bias. "I was brought here shortly after its completion—but before its testing. When the Ring installations were used, no one returned for me. I determined that I was on my own. Which is why it was possible to access my prioritization and control system, since I was, you might say, at loose ends, without clear-cut purpose after the activation . . ."

"Less about yourself and more about this shield world," Sooln said.

"Wait," Ussa put in. "The Ring installations. Do you know *where* these Rings are?"

"That information was taken from my memory when I was brought here. There were security concerns. I have only a partial knowledge of the Rings now. Much was eliminated. It's very disagreeable, having a gap in your mind. I don't recommend it. One always comes upon the gap and one probes and finds nothing where something should be. It has always seemed to me—"

"Try to stay focused," Ussa said.

"I do apologize. Many millennia here, with no one to converse with, left me overtalkative and perhaps a bit on the senile side, if the term can be applied to a machine."

"What do you know about the Rings, and the shield worlds?" Ussa said, gnashing his mandibles with exasperation.

"Only what I have told you before: that the Rings emanated a particular energy that would destroy sentient life—and yet the emanation was somehow intended to protect biodiversity across the galaxy. From . . . I don't know from what. I'm afraid that information was kept in what is now one of my gaps."

"But what do you know of the so-called . . . Great Journey?"

"That term is not specifically familiar to me."

Sooln looked at him. "I thought you didn't believe in the Great Journey."

"I don't," Ussa assured her. "But perhaps the Forerunners did. They went *somewhere*. I was just thinking that if I could prove the Great Journey is a myth, that the Ring installations were meant for something else . . . as weapons, as I suspect . . . then perhaps we could wrest some of the fools on Sanghelios away from the Covenant."

"Ah," said Enduring Bias. "I'm afraid information that would pertain to such an effort was kept in parts of my memory that—"

"Yes, yes," interrupted Ussa. "Which are now gaps. Go on, then—show us the visualization of the shield world's meta purpose."

"That is easily accomplished."

The shield world in the hologram had seams in its metallic shell. The seams, as Ussa and Sooln watched, began to leak light—white radiance seemed to race around the seam lines, outlining all the segments making up the shell. The light grew in intensity . . . and then the seam lines grew farther apart. The shield world seemed to explode in slow motion, as if the massive metallic sphere had been made of three-dimensional puzzle pieces and a host of invisible hands were plucking those pieces away from one another, moving them, all at the same speed, outward from the center of the semi-artificial world. It appeared like both a slow, fluid explosion and an organized disassembling, at once.

"This is happening more slowly than it would in real time," Enduring Bias explained. "You will note that some of the atmosphere and fluids are being discharged, at least outwardly. Hence it does look like a real explosion. Within airtight components of the shield world, the atmosphere remains."

"And from there?"

"From there, the components move to the next orbit out, which, as you recall, is largely made up of asteroids. The components would remain in communication. However, I cannot disclose with certainty that this process will work—it was not tested, and at this point the machinery may be faulty."

"So—if we tried it . . ."

"For what purpose? Why would you want to try it?" Enduring Bias asked.

"I don't know that I would. But for my own reasons, it is a possibility. In some situations. But—it could end badly? Lethally?"

"Certainly. The outcome could well be negative. I would calculate a forty-nine percent chance that the outcome would be lethal for all biological organisms on this world." After a moment it added chirpily, "Shall we try it? I would be curious to know if it works."

"No," Ussa grunted. "We will not attempt it. Unless we have to."

High Charity
850 BCE
The Age of Reconciliation

"Great Hierarch, Prophet of Excellent Redolence, it is an unbearable honor for me to be here."

"An interesting choice of words, Inner Conviction," said Excellent, with a fluttering, ancient *What means this?* gesture.

Mken had arranged the meeting, thinking that perhaps all the Hierarchs would be present to try to persuade Excellent Redolence against this mission. But judging by the setting and the Hierarch's pose, Excellent seemed to have guessed Mken's purpose.

They were in the San'Shyuum Hall of Sacred Guidance, where the Hierarch had positioned his elegantly articulated antigrav throne on a dais, so that he was looking down upon Mken. He was slouching a little, unconsciously expressing, it seemed to Mken, the time-honored overconfidence of those who rule and those who aspire to wider rule. His branching golden mantle glittered in the ambient illumination of the great hallway. The symbol of the seven Rings, in the Arrangement of Holiness, was projected in a holograph above him; a single Ring glowed from his crown at the center of his forehead. All this symbolism was of course meant to intimidate the Prophet of Inner Conviction, as were the Elite guards who stood, fully armed and shining in armor, to either side of the dais. The Hierarch was seated in the center of the dais—when the other Hierarchs were there, Excellent was usually seated to the right.

"Before I continue, O Excellent Redolence," said Mken with an assumed meekness, "should I wait for the other Hierarchs to arrive?" He knew perfectly well that Excellent had reserved the room, so to speak, for himself and his personal retinue alone, that the other two Hierarchs had not been informed of the meeting. But Mken wanted Excellent to be reminded of this violation of protocol.

"That won't be necessary; the other Hierarchs are fully briefed on the genetic restoration expedition," Excellent said with a dismissive, magisterial wave of his hand.

R'Noh drifted into the big chamber, deliberately moving with stately aplomb, as if to bask in the reflected glow of the Hierarch's authority.

"Ah, there you are, Minister," Excellent said silkily, with an *It is past time* gesture, but conveyed in a genial fashion. "You have consulted with the ship's captain?"

"I have, Great and Sacred Hierarch," R'Noh replied, genuflecting. "The ship is still being charged and victualed, but he anticipates readiness within this daily cycle."

"But—" Here Excellent turned his deceptively mild gaze upon Mken. "Is our Prophet of Inner Conviction in readiness?"

"I cannot be truly ready, O Hierarch, for a task I have little confidence in. I request consultation with the full triumvirate of Hierarchs, so that I may be of assistance in selecting another candidate for the expedition, if, indeed, the triumvirate approves—"

Excellent Redolence sat up straight, his long neck recoiling like a snake about to strike. "Mken 'Scre'ah'ben!" The use of Mken's original name was intended to put "The Prophet of Inner Conviction" in his place. "Do I understand that you are accusing a Hierarch of the Sacred Search of breaching Council protocol?"

R'Noh made a pleased sniggering sound at this scolding.

Mken kept his temper in check. "I imply nothing of the kind, O Hierarch. I am suggesting that the purpose of this journey is beneath us—and is not necessary. It is past time for a review of the need for a Roll of Celibates. Instead of a mad and risky expedition, let us scrutinize—"

Excellent slammed a fist onto the arm of his antigravity throne—accidentally triggering a spray of random holographic images and making his chair revolve once in the air.

Mken wanted to laugh, but given the situation, thought it unwise. "They are, after all, San'Shyuum, worthy of respect as our people, even though—"

Pretending the throne-spin hadn't happened, though even R'Noh had to suppress another snigger at the sight, Excellent Redolence jabbed an accusing finger at Mken and demanded, "Have you forgotten that these so-called Stoics have appropriated our homeworld, Janjur Qom—stolen it from the holy martyrs? It is an act of liberation, not abduction, to acquire females from them! And the Purifying Vision of the Holy Path, the Luminary associated with it—these alone should justify the attempt!"

"If perhaps we could involve the other Hierarchs—"

Excellent made a quick, snappish gesture that was rarely used, meaning *Go silent or die silent.* "I will hear no more of this political casuistry! The triumvirate has agreed that I am to oversee a restoration of new breeding stock! The method was not specified—therefore, I shall specify it myself!"

Excellent seemed to realize that he was exposing himself—that the raging tyrant who was the *real* Excellent Redolence preferred the appearance of a somber, witty San'Shyuum of subtle wisdom. He settled back in his throne and absently stroked the fur on one of his wattles. "You have unsettled me. I will brook no more insubordination. Here are my terms, 'Prophet of Inner Conviction.'" Mockery dripped from his tone as he used the title. "You may take your choice. You will suffer a severe, thorough, and perhaps not entirely unbiased inquiry into your exclusion from the Roll of Celibates—an exclusion that I believe to be fraudulently arranged—and you will suffer the legal consequences . . . or you will lead this expedition to Janjur Qom."

"With all due respect, Great Hierarch, I am scarcely a military commander."

"I beg to differ. You were in action on the Planet of Blue and Red, and in other places during the war. We have no one else available here with such experience. You oversaw purges and the appropriation of resources."

"That was long ago."

"Silence! Enough of this—make your choice!"

Mken took a long, deep breath. Then he bowed to the inevitable— as he bowed to Excellent Redolence. "I will lead the expedition suffused with an eagerness to serve you, Great Hierarch."

"Good. Go and prepare for departure as quickly as you can. Breathe not a word of this to anyone. Then report to launch bay thirty-three. Your staff has already been chosen for you. Including the Elites . . . my Sangheili . . . I am sending along with you . . ."

"Respectfully, Excellent Redolence, I will need to make a plan. Survey the state of the homeworld, choose the precise—"

"Once more you drag your heels! The survey is based on sound surveillance intelligence. The plan was made through specific modeling. It has all been completed. You are free, however, to refine it as you go. Now, leave my sight and prepare for departure."

Mken made a gesture of obeisance and turned away. Drifting his chair past R'Noh, he heard Excellent remark with a sneer,

"R'Noh, refresh my memory. Didn't this very 'Prophet of Inner Conviction' once denounce you as a capricious fool when you suggested a mission to obtain females from the Stoics?"

"Why, yes, yes he did, Great Hierarch!"

"Is it not an exquisite irony that now he must lead such a mission himself?"

"Oh, I agree," chuckled R'Noh, as Mken directed his chair through the doorway. "I find that quite exquisite!"

"Mken," said the Hierarch from behind him. "Remember that *no one* is to know about this mission . . . except those who must accompany you."

Mken paused, half turned. "Very well, Great Hierarch. But—when we return? Surely, then we must . . ."

"Yes, yes, once it is complete and you have returned, success in hand—then we will announce it. Success will protect the mission from expected criticism. Now, you go and see that it *is* a success!"

Mken gestured *Joyful obedience.* He went slowly from the room, to preserve as much dignity as remained to him . . . precious little.

After leaving the hall, he paused in an observation bubble, directing his chair to a window that looked out on the smeared purple of a nebula. To go out there and return to Janjur Qom . . . He'd dreamed of going there all his life. But under these circumstances . . . no.

The Stoics were not without their own military resources. What were the chances he would return alive from such a mission?

It seemed to him the chances were feeble.

And the likelihood was that he would die there, away from his beloved mate, never seeing his child. This was utter madness.

CHAPTER 5

High Charity
850 BCE
The Age of Reconciliation

O*n the blood of my father, on the blood of my sons, with each beat of each heart within my breast I swear to uphold the Covenant."*

Under the direction of the San'Shyuum known as R'Noh, a Sangheili ranger known as Vil 'Kthamee recited the oath with the other Sangheili, before setting foot on the corvette *Vengeful Vitality*, the vessel that would take them to Janjur Qom under the command of the Prophet of Inner Conviction. Vil always found the oath thrilling, but later, if he thought about it too much, he felt uncomfortable; he tasted a bitterness. The Covenant was relatively new, the Writ of Union was crafted not so long ago. And within memory the Sangheili had fought the San'Shyuum. How many of his bloodline, his egg brothers, had died under the blistering, murderous blasts of the Dreadnought?

And yet he served these same San'Shyuum.

Surrender? It was *not* surrender—the dishonor of such a

thing the Sangheili could not imagine; no, it was alliance—and it was the saving of Sanghelios.

Still, here was that bitter taste within his mandibles, when he thought of the fallen dead. Could they but speak, would they denounce the Sangheili as living without nobility?

Now there was a crueler irony: Vil lived on a great chunk of what had once been Janjur Qom. It was the homeworld of the San'Shyuum, the homeworld of those who had wiped out so many Sangheili. The great mass of stone and soil, about two mountains worth, taken up by the Dreadnought when it arose from Janjur Qom, had been removed from the keyship and formed into an asteroid; it was to be the foundation of the true pedestal of High Charity. And already there were warrens dug into it, sealed off subterranean fortresslike structures, airtight and almost self-sufficient, where lived Sangheili serving as guards, protectors of the San'Shyuum.

There were six trained Sangheili warriors, and their commander Trok 'Tanghil, filing into the corvette on the launch deck. Just before he stepped into the air lock Vil's gaze took in the sweeping, curved lines of the iridescent stealth corvette; it was in two linked tiers, its middle swollen like a Sangheili slitherer just after the creature had swallowed a hopping slug alive—as if something large was not yet digested in its belly. Like with all Covenant ships, loosely based on an obscure selection of Forerunner designs, there was something organic about the lines of the ship; it emulated the rippling forms found in nature.

Just inside, floating blithely from left to right, on some engineering mission, was a Huragok, a being that defied the contrast between machine and biological organism. The thing—they could not be called a species, not having evolved—had been artificially created, it was said, by the Forerunners themselves, who built them up with nanocellular intricacy to be repair and enhance mechanisms, to act as maintenance engineers for the devices known now as sacred relics. A Huragok's snaking head could seem slightly reminiscent of the San'Shyuum, to Vil anyway, but the Engineer organisms had three eyelike sensory nodes on either side of their heads. A large cluster of translucent pink and purple gas sacs—some for elevation, some for propulsion, some for chemical supply—humped over the creature's head; two probing, feathery anterior tentacles whipped forward. Each tentacle tip articulated into cilia, microscopically fine at the ends, for working within electroenergetic interfaces and other gear; from its underskirt below rippled four other work tentacles. The docile creatures seemed to desire nothing but food and work—and they'd made no resistance when tamed by the San'Shyuum.

The Huragok seemed to be coming along on the expedition—and Vil had worked with the creature before, more than once. He recognized it by the particular mottling of its air sacs. This Huragok was known as Floats Near Ceiling. It communicated with configurations of its tentacles and could read some hand signs and certain holographic insignia. The Huragok being part of the crew was good, as Floats Near Ceiling was efficient and Vil always found its presence to be curiously comforting. Perhaps they were soothing because the Huragok had no agenda but effecting repair, maintenance, following directions, and the like—the creatures were almost eerily trustworthy.

After stepping from the air lock into the ship, Vil saw the San'Shyuum leader known as Inner Conviction, the Prophet seated broodingly in his antigrav chair at the foot of the ramp leading up to the bridge of the corvette; an armed Steward behind him watched the Sangheili narrowly. R'Noh, the Minister of Anticipatory Security, wasn't coming on the voyage, but there were several other San'Shyuum on the stealth corvette: the captain, called Vervum, the communications officer, S'Prog, and a gunner named Mleer. But the vessel was outfitted for clandestine activities, not significant space battles, and it occurred to Vil that he and the other Sangheili outnumbered these San'Shyuum, who, after all, were of little use in a pitched hand-to-hand fight.

Flickering through Vil's mind came an unbidden daydream—he imagined he and his fellow Sangheili taking the ship, slaughtering the San'Shyuum, making their way in the corvette back to Sanghelios, settling in secret in some remote part of the world, or perhaps on one of the moons.

Instantly Vil was ashamed of himself. How could he even imagine such a thing? He had spoken an oath—many oaths, a taut and binding knot of vows—all to uphold the Covenant. He had bound his soul to the Covenant through those pledges. How could he even imagine rebelling?

I must reform my thinking—or turn myself in.

He must have no more treasonous fancies.

Vil carried his satchel and directed-energy rifle into the crew's quarters, stowing his gear under a bed, wondering if, after all, he would die on the alien soil of Janjur Qom. That they had some sort of assignment there was whispered in the barracks. They would be briefed when they reached orbit around their destination. But what it was, and why the ship was going alone to a world known to be seething with hostile apostates, was not known to any but the San'Shyuum.

The Refuge: An Uncharted Forerunner Shield World
850 BCE
The Age of Reconciliation

Tersa had to return to the hall of crystal columns to get his scan-cam. He'd forgotten it in his hurry to rush off to the midday meal. The food was mostly the local and quite edible vegetable matter and some artificial meat—the latter from the protein fabricator they had brought with them from Sanghelios. The protein mash was unappealing, but Tersa was young and his appetite was strong. There was an assortment of small fauna wandering the shield world—certain Sangheili had been tasked to use analyzers and discover if they were safe to eat. The Sangheili had high hopes of fresh meat, and soon.

Tersa needed the scancam in the next room slated for evaluation; it hadn't been of much use in the crystal columns chamber, the great transparent pillars, though clearly vibrating with energy, remaining stubbornly resistant to scan or analysis. Enduring Bias would have to be called to identify them, Sooln had said.

And there was Enduring Bias now, up ahead, floating between two columns. It must be here to confirm the use of the room. The shield planet was immense, and it was now well known that En-during Bias had lost some of its memory.

Oddly enough, it seemed to be emanating an image of the Ref-uge, the shield world itself, seen from space. And muttering to it-self in an unrecognizable language as it did so.

Or was the holograph what it seemed? Tersa began to doubt it when the flying AI seemed to make the image explode. Then come back together. Then explode again . . .

Tersa wasn't sure if he was authorized to talk to Enduring Bias. He was just a young Sangheili, and Enduring Bias was a living

Forerunner relic, a holy thing, and only Sooln and Ussa and, perhaps, Ernicka the Scar-Maker spoke to it, as far as Tersa knew. But Tersa had the curiosity as well as the appetite of the young, and he couldn't resist the chance, since no one else was around.

"Have you identified the use of this room?" Tersa asked, walking up.

"Oh!" Enduring Bias spun to face him, its three electric-blue lenses shining down at Tersa. "I was so absorbed in the external modeling, I didn't notice you come in. I really must realign my peripheral analyzers. I have much work to do on myself. I have been having trouble with internalized visual modeling—I find projecting works better now."

"What was that language you were speaking in?" Tersa asked.

"I have developed a habit here, in the course of millennia of conversing with myself as I work. I tend to use the language of the creators. Can I be of service to you?"

"Of service? To me?" Tersa was tempted. Perhaps he could ask Enduring Bias what the truth was about the Forerunners. Had it known them? Were they really gods? Supernatural creatures? If so, why did there seem to be a biological waste-disposal system here? Was there such a thing as sacred biological waste?

But a more pressing question came to mind. "Were you making pictures of this world blowing up, just now?"

"Yes and no."

"Can that be an answer—yes and no?"

"You've never noticed that many things are a case of both affirmative and negative? In fact, primitive computer systems tend to develop using codes made up of yes and no, one and zero, one one one zero one one zero zero—and the very structure of the universe might be said to be a fluctuation between yes and no, if we consider quantum effects in particle presence, and the original impulse of—"

"But—what about the picture? Of the planet being destroyed?"

"As to that, your leader, Ussa 'Xellus, requested of me to explore the feasibility of activating the Great Disassembler. Its processes may be regarded as a kind of explosion and then again, it is not a true explosion, but rather an orderly disassembling. However, there is inevitably an admixture of chaos."

"The Disassembler. Does it relate to this room?"

"You make an admirable intuitive leap, possibly the result of background consciousness calculus. Yes! This room is indeed the energy generator and focuser for the process of disassembling. I was here making certain that the process could go forward if needed. I ran a model to check the energy output with my projections of full disassembly. Happily, utter disassembly of this world seems entirely possible!"

"That's . . . good news. But—why would Ussa want that . . . that disassembly?"

"He has not informed me of his underlying purpose."

"Won't it kill us all if you just break it all apart in space?"

"Now, that is another question that's, if not answered affirmative or negative, is answered best by . . . perhaps and perhaps not."

"Oh. I see." Tersa felt a chill in his mandibles and down his spine.

"I must prioritize now, and depart from your ever-so-agreeable companionship. Sooln has transmitted a summons to me. Good algorithms to you, young Sangheili!"

And Tersa watched with growing dread as Enduring Bias flew away, talking obscurely to itself as it went.

Covenant Vessel *Vengeful Vitality*
Near High Charity
850 BCE
The Age of Reconciliation

The *Vengeful Vitality* hummed with energies held barely in check as it prepared to generate a slipspace portal. Mken, the Prophet of Inner Conviction, could feel the chained power of the vessel vibrating under his chair as he approached the rear launch deck. He wished he could step off the chair, here, but it would confuse the Sangheili.

It was a curious thing—one could not feel much, when the mighty Dreadnought, unthinkably gigantic as it was, traveled through space. But the smaller the vessel, the more one felt, as if the smaller ships were more reactive to gravitational fields, radiation, and the minute particles flitting through the void. Mken found that he enjoyed the sensation—there was something romantic about it. It must be like being on the naval vessels, sailing the seas of Janjur Qom—back in the old days, when San'Shyuum were physically strong, and the ships were made of wood.

Mken eased his chair closer to the insertion dropship. A relatively compact troop transport, the vessel was shaped like *eilifula*, the humpbacked shelled creatures found in San'Shyuum's oceans, a purplish-blue transport that, like the corvette, was capable of merging visually with a backdrop for stealth purposes. It had room in it for three San'Shyuum, Sangheili, and as many as ten San'Shyuum females in the specially fitted cargo chamber at the small ship's posterior. The females would not be terribly comfortable there—but their trip back to the ship would be a short one. They would either make it or be shot down in short order.

Trok 'Tanghil, the scarred old Sangheili commander, missing

part of one of his lower jaws due to some old military encounter, stood by the open hatch into the dropship; to his side stood a young Sangheili soldier Mken knew only as Vil. It was his impression that Trok was Vil's uncle. But with the Sangheili, he understood, an uncle was almost the same as a father—and sometimes *was* the father, though direct paternity wasn't revealed in the bloodline.

A Huragok was floating out the hatchway, and as it came it signed with a contortion of its lower tentacles to Vil. "Floats Near Ceiling signals that the vessel is in working order, in all systems."

"Perhaps the Prophet would like to inspect it himself?" Trok suggested.

"No," Mken said, glancing at Vil. The young Sangheili must be bright to have so quick a comprehension of Huragok sign language. "If the Huragok claims it's functional, then it is so. I would only perhaps collide my chair into some control panel and make it nonfunctional again."

"But you are scheduled to take part in the excursion expedition," Trok pointed out unnecessarily. "You will have to enter the vehicle at that time. Do you wish to have your chair adjusted? The Huragok could do it." Trok seemed to have an air of genuine puzzlement—he was apparently one of the more humorless Sangheili, of which there were many, and didn't realize that the Prophet of Inner Conviction had been indulging in self-deprecating humor.

"I was speaking lightly," said Mken. "Even a Prophet must do so occasionally." Especially when his future looked so doleful. "Who else is scheduled for the mission?"

"I am, Your Eminence," said Trok. "And the other San'Shyuum."

Mken pondered that. "I may alter the crew list for this leg of the mission. I strongly feel that the greatest danger is an attack on the dropship itself. I will need you to remain with the dropship—to protect it."

Trok grunted. "I see the wisdom of the Prophet."

"I shall take the Huragok with me—because there is a special relic we hope to find and take with us, and he may be of use. Ranger Vil 'Kthamee can come along to communicate with him. I have not that particular skill."

Vil seemed to tense at that, but Mken had made up his mind.

The image of the *Vengeful Vitality*'s pilot appeared in a holograph over Mken's chair panel. "Sir! We are about to enter slipspace. All passengers and crew are advised to take up stations."

"Very good, Captain. I'll be in my station quickly." He turned to the others. "You heard him. Get to your stations! We are on our way to Janjur Qom."

How long had it been, a thousand solar cycles, since a San'Shyuum descended from Reformists had set foot upon the homeworld?

His three-fingered hand shook as he tapped the arm of his chair and drifted toward his station. The true home of his people . . . and he was to see it.

There was a strong possibility he wouldn't come back alive . . .

But perhaps, after all, it was worth it.

CHAPTER 6

Covenant Vessel *Vengeful Vitality*
Orbiting Janjur Qom
850 BCE
The Age of Reconciliation

A world spread out below Mken. Clouds spiraled around a giant crater, the immense blue sea known as the Great Apothtea; the dark green of vegetation carpeted much of the main continent; outer regions were more rugged. Mken recognized a number of features from his studies of the old holograms. Was that not Zelfiss, where the fabled fortress of Granduin, undermined by the Stoics, had crumbled into the sea? And the crater—it was once the resting place of the Dreadnought, partly submerged below Apothtea's surface, but it was now the mark of the great ship's ascension; it was the scar where the Reformists had taken a god's fistful of the world as the mountain-high vessel rose to meet the stars.

The planet below was Janjur Qom.

Parts of Janjur Qom throbbed with life—with water, with greenery, with lights. Other parts seemed barrenly rocky. These regions, Mken supposed, might be the mark of the Forerunners' wrath—he'd found an ancient text referring to the punishment of his people's world, long ago, for their rebellion against the gods.

— 95 —

But most now held that the tale was only a myth, used to inspire fear in the defiant and explain the vagaries of the planet. Or was it true? Had the sacred ones, the makers of the Path to the Great Journey, been so furious with his people's sins that they burned vast populated areas of the planet away?

How could one follow a path laid down by such divines? Could a flame of punishment be a manifestation of the holy light of the cosmos?

Perhaps it could be. The fires of destruction were everywhere. Scourges wiped out entire species; droughts came and went; asteroids crashed murderously into inhabited planets.

And suns were known to destroy themselves.

Indeed, the very star at the center of this system—the sun that had warmed Janjur Qom for billions of solar cycles—was thought by some to be particularly unstable. Certain San'Shyuum astronomers had muttered darkly that the end was coming one day . . .

But the Great Journey promised transcendence, an escape from the inexorable arrow of time, from the endless erosion that is entropy. If the Great Journey was real . . .

But of course it was. Either that, or the Covenant, the Path—Mken's entire life—was meaningless.

Perhaps when he found the Purifying Vision of the Holy Path—if indeed the relic was where Excellent Redolence said it was—he might then see his way clearly. The relic would surely be a light of inspiration; so it was rumored to be.

But the sight of Janjur Qom itself moved him deeply. As he gazed at it, he thought, *Here is the mother I have never known. This is my true lineage. This is the womb of my people. A million solar cycles and more of San'Shyuum history took place here. This was where San'Shyuum emerged from the seas; where they began to farm, to build, to create civilization. Where they shed their blood as they struggled with one another for sovereignty.*

The soil of Janjur Qom was impregnated with the blood of Mken's ancestors. Over a millennia ago, Mken's Reformist family had fled from this world—had vaulted on the Dreadnought into the stars.

Gazing upon it now, for the first time in his life, Mken felt more moved than he had in many cycles. He felt an emotion welling from deep within—from the very cells, the genetic core of his being. *Janjur Qom!* He wanted to cry out, to weep with the glory and anguish of it.

But the cry went unvoiced. He had to continue his pose of austerity. He had to be the Prophet of Inner Conviction.

"You seem to be meditating deeply, Eminence," someone said, at his elbow. "I fear to disturb you but . . ."

Startled, Mken spun his chair about to find Vervum L'kosur, the ship's captain and coxswain, in an antigrav chair, gazing at him with his large, mocking dark eyes. It struck Mken that this Vervum was not at all in awe of the Prophet of Inner Conviction. And Mken instantly suspected that Vervum was R'Noh's man, was at least a spy for the Minister of Anticipatory Security. It was quite possible that Vervum was even an agent for that Ministry—surely R'Noh had been recruiting for his new intelligence fiefdom.

Vervum's chair was decorated with the holograms of the Covenant's military arm, like fringes of colored light, and he wore a uniform robe sewn with stars indicating the systems he'd served in.

"I see you served at the Planet of Red and Blue, as I did," Mken remarked, as he tried to get his composure back. "You were on the Dreadnought there?"

"I was on the planet, guarding the relic recovery team, O Prophet."

"Ah. You and the others did a fine job."

"The Sentinels did most of it. I regret that the seditious Ussa 'Xellus escaped your net, O Prophet."

Interesting, how Vervum put that. *Your net.* Laying it all on Mken's shoulders.

Yes. He was likely R'Noh's agent.

Mken made a mental note to beware of treachery from the captain of this vessel.

Could it be that R'Noh intended to let Inner Conviction do the work, take the risk here—and then eliminate him, have him assassinated on Janjur Qom, so that he was not present to take the credit for the mission's success?

If so, R'Noh was assuming too much. Mken himself doubted the mission's chances of success. There were too many imponderables on the planet below, too many Stoics. Too much toxic history between Stoics and Reformists.

And if they were successful, R'Noh was assuming far too much about Inner Conviction—that he was foolish enough to allow himself to be stabbed in the back.

I will not make it easy for you, R'Noh.

"Captain, have you been monitoring transmissions from Janjur Qom?"

"Yes. Their language is archaic but we manage to understand them. They do not seem to be aware of our orbital position. They have some satellites, some simple technology. But on the whole they seem to be the Stoics they were when our people left. Predictably, they have resisted progress. They don't appear to have the capability of penetrating our stealth shield."

"Then let us position the ship over our drop zone . . . and prepare the dropship for landing."

The Refuge: An Uncharted Shield World
850 BCE
The Age of Reconciliation

Tersa was finishing his scan of the cryptic, floating devices in Sub-level Four—a series of hovering three-dimensional rectangular cuboid objects that occasionally changed shape, becoming tetra-hedronal, octagonal, pyramidal, then back to rectangular cuboids. He had realized early on that the objects changed shape when he scanned them, or even when approached closely. They seemed aware of him, and again he had the uncanny feeling they were scrutinizing him rather than vice versa. If he spoke, muttering over his task, the objects emitted sweet chiming sounds, as if responding to him in some crystalline language.

He stepped back and looked around the enormous hall, a bit spooked by this place. He was occasionally unsettled by the shield world, especially when he was alone in the alien, artificial vaults and corridors, the chambers and galleries. The Forerunners, who had built this world, seemed everywhere—and nowhere. Their work was here, their artifacts, their architecture, the personality of their culture. Most of it seemed enigmatic to Tersa, and to most of the others, just as it should. Was it even permissible to understand the gods?

But sometimes Tersa felt that the Forerunners were somewhere near at hand, watching, perhaps just around a corner or hidden behind some panel. Absurd to think that, of course. They had all passed from this plane of existence—the Covenant said they had taken the Great Journey. Ussa said no one knew where the Forerunners went, or if they would ever be back, least of all the Covenant—but their traces were sacred to the Sangheili all the same.

He remembered what he'd heard from Enduring Bias about

the Disassembler. What was Ussa planning? Disassembling the shield world . . . it sounded like madness.

Put it out of your mind. You cannot possibly understand what Ussa intends.

But still . . .

'Crolon and 'Drem hurried up then—'Drem was a taller, spindlier Sangheili than most, wearing rusted armor and leather braces and boots from the almost extinct and quite vicious barbed *thremaleon* of Sanghelios. Wearing the spiky running lizard skin was an affectation, usually to give the impression of membership in a Victory or Death cult. *More mandible flappers than fighters, that Victory or Death bunch,* Tersa's uncle had said. *All boast.* 'Drem had the old runic tattoos of Victory or Death on his neck, too, Tersa saw.

Right now, 'Drem looked more like death than like victory—he looked shaken, his eyes shadowy, almost hollow. "I cannot abide this room," 'Drem said in a creaky voice. "I feel a vibration within me here. Not natural. Not right."

'Crolon nodded, "True enough."

'Drem had become a companion of 'Crolon's lately. They were an unpleasant pair, to most of the others. But 'Crolon was slippery and glib, and sometimes the adherents listened to him.

"I sense strangeness in here, too," Tersa admitted. "But if it was dangerous, Sooln would know. Enduring Bias would warn us. I'm sure there is no cause for concern."

"What could go wrong," 'Crolon wondered with acrid sarcasm, "in a room created by the gods? A room deep beneath the shell of an alien world? Why, *nothing* could go wrong there, I'm certain."

"I have been here for some time," Tersa said. "As you see— nothing has harmed me."

"Perhaps it is simply waiting," 'Drem said. "Perhaps it was waiting for more of us—for its little trap to be sprung."

Tersa stared at him. "Trap?"

"Indeed. Who knows what these things are for?"

"I have a theory," 'Crolon put in. "I wonder if these vibrating shapes could be for testing souls! You have seen how reactive they are. They could be probing us. The Forerunners—the gods, the messengers of the cosmos—could be using them to decide which of us live or die. If we are worthy or unworthy. When they decide . . ." He clashed his mandibles in the Sangheili version of a resigned shrug.

'Drem stepped back from the hovering geometrical figures—and then took another step back. "Those things can see . . . inside me? My soul?"

Tersa waved a hand, dismissing the idea. "That's 'Crolon's theory. More likely they are part of the shield world's energy system. Or used in communications."

"You are correct—they *are* used in communication!" said Enduring Bias, buzzing into the room.

The abrupt entry of Enduring Bias made 'Drem hiss and snarl, startled. "The dark angel slips up behind us . . . !"

"What an interesting cultural tang there is in that appellation—*dark angel*. I hardly know what to say," Enduring Bias remarked, turning to scan 'Drem in curiosity.

"What is it doing to me?" he muttered, backing away. "I feel a tingle! An intrusion!"

" 'Drem, it is only scanning you," 'Crolon said. "It is the eye of the Forerunners—a sacred relic."

"Relic, I am," said the machine. "The relic of an earlier age. But I have never felt sacred."

"You said I was correct about communications?" Tersa asked. Like youth of any race, he enjoyed being told he was right; it happened so rarely.

"Yes," said Enduring Bias. "These are communication dispensers. It was once called the chamber of sensitive geometries. These shapes generate a quantum action-at-a-distance field enabling instantaneous communication through barriers within the shield world. Of course, one must know the key. The entry phrase. I have lost that, I'm afraid. But we hope to rediscover it. Some of my files are restorable."

'Drem stared at the shifting hovering shapes. "Communication . . . and it is everywhere? So in a way, it watches whatever we do?"

"It *is aware of you*, wherever you are on the planet, would be a more precise way of putting it."

"I do not trust such a thing," 'Drem muttered. "Ussa has brought us here to live like that? It isn't right."

"He doesn't even know how to use these devices," Tersa said.

"So this machine says—but Sooln is Ussa's female. And she controls the machine."

"She certainly does not!" Enduring Bias said. "I resent the implication. I have a much higher purpose. I am programmed and instructed to do my best to monitor and even to repair this shield world. We do need some Engineers here. The Huragok would be most welcome. You don't have any Huragok with you, do you?"

"Huragok? What are those?" 'Crolon asked.

"You see their like in this reproduction," Enduring Bias said, projecting an image of a strange hovering creature composed of billowing spheres and tentacles. But it looked familiar.

"I have never seen one," said Tersa, "but in the wars, my uncle saw one when they raided a San'Shyuum ship. He told me about them . . . They are with the San'Shyuum now, fixing things."

"Are they?" Enduring Bias asked, its single, electric-blue eye glowing with renewed interest. "The San'Shyuum. Sooln told me of them. I believe them to be a race with certain ancient connections to my creators. The Huragok, now—they were taken from here, when the decision was made not to test this facility, but, sadly, no one consulted me. I need the Huragok. One could wish the San'Shyuum were the new occupants of this world, if indeed they have the Huragok handy . . ."

"What treachery is this?" 'Drem sputtered. "The San'Shyuum are the enemy—and this construct wishes to work for them instead of the Sangheili!"

"I was merely expressing what I think could be characterized as a wistful observation," Enduring Bias said.

"What does all that mean?" 'Drem demanded.

"It means," said 'Crolon thoughtfully, looking at the machine, "Enduring Bias does in fact wish the San'Shyuum were here. And it works closely with Ussa . . ."

"No. He just wants their Engineers," Tersa said, worried that some kind of rebellion was breaking out—and that he might be caught up in it. Or killed if he didn't take part. "He . . ."

"He? It's a he?" 'Drem said. He sniffed. "It's a thing. A mere construct."

"I have engaged a male tonality," Enduring Bias said. "It seems to generate more respect among those of your culture, for reasons quite unknown to me. I hypothesize a classic patriarchal structure, with the expected attempts to suppress the—"

"What I'm trying to say," Tersa interrupted, "is that Enduring Bias wants the Huragok here to repair things. To fix the machines."

"And to do some repair on myself," said Enduring Bias. "Yes. At this remove, as long as you do not damage this facility in any significant way, I am actually indifferent to the occupants. The creators seem to have departed. I know not where. I have been out of the communication spiral. Out of the discussion. Out of the loop."

"So—indifferent to occupants?" 'Crolon scratched a mandible. "You would condone the San'Shyuum being here?"

"Absolutely, though only if it meant access to the Huragok . . ." Enduring Bias said, at last becoming aware of some need for politesse. "I do not reject the Sangheili. Indeed, the one called Sooln 'Xellus has repaired some of my mechanism. And we have established a new rapport. After all, I've always been subject to the wishes of my programmers. And to some extent I have been reprogrammed."

"Sooln has reprogrammed you—and you desire the San'Shyuum were here if it meant the Huragok as well?" 'Crolon murmured. "I find that interesting."

"That is mixing what does not need mixing," Tersa said. And using an old Sangheili expression, he added, "It is mixing blood and oil."

"I certainly hope so," 'Crolon said. "I would never question Ussa's decisions. I just take note of this and that and . . . wonder. But I am loyal to Ussa and Sooln and to this—what was it Ussa said this morning? This 'mission of the new Sanghelios.'"

"I shouldn't have left the old Sanghelios!" 'Drem muttered. "This place seems more a trap than a refuge." Then he looked darkly at Tersa. "You will not speak of what you have heard here, childling," 'Drem said.

Tersa ground his teeth. "I am young—but no childling."

'Drem snorted. "Really, now? You still have egg yolk on your neck."

"Come, 'Drem," 'Crolon said. "It is time for the evening meal."

"It is swill—no real meat to it," 'Drem grumbled, following 'Crolon out.

Tersa looked at Enduring Bias. "I hope you don't casually repeat what you have heard here. If you do, you could cause bloodshed."

"That would be unsanitary," Enduring Bias said. "Most dis-agreeable."

With that, it flitted away. Tersa wondered if he should be the one to report the discussion—and if Ussa might misunderstand Tersa's part in what had been said.

Because it seemed to Tersa that subversion had taken place here. So far it was only words. But back on Sanghelios, Tersa had known words alone to cause more than one beheading.

CHAPTER 7

Reskolah, Janjur Qom
850 BCE
The Age of Reconciliation

They were concealed by the stealth field projected by the drop-ship, yet nothing was hidden from Mken; he could see the night-darkened world about them, gleaming in the starlight. Plaon, the old scarred moon, hadn't risen yet, but he could see creatures flapping in the sky; he could feel Janjur Qom's fragrant winds.

The Prophet of Inner Conviction felt a strange mix of buoyancy and oppression.

The air here seemed to speak to his most primal being. The smell of the vine-wreathed forest nearby—a botanical perfume, a mix of decay and new life that he'd never scented before—seemed impossibly familiar. His genetic makeup seemed to recognize it. Something deep in his brain responded, and it made him feel giddy, light-headed.

But the unmodified gravitational field of his homeworld was more than he could easily bear. High Charity had significantly lower gravity than this. He had overestimated the strength he'd built up on the keyship. Janjur Qom was not particularly large or dense—it was "Janjur Qom Normal." Unfortunately, Mken and his San'Shyuum peers from the Dreadnought were not Janjur Qom Normal. The Stoics here, or their descendants, would be stronger, more fit and muscular, more genetically diverse than Mken's own people. That made the locals particularly dangerous in a close engagement. Given the context, possibly even as dangerous as the Sangheili.

They hadn't wanted to drop straight down to the grotto. If the Stoics were monitoring them, it would give away one of the expedition's primary goals. And the Stoics must not learn why they were here, after all this time. So first they would see if they were being observed. Mken had chosen to approach the grotto circumspectly.

And this landing, some distance off from the first destination, gave Mken the time to get an intuitive grasp of Janjur Qom.

He had stepped away from the front ramp of the landed dropship, leaving his chair a few strides behind.

But here he felt like a toddling infant taking his first tentative steps. A notion came to him, that the homeworld itself was punishing him, and all his kind, for abandoning her. They had left their mother, Janjur Qom, and now she pressed the heavy hand of gravitation on them, to put them in their place.

Absurd. You're falling victim to a runaway imagination.

He glanced toward the Sangheili, like the young Ranger, Vil 'Kthamee, who moved about with such ease as they patrolled the perimeters of the camp around the turret and mobile combat barriers.

"Gravitation is more than we're used to here," grunted Captain Vervum, directing his own chair up to hover beside Mken. "I am surprised you trouble to leave your chair."

Mken gestured, *It's a minor difficulty.* "This is our homeworld. I wanted to feel it, as San'Shyuum would, in ancient times. I am also a historian."

"We are not here to study history," Vervum said.

"You are using a disrespectful tone I do not care for, Captain," said Mken.

"I meant no disrespect, O Prophet."

Mken gestured, *I choose not to be offended.* "The artificial gravity of the keyship is dialed lower—substantially lower, actually. I have often wondered if it should be higher, raised by degrees, over a solar cycle or two till we strengthen our bodies."

"Our limbs are not what they should be, trained or not, Your Eminence," Vervum said, his tone more respectful. "That is one reason we are here. For the replenishment of fresh blood—for improved physical form in our offspring."

"I have visited a number of worlds, most of them with lower gravity than this one. And I have found myself wondering if we should try harder to . . ."

But he decided not to go on. He had not forgotten that Vervum might well be an agent for R'Noh—and was quite likely an operative for the Ministry of Anticipatory Security. Mken didn't wish to say anything that could be willfully misconstrued as a heretical defiance of the Hierarchy.

Mken gestured, *I will speak of it another time.* But he didn't intend to do so.

A light spilled onto the mossy soil as the hatch of the dropship clicked open for them. "Almost time to head for our target," Vervum observed.

Mken realized he'd been stubbornly standing here, legs aching from the planet's heaviness, when he really wanted to go back to

his chair—he'd been delaying out of sheer unconscious prideful-
ness, merely because Vervum was there.

He sighed, turned, and slogged back to his chair, sitting on it
with a sigh of relief as the ambient gravity field reduced his body's
burden to what it was used to.

Settling back, Mken glanced at the sky, half expecting to see
some form of Stoic San'Shyuum overflight. The remote Eyes had
revealed that the Stoics had advanced little technologically since
the war. It was unclear why, though perhaps they felt further ad-
vancement, after the violent departure of the Dreadnought at the
hands of Reformists—which they clearly viewed as blasphemy—
might incur the wrath of the gods. Nevertheless, the Stoics possessed flying attack vehicles not terribly different from those at
the time of the war a millennium ago. They were simple, using
air compression and gas-igniting fuel to drive their vessels and
fire their weapons. Mken wasn't at all sure the *Vengeful Vitality*'s
stealth field was impervious to detection. On the way here, he'd
read the report on Stoic capabilities. They did possess some kind
of reflector scanning to detect vessels entering their atmosphere.
Once a remote Eye had been pursued by Stoic aircraft. And
the Stoics were likely well aware that there were hostile species
equipped with space travel in the galaxy—and they'd be watching for those hostiles. And for the possible return of the hated
Reformists.

What would the Stoics do if they captured Mken? Simply put
him to death? Or worse?

The thought of never seeing Cresanda again was already worse
than death to Mken. She was to have his child—who had been con-
ceived in a rare moment of profound biological intimacy, match-
ing their emotional intimacy. Scarcely ever did the San'Shyuum

females become fertile now. Something so rare and precious . . . and he might never see the child. He sighed. He was more scholar than fighter. But here he was, on a planet full of enemies.

His father had often said, *Whatever arises, the wise ones meet with a calm face.*

Mken looked at the sky again, saw nothing but a veering bony-winged *rakscraja*, its pale wings reflecting starlight. He tugged at a wattle, thinking, *First things first.*

The excursion team would take the dropship to the grotto of the Great Transition. And then, the village of Trellem.

Mken tried to remember what he'd read about the grotto. He knew it was associated with iconography of a legendary goddess, a mysterious Forerunner his people had long associated with re-birth. He assumed she was mythical—a symbol, merely. But who knew for certain?

Mken felt an attenuated, almost ghostly thrill, considering the possibility of entering the grotto of the Great Transition. Long ago it had been protected as sacred, and forbidden, by the Stoics. Remote-control Eyes sent to the planet from the Dread-nought suggested the grotto was now forgotten, overgrown and abandoned . . .

But there was the risk that it was still defended, after all this time.

He heard an odd fluting sound, and turned to see the Huragok floating along, like a sea creature somehow transferred to the air as it returned to the dropship—it had been checking the stealth field. Vil 'Kthamee was walking close behind the creature, as if gently herding it along. Certainly the young Sangheili—who didn't seem in the least inconvenienced by planetary gravity—had a peculiar rapport with the Huragok.

Trok 'Tanghil was already loading up the turret, while standing on guard with directed-energy rifles. Vervum was entering the vessel, preparing to pilot the humpbacked vehicle.

It remained only for Mken to follow them. With one more nervous look at the sky, Mken directed his chair through the small hatch into the excursion vehicle and gave the order to head for the grotto.

Vil 'Kthamee was strapped into a seat along the bulkhead, across from Loquen 'Nvong, who looked back at him with quiet, condescending amusement.

Turning away from Loquen, Vil peered out of a viewport. A rolling landscape of trees and other foliage—green and argent and turquoise—went unreeling below as the dropship flew just over the treetops. The stars glowed brightly overhead, lending a blue-white sheen to the colors. In the distance were the lights of a town. He saw one road, cracked and weedy. It was there, and gone. They passed over a river, where some massive, glossy amphibian rose into view, shook itself, then descended from sight. They flew onward.

"You're enjoying the view?" Loquen asked gruffly as he fingered his plasma rifle. The bifurcated rifle was pointed upward, but a quick motion of Loquen's hand could turn it toward Vil.

Glancing at Loquen, Vil flipped his hand noncommittally. "New world. I am as curious as the next Sangheili."

Vil was coming along to translate for the Huragok. He'd been surprised to see Loquen 'Nvong along on the dropship. Vil had understood the expedition was to avoid conflict of any kind. This was to be a clandestine mission. So why the large and dangerous Loquen, who was always spoiling for a fight?

Though Loquen was fairly young, the Sangheili warrior was arrogant—and Vil had seen him sacrifice other soldiers for his own glory. Loquen kept his mandibles half closed much of the time—a symbol, to a Sangheili, of warning: *Do not threaten me. I am on the alert.*

Vil heard Floats Near Ceiling tootling to get his attention. He glanced up, and, as it happened, the Huragok was in that moment truly floating near the ceiling of the dropship's fuselage. The Engineer organism flapped and flashed its tentacles—a question of some kind, rendered too fast for the Ranger to read. Vil signaled *Repeat.*

When the Huragok repeated its question, Vil had already touched the wrist holo interpreter. The device scancammed the Huragok, and holographically translated the symbols to Sangheili runes.

<<Much work,>> the Huragok was saying. <<How to begin? Have glimpsed world, outside, thousands of devices to repair.>>

Vil understood. He had heard how the San'Shyuum had broken up into two major factions, one leaving for the stars, to unravel the puzzle of every Forerunner relic discoverable out there, the other group remaining, now stifling any advances in technology, inheriting a world in which there were countless cryptic Forerunner relics, most needing repair. And somehow the Huragok had already sensed those mechanisms, outside. But how?

"How do you know what is out there?" Vil asked the Huragok. Vil had a scientific side that many Sangheili didn't share. The others were all technologically capable, but the more pragmatic—and that was most Sangheili males—lacked much curiosity as to the underlying principles of that technology.

<<Call to me,>> the Huragok responded.

"Call to you? How?" Vil tapped the translator module fixed to his hearing lobe to make it translate for verbal on his end.

<<Use the Engineer communication frequency. Receptivity to frequency integral. When in need of repair, creator-designed machines send out repair request signal. Was puzzled for a time when arrived. Had not experienced before. But remember being taught. Machines call to me.>>

Creator-designed. Meaning the Forerunners. Vil's cousin K'ckel had told him about it—cousin, or possibly brother, since Sangheili were raised in a way that made murky the identity of one's real father. K'ckel was a junior researcher in an armory on Qikost, one of Sanghelios's two moons. He had spoken to Vil about the distributed intelligences, found partly intact, machine intellects who had referred to "the creators." The term "creator" had helped increase the numinous aura of the Forerunners. Who were the final creators, if not the gods?

"The Prophet of Inner Conviction has his own plan for you," Vil told the Huragok at last.

Floats Near Ceiling fluted discontentedly. <<So much calls. So much and so many.>>

Vil could feel the dropship slowing. He looked out the viewport, and saw that it was descending into a ravine.

Just a few moments later, they were filing out the air lock into a muggy night. The air seemed without breeze—yet the plants about the dropship rustled as if wind-stirred. Something screeched as it flew overhead; smaller, insectlike creatures hummed near, away, and then nearer still.

Like the others, Vil had been treated with antibiotic, microscopic nanoagents, which protected them with astonishing efficiency, destroying all local antigens invading their system before any harm could be done. The air was breathable on Janjur Qom, the gravity bearable, at least to Sangheili. But the insectlike flying creatures grew bolder, and soon sucked at Vil's skin—they were tiny, almost diaphanous organisms that seemed to combine legs with wings. They died almost instantly when they drank his blood, not from nanoagents, he supposed, but because Sangheili blood was so very alien to this world.

But the San'Shyuum Prophet, up ahead and drifting along in his antigrav chair, was scratching at bites on his arms—his blood was a slightly exotic treat to the parasites.

With the floating Huragok beside him and a plasma rifle in his arms, Vil followed the San'Shyuum along a dark and dank trail that snaked from the center of the ravine toward the walls of stone to one side. The San'Shyuum, Inner Conviction and Captain Vervum, took the lead, with muted lights on their antigrav chairs. Loquen followed behind, and having the trigger-happy Sangheili in the rear made Vil a trifle nervous.

To either side was a high hedge of flexible-looking foliage that rustled as they came close to it; it quieted down when they were well past. Occasionally, tentacle-like shoots reached sinuously from the wall of foliage, and gently stroked at the interlopers, as if inspecting, perhaps tasting them. The San'Shyuum had warned them this might happen, but assured them the probes were harmless, merely investigatory on the part of the organisms—which were, actually, as much animal as they were plant. A large blossom lowered from somewhere overhead, opened wider, so that the eye within it could inspect them.

Unfamiliar smells barraged Vil's nostrils, some astringent, some cloyingly sweet, some hinting of decay. The familiar smells of mineral and water came to him, too. He felt the ancientness, the alienness of this planet. And something—as the plants shifted, the blossoms stared—that was almost a subcurrent of hostility from the world itself.

It was as if this entire planet, this Janjur Qom, was silently intoning, *You do not belong here, Sangheili. You are invasive, you are foreign to my living body. I will enwrap you, dissolve you away . . .*

Strange thought in a strange world. But he'd always been more imaginative than most Sangheili. His uncle had often taken him to task for it.

Suddenly the thin path opened out into a small meadow, knobbed with boulders. Beyond it, a beetling cliff loomed, its craggy embossments picked out by starlight.

They wended between the low boulders, approaching the base of the cliff wall. Above them, the top of the cliff was furred by another kind of plant—thick, dense, and brown.

As the expedition drew near, a cloud slipped away, somewhere overhead, and a little more light eased through to the rocky wall to expose a panel of somewhat eroded carvings, a kind of lintel above a roughly rectangular shadow so dark it must be the entrance to a passage. The Prophet of Inner Conviction aimed a light from his chair upward onto the images sculpted into the lintel. The bas-relief carving was divided in two, a row of figures seen on the right and left, in hieroglyphic profile, both groups facing inward toward a circular form enclosing a star.

The carven figures on the left were bipedal, vaguely hominid in shape. Their skulls and jaws seemed different from Sangheili or San'Shyuum, to Vil; it was difficult to see in the uneven light. The figures on the right were clearly San'Shyuum, though without antigrav chairs. They stood more upright than the San'Shyuum of the Dreadnought, and seemed more elegantly shaped.

Vil heard something move behind them—a heavy presence grunting as it shouldered through the undergrowth.

Loquen heard it at the same time. "Something's moving in that forest," he declared suddenly. "Not those bothersome plants— something large."

"There are many beasts on Janjur Qom," said Captain Vervum. "The Stoics have retreated to relatively small areas, and given up much over to the wilderness. Stay alert, but do not fire your weapon without definite cause."

"And keep your voice down," Inner Conviction admonished them. "Both of you."

And the Prophet of Inner Conviction directed his chair toward the darkness of the roughly rectangular opening ahead.

CHAPTER 8

Seeing Ernicka the Scar-Maker stalking across the high-ceilinged space of the Hall of Feasts, Tersa was tempted to simply walk up to him and report what he had heard 'Crolon and 'Drem saying at work.

It had seemed to Tersa that 'Drem and 'Crolon had been plotting insurrection there. Or perhaps they were only hinting at it, which was already dangerous enough.

The scarred Sangheili warrior—who always chose to be last to eat—was carrying a pot of protein mash from the synthesizer at the back of the Hall, setting it up on one of the makeshift tables. The room buzzed with conversation.

Still, Tersa hesitated. He hung back near the door, wondering if he would appear to Ernicka as a dishonorable informer if he told him what 'Crolon had said—repeated the implications 'Crolon had made suggesting that there was some obscure connection between Ussa, Sooln, and the San'Shyuum. 'Drem had been even more forthrightly suspicious of the Refuge—and by extension, of Ussa.

But when Tersa considered reporting the talk, imagined himself repeating it to Ernicka, it all sounded like mere grumbling. Perhaps it was . . .

But he'd felt a chill, listening to 'Crolon and 'Drem speak that way.

At Tersa's right sat 'Crolon and 'Drem themselves. They were usually among the first to eat. Now they were huddled together over their meals in close conversation. 'Crolon seemed to sense Tersa watching—he turned and looked directly at Tersa, then murmured something to 'Drem.

'Drem nodded, and the two of them rose and approached the young Sangheili. Attempting to ignore them, Tersa started toward the table area.

"One moment, young warrior," 'Crolon said affably. He and 'Drem blocked his way. "Do you have time for some wisdom?"

"Much time for much wisdom, and little for little," said Tersa, quoting his uncle. He looked back and forth between the two Sangheili. "Well, then?"

"It is the way you have been looking at us," 'Drem said. "Since the other day in that room with the talking shapes. And that damned machine—Enduring Bias."

"And how have I been looking at you?" Tersa asked.

" 'Drem is prone to making subjective judgments," 'Crolon said. "But I did want to make sure you did not misunderstand us. You did not imagine we said anything disloyal to Ussa, I'm sure . . . ?"

"I would not say disloyal," Tersa said, looking at the protein urn. He was getting hungry. His stomach was growling.

"What were you thinking of saying, then?" 'Drem asked. He had his head cocked to one side—he had the air of a Sangheili who thought himself sly.

"Ussa is a fair and impartial kaidon," Tersa said, irritated. "I'm sure you have nothing to hide from him. He would not jump to conclusions. It is not his way."

"And does that mean you *are* thinking about reporting us?" 'Drem demanded.

"I am thinking about my meal," Tersa said. "As well as when we finally get to hunt some of the life forms on this world. That is all."

He started to push past them, but 'Crolon put out a hand to stop him. "Just to be clear as a warm day," 'Crolon said, "let me remind you of your part in the discussion."

"My part?"

"Yes. You agreed with everything we said. In fact, you took the entire affair much further. I believe I recall your saying that we were in great danger here and you thought Ussa might be a traitor to his own people."

"What? I said nothing of the sort! The Flying Voice was there! He can report what was said."

"He was not present the entire time," 'Crolon said smoothly. " 'Drem and I are your seniors, and there are two of us to your one. If we report that you spoke treason, well . . . why should Ernicka and Ussa not believe us over you?"

Tersa looked at him in shock. "You would dishonor yourselves with that lie!"

"It is how I remember it as well," 'Drem said. "Or how I *will* remember it . . . if you say anything. If you attempt to betray us, we will see that it is you who are betrayed instead."

"It is just clan sense, right from the egg," 'Crolon said, patting Tersa's shoulder. "I think we understand one another now."

And with, that he and 'Drem walked away. Tersa found that he had lost his appetite.

Reskolah, Janjur Qom
850 BCE
The Age of Reconciliation

"You really believe this is it?" Vervum asked. "This is the grotto of the Great Transition?"

"There is little doubt of it," Mken said. "The carving on the lintel, over the entrance—exactly as described. The location is right. It must be here!"

"But—it's empty."

So it was—or so it seemed. The passage cut into the stone of the cliff had led them in about fifty strides—and then come to a blank wall. They had seen no further carvings, no idols or machinery—nothing but a cracked stone floor, grown here and there with some sort of orange fungus, and roughly hewn walls. Their Sangheili protector's boots echoed whenever the soldiers moved; the Huragok fluted and bobbed in the air, now and then gesturing at Vil. The other Sangheili, Loquen, seemed to spend most of his time staring back toward the entrance. He was convinced, it seemed, there was something dangerous nearby, and he could be right.

But Mken wasn't ready to give up just yet. He had brought the Huragok along for a reason.

"I half expected we would find it this way," said Mken.

He directed his antigrav chair over to the blank wall that had awaited them at the end of the passageway. Grimacing as he felt the gravitational pull increase, he rose from the chair and leaned forward, running his fingers along the wall.

"Your Eminence," Vil said, walking up. "Perhaps this isn't the end of the passage—perhaps this is the *real* door."

Mken looked at him with surprise. "An astute hypothesis. I was just thinking the same thing."

"If the Huragok could be allowed to investigate, Your Eminence . . ."

"Yes. But I was looking for something that could be investigated. I was hoping for some small inset, a triggering mechanism inside a slot, something. But so far . . ."

Vil turned to the Huragok and signaled with his holographic translator. The colored symbols appearing in the air between Vil and the Huragok added to the mix of shadow, color, and fleeting light cast by the San'Shyuum's chairs.

The Huragok tilted its head to take in the symbols, then made a fluting nose and whipped its tendrils about in response.

Vil clicked his mandibles in the affirmative. "Yes, Floats Near Ceiling is—"

"*What* floats near ceiling?" Vervum asked, puzzled.

"That is the Huragok's name: Floats Near Ceiling. It says that it has detected very small apertures, which only a Huragok's finest cilia could fit into. Floats Near Ceiling thinks the wall could not be opened without a Huragok present."

"Good—then let the Engineer test that theory," Mken said, stepping out of the way.

Vil signaled, and the Huragok drifted to the wall as leisurely as a cloud and ran its tentacle tips over the stone. It was methodical, starting near the ceiling, performing its tactile investigation in a grid down from there. Within a minute, it made a satisfied double grunting sound, and its tendril-tips seemed to sink impossibly into the wall.

It made a soft subvocal sound, almost a purring, so content was it to interact with the machinery, to analyze, to repair, to activate . . .

There was a breathless moment of waiting, so that Mken's thoughts drifted to the thing moving in the undergrowth outside, the possibility of Stoics becoming alert to this intrusion.

He sank back gratefully in his chair, checked his communication system, looking for a warning or a message of some kind from the orbiting *Vengeful Vitality*, which was scanning for hostile movement. The last message was: *No indication of enemy, and all is well. We remain alert.* It had been sent before Mken had led the way into the passage. He wasn't at all sure if he could get a clear transmitter signal through all this rock.

The Huragok drew back then—and the wall parted like a curtain, a seam appearing down the middle, widening, and the barrier slid away to the left and right.

"Splendid work!" Vervum said.

In the room beyond . . . was nothing. There were no stairs, no niches. Mken was stunned by disappointment. Part of him had hoped there might be vestiges of the Forerunners here . . . perhaps even the Purifying Vision of the Holy Path. The grotto was said to have been created solely to house that artifact.

"It has been removed. Looted," Vervum suggested.

Vil cleared his throat. "But there is dust on the floor, Captain, and no tracks in it. They would have needed a Huragok to get in, after all."

Once more Mken looked at Vil in surprise. He seemed both too young and too . . . *Sangheili* . . . to be so acute.

It might be that he tended to underestimate the Elites, and all the Sangheili. After all, they had already developed space travel between stars when the San'Shyuum discovered them. A current of scientific talent flowed under all the martial bristling.

Mken turned to the Huragok, which was making impatient trilling sounds as it flailed its tentacles. "What does it say?"

Vil pointed his translator toward the Huragok, to sort out the symbols.

As Mken watched, he spotted repeating patterns in the Huragok's tentacle configurations; each symbol went by with a flicker, hard to catch. Sometimes the tip of the tentacle became a corkscrew shape; sometimes it formed in a series of O and V shapes; other times it crossed with a second tentacle, making a living ideogram.

"It says it detects a signal from the room. Something is asking for repair and activation."

"That back wall—is it another door?" Mken wondered aloud.

Vil passed the question on to the Engineer. The Huragok replied in the negative and added, through Vil: <<Follow.>>

It drifted over to the farther wall and seemed to silently contemplate it in the eerie multicolored light from the antigrav chairs. Then it traced a small rectangular shape on the wall. Mken came closer and peered at the spot, which was almost dead center in the wall. It was just a little smoother than the surrounding stone. As he watched, Floats Near Ceiling caressed the space, whisper-thin cilia vanishing into unseen openings.

The rectangular shape gleamed within itself, the light rippling. Then it extruded from the wall with a faint grating sound. It was now a jutting brick shape. The Huragok made another adjustment on it, and Mken gasped as a hologram flared, the blue-silver circular icon shining up from the extrusion, the shape of a hoop big enough for a San'Shyuum to climb through.

Then the hoop shrank, becoming a circle at the center of another construction—Mken recognized it as something some runic symbols had only vaguely referred to in the past, said to be one of the greatest of Forerunner creations. It had six points emanating from the center, like the petals of a flower. At the center, a circular three-dimensional shape, another hoop shone at its core. The shape expanded, and Mken knew it as a "Halo," the first detailed sacred Ring he'd ever seen. He almost wept with joy upon seeing this. On the interior face of its hoop was the topography of a world. Land, hills, valleys, water courses, lakes, artificial structures, all beneath a translucent skin of atmosphere. The interior of the hoop was a living world . . .

Mken suddenly felt more like a true Prophet of Inner Conviction than he had in many a cycle. He was moved by these glowing, transparent symbols, floating and shifting over the block. The images were being projected upward from the brick shape that had extruded from the wall. It was a particularly fine and especially ancient holographic projector.

And truly it was a Purifying Vision.

But he doubted the projector could be a Luminary in itself. The small brick-shaped base and the hologram together comprised the Forerunner's Vision. Where, then, was the Luminary?

"This will bring confirmation," Mken whispered. "This will bring many to the Path. Those who see it will *believe*. The Halos are out there somewhere, waiting for us. And when we find them—when we activate them—it will be the commencement of the Great Journey. But we need the Luminary to find them, according to the ancient prophecies, inscribed in the corridors of the great Dreadnought."

"We need to leave," the scratching anomaly of Loquen's voice interrupted from the entry corridor. "Pull that device out of the wall, Your Eminence. I have just checked the entrance. There are several things out there. I cannot quite see them, but I don't think they're friendly. We are going to have to fight our way past them, before more of their kind come . . ." Loquen backed into view, his weapon pointed out the passageway.

Mken growled: "Ranger, this is a sacred moment, not a time for panic. Do not fire your weapon unless attacked."

"You—" Vervum indicated Vil. "Can this Engineer pull the Forerunner's Vision out of the wall without damaging it?"

Vil asked Floats Near Ceiling and the Huragok replied in the affirmative. "Yes, sir."

Mken said, "Tell it to retrieve it, and with exquisite care. To do no damage. And to shut down the hologram for now."

Vil translated, and the Huragok accomplished the extraction in seconds—evidently the holographic icon was intended to be movable, once discovered.

Vervum made a move toward the projector held in the Huragok's tentacle—but Mken pretended not to notice, and he took the Purifying Vision foundation device himself, slipping it into a pocket of his robe. "Good!"

"Now what, Your Eminence?" Vil asked.

"We need the Luminary!" Vervum said, irritation tightening his voice.

Mken gestured *Of course!* He turned to Vil. "Tell our talented friend Floats Near Ceiling to look for the Luminary—it may be behind that next wall. It can try the socket where the base of the Vision was."

Vil signaled; the Huragok fluted a reply, and stretched its two tentacles to probe within the socket. Moments passed. Then the Huragok made a chirping noise that sounded almost joyous.

The wall trembled and came apart, sliding neatly out of the way but along a crooked seam like puzzle pieces. Behind the wall, within an otherwise empty niche, hovered a gray metal device formed of symmetrical vanes trimmed in thin panels of blue light. The Forerunner workmanship was immediately obvious. To Mken, the Luminary seemed somehow alive as it shifted slightly in the air, turning a glowing cool-blue gaze at them. It was neither large nor small—a San'Shyuum could just clasp it within the scope of his arms. Its centerpiece was a globe of polished gray metal, within which glowed sentient blue light; its vanes were like stylized, intricately figured blades extending from the small globe, a divided vane atop, armlike extensions on the sides, as if it were some primitive hieroglyph of a sun god.

"Is that it?" Vervum asked. "The Luminary?"

Mken's response was breathless—he could hardly speak in his excitement. "Its design, overall, is consistent with a Luminary, though it's not entirely like the others . . . but I believe—*yes*! It must be! We must take it immediately back to the ship. The Dreadnought's inscriptions foretold, generations ago, that the Forerunners had designed a particular kind of Luminary, different from those we had encountered before—a kind capable of showing the way to the Holy Rings themselves. Some believed that one of these had been hidden here, under our people's very noses for ages. And at last, our faith has proven true. Back to the ship, put these relics in storage there—then on to the second part of our mission."

"No," Vervum said, moving his chair behind Loquen. "I do not think that is going to happen. There is something else planned for you, O Prophet of Inner Conviction . . ."

Mken turned his chair and was startled to see that Loquen was pointing his rifle at him—at the Prophet of Inner Conviction himself. And Vervum made the gesture, *Make peace with your ancestors.*

He had half expected treachery from Vervum, but not something this bold.

But so be it. Mken did have weaponry on his chair. Had they forgotten that?

He touched the arming node . . . and got no response.

"Oh, we already nullified your weapons," Vervum said with a soft sneer. "You shouldn't have walked away from your chair at that first landing."

"You have not really thought this through," Mken said. "Nor has the hidden hand who manipulates you. R'Noh supposes he can get me out of the way, take credit for everything that is accomplished here. But . . . it is not so simple." He was stalling. Thinking . . .

Vervum gestured, *Respectfully, you are mistaken.* He added an extra flip of the thumb to show the gesture was used in mockery. "You confirmed the site. You and the Huragok opened the repository for the Vision. You activated it and confirmed the Purifying Vision's nature. And you found the Luminary for us. And you really are superfluous when it comes to recruiting the females. We can do that. Hence . . . your usefulness is at an end. And the Ministry of Anticipatory Security"—he gave the gesture of wry amusement—"anticipates that you will inevitably become a security problem."

"Oh—on what basis does it foresee that?" Mken noticed that Vil, off to the side, was signaling the Huragok.

"It's of no import now. Surrender the Vision to me. Otherwise it may be damaged when we execute you."

Mken realized he might have to comply. The Vision was more important than he was.

The Huragok drifted toward the niche, placing itself between Loquen and the Luminary as if to protect it. Vil backed toward the same wall. Mken took the cue and backed with them—and made up his mind to defiance. "No, I'm not going to give the Vision to you, Vervum, nor the Luminary. You are not authorized to take them."

Vervum snorted. "Authorized? I'm authorizing myself. Loquen, do what must be done. I believe I can communicate with the Huragok. So get rid of the Ranger as well."

Loquen turned his rifle toward Vil. "This one first, then—he's armed."

The directed-energy rifles were divided into upper and lower parts. They were jawlike—perhaps a design unconsciously mimicking a Sangheili's mandibles—and by his expression, it seemed as though Vil had never before looked into them from the point of view of a target.

Loquen fired, but Vil was already reflexively stepping aside, aiming his directed-energy rifle, and he launched a spike of super-heated plasma.

The other Sangheili was moving, too—and Vil's shot burned into Loquen's left shoulder. Loquen clashed his mandibles in pain and staggered back, his return fire searing over Vil's head.

A bright beam of energy hummed from the arm of Vervum's antigrav chair. But Vervum was no expert with chair armament, and the blast burned along Vil's ribs. Vil's armor deflected most of it; there was agony but no serious injury.

The Huragok meanwhile was caressing the rock wall to one side, and suddenly the stone barricade began to close. The chamber was being resealed.

Vil fired again, but Loquen had drawn back into the shadows, a bad target, and for a moment it seemed as though Vil had felt an innate reluctance to actually shoot at Vervum, one of his superiors, let alone at a San'Shyuum and the captain of the vessel.

Instead Vil deliberately fired past Vervum and into the darkness, sending several bolts out of the passage and into the undergrowth.

Then the stone doors sealed shut.

CHAPTER 9

The Refuge: An Uncharted Shield World
850 BCE
The Age of Reconciliation

Her name was Lnur 'Mol, and Tersa knew perfectly well that he should not be staring at her. She was busily serving out pots of foodstuff to the workers. She had no time for him. He should not be staring at the gleam of her mandible teeth—those teeth so sharp, so white. He should not be considering the slender lineaments of her figure, the jewel-like gleaming of her silver-green eyes, the perfect symmetrical arrangement of her four jaws. She wore no armor, except some neat trappings of leather.

No. Staring at Lnur was not advisable. He had only met her a few times, had not the courage to speak much to her; he hadn't initiated courting rituals. And Tersa had tasks to complete, helping Ernicka repair the burnblades. Lnur was in the workshop, on Level Two, only to bring in foodstuff for the five Sangheili males at work here.

She brought him his pot of protein mash—and surprised him by making a little conversation. "Is that one done?" she asked, looking at it closely. "Both my egg siblings went into weapons design and repair. I do enjoy looking at them myself."

"I think I shall test this one," he said.

He inserted the charger and squeezed the activator. The sword's metal blade hummed within itself. As they watched, it took on a slight red color as it heated up. It charred what it didn't cut without cauterizing.

"It looks as if it's functioning," she said.

Her voice was mellifluous. To Tersa, it was like listening to music.

"Would you like to try it out?" he asked, nodding toward the synthetic-wood target board across the room.

Female Sangheili weren't recruited as warriors, but they all knew the rudiments of combat so they could defend home and eggs in case of invasion while the males were away.

She glanced self-consciously at the males working near Tersa. Ernicka was carefully not looking at her or Tersa. The others watched covertly with closed-jaw smirks of amusement.

Then Lnur straightened her shoulders and said boldly, "Yes. Thank you. Should it ever be necessary . . ."

Tersa warmed to her even more, then—her refusal to be completely cowed by the ancient gender roles was strangely attractive. It suggested she might be capable of bold intimacy, as well as bold action.

But of course, he mused as they walked over to the testing target, Lnur was still Sangheili—and he had never heard of a Sangheili female truly challenging the old patriarchal order. Sooln was perhaps more active in the technological world than many females; she gave her counsel to Ussa 'Xellus himself. But she didn't go too far. Privately, he wondered if the time would come when some Sangheili female would try to rebel in a more significant way. But of course she would be quickly put to death.

The very thought disturbed him.

Tersa stepped up to the target, once more activating the burner element in the sword, and gave it a tentative slash. The target was fittingly shaped like a San'Shyuum—the only enemy any of them had known for decades—and the blade cut and burned at once into the neck of the figure.

"It seems to work," he said. He glanced at Ernicka, working a few tables away. Ernicka seemed to be pretending to be unaware of Tersa and Lnur. "Here, Lnur. You give it a try."

He carefully handed it over to her and stood back—perhaps a little more than he would if he were with an experienced soldier.

She gave him a glance of mild reproach and then swung viciously at the target. The blade sizzled and cut halfway through the San'Shyuum shape's neck.

She gave it a cunning twist of her wrist and the sword came free, leaving a trail of smoke in the air.

"You have fashioned this in dangerously fine shape!" she said. It was a traditional compliment to an arms worker.

"Has he, now?" said 'Crolon, walking in. He was carrying a small crate of swords to be upgraded. 'Crolon paused to look at the two young Sangheili, and at the target Lnur had slashed. "You seem to have some considerable experience of weapons, young female."

"My mother taught me . . . For the—"

"I know, for the defense of home and eggs," 'Crolon interjected with amusement. "How often I've heard that excuse for a female not knowing her place."

Tersa felt anger rise up in him, like boiling water through a tube. He took the sword from Lnur. "'Crolon . . . you're a swamp *skorken* nipping at a wader. You need to apologize to my friend. Or perhaps take one of those swords from your box."

The room fell silent, Ernicka watching narrowly from his worktable. 'Crolon looked at Tersa with surprise. "So! There are teeth in your jaws after all! Interesting. And interesting, too, this socially corrosive activity you're engaged in here. I will not fight with you, young Sangheili—not so you can caper impressively in front of a female."

Lnur gave an embarrassed gasp at that.

'Crolon went on. "Ussa has ordered us not to waste our fighting on one another—not without grand provocation or permission."

"On the contrary," said Tersa. "You have been provoking me, threatening me—and now you've insulted my friend. If you continue, I will ask Ernicka's permission."

"How dare you." 'Crolon gave Tersa a coldly glittering look and then walked to the table, dropping off the crate, without another word.

Ernicka was looking at Tersa with a mix of approval and irritation. "Back to work, Tersa!" he called out.

"Coming!"

"I'm sorry if I got you in trouble," Lnur murmured.

"I'm sorry I embarrassed you!" Tersa whispered ruefully. "I shouldn't have said that you were . . . assumed you were . . . a friend. I mean . . . I scarcely know you . . . I mean, I did not intend any . . ."

"It is all right," she said. "If it is up to me—you *are* my friend."

She turned and walked out the door.

With a great effort, Tersa managed not to watch as she left.

Reskolah, Janjur Qom
850 BCE
The Age of Reconciliation

Mken, Vil, and Floats Near Ceiling found themselves locked away inside the grotto.

The Huragok had triggered the wall to close off the inner chamber; it seemed a permanent seal, a seamless barrier between them and their enemies. Loquen and Vervum were outside . . . and beyond them, something moved in slippery camouflage through the undergrowth. Something dangerous.

The glow of Mken's antigrav chair and the Luminary lent a weak light to the room. The Huragok fluted mournfully and flicked its tentacles at Vil 'Kthamee. Mken waited nervously for the translation.

Vil grunted. "He is able to use the hidden devices in the walls—he can sense some of what is going on out there. It is as I hoped . . . but I may wish later I had not done it."

"Explain," demanded the Prophet of Inner Conviction.

"I fired past Loquen and the captain, out through the door, into the undergrowth, to stir up those who are hunting out there. So they would think Loquen was the one firing at them. And so that it would be they who would destroy the San'Shyuum—and not me."

Mken was impressed by Vil 'Kthamee's strategic thinking, and his honesty. The young Ranger wasn't foolish enough to kill a San'Shyuum and still hope to avoid punishment, whatever his motives. "And you managed to convince the Huragok to seal us in so we would be safe . . . but can it get us out again?"

"Yes, so it says." Vil signed to Floats Near Ceiling. It responded. "The Huragok says they are fighting out there now . . . something is firing projectiles at them . . . Loquen and the captain are firing back. Ah—Vervum . . . he has been killed."

Mken felt a chill at that. The *Vengeful Vitality* could be instructed by anyone who knew the vessel's command codes to return to the Dreadnought—and Mken had those codes. But Vervum had been an agent of the Minister of Anticipatory Security.

Mken had hoped to outmaneuver Vervum rather than kill him, and so avoid having to explain everything to the Hierarchs. The tale of Vervum's death could easily be twisted against him when R'Noh and Excellent Redolence got hold of it.

The Huragok was now signaling again. Vil translated: "Now . . . Loquen is firing his weapon, and running into the forest. The hostiles are coming into the grotto! They are San'Shyuum—but different from those we know from High Charity. They do not use chairs. They are more . . ." The Ranger paused, evidently deciding, out of instinctive politesse, not to quote the Huragok contrasting the two breeds of San'Shyuum. "They have projectile weapons. Perhaps gas fired. One of them now takes Vervum—and the chair. But this they must carry. The chair is broken. The Huragok wishes it could fix it . . ."

"Only what is relevant, please, Ranger."

"Yes, Your Eminence. They are departing the grotto—they do not seem to be aware of this room."

"With luck, they don't know you and I are here, then. Perhaps they think our group has split up."

"Yes, Eminence. I suspect they're going to look for us elsewhere."

He turned and looked at the Luminary—and again it seemed as if it looked silently back at him. "Now . . ."

Mken directed his chair to approach the Luminary. He spread his arms, reaching for the sacred relic. And it surprised him by floating toward him and turning, then settling into his grasp. It was almost as if he held it in his lap. "I'm clasping the ages," he murmured. "The past and the future."

He was profoundly moved. To find an artifact this important, this fully intact . . .

"It is a beautiful relic," Vil said reverently, looking at the Luminary.

"Yes. You must not speak of it, back on High Charity—not with anyone unauthorized. Do you understand?"

"I do, Your Eminence."

"Good—the Huragok can open the outer wall and we'll be on our way."

"To Crellum, Your Eminence?"

Mken found himself wondering suddenly if they should go to Crellum at all. Wasn't it more important to get these sacred artifacts away from Janjur Qom? He had the Luminary. The females seemed almost unnecessary in comparison. But even as he'd argued with R'Noh and Excellent Redolence back at High Charity, he'd known that the fresh genetic material the women would bring could be vital. He'd been reluctant to take on that part of this mission. But he was here now. And if he didn't come back with the females, R'Noh and Excellent Redolence might retaliate: they might block Cresanda's right to have their child. She could be at risk of being incarcerated.

He must go on with it.

"Yes," Mken said. "We will go to Crellum and retrieve the females. May the spirit of the Great Journey protect us. Now—tell the Huragok to get us out of here. The air is growing stale."

Vil translated the command, and the Huragok opened the wall. Moonlight and some cool air reached them from the passageway back to the meadow. A nocturnal flyer gave a trilling cry, somewhere distant.

They watched and listened. There was nothing else—no sign of Stoics outside, no enemy at all. The camouflaging wall had worked. Unconsciously, Mken hugged the Luminary a little closer. "Good. Let's get on with this. Back to the dropship."

"And then to the corvette, Your Eminence? To store these relics?"

Mken was tempted. However . . .

"No—there's no time. We have the rest of our mission to complete. And the Stoics will not expect us to go to Crellum. Or so I hope."

What remained of the grotto expedition returned to the dropship without incident, though with every step along the trail, Mken expected an attack from the darkness.

As they arrived at the dropship, he saw that clouds had gathered, swept in on a soft east wind, and the moon was rising to join them.

Vil saluted Trok 'Tanghil as they approached, but Trok was gawping at the Luminary clasped to Mken's chest. "Is that . . . ?"

"It is what it should be," said Mken briskly. "That is all you need to know. Everyone board the dropship. Get ready to take off!"

Trok blinked. "Certainly, but—should we wait for the captain, Your Eminence, and the Ranger Loquen?"

Mken hesitated, wondering if he should trust Trok with the full truth. But it was better to say too little instead of too much. "The captain was killed by the Stoic primitives. And the Ranger, the one called Loquen, ran into the forest. We believe he is likely dead."

Trok scratched at his broken mandible. He seemed to have difficulty comprehending. "He *ran*? You mean—he was trying to flank the enemy?"

"No. He panicked."

Trok appeared confounded. "He was impulsive, but I've never known him to be dishonorable!"

Mken waved away the subject. "We have no time for this discussion. We must be off for Crellum."

"Just as you say, Great Prophet, but"—Trok peered at the dark undergrowth—"do you think you were followed?"

"Have you any indication the *Vengeful Vitality* was discovered?"

"Our stealth field seems to have worked so far, O Prophet."

"Then probably we're safe for the moment. They found some of us—they didn't discover the others. Or so I conjecture. Trok, can you pilot the *Vengeful Vitality* when the time comes?"

"Indeed, I can. I am not the expert that Vervum is . . . or was."

"You will act as captain, then, when the time comes. Hurry!"

Vil 'Kthamee helped Mleer store the turret in the dropship's armaments locker. At the opposite bulkhead Mken was placing the base of the Purifying Vision in a relic storage cabinet, and then eased the Luminary in beside it. He fastened the protective webbing around the device, and then locked it away.

Vil hurried aft, made sure the Huragok had its tentacles firmly clinging to its wall grips, then went forward to his assigned place.

As he got strapped into his seat, Vil looked around, taking stock.

There were six Sangheili left, and all were at their stations as the dropship rose humming into the air, Trok piloting up front.

"Trok!" Inner Conviction called. "Take us up—we'll travel as high as we can."

They ascended steeply. Vil watched through a port as the small vessel rose above the thin cloud cover. Now, silvered by the light of Plaon, Janjur Qom's moon, the clouds looked like a shining field of snow.

Vil wondered if Loquen had been captured by the Stoics. The San'Shyuum now inhabiting Janjur Qom were said to be more savage than those on High Charity. They would be quick to torture, he supposed.

Loquen might not be as resilient as everyone supposed. After all, he had fled into the jungle, when most Sangheili would have chosen to fight to the death. What would Loquen tell them if he were caught and came under the knife? Did he know enough to give the Stoics the location of High Charity? Would they even understand his speech?

The Dreadnought could be moved, even now—but with High Charity only partly completed, it might very well be vulnerable, if somehow the Stoics possessed the means.

Then another thought struck Vil: Suppose he himself was taken by the Stoics? What would he tell them under duress?

Nothing. He, Vil 'Kthamee, would not be taken alive. Not if he could choose. If by some mischance they'd struck him unconscious, and he found himself captured, he would never reveal anything, come what may.

But Loquen? Vil knew that a habitual display of fierceness could camouflage fear. He suspected that Loquen, if still alive, could not be trusted.

CHAPTER 10

The Refuge: An Uncharted Shield World
850 BCE
The Age of Reconciliation

Tersa and Lnur were in Ussa's Garden, on the eco level of the shield world. She had a hand in the crook of his right arm, an ancient way for a female to walk with a male, an informal courting that carried with it as yet no commitment. But even this casual touch made Tersa's nostrils flare; he couldn't keep from occasionally daydreaming about her . . .

What would it be like to raise childlings within the steel womb of the Refuge? Would they never see a true sky?

The artificial sun within the shield world illuminated the small trees, the rugged stone outcroppings, the flowing water, the light safely refracted and filtered by translucent energy fields so there was no dangerous radiation or glare. Overhead, the icicle shapes of the cryptic devices jutting from the distant metal concave ceiling gleamed dully; shadows crisscrossed oddly here and there, random stripes across the garden area. Something rustled softly in the brush.

"Tersa—at times I wonder if that solid-seeming metal up

there will simply break open all of a sudden, and Covenant ships will come for us. Could they have followed us here somehow?"

"I believe—*I have* to believe—that Ussa 'Xellus took every precaution. He would have left no trail—and we are a long way from Sanghelios. No, this is precisely what we call it. Refuge."

Privately, Tersa thought that there was no knowing for certain. He reckoned that the Covenant had a great many resources; the San'Shyuum were cunning, and the kaidons of the city states back on Sanghelios would never cease their search for the traitorous Ussa 'Xellus. Separate clans, separate cities—that was permitted. But those who dared renounce Sanghelios forever went gratingly against the cultural grain.

But it was Tersa's instinct to at least attempt to protect Lnur from those worries.

As if an omen, a shadow fell over them—but it was just a passing robotic conveyance, flying quickly past overhead. It was gone in an instant, taking its shadow with it.

"Will we really be here for the rest of our lives, do you think?" she asked.

"I do not know. I would like to think we'd use this as a base—and when the time was right, make some kind of sally and perhaps harass the Covenant, or just some exploration in this star system. It would not be natural for Sangheili to have no possible adversary, nothing to test ourselves against."

"I agree with you there—to just vegetate in here, studying, never pitting ourselves against anything . . . we'd degenerate."

They walked on, following a stream that went down a slight slope. After a few thoughtful moments, Tersa said, "There are not that many of us here—we need to stay unified. But a Sangheili warrior must test himself against an enemy. It has occurred to me that if we do not find enemies on the outside, we will find them here. We could become divided, factionalize—and that would be a volatile situation in a self-contained world such as this. It would be almost like a mutiny on a spacecraft. A high risk for everyone. The wrong kind of risk."

"I have had the same thought—especially after that encounter with 'Crolon. I've heard rumors about him, and a few others . . ."

He glanced at her. She was young, and occasionally he'd heard her engage in hearsay—he didn't want to encourage it. Hearsay could lead to the very thing that they'd been speaking of. It could be the seed of factionalism, division, mutiny, and ultimately the failure of the colony.

"I have no liking for 'Crolon," she went on ruefully. "The females in my clan have a strong protector-of-eggs tradition." She glanced at him. "Very strong."

"Yes? More than is . . . orthodox?"

She hesitated. "I will be direct with you, though it's taking a chance. Yes. More than is orthodox." She then added with a certain defiance: "We believe females can become warriors. And more. But . . . it is not something we speak openly about—at least not with males."

He felt an internal flutter, a mix of astonishment and admiration. What Lnur had said was heretical, but also brave. And "between his hearts," as the Sangheili saying went, he knew she was right.

"Perhaps, hearing that," she went on, a little louder as the sound of a waterfall increased from up ahead, "you would not want to walk with me anymore—perhaps you would not care to be seen with me at all. I wouldn't blame you. But . . . I wanted you to know."

"I suppose I *did* know—the way you took to that burnblade. Lnur, I am honored you trusted me."

She pursed her mandibles in a combination of amusement and appreciation. "You do know the right things to say, Tersa . . . at least to me."

Hearing that, Tersa felt a subtle thrill of confirmation, a recognition of destiny perhaps, like an energy charge all about them . . .

They'd come to the edge of a small bluff overlooking a dale. The stream tumbled over the cliff, plunging just far enough down to make the waterfall sound louder.

Tersa then heard something penetrating the burring splash of the waterfall. Voices. 'Crolon—and 'Drem. And someone else.

He couldn't quite make out what they were saying. "Do you hear voices?"

"Yes. Is that . . . 'Crolon?"

Tersa and Lnur looked at each other. Then in silent mutual agreement they eased closer to the edge of the bluff and looked over, toward the pool below.

There were four Sangheili gathered down there—'Crolon, 'Drem, Scorinn, and Gmezza the Limper. Scorinn was a female; Gmezza the Limper, so nicknamed because of an injury that had made his right leg a little shorter than the left, was her mate.

From here, the voices carried up the cliff side, though blurred by the sound of the falls. ". . . If we fail to take action, we will all die either way," 'Crolon was saying. The next phrase was partly obscured by the noise of the waterfall. Tersa heard only ". . . alternative, so far as . . ."

"But Scorinn and I—we would need proof. This idea that Ussa will commit a mass . . ." Tersa lost consistent track of Gmezza's voice then. ". . . hard to . . . cannot go about . . . we could all be executed . . ."

"What 'Crolon says is true!" 'Drem said insistently, his voice loud enough to cut through the waterfall's hiss and splash. "You notice Ussa rarely allows us to carry weapons. Why? And that flying construct is in on it! It wants to summon the San'Shyuum!"

"That doesn't make sense," said Scorinn. "If Ussa plans what you say, why would he summon—"

"Silence, female, the males are speaking!" barked 'Drem.

"'Drem!" warned the Limper. "That is my mate—"

"Gmezza," put in 'Crolon. "Did I not hear you mention yesterday that this place was a mistake? I would hate to have to . . ."

"Look! Someone is up there, listening!" 'Drem cried. "At the top of the waterfall!"

Lnur instinctively tried to jerk back—and her foot slipped. She tottered on the edge of the cliff.

Tersa grabbed her arm and steadied her. "We need to leave now."

They hurried away, Tersa wishing Ussa had not forbidden the carrying of weapons without permission. Hunting parties were allowed. There were furred and feathered creatures in the stony, tree-flecked level of the Refuge, most unfamiliar but none dangerous—and many had been shown by scanners to be edible. The colony would rarely need the protein synthesizer from this time forward.

The weapons order was controversial, and almost inimical to a Sangheili. But Ussa was concerned about close confines, fights flaring that would only divide a relatively small settlement and weaken it when the time came to confront a real enemy. Ussa had declared that weapons would be issued if the shield world were attacked; at times they were permitted for practice sessions with targets, and sparring.

But Tersa needed one right now. 'Crolon might well be pursuing them. If, as it seemed, he'd been plotting insurrection, he'd want to know immediately who had overheard them. He had likely witnessed Lnur on the cliff's edge, at the very least. She was in danger . . .

Lnur seemed to be thinking the same way. She paused, picked up a broken limb from under a tree, desiccated and lightened by time, and gave it a good grip.

Her timing was excellent—'Drem was suddenly there, leaping down from a boulder to block their way. He had a work knife in his hand—something used in construction, but deadly enough. Breathing hard, he hissed, "The others are slower, but they'll soon be here! We'll have a word with you!"

And he brandished the blade.

Tersa stepped in front of Lnur. "Get out of the way, you fool!"

'Drem snarled, "You would insult me?" He rushed in, slashing at Tersa, who easily sidestepped the attack. The evasion gave Lnur a chance to step in and swing the club. She caught 'Drem solidly on the side of the head with it.

'Drem spun and went down, groaning, clutching his head.

"Good aim!" Tersa said admiringly.

"Come on!" Lnur said, leaping over 'Drem and hurrying off.

'Drem was starting to sit up, once more wielding the knife. Tersa kicked 'Drem's wrist, hard enough to send the knife spinning from his grip. Then he rushed after Lnur.

It didn't feel honorable, not to stay and engage in full combat with 'Drem, but somehow it also wouldn't have been right to linger and kill him. Three of 'Drem's companions were coming, and Lnur would be unprotected if they set upon her.

But then again, it appeared she didn't need much protection. Perhaps, he thought, she should be protecting *him*.

"I wonder," Tersa said, when he caught up with Lnur, "if we should've killed him."

"Yes, I wonder about that, too."

The dropship was moving through the night as slowly as possible, so as not to attract attention. Its occupants were following the contours of a deep ravine through a verdant tableland. A river ran below them—but Mken 'Scre'ah'ben was not sightseeing, not in that way.

Hunched uneasily in his antigrav chair, behind Trok 'Tanghil, who was now piloting the craft, Mken stared into the topographical hologram of Crellum projected over his chair. The image was being transmitted from the orbiting *Vengeful Vitality*, its scanners penetrating the cloud cover. Waving his hand over the holoswitches, he turned the image this way and that, expanding it to include a goodly distance from the settlement. Crellum was merely a double row of oval wooden and plaster houses, a fishing community curving along the edge of a large lake, some of the houses on stilts over the water. Some part of Mken's scholarly mind noted that the edifices were old-style, their outlines evoking the shape of an average San'Shyuum's skull seen from above.

But mostly he was scanning for movement, shifting the image through several spectra, looking for heat signatures. He could see a number of figures moving down the lane between the houses; animals that must be *garfren*, thick-bodied stock animals kept mostly for milk, shone from a kind of corral. He had a treasured *garfren*-fur coverlet on his bed, back on the Dreadnought. Was Cresanda snuggled under it now, tossing and turning, trying to sleep as she worried about him?

Don't think about her now, he chided himself, looking more intently at the hologram.

Cupping the village was thick undergrowth, with every so often a larger tree looking lonely among the shrubs—most of the forest that had once stood there had been logged off many centuries ago. Something was moving rather oddly through the undergrowth, several shapes of the same kind, ones he did not recognize. Mixed in with it were other body signatures that might be San'Shyuum.

But he saw nothing that looked like an armed force, no over-flights, no aircraft, nothing that looked like turret emplacements.

Trok 'Tanghil glanced over his shoulder. "How lies the land, Your Eminence? Are the hostiles aroused?"

"If they've set a trap for us, it's too cunning for me to penetrate. It's time to move in—and take our chances. The females should be awaiting us."

"Can our . . . our special guests really be waiting for us?" Trok asked, turning his gaze to the windshield and steering the vessel out of the ravine.

"The message was sent via holo, through an Eye . . . and two of them responded. The latest message indicates that seven others are also willing. There are almost no young males in this part of Reskolah—and when they *are* about, apparently they treat the females barbarically."

"The settlement's males have died in battle?"

"They were conscripted—whether they are dead, we don't know."

"We are approaching possible landing site one . . . It appears to be clear. Our stealth field must be doing its job."

"Good. Then let us land. Deploy the Rangers and the others the instant we set down."

"So it will be, Your Eminence."

The cloud cover had fractured for the time being, letting the moonlight come unsteadily through to dance on the small waves of the broad lake. Accompanied by three Sangheili, Mken tramped along the curving beach toward the small settlement of Crellum. He was supported by an antigrav belt, which was not as efficient as the chair. Still, the chair's holo instrumentation glow would have put any local Stoic soldiers on alert: *Here is the Reformist invader you're looking for.*

And Mken knew they were indeed searching for him. By now they'd have realized that the two encountered outside the grotto couldn't be the only ones planetside.

With Mken were Commander Trok 'Tanghil, and two Sangheili Rangers: Vil 'Kthamee and a stocky, frightened-looking Ziln 'Klel, the latter clutching his rifle close to his chest. The Sangheili had a reputation for being insanely brave, but somehow R'Noh had assigned a couple of shaky Rangers to the expedition—Loquen and now this one. More of R'Noh's treachery, probably—but the Minister of Anticipatory Security hadn't counted on the resourcefulness of Vil 'Kthamee, someone who had a great destiny to fulfill. Mken would see to that.

Mken hoped the dropship was safe with the others—it was underdefended, and if it was taken down, despite the stealth field, this mission would be useless.

The Prophet of Inner Conviction stopped and his armed entourage paused at his signal. He didn't want to blunder into a trap. He listened, and heard only faint voices, carried across lapping waves. He could smell the tarn's living waters; he heard the grunt and splash of some large creature out there, perhaps a hungry *ilpdor*. The immense six-legged predators were amphibious—he hoped they didn't come to shore to try for a taste of his expedition. It would take their plasma rifles to kill the creature, and that would attract unwanted attention.

Lamps in Crellum shone from windows with power collected

during the day from the energy of the sun—gathered by plants carpeted on the roof, according to the corvette's analysis scans; the lights made circles of illumination shaped by the round windows in the lozenge-shaped houses. Mken could see boats tied up, clacking against pilings with the movements of waves, and light reflected from the water around the houses on stilts. Occasionally he glimpsed San'Shyuum walking by, silhouetted against the lights. He saw only one who seemed male, and the fellow moved haltingly, as if quite elderly.

We are fools to be here, he thought. *And what if something happens to the Purifying Vision and the Luminary back at the dropship? We should take it to orbit. I should be studying both—not fumbling about a primitive settlement.*

But he was appointed to pick up their charges at a certain hour. He must be there on time . . .

He sighed. "Let us go on."

He led the way, trudging along, wishing he had a more powerful antigrav belt.

The message had said they were to meet a female named Lilumna just outside the village along the shore. And up ahead—was that not the dark silhouette of a female San'Shyuum?

Yes. There was something, too, about her posture, her body language, that expressed nervousness, alertness—waiting.

"That is probably her," Mken whispered. "Do not get nervous with those weapons. Stay here."

He hobbled toward her, hand casually resting on the pistol holstered at his hip. But he wasn't much good with it. The antigrav chairs had their own weapons and did much of the aiming, too.

By the Great Journey, but this could end badly . . .

The San'Shyuum female looked more frightened than dangerous, however, as Mken approached her.

"Are you Lilumna?" he asked gently.

She stared at him. Then, her big eyes catching a flash of moonlight, she came a little closer. "Yes," she said, her voice unsteady. "Are you . . . ?"

"Yes. My name is Mken—I am from off-planet. From High Charity. I am the one sent for you."

She stared at him, then came a little closer. She was wearing a robe that was loose up above, clinging to her lower parts, sewn with the ancient home symbols of Reskolah and ancient symbols of fertility. It was a traditional robe worn by San'Shyuum females seeking mates.

Lilumna looked him up and down, frowning. "You seem . . . not entirely well. Is everyone like you there?" Her accent was thick, her word usage not entirely familiar, but he made out what she was saying, and she seemed to understand him.

He winced inwardly at her blunt assessment. "It is merely that—I am not used to the higher gravity here." That wasn't the full explanation. But if he admitted that the typical Reformist San'Shyuum was feebler than the males she knew here on Janjur Qom, she might never come with him, and his mission would fail. Feeling obscurely guilty, he went on. "We are not all alike, no. Are you and the others still willing to come with us?"

She made a sinuous motion with her snaking neck and a hand gesture that was still the same with San'Shyuum, even on High Charity. It meant, *I have decided. It will be done.*

"Excellent, Lilumna. But I must ask—are there soldiers here? Anyone looking for off-worlders?"

"I've seen no one like that tonight. But there was a *folasteed* patrol this afternoon, asking questions. None of us spoke to them—they're brutal. We all despise them quite thoroughly and completely. They are a good deal of the reason we want to leave

Janjur Qom. And there are so few males that one would care to mate with. And as for me . . ." She looked at the sky. "I want to see what is up there, beyond the moon."

"You will," he assured her, even as he wondered what a *folasteed* patrol might be. The word was unfamiliar to him. "Can you signal the others?"

Lilumna seemed to waver. Then she hand-gestured a shrug. "They asked me to meet you—I must decide. I have always been intuitive. You seem honest enough. I will simply have to trust you are not some sort of slaver."

"I am not a slaver, and you will not be slaves. You will be offered the chance to meet many males, to make the acquaintance of powerful Prophets of the Great Journey, who seek new mates."

Lilumna pointed at the lake. "The others are watching us—they're out there." She took a deep breath and seemed to make her decision. She raised both hands over her head, and made *It's safe to come* gestures with both of them.

"I don't see anyone . . ."

"There—" Lilumna said. "Now do you see them?"

Then he saw the *ilpdor*—its legs moving rhythmically as it swam toward them, mouth agape . . .

Was this Lilumna here to feed him to a giant aquatic predator?

It seemed absurd. But still the great scaly beast bore down upon them . . .

CHAPTER 11

Y ou are under arrest, Tersa," said Ernicka the Scar-Maker. "And you, too, Lnur 'Mol. I am sorry, but it must be so. The kaidon demands you submit—or die."

They had come to the Hall of Feasts, not sure what to expect. The hostile stares of Sangheili should have warned them. And then Ernicka had come in from behind them, a plasma rifle in his hands.

Tersa was carrying a burnblade. He put a hand on the sword grip, prepared to draw it. Ernicka raised his rifle—

"Please, if you value me," Lnur said, her voice barely audible. "Give up the weapon. We must trust in Ussa."

Tersa hated the thought of surrendering to a court where he would be slandered, where the king and prince of Sangheili liars, 'Crolon and 'Drem, would be pointing accusing claws.

But . . . Lnur had said the one thing that disarmed him. He valued her above all things.

He muttered assent, drew the weapon, reversed it, offering it pommel first to Ernicka.

The weathered Sangheili lowered his rifle and took the burnblade. "A wise choice. Come with me."

He seemed to trust in their honor, walking ahead of them to Strategy Hall, where Ussa held court.

The rectangular room had been one of several parts of the shield world that hadn't appeared to be completed by the Forerunners. Enduring Bias had explained that despite this, in some ways, it was one of the Forerunner's most advanced constructions. There were materials, technologies, found here that were not found elsewhere. They'd been newly developed, just when the Flood, as Enduring Bias called it, had threatened to overwhelm the galaxy. That great war had left this shield world unfinished, populated only by small creatures seeded here to complete the ecology.

Strategy Hall was therefore only a large empty room with steel-colored walls and a crystalline ceiling emitting a soft light. At one end, Ussa's court attendants had erected a broad podium of extraneous plastics found about the shield world. Here, as Ernicka, Lnur, and Tersa strode up to it, the kaidon sat on a simple wooden chair, constructed from the trees up on the eco level.

Behind Ussa, on the wall, was a half-finished painting of Sanghelios beside the metal-jacketed world of the Refuge—the new symbol of their colony. The mural was Sooln's work-in-progress.

Ussa shifted pensively in his chair and looked balefully at them. "I have heard an accusation from 'Crolon and 'Drem. That you are conspiring against me. That you attacked 'Drem, tried to murder him, to quiet him about it. That's the kernel of it, though of course he was tiresomely loquacious. What have you to say?"

" 'Crolon and 'Drem are lying to cover up their own perfidy," declared Tersa. "I have heard them speak sedition time and again. They were trying to recruit Gmezza and Scorinn."

Lnur looked reproachfully at Tersa. Scorinn was Lnur's aunt, and a kind of second mother to her. She'd asked that Scorinn not be dragged into this—but Tersa had made no promises and now he felt he had no choice. Scorinn and Gmezza might well be trusted to tell the truth.

"Gmezza and Scorinn . . ." Ussa ran a thoughtful thumb along a mandible. "I have not heard this."

"And if they were there," Lnur asked, "why didn't 'Crolon say so?"

"Yes, one wonders," Ussa said. "But if they were speaking of treason, why didn't you come to me with this?"

Tersa sighed. "We were talking about it, Great Kaidon. But—Lnur was worried about her relation, about Scorinn. And we knew it would be our word against theirs. I would have come if I'd had more proof—and if we'd heard them speaking clearly. But some parts of it we weren't sure of . . . we only overheard them from a distance . . . we didn't want to cause executions without better proof."

"Particularly not the execution of Scorinn?" Ussa grunted. "Well, we shall have Gmezza and Scorinn here. Ernicka—send for them!"

"It will be done, Ussa," Ernicka said, signaling the guardsmen at the door.

"There is another who can speak for us, Great Ussa," Tersa said. "Enduring Bias!"

"Indeed?" Ussa seemed distracted as he replied. "Sooln was looking for the Flying Voice earlier and he was not easily found. That's usually the case when he's inspecting the outer shell. But we shall find him. It may take some time. In the meantime . . . sit over there, on the floor, and wait. I will have water and food brought for us all. And we shall see if you are to live or die."

Reskolah, Janjur Qom
850 BCE
The Age of Reconciliation

Mken hadn't quite gotten over his astonishment. He'd been surprised to see eight female San'Shyuum riding the *ilpdor*. He'd never heard of one of the immense predators being trained, in any way. But it seemed this one was. Low slung but broad, it lurched along the sandy beach with the San'Shyuum females lined up, straddling its back—with variants in the color of the shiny cloth, they were all dressed in the traditional *I am willing to consider mating* garb.

They seemed perfectly comfortable riding the giant carnivorous amphibian—but the *ilpdor* seemed clumsy as it trotted along, its webbed, clawed feet not as comfortable on land as in the water. It reeked of scaly amphibian and muck, trailing bits of seaweed and some kind of clutched-on parasite like a grotesque skirt as it waddled up the shore.

Feeling an uncomfortable combination of fatigue and anxious tension, Mken walked a safe distance to the right of the scaly six-legged creature's wide, toothy jaws. A lolling blue tongue whipped out from time to time, licking at rows of fangs as the *ilpdor* rolled its faceted eyes toward him. Mken couldn't get over the feeling that it was imagining what he might taste like.

To Mken's right was Lilumna, walking with a vigor that put his own trudging to shame; flanking her were the three Sangheili. Vil 'Kthamee glanced from time to time at the females riding the *ilpdor.* The Sangheili Ranger seemed amused, if Mken judged that clamping of mandibles right—but it was hard to tell when a Sangheili was amused.

"Lilumna," Mken said softly, "I flatter myself that I know a good deal about Janjur Qom—though I was never here before today. But I can recall no accounts of an *ilpdor* having been tamed."

"It is not exactly tamed; it is more like a partnership. Large fish have become scarce in the lake—the males from the capital city have dragged nets along it, numerous times, and reduced them. My sister, Burenn—she rides there in front—found this creature starving when it was but small. If it had been larger, it would have snapped her up and eaten her. But she fed it the meat and cheese of the *garfren* and somehow it bonded with her. Now it helps us catch what fish are left, driving them toward our nets. We feed it, and it keeps the worst of the depredations at bay. We have named it Erb. We can't keep it out of the water long, but—"

"Your Eminence!" called Trok softly. "We've come to the turning! The signal confirms it—the dropship is this way."

"Thank the Journeyers for the signal, then," muttered Mken. He glanced at the sky. The clouds had closed up again and there was little light. "I can't see where I am . . ."

In a few hours, perhaps much less, it would be dawn—and then there would be all too much light. They must get to the dropship quickly as possible before they were spotted.

They followed Trok off the beach, onto the trail threading through the undergrowth. The *ilpdor* grunted and whined, seeming reluctant to go so far from the lake. Burenn slapped Erb's neck and bent over to whisper to it, urging the great predator on.

It sniffed sadly but tagged along after the Prophet of Inner Conviction and his Sangheili guardians, on into the thick, restless brush.

As the odd procession wound its way up the trail, vines licked out and seemed to snuffle at them. Erb snapped at the probing vines, driving them back.

They were within a hundred paces of the dropship when the enemy found them.

It was hard to tell what they were at first. "Soldiers!" Burenn shouted. "They're coming on *folasteed*!"

But Mken, in his weariness, had forgotten to find out just what *folasteeds* might be. At first they were just the rough shape of a four-legged riding animal emerging from the brush—about ten of them. There was a zipping sound, and a peculiar reorientation of the undergrowth. He heard someone or something yowling—it sounded like a cry of agony.

Then the clouds parted and moonlight flooded the glen. Mken saw San'Shyuum in armor, carrying large, clumsy-looking projectile rifles, and riding on . . . what was that, exactly?

The *folasteeds* were made of the underbrush itself—it was as if the thick vines and plants, the smaller trees, the shrubs, all merged together beneath the riders. The riders were carried along on rough four-legged shapes, with heads and torsos, their general outline like steeds found, in variations, on many planets—but these were constantly taking form and falling back into the brush. The outline of the steed continued consistently under the riders— the riders passed along, the steeds formed from the brush they came to. It was as if the forest itself was constantly creating riding mounts *from itself* for the soldiers; as if the riders were sliding along on living plants rather than each riding a single steed.

"What are they?" Mken blurted.

"At a guess—gene-forging!" Vil 'Kthamee muttered, firing his weapon. "The plants have been redesigned to work for the Stoics!"

That made a sort of blurred sense to Mken—the Stoics had

drawn a line when it came to hardware technology. They were allowed so much, and no more. So their scientists had digressed into wild botanical genetic engineering experiments.

The *folasteeds* were almost upon them.

Drawing his sidearm, Mken shouted, "Lilumna! Get back, behind Erb! Keep all the females back!" He fired his plasma pistol toward the riders, not at all sure if he was hitting what he was aiming at. More illumination came in staccato strobing from the plasma rifles, which spat luminous bright energy at the onrushing patrol.

And that's when Mken saw Loquen—he was being carried along by vines himself, not by a *folasteed*, but by a plethora of vegetable cords that whipped from the grass to pass him along, one thicket to the next. He screamed as the vines tore off shreds of his hide, as two other vines probed into his eye sockets. Loquen was being displayed here, Mken realized, to frighten them—to make them lose heart.

"Let me *go!*" Loquen shrieked. "I showed you where they were to be! *Let me go now!*"

But the vines tore Loquen to pieces in seconds, flinging the steaming, spurting chunks at the Sangheili and the Prophet of Inner Conviction.

The riders circled the small party of outworlders now, the steeds tearing up roots when they needed to cross the path, reinforcing from more plant matter beyond it, bellowing.

Vil fired at the riders, his aim unerring. One of them went down, his eyes burned away. Another fell from his steed and rolled, clutching at a charred midsection.

Ziln 'Klel shouted defiance, putting aside his fears and rushing at the enemy, firing his weapon . . .

Mken staggered back from the onslaught as projectiles hissed past him. He fired his pistol till it burned his fingers overheating. One of the riders fell, roaring in pain.

A projectile struck Ziln 'Klel in the torso, making him cry out and stagger—another caught him in the head, blowing it apart. His body fell limply, like a thing of rags.

Trok fell then, grunting with pain as he was hit by a projectile—shot but not killed, not yet. His weapon was drained of power and, lying on his back, he drew his burnblade. Projectiles flashed past Mken and he knew his time was about to come. They could not miss forever.

Then there was a gurgling roar and the *ilpdor* was among the enemy, ridden now by Burenn alone. She shouted commands and clutched at its neck as it reared back on its hind four legs, slashing with its front talons, its huge jaw snapping. It tore into vines and soldiers, ripping them from their steeds, shaking them to break their necks, throwing them aside.

Vil was hurtling grenades—they exploded in enormous blossoms of blue-white incandescence, as if mocking the living plants around them, and two of the riders went down, their steeds blasted apart, armor ruptured . . .

Another rider—the last of them—leapt from his mount, firing his weapon over and over into the throat of the *ilpdor* as he came skidding off the *folasteed* along the trail.

The *ilpdor*, spurting green blood, thrust toward its tormenter and crunched his head in its jaws . . . and then Erb staggered and tipped to one side. Burenn jumped free at the last moment, just evading a crushed leg.

Erb shuddered, and gasped, and spat out an enemy's head . . . and then died.

Weeping, Burenn knelt by the hideous, reeking beast, hugging its bloody head to her chest.

"Come, Burenn," Mken said, dazedly helping Trok to his feet. The commander was shot through a thigh, but he would likely get back to High Charity alive, if any of them did. "We must go. The dropship is near. We must all hurry. Where are the other females?"

"We're here," said Lilumna, leading the other six female San'Shyuum from the shadows. "We must flee." She pulled her sister, Burenn, to her feet and hugged her. "The plants have no real mind—they are controlled by the riders. But they can feel threatened. They may attack us—and soon."

The San'Shyuum gunner Mleer came hobbling up then, looking around wide-eyed. "I saw the battle! Are there more of them?"

"And what if there were?" Trok growled at him. "What use were you?"

"I didn't know if I should leave the ship—my orders."

"He's right, Trok," Mken said, helping the warrior trudge toward the vessel. "Mleer, help Trok back to the dropship. I need to know the relics are safe. Let us leave Janjur Qom . . . as quickly as we can."

They would leave their true home for a mere substitute—for High Charity. But they had the females. And they had both the Purifying Vision and the rare Luminary. He would especially take that in triumph back to R'Noh, and somehow manage not to simply throw it in the Minister's face.

CHAPTER 12

'Crolon, 'Drem, Gmezza, and Scorinn had been summoned to Strategy Hall to face Ussa 'Xellus. Tersa, standing with Lnur off to the side, watched them closely. 'Crolon and 'Drem looked sullen, Gmezza and Scorinn frightened.

"We did not speak of sedition, Great Ussa," said Gmezza. He took a limping step closer to the podium where Ussa sat, half slumped in his chair, listening closely.

Ernicka the Scar-Maker, expression like a storm cloud, stepped between them.

"It is quite all right, Ernicka," Ussa said, glancing to all who stood before him, his eyes lingering a bit longer on Lnur. "He is not armed. Nor am I afraid of him."

"We simply requested more explanation," said Scorinn, her eyes cast down. "We wondered why . . . We heard rumors . . . We . . . I apologize, Kaidon, that we . . ."

"I do not tolerate sedition," Ussa said. "If I am leader here, then it is truly so. If I am not to be accepted, so be it. But those who wish me to be leader must accept my word. Nothing else is possible here. And that is the way of a clan and a kaidon. But . . . not every doubt can be considered treason. If it were, we would all have to be executed at some point." He looked at 'Crolon and 'Drem. "I have heard from Gmezza and Tersa that you two suggested that I was planning to destroy everyone . . . to annihilate the shield world. That I was planning to invite the San'Shyuum to be my allies."

"Oh, but we didn't say *that*," said 'Crolon smoothly. "We were misheard. The sound of the waterfall obscured us perhaps. We had heard Tersa there speaking of a method for dismantling the planet— this shield world—and we heard the machine called Enduring Bias discussing the San'Shyuum fondly. But we were actually concerned about Tersa, not about you, Great Ussa. In fact—"

"Did I hear someone use my informal designation?" called Enduring Bias, zipping into the room. The Flying Voice flew in over their heads and hovered over the dais, turning to look at the group gathered before Ussa. "Someone was inaccurately paraphrasing me, I suspect. And not the first time."

"You are familiar, now, with our customs, Enduring Bias," Ussa said, not looking at the device as he spoke. "You know what we regard as breaking our rules and those rules respecting sedition— treason, treachery, dangerous levels of disloyalty. There are some fine lines, in some cases—but perhaps you are aware of remarks by these two"—he nodded toward 'Crolon and 'Drem—"which might fit into the category of treason or treachery."

"If you will kindly allow me a moment or two, I will interface with the facility's observation cells . . ."

"Observation cells?" Ussa said. "What is that? I do not know the term."

"I have informed Sooln about them," said Enduring Bias. "The observation cells are organized by the communications center—the Chamber of Sensitive Geometries. The cells are implanted into the walls throughout the facility. It was one more special innovation for this facility—a marvel, really. As we've chatted, I've organized a short selection of interesting observations of the two Sangheili in question."

And then Enduring Bias projected holographic surveillance footage of 'Crolon and 'Drem speaking. It started with their conversation with Tersa in the Chamber of Sensitive Geometries, went to their discussion with him in the Hall of Feasts, including the suggestion that they would falsify testimony against him if necessary. It went to a private conversation they had in a corner of a dormitory, in which 'Drem remarked, "If we're to save us from the madness of Ussa—he must die!" and 'Crolon replied, "Keep your voice low, my friend. But I will just say—I do not disagree. We must organize people against him. And someone must be selected as the new kaidon. I was thinking I myself might be suitable . . ."

"I have heard enough," Ussa said firmly, glowering at 'Crolon.

"But there is much more!" Enduring Bias said.

"That will be sufficient."

"You believe this dark angel?" 'Drem demanded, looking around desperately. "That machine—over flesh-and-blood Sangheili? I knew it was something demonic about it. I could feel it!"

"Oh, 'Drem!" 'Crolon said soothingly. "Ussa would never be so foolish as to trust a machine over his brethren in flesh and blood! He will naturally suspect that the Flying Voice has fabricated this imagery, these apparent conversations—surely the device has the capability."

"I *do* have such a capability," said Enduring Bias. "However, it was not necessary, since these real conversations took place."

"That thing cannot be from the Forerunners!" 'Drem shouted,

pointing, backing toward the door. "It is from . . . the San'Shyuum! It is from our enemies!"

"Ernicka, take those two into custody," Ussa said, indicating 'Crolon and 'Drem. "Lock them in storage room seven. We will call a convocation for their execution shortly."

"No!" 'Drem turned to run, and Ernicka rushed after him, drawing his burnblade. He threw the weapon, and its shaft cut into 'Drem's spine. The Sangheili fell and thrashed in agony, wailing.

Tersa found 'Drem's writhing to be a distasteful sight. So did Ussa, apparently. Ussa said, "Ernicka—finish what you have started."

Ernicka walked over and pulled the searing blade from 'Drem—and then, in one smooth motion, severed the traitor's head from his neck.

'Crolon was staring at this in desperation. "Great Kaidon . . . I . . ."

"Take along a sentry, and escort the one who lives to the store-room, Ernicka," Ussa said.

Ernicka turned menacingly to 'Crolon. "You heard the kaidon." He brandished the burnblade. "Go. I follow."

'Crolon walked unsteadily from the room—stumbling as he went in the spreading pool of 'Drem's blood, so that he nearly fell into it face-first.

Ernicka grabbed 'Crolon's arm and, keeping a solid grip, escorted him from the hall.

"As for you four," Ussa said, turning to Tersa, Lnur, Gmezza, and Scorinn. "You should know that while there is a mechanism for disassembling this world, it does not relate to . . . destroying it." Ussa hesitated as if he were not sure himself that this was entirely true. Then he went on. "You must simply trust me."

"I always have, Great Ussa," said Tersa. "And today I've seen that my trust was well founded."

Ussa pointed at Gmezza. "And mind what you babble about with others . . . you and your mate!"

"Yes, Kaidon!"

"Now, go about your business! The four of you are wearying me. I wish to consult with Enduring Bias alone. New questions have arisen . . ."

Vengeful Vitality
In Orbit Around Janjur Qom
850 BCE
The Age of Reconciliation

"Commander . . . are we ready to leave orbit yet?" Mken asked nervously, watching the scan monitor. So far there were no signs of an attack from the surface. But the Stoics had enough technology to be dangerous—perhaps even to a ship such as the *Vengeful Vitality*, which was in the same orbit since it first arrived. Janjur Qom glowed magnificently in a viewport, but now Mken wanted very much to leave it behind.

Trok 'Tanghil shifted in the captain's seat to ease the pain of his wound. The projectile had been removed, and he'd been salved and bandaged, but Mken knew the old warrior was still in agony. Trok squinted at a readout and grunted to himself. "I did warn you that I had not the expertise Vervum had, Your Eminence. It appears he locked down the engines. I believe I can get under way shortly, but . . ."

"I know you are injured, Trok, but you are also the only one competent enough to do this."

"I was not complaining of my wound, Your Eminence," Trok muttered. "I am merely saying it will take a little longer."

"I know—never mind. Just do it as quickly as you can. I will check on the females."

They had lowered the ship's artificial gravity to match High Charity's, so Mken got out of his chair and made his way on foot back to the corvette's hold, retrofitted for the comfort of passengers.

He was visiting the females mostly to keep himself busy. His mind was tormented with questions about the Luminary. As he went along the corridor, his hand went to the projector base for the Purifying Vision in his robe pocket. He couldn't carry the Luminary about with him, not handily, but at least he could keep the Purifying Vision close. He was going to take it to an officer's cabin and peruse the hologram again.

It was unbelievably precious. He'd accessed the Luminary just long enough to know that it did indeed contain galactic coordinates for the Halos of legend, specifications for the devices and their manufacture, as well as where they had originated from and data on their ultimate purpose. He hadn't delved deeply into it—he needed the help of other Prophets with more expertise in sacred relic technology. But at some point, on the way back to High Charity, why not examine the Luminary again? It was still in the dropship, safely in *Vengeful Vitality*'s deployment hold. He could almost hear it calling to him.

Mken found the nine females strapped tensely in the cushioned seats, four on one side and five on the other, along the fuselage of the vessel. Lilumna was gazing in awe out a port at Janjur Qom.

Mken turned to Lilumna's sister, Burenn. "I wanted to say thank you. You saved our lives, bringing your . . . your *friend* Erb into the fight."

Burenn's voice trembled as she replied. "I had hoped my mother would care for Erb. And now . . ."

"I want you to know—if I were to have a daughter, I would want her to be like you. I thank you again—we all do." He turned to Lilumna, still gazing at Janjur Qom. "So, what do you think of it?" Mken asked.

"It is so vast, so shining . . ." Lilumna shook her head. "I knew—we have some basics about our world, and yet . . . I didn't know. Until you see it . . ."

"Yes. I do understand," said Mken.

"There's something else you may not understand," said Lilumna, looking at him. "When I gaze at it, I-I don't want to leave it. Suddenly I realize how large our homeworld is. There must be better San'Shyuum than those in Reskolah. There must be more males—better ones! They must be there on Janjur Qom somewhere! Burenn and I—we are not certain we want to go with you now!"

Mken made a hand gesture of sad commiseration. "I understand how you feel. But—we are committed. You must believe me when I tell you we cannot return to Janjur Qom. We are going to High Charity." He cleared his throat and tugged on a wattle, hesitating—but he decided he must say it. "Outside the door I just came through, there are two armed guards. They will not let you leave this hold until we are through slipspace—and well on our way."

"So . . . we *are* slaves after all!"

"No! Absolutely not. I assure you of this. But here, you must follow the rules of this ship. And I command this vessel, for now. I must insist you remain here. You will not be enslaved on High Charity—of that, I promise you."

Mken turned away from her and slipped through the door, closing it behind him. He looked at Vil 'Kthamee and Mleer, waiting outside, and wondered what would happen if they had to use their weapons to keep the females in check. Would Lilumna be shot down?

Would Vil be forced to actually kill her?

His gut clenching at the thought, Mken turned away, heading for the bridge.

"Your Eminence," came Trok's voice on the communicator in his collar. "I have the ship ready to depart."

"Then go! Take us out of orbit!"

Mken had just reached the bridge when he heard the screech of warning from the scanners and looked at the monitor to see the large projectile coming at the *Vengeful Vitality*.

The corvette had only begun to move from Janjur Qom's orbit when the missile struck.

The deck rocked, the ship shuddered, a roar reverberated along its hallways, a shock wave reaching the bridge—and Mken, flailing, fell heavily onto his side.

"We're hit!" Trok shouted, trying to regain control of the vessel. "An indirect hit! Straight from Janjur Qom! If we hadn't already started on our way, we'd be done for . . ."

"How much damage?" Mken asked, trying to stand.

"Some—in hold twelve!"

The realization struck Mken like another projectile. *They'd been hit close to hold eleven—close to the deployment hold where the dropship was stored.*

And the sacred Luminary was in the dropship.

Mken managed to stand, grimacing with pain, and staggered back into the corridor. "Get us out of here!" he shouted, as he stumbled his way toward the rear of the *Vengeful Vitality*. The corvette was still shaking—some part of it was depressurizing, its artificial atmosphere sucking into space. Mken knew that section would be automatically closed off by the ship's life-support response mechanism—but the precious air jetting from the breach destabilized the ship. It fishtailed in space, twisting this way and that, its artificial gravity rippling with inertia, so Mken was sent bouncing and bruising from one bulkhead to another as he worked his way to the aft.

Somewhere, an alarm went off, an automatic announcement made in a carefree tone, *"Holds ten and eleven are experiencing rapid decompression. Evacuate to pressure-sealed areas. A danger of sudden death due to an absence of atmospheric pressure applies to personnel who fail to evacuate holds ten and eleven. Holds ten and eleven are experiencing rapid decompression. Evacuate to . . ."*

"Your Eminence!" Vil 'Kthamee cried as Mken came through the hatchway. "Are you all right?"

Mleer was gaping at him; Mken realized he was bleeding. "Never mind! The females! Get them out—crowd them up into the crew's quarters!"

"Yes, Your Eminence!" Mleer said.

Vil 'Kthamee opened the metal door and they stepped through to find the females up and clutching at the straps that held them in place, several of them cursing Lilumna and Burenn for talking them into making this hellish journey.

The corvette lurched again, metal squealing. Vil and Mleer unhooked the females, and sent them toward the front of the ship, one by one.

"What happened?" Lilumna demanded as Mken pushed past. Her voice was barely audible over the alarm and announcement. *"Holds ten and eleven are experiencing rapid decompression . . ."*

"A missile, from the surface!" Mken shouted as he got his footing and hurried toward the hatch to the deployment hold.

She looked around wildly, calling after him, "Is this only the beginning?"

"I think we're out of range now . . ." That of course was just a guess. They knew so little about the Stoics' military capability. "Follow Vil 'Kthamee!"

Burenn was at the back of this compartment, where Mleer was just helping her stand, when Mken reached the door to the deployment hold. She'd struck her head when the ship was shaken about, and blood streamed into her eyes.

But at least the vessel was pitching less. It was easier for Mken to move. He was only badly bruised from the initial impact—and he was charged with purpose, able to ignore the pain.

"This way!" Mleer shouted at the females, hurriedly leading the way toward the ship's bridge.

Mken checked the pressure indicator on the door to hold eleven and found the pressure normal. But beyond that . . .

His pulse raced madly as he thought about the implications of the Luminary, the sacred artifact that held the Covenant's key to the Great Journey, now threatened by the void of space.

Mken palmed the door open. It slid aside and he went through. He sealed it behind him, then turned to the racks and lockers along the walls; they contained everything he needed: pressure suits, atmospheric chargers, tools.

"Holds ten and eleven are experiencing rapid decompression. Evacuate to pressure-sealed areas. A danger of sudden death—"

"Trok!" Mken shouted, hurrying to the lockers. "Are you hearing me?"

"Yes, Your Eminence!" came the voice from Mken's collar communicator.

"Then find a way to shut off those alarms and that cursed announcement! I have to concentrate!"

"Immediately, Your Eminence!"

It wasn't quite immediately, but when Mken had the boots off, the clangor and looping announcement fell silent. He could hear thumping, creaking from the deployment hold.

Hurry!

Hands shaking, Mken dragged on the pressure suit—it was designed to be donned quickly, edging itself onto his limbs and torso with self-guiding intelligent materials sensors. As he dressed, he called Trok on the communicator. "Trok! What's the ship's status?"

"Engines are online, but working at one-quarter power. *Vitality* is preparing to form a slipspace aperture, but it's taking time. There have been no follow-up attacks from the surface of the planet."

"They must have seen us when we took off at dawn—enough sunlight can compromise the stealth field. We're fortunate to have gotten away at all."

"The Huragok is working to repair the power lines. We hope to be at full power shortly, Your Eminence."

"What's the status of the deployment hold?"

"Stand by, please, while I check the . . ." He sputtered something unintelligible in some dialect of Sangheili. A curse of some sort. And then: "We had a temporary seal on the breach . . . but the seal has just broken down! The hold is once more decompressing!"

Mken heard a high-pitched grating sound from the deployment hold and his mouth went bone dry. Holding the helmet in his hands, he rushed to the door and into the next chamber, and looked through the window. To his right, he could see the gash the missile had made in the metal skin of the ship, sharp curled pieces of hull bent inward. He glimpsed stars flashing beyond the rent in the bulkhead; within the hold—which was actually a small hangar for the dropship—unidentifiable debris, scraps of metal and detritus, had once more begun whirling toward the breach in the hull. The last of it was drawing the overturned dropship with it, making it move gratingly, a little at a time, toward the gash in the bulkhead. The dropship was breaking up as he watched—pieces of it were tearing off, flying out into the ravenous void of space.

He put the helmet on, then turned at the chime from the door behind him. Hadn't he sealed that door?

It was opening, and Burenn was stepping through, the San'Shyuum female dazedly looking around. "Mken . . . if you please . . . I am . . ."

"Get out of here! I'm about to decompress this room! Get out!"

"I can't!" She blinked, seeming about to keel over, and leaned against the doorframe. "Mleer left me . . . the door sealed—it's locked! I can't get out!"

"Then wait for me there! Get back in that room and close that door!"

"I didn't open it."

"What?"

"It opened and I came through . . ."

"Trok!" Mken shouted, turning to look through the small window in the hatchway door again. In the hangar, the dropship was now banging against the breach in the hull—which looked as if it was about to deliver it into space, like a female delivering an offspring from her womb.

"Yes, Your Eminence?" came Trok's voice.

"Why are there doors unsealing on their own down here?"

"It's the life-support system—the damage to the ship has caused a power pulse that has reset it. Some of the doors are not sealing, and are opening of their own accord—the ship's computer seems to be prioritizing to close those doors necessary to save the rest of the vessel! The Huragok is trying to control it but . . ."

"Please . . ." Burenn sobbed. Mken turned and saw her collapsing limply to the floor. And she was blocking the opposite door. It wouldn't close with her there. If she was left lying in that spot when he opened the door to the deployment hold, she would be taken violently along with the decompressing air into the vacuum. And there was no time to get her into a life-support suit.

Mken turned to the window in the door to the deployment hold—and saw the dropship, now in pieces, blocking the gash . . . but he could see the hull buckling. And something else. Half seen in the partly shattered dropship was the glimmering blue of the sacred Luminary. It was in danger of being lost forever.

If he didn't get Burenn into the other room when he opened this door, she would die. If he did take time to help her, he would very likely lose the Luminary.

The Luminary was more important. But . . . Burenn had saved his life back on Janjur Qom. Had saved the entire expedition. And was the biological artifact of her healthy genetic material less important than the Luminary?

Yes. Leave her! Get to the Luminary.

But . . .

Inwardly calling on the spirits of the Forerunners for help, Mken turned furiously to Burenn, went to her as quickly as he could in the lumbering pressure suit. He could see that she was breathing—she was still alive. He dragged her through the door, away from the aft of the ship and into the room where the other females had been seated. The San'Shyuum females had all gone to safer berths forward, and so had that panicky oaf Mleer.

"Trok! Can the door to twelve be resealed?"

"The Huragok is working on it, Your Eminence!"

Mken wanted to scream with frustration. "Get it done quickly! We are about to lose the Luminary!" He put on his pressure suit's helmet and returned to the next room and the door to the deployment hold.

He got there just in time to see the breached hull explode outward, the pieces of the dropship flying out into space. It was unable to resist the powerful suction, and was drawn inexorably out into the vacuum.

"Trok! The Luminary! Can you track it? The pieces of the dropship, the Luminary, they should be in the same gravity well! Can we . . . can we go back? Can we . . ."

There was a long crackling pause. Finally, Trok reported, "I'm sorry, Your Eminence. Our instruments are following everything that was expelled from the hold. It's falling back toward Janjur Qom. The Luminary with it—its energy field is quite distinctive. It is plunging into the atmosphere of the planet . . . we have lost it."

"No, Trok. No. I cannot bear that. Look again. Please."

"I'm sorry, Your Eminence. It is too late."

CHAPTER 13

Ussa 'Xellus was just waking up, his first thought that today he must contend with the execution of the traitor 'Crolon . . . and then attempt to ease any fears among his people, who had come to call themselves "Ussans." He needed to make sure they remained unified.

Sooln came into the sleeping chamber, her eyes glinting with alarm.

"Ussa, 'Crolon is gone!"

"What?"

"He's gotten away!"

"When? How did this happen?"

"We are not sure—at some point as most of us slept. I don't know how he did it."

"Summon Enduring Bias."

Minutes later, Ussa and Sooln were hurrying up to the storeroom they'd used as a jail cell. Enduring Bias was already hovering by the open door. "This is all quite interesting. But I should inform you . . ."

Ussa was staring at a small puddle of blood on the metal deck in the otherwise empty storeroom. "We had the door locked—a guard was stationed outside."

"I merely wanted to say—" Enduring Bias began again.

Sooln turned to the Flying Voice, interrupting. "Can you show us what happened?"

"Yes. I have only just now retrieved the relevant data. This was recorded earlier." The Flying Voice angled itself so its lens was focused downward and it projected a holographic image showing the exterior of the cell seen from near the ceiling. There was a sentry, a Sangheili Ussa knew as 'Kwari, leaning on the cell door, half-asleep. When the storage room was selected for a jail, small holes had been drilled in the door to allow sufficient air for prisoners. 'Kwari had removed his armored helmet and placed it on the floor.

Suddenly a thin metal blade, slimmer than a childling's clawnail, thrust through one of the holes and into 'Kwari's hearing membrane. 'Kwari shrieked in pain and fury and they heard 'Crolon jeering, clacking his mandibles mockingly.

"*Coward!*" shouted 'Crolon, withdrawing the blade. "*That is what happens to the dishonorable!*"

Furious, 'Kwari did just what 'Crolon must have hoped he'd do—he turned and unlocked the door, then started in, drawing his burnblade. "I'll punish you for that! They'll find just enough alive to execute!"

And then 'Kwari screamed in agony, staggering backward. The slim blade had been driven into 'Kwari's right eye, all the way to the hilt.

'Crolon wrested the sword from the dying sentry, severed his head, and sprinted away.

"That fool . . ." Ussa muttered.

"Where has he gone?" Sooln asked, turning to Enduring Bias.

"That is what I have been trying to tell you, Ussa 'Xellus—he has gone to craft launching. He was there for some minutes before I detected it. I cannot watch everything at once, you know. I must access specific visual data before I can—"

"Craft launching!" Ussa burst out. Unconsciously, he drew his burnblade. " 'Crolon is an engineer . . . he could fly one of the smaller vessels! If he chooses the right one, it will almost fly itself."

Something floated into the corridor near Ussa then, and slowed down. It was one of the flying freight movers, really just a shallow open box large enough for a moderate load of material. "Enter the mover," Enduring Bias chirped, "and I will transport you there."

"Should we not get some aid from the others?" Sooln asked.

"There is no time for that," Ussa said, striding to the mover.

"Then—simply shut down the hangar door for craft launching!" Sooln told the AI as she and Ussa climbed into the freight mover.

"I regret to report that he has sabotaged the hangar controls," Enduring Bias said as they flew along the hall toward the elevator shaft that would take them up to craft launching. The Flying Voice soared along right above them.

"That means 'Crolon is trapped there himself!" Ussa pointed out.

"Perhaps not. Though I do not seem to have control over it, he has been able to enable an emergency escape fail-safe, so the door is controlled only by remote signal from within the vessel."

They were ascending the shaft now, with dizzying speed. The mover wobbled with air pressure and Ussa held on to Sooln with one hand, the other gripping the rail of the freight mover.

Then they slowed, and switched to horizontal movement, along a gray metal corridor. The freight mover and Enduring Bias passed through an open door and into a control center that over-looked the hangar. The mover slowed and Ussa vaulted out, run-ning to the window.

Below he could see three vessels, one of them the small inter-stellar craft the *Clan's Blade*. And it was the *Blade* that was glow-ing at the control area—as the wall melted away, on a signal from the ship.

"He's on the *Clan's Blade*!" Ussa shouted.

"Yes, and I am afraid the hangar is responding to his plasma en-gine activation. It knows he wishes to leave—and it arranges his exit."

"There has to be a way to stop it!" Ussa said, looking around the control room. But none of the equipment here was known to him. There were arcanely glowing three-dimensional sym-bols slowly revolving over panels of some unknown material. He wouldn't know how to operate the controls here, either way. And one of the panels had been smashed—pried open by a burnblade, by the look of it.

"Can either of you get this working again?" Ussa asked.

"No, not without much study," Sooln said. "He was probably just guessing what to sabotage."

"I could do it," said Enduring Bias. "If I had a Huragok here. Can we import one? That would be splendid. We could use the Engineer for a good many critical repairs."

"Look, 'Crolon is already gone," Sooln said, gazing through the window.

Ussa followed her gaze and saw that the *Clan's Blade* had glided through the opening and was ascending a ramp, to the outer shell.

"Maybe we can get up there and bring him down . . ."

"I do have a short-range energy focuser that can be used for destructive purposes," the Flying Voice replied. "But it will not reach the vessel . . . which is already ascending to orbit."

"If he's gone, he's gone," Sooln muttered, turning away. "But . . . what will he do, Ussa? Will he return to the Covenant?"

"It is not likely, in my opinion," Ussa said. "'Crolon is very much oriented to his own survival. The Covenant might execute him simply for allying with us to begin with. He will search for some safe place to hide himself."

But Ussa wasn't certain of this. 'Crolon could get the coordinates of the shield world from the *Clan's Blade* itself. Suppose he tried to barter those coordinates to the Covenant in exchange for his life? What then?

"Perhaps we should attempt to find some other place to take our people to," Sooln suggested, her voice heavy with reluctance.

"We might choose to do that," Ussa said, turning away from the window. "I will give it thought. However, there is an alternative— even if the Covenant finds us here . . . and perhaps in the long run, it might be for the best."

The Dreadnought, High Charity
850 BCE
The Age of Reconciliation

"Why should we believe a Sangheili, O Prophet of Inner Conviction?" Excellent Redolence sounded urbanely bored as he asked the question.

Mken sensed the Sangheili beside him tensing at this sneering rhetoric. "I don't understand the question, Excellent Redolence," Mken said, though he in fact understood all too well.

Excellent's large, hooded eyes rolled to take in the Sangheili,

Vil 'Kthamee and Trok 'Tanghil, who stood to Mken's right, the three of them appearing in the High Council Chamber.

The High Council was intended to include a select number of San'Shyuum and Sangheili, government delegates ordained as part of the Writ of Union, but for now the only authorities on the glassy, translucent platform were merely the triumvirate of the Hierarchs. There were the three of them in their hovering gravity thrones—great cups of circular metal that comfortably gripped the lower half of each San'Shyuum Hierarch, and that also discreetly included, Mken knew, gravity cannons that could annihilate him in an instant, if the Hierarch chose.

The Hierarchs were lined up along the platform in their nearly weightless chairs. Behind the triumvirate was a decorative backdrop of glowing violet and blue panels. Each Hierarch wore a loose-sleeved robe with similar colors to the panels; their hands, three fingers and thumb, were poised near the controls of the thrones. On their heads were golden helmets, each headdress closely following the shape of the forehead and displaying a glowing blue hologram in the shape of a halo. From the throne's backing behind the Hierarchs' collars rose great forking figures of gold that overtopped their heads.

On Mken's far left was the Prophet of the Glorious Journey, who was rather slender, with his back hunched, his eyes set widely apart in an almost triangular face. Then came the Prophet of Unity, middle-aged and sitting up straight in his throne, eyes glittering with intelligence. And in the third gravity throne sat Excellent Redolence. Standing, arms crossed beside the dais, facing Mken, was the Minister of Anticipatory Security, R'Noh Custo. R'Noh looked pensive, shifting nervously from foot to foot. His expression was angry, defiant—but his bearing was fearful.

The testimony from Vil 'Kthamee and Mken had been damning. Trok hadn't been there, in the grotto, when R'Noh's agent, Vervum, had tried to assassinate Mken—but he had seen Vervum tamper with the weaponry on Mken's antigrav chair. He had supposed Vervum was merely adjusting it. But given the testimony, it did sound as if Vervum had disabled the chair's armaments.

"You do not understand my question!" Excellent Redolence said in mock astonishment. "Really!"

Mken glanced at the Sangheili. "Excellent Redolence, with all due respect." He made the hand gesture of respect, as well, to re-emphasize he didn't want to offend the Hierarchs. It wouldn't help Cresanda to have her husband disintegrated with a gravity cannon. "The Sangheili are our allies in the Covenant. We must trust them and they in turn must trust us. Trok 'Tanghil here is a well-respected commander. Ranger 'Kthamee earned my respect. He saved my life."

"You are at least partly right," said the Prophet of Unity. "The Covenant must be based on mutual respect. I'm sure that Excellent Redolence did not intend it quite the way it sounded. The Sangheili are indeed our allies. But let us look at the situation. You were asked by a Hierarch to bring back a group of female San'Shyuum; this you accomplished. You were asked to bring back the legendary Purifying Vision—and its accompanying Luminary. You claim you had the Luminary, and yet it is lost. How you could lose anything so unspeakably precious passes understanding. Is it any wonder that we ask ourselves if you have muddied the story to avoid blame?"

"I accept all responsibility," said Mken. "I was in charge of the expedition. But you have heard Trok 'Tanghil say that the word of this young Ranger can be trusted. And he testified as to what happened. The Huragok can also be consulted."

"The Huragok!" Excellent Redolence jeered. "Now we're consulting artificial organisms created to fix machines!"

"It is true that we cannot admit a Huragok as a witness," said the Prophet of the Glorious Journey blandly, waving a dismissive hand at the notion. "They are almost without volition—too easily influenced. And difficult to communicate with."

Vil 'Kthamee stirred and opened his mouth to speak, and Mken thought he was going to argue about the possibility of communicating with Floats Near Ceiling, so he reached over and squeezed the Sangheili's shoulder in warning. Vil clamped his mandibles and merely growled softly to himself.

The Prophet of Unity, thoughtfully tugging a wattle, said, "Huragoks aside, we cannot ignore the . . . the *probability* that Vervum, an agent of the Ministry of Anticipatory Security, attempted to assassinate the Prophet of Inner Conviction."

"And it was that attempt, and its aftermath, that delayed us, O High Prophet," said Mken, ceremoniously gesturing to show respect and agreement. "Had we not been delayed, I believe we could have safely eluded the Stoics. And had we left without having a battle with the Stoic *folasteed* patrol, we likely would have left Janjur Qom in time to avoid the missile attack, which cost us the Luminary."

"If you had properly stored the Luminary in another part of the vessel," said Excellent Redolence, "you would have it here now. That is—if you ever had it at all."

Mken clenched his fists. He wanted badly to use his own chair's weaponry on Redolence. Instead he gestured, *So you say.*

"You have all seen the damage to the ship," said someone behind Mken. He turned to see old Qurlom floating into the room on his gravity chair. "The *Vengeful Vitality*'s systems recorded the presence of the Luminary."

"Qurlom," Excellent Redolence snarled, "you are no longer a Hierarch, and you have no right to—"

"Oh, but I do have the right!" Qurlom said. "Look at the Book of Hierarchs. Review the rules! I am not active—I am retired. But I am still allowed to voice an opinion here when I choose. And my opinion is, this is all a waste of time. Mken has done nothing wrong. He acted heroically! The Great Journey has blessed him . . . and the gods of the Journey have decreed, quite evidently, that we have not yet earned a Luminary that will show us the whereabouts of the Halos. But I have just come from viewing the Purifying Vision. Have you all seen it? That is—the exhibition of images within the device?"

"We have," said the Prophet of Unity.

"Then you would have to be blind not to know what it is telling us!" Qurlom said. "The loss of the Luminary is a judgment upon us from on high! We are not yet worthy! But the Purifying Vision informs us that we are on the Path—and it gives us clues . . . which one day may lead us to Halo!"

"I respect Qurlom's theological acumen," said Great Journey. "It is long tested and always righteous. Thus I vote that we rule that the Prophet of Inner Conviction is found blameless for the loss of the Luminary."

"And what of the attempted assassination?" Qurlom demanded. "I know the story from Inner Conviction's own lips. And who is to blame? The Ministry of Anticipatory Security—surely a dangerous concept in itself—and that fool, R'Noh!" Qurlom pointed a long, arthritically warped finger at R'Noh. "Let this absurd new Ministry be eliminated—and its Minister demoted to a third administrative assistant in Sewage Treatment! If we cannot prove that he was behind the assassination attempt, we may yet infer it! Let him be sent to the hinterlands of the galaxy, to oversee a mine! And then we may have a modicum of justice!"

"I . . . no!" R'Noh said. "I . . . it wasn't . . ."

"Silence!" Excellent Redolence had turned in his throne and was bellowing at R'Noh. "One word more and I will push for your execution! Clearly you have let your personal dislike for Inner Conviction blur your ministerial agenda! Go! And say no more!"

Mken grunted to himself, hearing Excellent's emphatic command to R'Noh to *say no more*. Clearly the Hierarch was trying to quiet R'Noh before the former Minister blurted something that implicated his true master.

Shaking, R'Noh gawped up at Excellent, who glared back darkly, his body language silently radiating warning even as his fingers slid toward the controls of his throne's cannon.

R'Noh noticed the motion and turned away. He strode out of the Hall, muttering inaudibly.

"Perhaps," said Unity, "we should all view the Purifying Vision again."

"We should, High Prophet of Unity," said Qurlom. "But something else has come up—we may have an indication where Ussa 'Xellus might be. I have received intelligence that the traitor could well be on an uncharted world, and not just that: one of those formerly inhabited by the Forerunners."

"Intriguing—and dismaying!" cried Excellent Redolence. "Heresy! This despicable creature dares to defile the creation of the Forerunners!" He turned and gave Mken a look that was superficially sympathetic—but that look had levels, deep dark levels, within it. "We shall have to take it back. And I think I know just the San'Shyuum to restore order to the Covenant. My apologies that you will have to leave High Charity so soon after returning to it . . ."

"Cresanda," Mken said in relief as she came into the front room of their living quarters. She wore a blossom-filigreed antigrav belt over her robe; she rarely used a chair. Mken was standing by his own antigrav chair, one hand on it, breathing hard. He'd been doing knee bends, holding on to the chair—he was still thinking about how weak he'd felt, physically, in the gravitational field of the San'Shyuum homeworld.

Cresanda looked at him wryly. "You have been exercising again." She took off her wrap and hung it on a peg. She had worn her maternal wrap, not because she was pregnant—there was a special shawl for that—but because as a wedded San'Shyuum female guiding young unmarried females, she had a proper appearance to keep up. She'd been assigned to help the young, would-be brides from Janjur Qom in adjusting to their new life on High Charity.

Mken slipped into his chair and puffed out his cheeks. "Enough for today. How are the new females, Lilumna and the others?"

"They've resigned themselves to staying—and marrying here."

" 'Resigned themselves' sounds less than enthusiastic."

"There is a certain homesickness. But they're also excited, and quite bedazzled by this place."

"Have they met anyone?"

"They've only been here a handful of days, my darling." She came to stand near him, putting her arm around his neck. "Of course, they have possible suitors—but have only seen them on the promenade. That kind of thing. They were a bit appalled by the physical aspect of some of our males. I take it the Janjur Qom males are rather burlier and straighter in posture. But they enjoy the courtesy, the gentleness of the males they've met. I think it will be all right."

"Hmm. If Excellent has his way, some laboratory form of procreation might be considered."

"His ideas are always in repugnantly bad taste."

"Yes. I find his latest one regarding *me* to be especially in bad taste."

"Are they really going to make you lead that expedition? You've only been back so short a time—you nearly got killed twice on the last one. And that was the homeworld!"

"Oddly enough, the homeworld is one of the most dangerous places I've ever visited. But yes—it has just been confirmed. Excellent has convinced the other Hierarchs I am to be the Prophet in charge of the expedition because, as he says, I 'allowed Ussa 'Xellus to get away' long ago and now I must atone. He is hoping I'll get killed out there. He knows I suspect he was behind Vervum's attempt to assassinate me. That is—he was behind R'Noh's little plot. One puppeteer puppeteering another. Yes, Cresanda." He sighed. "You see, a certain Sangheili, one Salus 'Crolon, has been captured in a vessel associated with Ussa 'Xellus. He has gallantly offered to show us where this mysterious Forerunner world lies—not that we need his help. The information is in that vessel's records. But 'Crolon may be useful yet . . ."

"You are going to this place?"

"I am—when we assemble the fleet. Very soon, with a sizable force. And I am going to have to confront Ussa 'Xellus once more . . ."

CHAPTER 14

The Refuge: An Uncharted Shield World
Strategy Hall
850 BCE
The Age of Reconciliation

Ussa 'Xellus found his mate, Sooln, with Enduring Bias on the eco level. The Flying Voice was floating just above Sooln, listening to her as she pointed at the stream. He didn't ask what they were doing there, or what they were talking about. It didn't matter anymore.

"Ussa!" she said, as she jumped over the stream to join them. She looked closely at him as he walked up. "Is something wrong?"

"I am very much afraid, Sooln, that the choice has been taken from us. It is too late to leave the Refuge. It seems that Salus 'Crolon has indeed approached the Covenant—or was caught by them. The Covenant fleet is here. It is in orbit around this very planetoid."

"That is grave news," Enduring Bias allowed. "But then again, it presents some interesting possibilities."

"I am afraid the possibilities might be altogether too interesting," Ussa said, looking at the curved metal-colored sky, at the jutting structures like stylized stalactites that seemed to emanate a barely visible inner light.

"How curious to have gotten used to this strange place," Sooln remarked. "But I have missed Sanghelios. Perhaps this is our chance to go back there."

Sooln looked at him. He didn't have to see it—he could feel her looking at him. He said, "Sooln—we'll never live long enough to go back to Sanghelios."

She came and took his hands in hers. "You mean—we will die here today? Or . . . tomorrow? The Covenant will—"

"I don't know if we'll die today, or tomorrow—or after many cycles. I just don't think we'll ever be able to go back to Sanghelios. My hope is . . . that the grandchildren or great-grandchildren of our people, here in the Refuge, will someday be able to go back there."

"So—you're going to activate the Disassembler? We're not sure of the effects. Enduring Bias tells me that it hasn't been tested . . ."

"That is correct!" chimed in Enduring Bias. "Which is why I advocate the experiment. Existence can be burdensome. Why not take a grand risk to see a world unfold?"

Ussa glanced up at the Flying Voice, thinking, *What an odd, anomalous remark for the machine to make. Is it breaking down?*

But aloud he said, "Let us speak to the Covenant fleet first, before we take an irreversible step, Sooln. Who knows? They may want to negotiate. Strange things happen sometimes . . ."

Covenant Carrier *Pledge of Holiness*
In Orbit Around the Refuge, a Formerly Uncharted Shield World
850 BCE
The Age of Reconciliation

Many day cycles later, the Prophet of Inner Conviction sat in the bridge of the *Pledge of Holiness*, gazing through the viewport. He was hunched in his antigrav chair, gazing out at the gray metal curve of the shield world, as described by Salus 'Crolon during his intital interrogations; a thin film of trace atmosphere clinging to the planetoid gave off a sheen of reflected sunlight. "What else is of interest in this system?" he asked.

"Gas giants, sir, none so far exploited," said Trok 'Tanghil, acting captain of the vessel, as Mken didn't trust anyone else at the moment. "Little of interest. There's an extensive asteroid belt that might be mineable. It is so dense in places I chose to enter the system not in accordance with the usual trajectory, when we exited slipspace."

"Vil 'Kthamee," Mken said, "you can research what else, if anything, is known about this star system. There will be time."

"Yes, Your Eminence." Vil, standing behind Mken, was now the Prophet of Inner Conviction's personal bodyguard, his assistant, and his official translator for all interaction with Huragok. Such a rapid ascent through the ranks was not unheard of, but in this case, Mken had simply insisted on it.

Glancing at the holodisplay, Mken spotted the luminous ovals that indicated other ships in the Covenant fleet taking their places; in the holo, they looked like some of the minuscule insectoid creatures he'd seen on Janjur Qom. How odd.

He felt a stab of anguish when he thought of his homeworld, so full of treasures, and so lost to him. The Luminary—gone. Perhaps it was, after all, as Qurlom had suggested. They were not yet ready for the Luminary that showed the whereabouts of the Sacred Rings, and so it had been taken from them.

Leaning forward, Mken looked through the bridge's viewport, and saw well to their right two of the Covenant's fleet, looking more formidable in reality than flying insects. They were powerful, recently built warships. He sometimes thought it a pity that negotiations with the Sangheili had required the decommissioning of the Dreadnought as a vessel of war. Were these earlier times, Mken might have utilized the Dreadnought's array of Sentinels, but nearly all of those had been destroyed during the war with the Sangheili. In fact, only a handful remained on High Charity, now more relics for a museum than weapons. But then again, their original function was what the Sangheili were for now anyway.

Mleer, walking with an antigrav belt, escorted a Sangheili in, keeping a plasma pistol trained on the fellow. Looking ragged, the Sangheili had his hands clasped into restraints in front of him. To Mken he appeared shifty, worried, and calculating.

"Is this the one called Salus 'Crolon?" Mken asked.

"Yes, it is he, Your Eminence," said Mleer.

Salus 'Crolon cringed in front of Mken, bowing again and again. "I am relieved at having been rescued by the Covenant from Ussa 'Xellus, Your Eminence! I am honored, nay, *blessed* to be in your presence!"

"Enough of that rubbish," Mken said. "I am wondering if we should use you to negotiate with Ussa 'Xellus, since you know him so well. He is, I believe, the leader of these rebels?"

"He is, Your Eminence, their leader—their dictator, in fact. He has absolute power over them. I am afraid that it might be . . . counterproductive for me to act as negotiator. He already knows that I was a great supporter of the holy and sacred Covenant, that I believed with all my being in the Great Journey. That I fled his new world in the hopes of rejoining with the Covenant. So I do not believe he is likely to negotiate through me. I can demand his surrender for you, if you like—I would rather enjoy that, but—"

"Yes, yes, I understand. Perhaps you can tell me what use you are to me, then? During our interrogations, you referred to numerous Forerunner artifacts down below . . . relics of all kinds. Indeed it looks as if the entire world before us is a relic."

"It very nearly is, Your Eminence," 'Crolon said, looking out the viewport. "Ussa 'Xellus and his mate, Sooln, kept their intimate knowledge of the workings of the Refuge's mechanisms to themselves—or rather between themselves and that diabolic intelligence they have made a deal with who—"

'Crolon broke off then. Perhaps it had occurred to him that what he was referring to was in fact a sacred relic itself.

"What diabolic intelligence is that?" Mken asked.

"I . . . the thing is not innately diabolic. But . . . under the influence of Sooln and Ussa, it has become, I suspect, blighted, desecrated, misdirected. It is known as Enduring Bias. It is a construct that watches everyone, is forever watching . . . and never ceases." His mandibles gnashed bitterly.

Mken snorted. "If you are such a great supporter of the Covenant, how did you end up with Ussa 'Xellus in the first place?"

"I was attempting to act as an agent for the Covenant, Your Eminence!"

"Yes, I am aware you made that claim. But Qurlom and the others examined our records. None of the Covenant on Sanghelios was able to confirm you were an agent. Indeed, our only agent appears to have met an unfortunate end."

"Records are sloppily kept on Sanghelios," 'Crolon said. "I am faithful to the Covenant."

Mken turned to Vil 'Kthamee. "You're a Sangheili, and I daresay a good judge of character. What do you think?"

"I think he is a liar, Your Eminence."

Mken looked inquiringly at Trok 'Tanghil.

"I agree with Vil 'Kthamee," Trok said simply. "This traitor speaks so much only because he hopes to dazzle with words."

"I, however, am less than dazzled," Mken said. "Mleer, keep this Sangheili under lock and key, in the corridor. You need not watch him yourself; get some underguards to do it. Report what you've heard here to sentry overwatch and let them keep an eye on him."

This was an exquisitely difficult situation. If he destroyed the shield world, he was eradicating a sacred relic—and all other possible relics it might contain. But if he invaded instead, they could be here for a good long time, fighting their way through a strange environment, confronted by an enemy that knew this place now very well.

Perhaps they could be persuaded to surrender.

But from what he knew firsthand of Ussa 'Xellus, Mken strongly doubted it.

Ussa 'Xellus was in the designated Strategy Hall, standing beside his kaidon's chair and, in fact, quite aptly talking with Ernicka the Scar-Maker about strategy—when Enduring Bias flew rapidly into the room. The living device zipped into the capacious hall so quickly Ussa thought it might crash into the back wall.

But the Flying Voice came to a neat stop in midair and reported, "Ussa 'Xellus—I am receiving a transmission for you. It is from the fleet in orbit around the world you now call the Refuge."

"What kind of transmission?"

"It is an instantaneous holographic image with sound; if you respond, the sender will see and hear you."

Ernicka growled at this. "You are about to transmit images from within this facility to the enemy?" He drew his sidearm, as if considering firing on the Flying Voice. "Can those fools 'Drem and 'Crolon have been right about this construct, Ussa?"

"Oh?" Enduring Bias sounded puzzled. "I assure you that I have not revealed any information that would put you at a tactical disadvantage or threaten this installation."

Sooln was striding in. "Enduring Bias is telling the truth. He will not betray us."

"I am glad you are so very confident of that," said Ussa dryly. "But I do believe we are forced to accept its word . . . for all the good the word of a machine may be."

"Is my word not shown to be better than that of some Sangheili you know?" asked Enduring Bias.

"You make a good point," said Ussa. He was tired, and fear for his clans squirmed painfully deep in his belly. But he did what he had to. He remained objective, and tried to see the next step before he had to take it.

"Enduring Bias has so much information about this world," Sooln said, turning to Ernicka, "that he could have uploaded the entire schematic of the Refuge to the enemy already if he had wanted to."

Ernicka grunted. "He . . . *it* . . . whatever the thing may be . . . I suppose we must continue to trust it."

"Enduring Bias," said Ussa, settling into his chair. "Enable the transmission. Theirs to me, mine to them. Show them only me, and nothing more."

"What if they trace the signal?" Ernicka said. "They could fire directly upon you!"

"We are too deep underground for any efficient attack from orbit on one spot," said Sooln. "If they want to attack us, they'll have to either obliterate the entire planetoid—or invade it."

"I will see to it that the transmission is sent from many places at once," said Enduring Bias.

"So be it," Ussa said.

Enduring Bias approached, hovered in front of Ussa 'Xellus, angled its lenses downward, and projected a holographic image in front of him. Ussa saw a life-size image of a San'Shyuum in a golden, ornamental helmet. A Prophet, then. The San'Shyuum was sitting in an antigrav chair—not the kind used by a Hierarch. The San'Shyuum shifted his weight on the chair, and Ussa heard him speak.

"I am known as the Prophet of Inner Conviction," said the San'Shyuum. "Can you see and hear me?"

"I see and hear you," said Ussa.

"And I recognize you, Ussa 'Xellus. Do you remember me?"

"I do not."

"We did not meet directly—but we nevertheless encountered each other on the Planet of Red and Blue. We observed each other from afar, I believe."

"Truly? Then you are . . . Mken 'Scre'ah'ben?"

"I am known by that name as well. I am at this instant alone in my quarters of this vessel. I wished no one on my side to hear our conversation. I choose not to be concerned about who might be listening at your end. But since I am alone here, you need not call me Prophet of Inner Conviction or Your Eminence."

"How generous of you."

"It is hard to tell when a Sangheili is engaging in mockery. I cannot read their faces or voices as well as those of my own people. So if that was intended as mockery, it was wasted on me. If you like, you may simply call me Mken—because I believe we must speak as two rational beings meeting face-to-face, both seriously and informally."

"Very well. You may call me Ussa . . . but do not imagine informality means weakness. Let us move on to our colloquy."

"Here is my offer, then, Ussa: if you and your people surrender, I will attempt to obtain permission to return all of your people, unharmed, to Sanghelios and have them repatriated there. You and your mate must surrender to judgment . . . and most likely execution. But your people, I trust, will be safe."

Ussa hesitated. This was a better offer than he had expected. *Your people, I trust, will be safe.* Could he trust this San'Shyuum?

But it didn't matter, really. He couldn't surrender. That was the entire point.

"I took up this fight for several reasons, but chief among them, Mken, was that the Sangheili should never surrender."

"But can the Sangheili . . . make peace? It must be possible! If you could not make peace, your species would have been destroyed long ago. There are thousands of Sangheili here, in this fleet, eager to see you punished—because you betrayed their peace, their solemn oath of the Writ of Union. Most of those who will see you in battle if I give the word are Sangheili."

"They are not true Sangheili. *We* are—we can make peace, if it does not involve surrender. We can agree on mutual withdrawal, you and I, and we will go elsewhere. And there will be peace."

"I cannot offer you that—we cannot withdraw. But I can promise that if you release your people from your control, and let them return to Sanghelios, I will use all of my considerable influence to see they are treated well, and released to resume their lives on the Sangheili homeworld. You will allow yourself to be captured—it need not be a symbolic surrender. You and your mate. And you will be subject to the justice of the Covenant."

"And I will be executed."

"Or perhaps allowed to fight to the death, in an arena. It is heard of, I believe, on Sanghelios."

Ussa simply could not trust the other San'Shyuum—even if,

perhaps, this one was sincere. "When you first put the proposition to me, you said, 'I will attempt to obtain permission.' Cunning to put it that way! You and I know you would be unlikely to obtain such permission. I foresee my people would be *exterminated*, if I . . . allowed myself to be captured, as you offered."

"I am not a Hierarch, but I am not without influence. I would do everything in my power to see that your people were not harmed."

"The Covenant on Sanghelios would regard them as a security risk. They would not allow that. I know my own people—or those who used to be my people. Every last one of us would be executed. And the San'Shyuum would probably make the same calculation."

Now it was Mken's turn to hesitate. He shifted in his antigrav chair and admitted, "I cannot disagree with your logic. But . . . anyone can be persuaded."

"I am afraid I cannot trust my people to yours. Or even to my own kind on Sanghelios."

"If you do not surrender, you will all perish. Your best hope is to trust me."

"I cannot actually speak for all of my people—I think most would submit to returning to Sanghelios if I asked them to. I am not at all certain I need to do so. I am dubious, Mken, that you can destroy us so handily, unless you are also willing to destroy the greatest repository of sacred relics you have ever encountered."

Once more Mken paused, tugging thoughtfully on a wattle. "For all we know, there are no relics within that shell. It could be largely empty."

"I think you know better—because you cannot have risen on high without some understanding of the Forerunners."

"No one," Mken averred, "truly understands the Forerunners. To suppose we understand them is tantamount to heresy."

Ussa leaned forward in his kaidon's throne and pointed a

finger at Mken. "I tell you that this place is alive with Forerunner secrets. And that is a warning! If you do not retreat . . . if you press an attack on us . . . we will destroy all that is here! And who will be to blame? Ultimately, that would fall upon the Prophet of Inner Conviction!"

The San'Shyuum made a soft sound that was like the gurgling of a narrow stream. Perhaps it was amusement . . . or disdain. "It may be so, Ussa. But would you, who rebelled to protect the Sangheili way with sacred artifacts, actually possess the conviction to destroy them?"

"Is that why you suppose we rebelled? We acted as such because the Sangheili must not surrender to the San'Shyuum—and the Covenant is based on foolishness. *The Great Journey.* Where is your proof of this Journey, for anyone but the Forerunners? We hold these relics to be precious and sacred, but we use them ourselves in this very world. It is the freedom, the independence of our people that we fight for, Mken!"

Mken appeared shaken by this blasphemous mockery. But he decided this was no time to engage in theological argument. "If it's freedom you fight for, then let your people fight for it back on Sanghelios. You will die knowing they have a chance to be free there."

"Now, Mken, you are misleading me. You have as much as admitted you can guarantee no such thing. No, I think that we will not bargain with you."

Mken paused, then said: "I will say something now, and I care not who hears this. Why do you think I speak to you this way, Ussa 'Xellus? I will tell you truly—it is because I *admire* you. You have always found your own path, following your own heartfelt beliefs. You have fought bravely; you have evaded us with cunning, with forethought and wisdom. You have greatness! I wish we could have that same greatness in the Covenant. You are greater, in your way, than any San'Shyuum I know. I would not lie to such as you."

Ussa was taken aback. But like Mken, he could not easily judge the sincerity of another sentient species. *By their actions you will know them* was an ancient Sangheili precept. He could not know if this San'Shyuum was being forthright until he could prove it. He must assume Mken's protestations of admiration were just manipulative guile.

"I cannot trust you, whatever savory words you use, Mken. I tell you that if you attack us, and we believe we cannot win the battle . . . we will win, nevertheless. Even though it means our own destruction—this world and all that is in it . . . even as we destroy ourselves!"

"I cannot simply remove the fleet, Ussa. The Hierarchs have commanded me to take you prisoner for judgment—or destroy you. I am bound to the Covenant. Supposing you are capable of such a deed . . . no, it is unthinkable. There must be an alternative."

"I offer you this, then. If you withdraw, we will hand over relics from this world—wonder after wonder, courtesy of the Forerunners. We will give them to you one at a time. A few every circuit of this world around the sun."

Mken seemed to ponder. At last he said, "I do not think the Hierarchs would accept such an arrangement. They would feel that the entire Covenant was stymied by a small group of rebels. If word got out . . . no, it could not be borne. And then I could not persuade them to trust you. Nor could the Sangheili."

"So we've come to the end, then. We cannot trust you, and you cannot trust us."

"That is how it seems. And yet I *do* trust you, Ussa. You radiate integrity. It is the *others* who would not share that trust. I must ask you a final time—surrender, for the sake of your people."

Ussa gnashed his mandibles. "My people would end up tortured and executed in the hands of the Covenant! I am done discussing this. It is hopeless. You cannot strike at this world without destroying countless sacred relics. If you try to invade it . . . we will destroy it. And all of the invaders along with it. Bias! End this transmission!"

And the holograph switched off. Mken 'Scre'ah'ben vanished—and Ussa 'Xellus never saw him again.

Covenant Carrier *Pledge of Holiness*
In Orbit Around the Refuge, a Formerly Uncharted Shield World
850 BCE
The Age of Reconciliation

"Were you careful to use the stealth fields, Trok?" Mken asked. They were in the command center of the *Pledge of Holiness*, above and behind the vessel's bridge—a wide, low-ceilinged room, a half circle lined by displays and holoprojectors. Several communications officers stood at their stations, awaiting orders and dutifully observing screens holding information that they didn't quite comprehend—the world before them was eerily mysterious.

"We did, Your Eminence," said Trok 'Tanghil, glancing at Vil 'Kthamee, who stood behind Mken. "However, we seemed to be tracked the entire way. The intelligence construct utilized by Ussa 'Xellus may be using Forerunner technology to see past our stealth fields. Even so, we have landed three hundred Sangheili, and six Sentinels, with a hundred Sangheili and two Sentinels each at three points . . . here, here, and here . . ." He pointed at the schematic of what was known of this world, provided by scans and, to some extent, Salus 'Crolon's limited knowledge. "We found entry where he suggested we might—but it worries me that we were not attacked upon our arrival . . ."

"Yes. It's worrisome. And where is that wretch Salus 'Crolon?"

"He has gone along to guide the troops at Point One. He was quite reluctant to make the journey."

"No doubt." Mken cleared his throat and pondered. "If they're tracking us, you may be assured they're waiting for their moment. The right ground for assault. The Covenant will be met by the rebel troops—"

"Look!" Trok pointed at the three-dimensional image, where red circles pulsed and expanded. "It's begun! Contact with the enemy! 'Tskelk, what is the report from Point One?"

'Tskelk, the Sangheili communications officer on Mken's right, seemed to be communing with his holodisplay. After a few moments he said, "There is stiff resistance at Entry Point One. It seems there is an ambush! I'm not sure from this report if—"

"Enough," ordered Mken. "I want to hear it—and see if we have a visual signal."

"It shall be done, Your Eminence."

The transmitted image quickly appeared, bleary from motion, an uneven three-dimensional view apparently shot from someone's helmet. Mken could see plasma rifles flickering out jets of energy, burnblades flaring and slashing on the perimeters. "They waited till we broke through the shell and then came at us from three sides!" said a Sangheili breathlessly.

Mken saw Salus 'Crolon then, running toward the camera. "They're coming for me! They've seen me! We must pull back to a safer vantage! Quickly—!"

Then three Ussan Sangheili converged on 'Crolon—they wore the colors of Ussa on their chests; evidently it was an image of the shield world beside Sanghelios. They wielded their burnblades, hacking him into steaming, smoking pieces.

"So much for Salus 'Crolon," Trok muttered.

The Covenant Elite transmitting the image was firing his weapon in hot blue flashes at the oncoming Sangheili rebels. He gasped his report as he fired. "There aren't many of them, but they are aggressive and effect—" He didn't finish, the slash of a burnblade cutting him off, the image winking out.

"We can send another nine hundred troops, Your Eminence," said Ernicka.

"Yes, it's better if—"

Then another image appeared—it was Ussa 'Xellus himself, with smoke rising around him, shouts in the background, a glowing rifle in his hands. "You! Prophet of Inner Conviction! Are you there? I cannot see you—but surely you see me!"

"Yes, I see you!" declared Mken, intrigued. "Can you hear me?"

"Your voice comes through faintly. I wish to tell you that I have anticipated you would send in overwhelming reinforcements. We have driven the Covenant back for the moment, but it cannot continue. For this reason, I am giving the order. This planetoid will be lost to you forever! No one who remains here will survive. I am giving your forces an opportunity to retreat—*not* to surrender. Take them aboard! Otherwise they will die. No more negotiations!"

And then Ussa blinked out.

All the Sangheili were staring at Mken, wondering what his order would be—and not daring to give advice.

"Order our people to retreat, taking their wounded with them!" Mken said firmly. "Back into the landing vessels. Leave three Eyes to observe, and send us what information they can. Then prepare another six hundred troops for the second stage of the invasion . . ."

"It will be as you command, Your Eminence," said Trok.

Trok conveyed the orders as Mken contemplated whether those additional troops would be needed. He suspected not. Somehow, all his research on Ussa 'Xellus suggested the rebel leader was capable of unusual mercy for a Sangheili—the mark of a great sentient being. In fact, Ussa's only real mistake was taking mercy too far, in tolerating Salus 'Crolon when he must have known that Sangheili was a liability.

Minutes passed—and then Trok announced, "The three troop movers are en route . . . No returning fire from the planet . . . that is surprising . . . they seem to be genuinely allowing the retreat . . ."

"It is not surprising," Mken murmured. "This is on Ussa's orders."

The Eyes sent images from within the shield world where they, too, met with no resistance.

But there was also no sign of Ussa's people.

On and on the Eyes searched, returning tantalizing images of Forerunner artifacts and relics. There was nothing except empty corridors, rooms filled with cryptic devices, and a great gardenlike open area where flying creatures unfamiliar to Mken flapped about.

And then it happened. The walls seemed to shimmer . . . and melt. Waves of heat surged over the Eyes, and each remote device's signal snuffed out. The image went black.

"Show me the entire world," Mken ordered. And as the image of the metal-sheathed planetoid appeared in three dimensions, floating above them, Mken said, "And order the fleet: general withdrawal, pull back, but stay within the system, at ready, facing the enemy. Make it a safe distance, whatever you judge that to be, Trok. But close enough that we can still view it."

The shield world dwindled, shrank to what seemed a quarter of its size as they drew back.

Then the cracks showed.

They were seams, really, glowing from within the planet, blue in some places, red in others. The curved, neatly fitted segments of which the Refuge was made were edging apart from one another, releasing fantastic shimmering energies in the gaps, light that stretched out from the cracking planetoid like the rippling skirts of an aurora. Molten metal gushed from the widening seams in the planet's sheath, like reverse meteorites spat into space, and the planetoid shimmered in the release of heat energy.

The molten metal soon became a bubbling cloud of minerals, metal droplets, and searing gas around the shield world—and beyond that, Mken assumed, the rebel Sangheili were dying or, more likely, already dead.

"Oh, by the Journey," Mken muttered. "He did it. He's destroying all those lives—and all those relics. Gone."

As if it had heard him, the planetoid confirmed Mken's lament—it exploded.

The roiling fireball became an expanding, uneven fog of burning fragments, murky segments of planetoid that spun away into the void.

"Nothing and no one could have survived that," said Vil 'Kthamee, his voice hoarse.

"You are correct," Mken said. "The relics—the rebels. All gone. Annihilated. And at what cost . . ."

"Your Eminence, fragments of the planet are spinning our way, highly volatile," said 'Tskelk. "I'm getting reports of significant collision hazard from across the fleet!"

"Tell them to take evasive action," said Mken.

Mken went to the bridge, to consult with the undercaptain. But the fleet was undamaged. The shield world was in smoldering fragments, joining the nearby asteroid belt.

Viewing the monitors, as they searched the area after the

planetary blast had culminated, Mken noticed that dozens of large, distinctive metal-cored shapes were distributed through the area. Mken half expected to find escape craft, at least some sign of life. Surely Ussa 'Xellus would have prepared something. Had he really sacrificed himself—and all his people—for the sake of honor? They must have come to their senses—they must be there, somewhere.

But he saw no trace of conscious movement. Fragments spun, flame jetted as gases burned away from the ruptured planetoid. Were those incandescent specks the Sangheili burning up, their lives being extinguished?

He couldn't be sure. But the fragments of the planetoid glowed with a radiation that suggested no life was possible here.

Still . . . they might not be as lifeless as they seemed. The metal-edged sections within the burning debris seemed to edge toward the safer emptiness of space. Their movement subtly—ever so subtly—suggested sprawling but organized trajectories. Perhaps . . .

"Sir?" asked Trok 'Tanghil, coming to stand beside him. "Shall we continue the survey?"

Perhaps it was a rational decision. Perhaps it was not. But Mken made it in an instant.

"No. Order the fleet to return to High Charity. I shall prepare my report. I expect it will not be well received—especially by Excellent Redolence. But Ussa 'Xellus is gone. That is the important thing."

He turned away, and wondered at that himself. If his suspicion was right—was he now engaging in treason?

But he had no real proof.

So perhaps it was better to let the broken circle spin onward, untouched, into the space beyond their view.

If Ussa 'Xellus was alive, the Covenant would likely never hear from him again.

And Mken had a life to live. He had Cresanda to return to, after all. Why, then, court trouble?

Within the Broken Circle
Strategy Hall
850 BCE

The freight movers were not comfortable but they did their job: they kept Ussa 'Xellus and Sooln and Tersa and Lnur and the others stable within the largest section of the disassembled shield world. The walls rotated sickeningly around them; wind, driven by the turning of the segments, blew and skirled past. The lights blinked, going on and off, but valiantly shining most of the time. Ernicka the Scar-Maker, looking quite ill, clutched at the side of the shallow box shape of the freight mover. Dozens of other freight movers carried hundreds of other Ussans nearby.

Enduring Bias hovered overhead, chattering happily to itself about how well the experiment was going, positive results, and status reports chirped in the strange tongue of the Forerunners. All dangerous radiation released was redirected outward, away from the Sangheili.

"Great Ussa, we live yet!" Tersa said, as if surprised. He was clinging to the side of the freight mover nearby.

"You find that surprising?" Ussa asked. But he was rather nauseated and wished the whirling and jolting of their section of the disassembled shield world would slow and stop, as per plan. "Bias! How much longer will we have to endure this much motion?"

"Until the fleet is gone—then I will give the command for stabilization fields," the Flying Voice responded.

"How much of the Refuge did we lose?" Lnur asked.

"A fair amount," answered Enduring Bias. "But all according to the design of the Forerunners. They were concerned to design a place that could elude the Flood even if some of the parasite survived the Great Purification."

"Have you restored some parts of your memory?" Sooln asked. "That sounds like new information."

"What does?" asked Enduring curiously.

"What you said about . . . the Flood? What's that?"

"Did I say something about the Flood? Oh dear. I've been having these intervals, these lapses—jolts of lost history spurting up and then breaking apart . . . I wonder how much longer I can last . . ."

"We need you," Ussa reminded the Flying Voice. "We need you to set things in proper orbit. To sketch in the circle so that it's distributed around the sun, within the asteroid belt. So the Covenant can never find us . . . and so we can travel between the segments. We will make a new colony, as the Forerunners foresaw . . . and we will need you for that."

"I hope to be of use," Enduring Bias said. "But that will be only as long as I can, and no longer. Entropy sharpens the arrow of time, and it flies ever faster for me."

"The Flying Voice really is beginning to sound a bit off," muttered Lnur.

"We'll make it," Ussa said. "I have a vision of how it will work. The molten parts of the planetoid hid us—and the solidified melt camouflages the colony's segments. We will be safe here. The true Sangheili will grow in numbers and in strength. We will learn how to harness the power of the Forerunners. And those who follow us will one day take Sanghelios back."

PART TWO

An Invitation to the
Dance of Chaos

CHAPTER 15

**From the Prophet of Clarity's Notes on the History of the Covenant
An Account Not to Be Made Public Until
the Passing of the Prophet of Clarity
Composed in 2552 CE
Originally written in the language of the San'Shyuum**

. . . *and so, imperceptibly yet epochally, the Age of Discovery came to a close, with the understanding that the Great Ones had left traces for us to follow, clues to the Great Journey, a quest that would lead the faithful through a wondrous transfiguration allowing elevation to the level of the divine, and a reunification with the Great Ones, those we also call the Forerunners.*

But the Age of Reconciliation, preceding the Age of Discovery, now comes to this writer's mind, for Reconciliation was the time of the Writ of Union, and an end to the conflict between the San'Shyuum and the Sangheili. It is true, as reported in the secret writings of my ancestor the Prophet of Inner Conviction, that there was some short-lived rebellion and a violent purging that immediately followed, an event we now simply call the Rending; that a certain Sangheili faction, led by one Ussa 'Xellus, tried to foment a resistance to the Writ and, ultimately, the Covenant. He and his followers are said to have been annihilated by a mighty and blasphemous act of mass suicide, their deliberate destruction of the planetoid they called the Refuge, which we now suspect to have been a shield world constructed by the Great Ones. This was the end of the initial Sangheili resistance—thereafter, their warlike race became the enforcers of the will of the Covenant. Here followed the beginning of the Sangheili, whom we referred to as the Elites, of the High Council of Sangheili and San'Shyuum, and the beginning of a great construction, the creation of the homeworld that is now High Charity—a Holy City free to move about in the void, a world and a power, formed around the keyship of the Great Ones and sacred land derived from Janjur Qom herself, which brings the mercy of deliverance to the converted throughout the galaxy. Thus was the Age of Reconciliation the true seed of the Age of Conversion.

The new Age was vested in the adaptation of all other sentient species that came to our attention, a conversion that came about through the domination of revelation itself and, when necessary, conquest.

Among the most difficult to convert were the formidable Mgalekgolo (also known as Hunters) from the rings of the gas giant Te, creatures formed on different principle from most, sentient worms with a collective mind capable of agglomerating small colonies into fighting beings. At long last, as the murals tell us, faced with possible extinction, they were tamed and became subjects of the Covenant.

The flying Yanme'e, simply called Drones by some, tend to a hivelike society, eusocial and separated by castes, each with its own tasks, subject to the will of a matriarchal queen. They are insectoid, but large, as are many creatures of the Covenant.

They were conquered on their planet Palamok, and a convocation of Hive Queens consigned their drones into our service.

The Kig-Yar were next to be incorporated into the Covenant. These long-snouted, toothy, crested creatures are a mix of bestial and civilized; they were found on the moon Eayn, which orbits the planet Chu'ot. They are at once ferocious and cowardly, fierce and yet scatter-witted. Yet some are effective snipers, and, once drawn into the Covenant they have proven loyal, though they are quarrelsome with the Unggoy and others at times.

From Balaho came the small methane-breathing Unggoy— the Grunts of the Covenant. They are a mix of clever and ludicrous, to my eyes . . . and to my hearing. They were conquered with little resistance at first; but there was, once upon a time, an Unggoy rebellion. And sometimes they show a surprising spirit of independence. But they are among the Covenant's most devoted seekers after the Great Journey, sacrificing themselves in great numbers on the battlefield, so prolific that more seem always ready to throw themselves upon the altar of war.

Then, from the three-mooned planet Doisac came the big, brutish Jiralhanae. Vicious fighters, their wars had reduced them from a higher civilization to one hampered by only feeble technology—thus their resistance to the Covenant was short-lived. Added to this, they seemed to have an unfilled hunger for some theological meaning, and they quickly adopted the worship of the Great Ones and set out upon the Path to the Great Journey. They are like overgrown carnivorous primates, sometimes given to feeding on the meat of fallen enemies at the conclusion of battle; they are massively muscled, thumping about on enormous two-toed feet. The hulking creatures, now known as Brutes, are prone to feuds and megalomania, and *while they are most useful in a battle, especially in close combat, they are known to privately jeer at the other members of the Covenant—except the San'Shyuum, thank the Great Ones, of whom they are in awe. They seem to have a particular dislike of the Sangheili, and are known to resent the high place the Elites have taken. In truth, I trust them not. It may be that . . .*

(The text here is damaged, interrupted. It continues thus:)

. . . the war with the humans has for much of its history gone well, though lately events are taking a disturbing turn.

We have destroyed many of their colony worlds without quarter or relent since the very beginning, having discovered their colonies before they found us. Their discovery was really one of chance, by way of the predations of a Kig-Yar missionary vessel, when they came upon a world the humans called Harvest.

Signals consistent with Forerunner presence were detected there, but no intact artifacts were found. The Hierarchs concluded that the humans had sacrilegiously destroyed the holy relics—after violence erupted between emissaries of the Covenant and the humans, the Hierarchs decided, for reasons unknown to me, that the humans were so dangerous and heretical they must be wiped out completely. They declared the humans vermin, claiming that they were intent on desecrating Forerunner vestiges. I will only note that, curiously enough, other members of the Covenant, when first discovered, were thought dangerous and heretical—and yet allowed to join us.

After a furious battle, the planet Harvest was subjected to plasma bombardment and glassed, but not before many of the humans had escaped. More human colony worlds were found and destroyed. Yet we could not, for many cycles, locate their homeworld, something we had learned was called Earth.

Solar cycles of war followed as we fought our way from one human colony to the next, wiping them out. We took grievous losses at times in those cycles, but the humans won only a sparse number of battles. We were an unstoppable force, rolling over their civilization, which seemed over time to have encompassed impressively large portions of the galaxy.

Then came the planet they called Reach, which we supposed to be the cradle, the homeworld. It was not. Though the planet was eventually glassed, the events that followed began to set the war in a new, alarming direction.

A human vessel, fleeing this world Reach as it burned, came upon the first Sacred Ring—our Fleet of Particular Justice followed the humans to what we now know was Alpha Halo, discovering it at almost the same time. A great battle was fought on the Sacred Ring and it was ultimately destroyed.

The destruction of a Halo was a wounding of hope. We all experienced its loss with a deeply resonant grief.

There is yet the dream of finding. Perhaps we shall find other Rings someday—but that hope in my lifetime may be impossible. In the meantime, the humans continue to create obstacles to the Great Journey . . .

(Interruption in the text due to damage.)

. . . and so, given our willingness to incorporate other races within the Covenant, I have been confidentially puzzled about the Hierarchs' dismissal of any possibility of offering the humans and their colonies a proper place in the Covenant, at the very least in order to quell the endless bloodshed.

Indeed, the humans were declared by the Hierarchs to be heretics, an affront to the sacred mission of the Covenant. Could it be because their energy, their expansionism, might possibly make them competitors for the Sacred Rings? But why could the humans, like the Sangheili long ago, not become allies in the search for the Great Journey? Their resourcefulness could be extremely valuable to us. And yet aggression has always been our first reaction to the humans.

Madness, for me to write what I have just written! But within me is the seed of centuries of historians. I have worked as communication engineer; I have been recently promoted to supervisor over a number of combat squads. And I am now being considered as an aide to a Hierarch, the High Prophet of Truth. But the deep desire for truth and knowledge, to make an accounting of the San'Shyuum's doings in the galaxy, is in my blood, my soul. I have always sought clarity—hence the name I chose for myself.

Still, I take a tremendous risk writing these words, as heretical as they may sound. Thus, as my ancestor Mken 'Scre'ah'ben did with his own accounts, I will keep them locked away, at least for now.

High Charity
The Hanging Gardens
2552 CE
The Age of Reclamation

Zo Resken, the Prophet of Clarity, was using his antigrav belt to walk with unusual companions in the Hanging Gardens. He was a fairly young San'Shyuum and not particularly highly placed, so it was odd to see him associating socially with the two Sangheili by his side. Uncommon but not unheard of. Still, if anyone noticed, they'd assume the Elites were most likely his personal protection. These Elites, however, were far more than that—G'torik 'Klemmee was an important commander, and Torg 'Gransamee a High Councilor. Torg was called G'torik's uncle, according to Sangheili custom . . . though in fact he was most likely G'torik's father, or so Clarity believed.

Zo looked around, unable to appreciate the spectacular view of High Charity from the Hanging Gardens. He was too concerned about unfriendly listeners. Two bored-looking Jiralhanae patrolled with heavy strides on a farther platform, hulking figures armed with spike rifles, native brutish weapons the Sangheili frowned upon but allowed in low numbers. A few dwarfish Unggoy were working in one of the gardens below, seeming to be arguing with a long-snouted toothy Kig-Yar. No one close enough to hear them, no surveillance drones in view either.

Zo, G'torik, and Torg had come here to the gardens to speak, as the spaces were wide around them; the greenery, blossoms and ponds, and artfully arranged stones were high platforms linked by gravity bridges—no one would hear their conversation.

"As you well know, Alpha Halo has been destroyed," Zo Resken said glumly as they paused by a pond. Something finned and golden wriggled in the water, like a bright thought in a dark mind. "For a time, some wondered if it was the judgment of the gods. If we were not worthy of the Sacred Rings. Once, millennia ago, a unique Luminary was found—it might have changed everything for us. But it was lost, and it was believed that the loss was also a sign of our unworthiness . . ." He decided to say no more about the Luminary the Prophet of Inner Conviction had discovered on the homeworld Janjur Qom—he wasn't ready to discuss Mken's secret writings with anyone from the Covenant just yet.

"In my opinion," growled the elderly Torg 'Gransamee, "if there was unworthiness that cost Alpha Halo, it wasn't spiritual—it was military."

"Perhaps it's not for us to say," said G'torik gently—his way of reminding his uncle that they were speaking to a Prophet.

"Don't be concerned about speaking freely with me," Zo said softly, glancing around again. "That is precisely why we are here. To discuss freely our allegiances."

Musing, Zo glanced up, noticing two San'Shyuum who drifted by in rather gaudy antigrav chairs, deep in concentration. Both had the features of San'Shyuum in youth, with the nose protuberance, the closer eyes, the stronger chin, shorter necks. He'd been a little startled when he'd first seen humans—they reminded him of the young adults of his own species.

The two, though, rode their chairs around a corner, leaving Zo to peer past a small flock of angular Yanme'e winging aloft—creatures like giant insects with transparent, speed-blurred wings—and gaze out through the filmy transparent field that held in the atmospheric pressure for High Charity. On a personal display he had brought with him, he pulled up sensor images captured from what remained of the Holy Ring, and he could see the debris field of the remains of the Halo, spinning: a vast churning sea of fragments and liquids, of soil and metals, of Covenant bodies and pieces of those bodies, of machines that would never be fully understood. Sacred relics—and one of the largest they'd ever encountered, the Sacred Ring itself, now destroyed. The sight was like a great heavy fist pressing on his heart. High Charity, the great habitat that also acted as a gigantic space-faring vessel, had been stationed at the site of the cataclysm a short time before yet another discovery had rocked the Covenant—Delta Halo. It seemed almost inconceivable that a second Sacred Ring was discovered in such a short time. Such sorrow mixed with newfound jubilation was almost too much to bear for Zo. But around the time High Charity had reached this new Ring, the word came that another catastrophe had struck—a high-level assassination.

"And now," G'torik said, "the High Prophet of Regret has been killed . . . murdered by the Demon on Delta Halo." It was his turn to look around nervously before he went on. "With perhaps aid from someone else . . ."

"But Regret did put himself in danger," said Zo, changing his display to the space presently outside of High Charity, where the immense band of Delta Halo rose up toward High Charity. "Perhaps it was ambition, perhaps holy zeal—but he did not confer with the other Hierarchs before taking fifteen warships to seek the Ark . . ." The Ark—potentially the greatest creation of the Forerunners, an unthinkably massive star-shaped device, bigger than many a world, capable of activating all Halos everywhere and commencing the Purification for the Great Journey across the galaxy. Also, according to legend, it was the final refuge of the Forerunners during their great battle with the parasite known as the Flood.

And Regret somehow found the portal to the Ark—how exactly remained unknown. But when he arrived with the Fleet of Sacred Consecration at the portal site, he quickly discovered that it was the cradle planet of the humans themselves. It was the world called Earth.

The humans were dangerous, and numerous.

Zo added bitterly: "Regret fled in a rather haphazard way to Delta Halo . . . and he clumsily allowed the humans to follow him. Including the Demon. It was he who murdered Regret . . ."

Zo had great respect for the High Prophet of Regret—but who could not be angry at him now for his foolhardiness?

"Did the Demon perish as well?" G'torik asked.

"No body was found. Some say it is likely he was killed when we scorched the site of this treachery."

"We have regretted underestimating that one before," said Torg. "I myself do not assume that a thing like that could ever die."

"What was it you said a moment ago?" murmured Zo, looking to see that the Jiralhanae were not close by. "That someone else may have aided the Demon?"

"Perhaps opened the door for the assassin," muttered G'torik. "The word among Elites who were there is that hundreds of fresh troops were coming in on Phantoms to protect Regret—reinforcements who could have saved the High Prophet! But the Phantoms were withdrawn before off-loading their troops. And the order came from . . ."

He seemed hesitant to say the name. But they were meeting here because of Zo's connection to the one who'd likely given the order: Ord Casto. Or more commonly known as the High Prophet of Truth.

"So it is said," Torg put in. "Why did he do it, Prophet?"

Why indeed? Zo squirmed inwardly, wondering. There was something so convenient in the loss of the High Prophet of Regret now. Truth had to share power before with two Hierarchs . . . now there was but one other. And that other, in his dotage, was obsessed with holy contemplation.

And why was Truth spending so much time in private discussions with high-level Brutes like Tartarus?

But aloud Zo said, "I can only guess. It may be that Truth took it upon himself to punish Regret for his brash expedition to Earth. There are hints of another reason . . ." There came a soft chime then at his collar communicator. A summons. "I must go—Truth has need of me. I suspect that Tartarus is about to arrive."

Zo was the High Prophet's Secondary Administrator—the

title had sounded grander when he was first appointed to the position. But Zo had found himself relegated to the role of little more than a lowly assistant. Possibly Truth wanted Clarity as a buffer between himself and the Elites. Zo had been fortunate enough to be present at the discovery of the Sacred Ring—Alpha Halo—and had been engaged in overseeing combat units of Elites in their attempts to repel the humans. He was known for his rapport with Sangheili. He had just managed to help his troops honorably escape the destruction that followed, when the Demon culminated the humans' blasphemies by destroying the Sacred Ring.

And how had all that been rewarded? Appointment to Secondary Administrator.

"Thank you for speaking to us," Torg said. "Events have unsettled us—and there is a reason the Elites trust you. Will you tell us what you learn?"

"I can promise nothing, but I am so inclined, yes." Zo did not wish to become a spy for the Sangheili. But then again—they were eyes and ears for him, too. With the discovery of Delta Halo in the wake of the first Ring's tragic end, it seemed reasonable to solidify old alliances rather than weaken them.

And he had his own ambitions.

High Charity
The Palace of the Hierarchs
2552 CE
The Age of Reclamation

Seated in his antigrav chair in the entryway of the private reception chamber, the Prophet of Clarity was nervous—soon he would have to deal with the Brute chieftain Tartarus—while at his back, in the room behind the Hierarchs' private reception hall, was the High Prophet of Truth himself.

He was still shaken by the report of Regret's death. At the very least, it confirmed his intuition of the ruthlessness of Ord Casto, the High Prophet of Truth, if certain mounting suspicions proved true.

If Truth was ruthless, then he was also clinically careful. Truth, like most Prophets, was almost superstitiously confident in technology, and Zo had supposed him unlikely to suspect anyone had tampered with his chair's communicator. But there was a chance that assumption was wrong. Truth might be careful enough to sweep for surveillance.

Zo had felt a certain resentment, relegated to his new station. He was looking for information, something he could use to advance his own agenda. Why should he not someday be a Hierarch? Knowledge could be power. And Zo had certain technological skills—he had begun his career as a communications officer, after all, and had that very morning used his expertise to secretly implant a share-input directive into the communicator within Truth's chair. Properly triggered, it would silently switch on, transmitting Truth's conversations, both in person and remotely, directly to and only to Zo. If Truth learned that the Prophet of Clarity was secretly eavesdropping, he would likely have him killed. He might use his throne's weaponry to do it personally. But if clear evidence of infidelity to the Covenant's millennia-old promise were to be discovered, it might provide Zo with distinct opportunities. Then again, with Regret's untimely departure, it might simply be wiser for him to posture for that vacancy. In light of Delta Halo's discovery and the near certain end to the humans' resistance once the Covenant crushed Earth, it would seem that the Great Journey was finally upon them and such political ambitions were, at best, petty and even sinful. Nevertheless, what was done was done.

Clarity tried to imagine how he might deny responsibility if the implant was found, but doubted he would be believed. It now struck him that he had taken an incredible risk.

Zo remained nervous about Tartarus's impending arrival.

At first, Clarity had been engaged here as a kind of buffering subaltern between Truth and the Minor Prophet of Stewardship, who had been for a time given control of the Fleet of Particular Justice's military assets. The destruction of Alpha Halo would claim the Stewardship's life, as well as most of the others, and Zo would live with the shame they all felt over what had taken place.

But lately, Clarity had become little more than a doorkeeper. And most of the visitors entering these days seemed to be Jiralhanae.

Zo glanced around to see that everything was in order. The translucent floors were burnished; the drapery, with the image of a circle within which was the continental tracery of Oth Sonin, the homeworld of Jiralhanae, was hung to one side of the dais where Truth received visitors. The drapery was a sop, really, an honorific banner to make high Jiralhanae feel important when they visited.

It seemed superfluous—the arrogant, violent Tartarus forever radiated a sense of his own importance. He showed a rote respect for all the Prophets, but seemed to regard himself as not only Jiralhanae chieftain, but chief among all Covenant soldiers. It was the High Prophet of Truth who had elevated Tartarus to head the Jiralhanae forces within the Covenant, and so Tartarus showed special deference to Truth. But to Zo, the chieftain seemed to be barely holding himself back from using his enormous gravity hammer, the legendary Fist of Rukt, on lesser Covenant. Tartarus seemed a true believer in the Covenant's mission—especially in his own elevation to the Great Journey. And only that unquestioning belief kept his hammer in check.

Hearing a whirring sound, Zo spun his chair about and was only slightly relieved to see it was the High Prophet of Truth, throne humming as he approached from the corridor. Ord Casto was in his full regalia, his antigrav throne, his high fluted gold collar, his golden helmet. His heavy-lidded, wide-set eyes looked critically at Zo as he approached.

Truth turned to him, cocking his head as he asked brightly, "Ah, Clarity—I trust you have been exact in your protocol? Only to serve as a reminder, it is best that we say nothing of these meetings with Tartarus; as you are well aware, petty jealousies sometimes simmer in the Covenant. One doesn't want to encourage them."

"I have spoken of it to no one, Your Eminence."

"Not even his holiness, the High Prophet of Mercy?"

"Not even him, O High Prophet of Truth."

Truth sat back in his throne. "Good." He added lightly, "We need not trouble the High Prophet of Mercy with all these scheduling details and military logistics. So—the chieftain of the Jiralhanae will be here any moment, with Exquisite Devotion."

"The Prophet of Exquisite Devotion?" He had heard nothing of Exquisite coming here. I'ra Be'Ar was a prominent High Councilor, was rumored to be in line to become a Hierarch someday. He was a crony of Truth's, but it was curious that he should be here for a meeting along with Tartarus.

This was shaping up to be very unpleasant. First Tartarus, now Exquisite Devotion. There was something about that San'Shyuum that made Zo queasy whenever he encountered him. For a moment, Clarity wondered if Truth would be so brazen as to consider a replacement for Regret so soon after the High Prophet had been struck down. Ultimately, it was the Council's decision, but Exquisite entertained many allegiances there among his own species.

"Yes. Exquisite will be here. Certain changes have been arranged. See that Tartarus has all the refreshment he desires—and offer the Prophet something made to his liking."

"It is an honor to do your bidding, Your Eminence."

"We all serve the Path together, according to our stations. We do have the Jiralhanae, ah, *beverage* on hand?"

"We do, Your Eminence."

Jiralhanae typically drank a thick red noxious liquid that Truth kept entirely for the top-level Brutes—it was said to be toxic to other species. Probably, Zo thought acidly, Tartarus would have been just as happy to drink the blood of his enemies, fresh from their wounds.

"I shall be in the back chamber," Truth said. "When they arrive, do not enter, simply signal his arrival first." Truth cleared his throat. "Clarity, here is something else. Best if you treat Exquisite with the utmost respect."

"Always, Your Eminence. Should I record the purpose of *his* visit?"

"No, do not record this cycle's meetings at all. In confidence, my dear Clarity, Exquisite will be taking a critical new post in High Charity. The loss of the first Ring was an unspeakable tragedy, but finding the second Ring and the human homeworld, as well as the gateway to the Ark, can be nothing short of a sign from the gods. As we secure these sites and begin to initiate the culmination of the Path, all that we've worked for over the centuries, it will require a dramatic restructuring of our governance. For this reason, I will have no need of your administrative services here on High Charity any longer—I am transferring you to Exquisite's authority, who will be overseeing much of the Holy City's governance while the

High Prophets and the High Council commit themselves to the holy task of commencing the Great Journey. Please do whatever he asks of you, without question."

Zo felt a sickly giddiness at the thought of serving under Exquisite Devotion. From bad to worse, in only a few moments.

"Now, Clarity—stand by in case I need anything."

"It would be an honor, Your Eminence."

As a sort of afterthought, Truth said, "It is a great tragedy, the loss of the glorious High Prophet of Regret, is it not?"

"A tragedy that will stain our history, Your Eminence, even at such a sacred time as the culmination of the Journey."

"Yes. Yes indeed. Though it grieves us, such must have been the payment for our final victory. Often sacrifice precedes salvation."

Truth's eyes flickered with something that might be a secret amusement, then floated his throne into the reception chamber.

Zo resumed his place in the doorway. He gnawed a knuckle, having difficulty accepting this sudden reassignment to the one Prophet he truly disliked. Wasn't this a kind of demotion? Perhaps he should ask Truth if he had done something amiss; certainly he still needed some assistance. But one did not question the High Prophet's decisions.

Zo heard a clomping sound, looked up to see the massive form of the white-bearded Tartarus striding along the columned hallway toward him, battle hammer propped on one shoulder. The hallway echoed with the heavy clop of the Jiralhanae's two-toed boots as he strode past a series of Honor Guards stationed farther down. The Elites serving as Truth's protectors had come to accept the Brute chief's comings and goings. Though they held complete loyalty to the Hierarch, Zo sometimes considered whether or not they secretly wondered what the purpose was with the Jiralhanae, as he had.

Where was Exquisite Devotion? Perhaps he wasn't coming after all?

Tartarus stalked nearer, his silvery skull ruff wagging with each step; his albinoid skin threw back the light with a dull sheen; his sharp teeth seemed perpetually bared in a red mouth that stood out from his dead-white skin and the pale fur somewhat uncommon to Brutes under his heavy bandoliers. There was something about Jiralhanae, something primatelike, that made Zo consider they looked like more primitive though much larger versions of the humans.

Then Zo's heart sank as he heard the querulous voice of the Prophet of Exquisite Devotion. "Tartarus! Do wait for me, if you please."

Tartarus turned, and Exquisite's antigrav chair accelerated to catch up with the Jiralhanae.

The ornate seat was a bit too much like a throne, Zo thought.

Twenty strides more and Tartarus was there, glaring down at Zo with intense eyes. "Greetings, Prophet of Clarity. The Hierarch is expecting me."

"I will inform him that you and the High Councilor are here, Chieftain Tartarus," said Zo mildly, gesturing, *Much respect to you both.*

"Yes, please do," said Exquisite. His voice varied between a cranky purr and a whine, but his face was always frozen in a bilious look of enforced benevolence.

Zo turned his chair and floated over to the door in the wall behind the dais. He tapped on the door. He could have signaled Truth on a communicator, but this ancient practice was more in keeping with protocol. "Your Nobility? Your visitors have arrived."

Truth's voice came fuzzily through the door. "Very good, Clarity. Serve them in the meantime. I will come out in a few moments."

Zo turned and saw that Tartarus and the Prophet had already come in. Exquisite had tented his hands and was gazing about him; the chieftain was standing stiffly in the midst of the mirror-walled chamber, scratching in his brushy ruff with one horny, four-fingered hand, the other still clasping the hammer. "I believe," Tartarus rumbled, "that the High Prophet of Truth customarily keeps a refreshment for me?" He looked around impatiently for it, fingering his hammer.

Zo gestured, *I comply with joy.* "Certainly . . . And some tea for you, High Councilor?"

"If you please, a bit of the sea flower, with a touch of sky spice."

Zo hurried to a cabinet near the entryway, found the proper bottle, poured the muskily odorous red fluid into the glass. He ordered the tea, with the proper herb and spice, and the refreshment panel hissed it instantly into the cup.

Zo returned, a drink in each hand. Tartarus snatched his and drank it down almost before Zo had come to a complete stop in front of him. Exquisite received his own cup with delicate aplomb.

"Exquisite Devotion," called Truth as he floated his throne from the back room. "Tartarus, Chieftain of the Brutes."

"High One!" Tartarus said gruffly, bowing deeply.

"Your Eminence," said Exquisite, making the gesture of grand respect with his free hand.

"I see you both have found the refreshments. I, too, needed something to soothe my mind. A Sacred Ring destroyed, forever lost—were it not for Delta Halo and the gateway to the Ark, these would be considered grave times indeed! Leave us, Second Administrator—see to my messages. I would speak with the Chieftain in private."

"It will be an honor, Your Eminence," said Zo as he took the empty cup from Tartarus.

The High Prophet made an imperious gesture with his three-fingered hand and Tartarus straightened up and approached him.

Still sipping tea, Exquisite Devotion silently approached the dais.

Zo left the room, closing the door, and then went into his own small work alcove to one side. He hesitated. Should he activate the device he had planted? It was dangerous . . .

But he valued information and insight. It was in his nature to want to know, especially given the recent changes and the constant peril that seemed to saturate these times. And there was the possibility of putting the information to good use . . .

He put the Brute's cup aside, reached to his collar, inputted the surveillance code, and listened. The device crisply responded. He turned the volume down low in case a guard walked by.

"Noble Hierarch, are we now ready to take action?" demanded Tartarus. "The Jiralhanae in my confidence are hungry for it—and I am impatient to set our plans into motion. The true consummation of the Great Ones must be near at hand."

"I agree," said Exquisite. "Time is of the essence now."

"It will be soon," Truth assured them. "Events crowd upon us. The High Prophet of Regret has been murdered, and by the Demon responsible for the destruction of the Sacred Ring, no less. This blasphemous assault demanded conclusive action, and the site was purged by our ships, though the Demon's fate remains in question. Our plans will proceed. But secrecy, for now, is still a requisite."

"I speak only the words you permit me, High One," rumbled the Jiralhanae.

"My discretion is well known to you, Your Eminence," said Exquisite.

"Yes. One must be careful. Matters are in flux. Regret is gone . . ." Truth seemed to muse over the realization. "Quite gone . . ."

Truth, Zo noted, sounded impassive about Regret's death—and was there even a touch of glee? Had not Truth and Regret, alongside the High Prophet of Mercy, served together as the triumvirate of Hierarchs?

Despite his feelings about all that had occurred in the wake of the Fleet of Sacred Consecration's demise, Zo himself had some sadness at the loss of Regret—as the former Vice Minister of Tranquility, Regret had treated Zo well.

Perhaps G'torik had been right, and Truth had abandoned Regret as punishment.

"And who failed to protect Regret, High One?" sneered Tartarus. "Is it not clearly the Elites?"

"An Honor Guard made up of Elites, as you well know, was there to protect him. This regrettable death has opened the door for us all, however. Already the forces around the human world have been . . . *changed*; the Brutes now control those fleets, and the Elites suspect nothing at all. Their myopic focus on this newly discovered Ring has blinded them to our movements regarding the human homeworld, Earth."

"What comes next will not have the same effect—it will open their eyes," Exquisite pointed out.

"No matter. Our plans will be put into action, and the Jiralhanae will have their rightful place. But let us say no more here, even this place . . ."

Zo gnawed again on a bony knuckle. Did Truth suspect Zo of eavesdropping? Perhaps it hadn't gone that far. But it seemed suspicion was in the air. And if Truth acted on that suspicion, Zo might be exposed. Perhaps he might undergo torture. Certainly death.

Zo sat back, expelling a long breath. His hands were shaking on the arms of the chair and he clasped them for steadiness, as what he'd overheard now began to sink in.

The High Prophet of Truth had been highly secretive of late. And now he was discussing what sounded like a kind of decisive action with Tartarus and Exquisite Devotion. A change of the Covenant guard? Such a thing was unheard of. The Sangheili had always served as the iron fist of the Covenant; that arrangement was the very foundation of the Writ of Union. This proposed new order was clearly something Truth had not wanted the other Hierarchs to know about, nor the Council.

And now one of those Hierarchs was gone.

Zo had often observed Truth's well-veiled impatience when the other two in the triumvirate thwarted his wishes. It could be that the High Prophet of Truth reckoned the Covenant could be governed by only one Hierarch. But why now? Why at the end of all things, and the consummation of the Journey?

And whom would Truth sacrifice so that he could reach that goal?

Quite possibly, whomever he had to, and in any way he could.

The Refuge, the Ussan Colony
Primary Refuge
2552 CE
The Age of Reclamation

Bal'Tol 'Xellus, leader of Sangheili Ussans, sat in his oval meditation chamber, gazing out through the viewport at the asteroid belt, with its dull gray metallic fragments of the ancient Ussan colony. The view was enhanced by magnification nodes impregnated in the glass—usually the asteroid belt was not dense enough to see with the naked eye. Bal'Tol watched as gigantic chunks of stone and ice slowly spun in their endless danceline, an orbital circling of the system's sun, broken moons, shattered planetoids, fragmented comets, an unruly belt yet overall in a perfect ellipse around the sun. It signified chaos within order.

At intervals in the asteroid belt were intact sections of his colony, most of them not turning in place at all, though they followed the curving trail of the belt's orbit. All but a few were kept from spinning by stabilizers. But like the asteroids, the colony sections were part of the dance of chaos, which found unitary equanimity in orbital grace. Counting Primary and Combat Section, there were fifteen areas to the Refuge—fourteen that were intact enough to be occupied—the largest being Primary Section.

There had been only a little more than four hundred Ussans who'd come here centuries earlier; their descendants now numbered 3,210. Primary Section had almost four hundred Sangheili living there. The other sections ranged in population from one hundred to just under two hundred. The colony's sections—odd geometrical shapes formed of cuboids and rectangular segments and the occasional cone—had once been connected, unified by the stone of a planetoid and the cohesion of Forerunner engineering. The Disassembly process initiated long ago had taken everything apart—exactly as the Forerunners had hoped it would—and scattered the sections throughout the asteroid belt. The asteroids were camouflage, a hiding place from the ancient threat older than the Covenant, and later from the Covenant itself.

But to Bal'Tol, now the separated sections of colony seemed to symbolize individual Sangheili going through life in their own chaotic orbits, trying to find centeredness, their self-awareness, stability, functionality, harmony . . . orbital grace. The method was said to have come from a prisoner from a far planet who had stumbled on their colony long ago. The meditation had been handed down for numerous generations and taught to Bal'Tol by his uncle, N'Zursa 'Xellus, the previous kaidon.

And at N'Zursa's death, Bal'Tol had become kaidon. He had taken the oath—he, too, could allow no contact with other sentient species. No others had ever found their way into the colony. If they did, they would be imprisoned or, more wisely, immediately executed.

Who knew? Perhaps those few contacts had caused the Blood Sickness. The blight had taken his Limtee. Bal'Tol himself had found her, his intended mate, dead in her sleeping chamber . . .

Bal'Tol sighed. The memory of Limtee's passing disrupted his meditation. He could now not return to an unblemished contemplative state.

Instead, he would go and consult C'tenz to see if there was a report on the 'Greftus Faction.

If there was a rebellion, a rebirth of the Way of 'Greftus, then Bal'Tol had another oath to fulfill. The rebellion must be ruthlessly put down.

Bal'Tol stood, stretched, and went broodingly through the door, out into the corridor. He nodded to a pair of guards, who saluted him as he passed, and then fell in behind him, as per security protocol.

As he walked to the Hall of Strategy, Bal'Tol noted a certain unevenness in the distribution of artificial gravity in this outer edge of the Primary Refuge. One had to step carefully. He must have the repair team examine the graviton generators. They did not understand the underlying principles well enough to create new ones; they were merely able to sometimes repair individual parts, and there was a diminishing store of spares, to be found in some places. Some of the Refuge sections had been deserted, and their parts could easily be cannibalized. The 'Greftus Faction had been right about one thing: the colony was giving way to entropy, as all things must in time. Thousands of solar cycles had passed since the Disassembly. Ussa 'Xellus's account of it, now difficult to read due to the ancient dialect it was written in, seemed to imply that the colony's sections had once been part of a great sphere, created by the near-mythical Forerunners, who had constructed it as the last of a series of protective worlds. They had made the Refuge distinct from the others—hidden within the sphere had been a new reordering, an altered blueprint for survival, should its destruction as a sphere become necessary. But the constant gravitational stress as the sections spun through the camouflaging asteroid belt, the inner exertion of artificial gravity, the exposure of section panels to solar radiation, as well as simple alloy fatigue, had gradually weakened parts of what had once seemed almost indestructible. Without repair, the sections would fall apart, and the colony would perish.

It would seem that even the Forerunners were not infallible.

The 'Greftus Faction, named after the long-dead rebel leader from the Fifth Section of the Refuge, 'Insa 'Greftus, had cried apocalypse when the decay had become evident, had declared that the Forgotten Gods, as they called them—supposed entities channeled psychically by 'Greftus—wanted the Sangheili to depart the colony. Ancient ships still survived in the Primary Section. Why not use one to explore and find the fabled homeworld Sanghelios? The Forgotten Gods supposedly told 'Greftus of the way back to that ancient place, which some thought of as purely mythological.

Bal'Tol's uncle N'Zursa had dismissed all 'Greftus's claims as the ravings of a Sangheili addled with the Blood Sickness. It was known that the Blood Sick were subject to madness, to hallucinations and paranoia.

There were no Forgotten Gods, N'Zursa declared, and 'Greftus did not know the way to Sanghelios. One day, perhaps, the path to the homeworld would be discovered—but until then, the colony must remain intact. The Refuge must tend its farms in the eco levels; it must cleanse its atmospheric filters; it must engage in such battle competitions as were decreed in the Combat Section; it must enhance travel between the various sections of the Refuge so that proper breeding could take place. Abandoning the colony was not an option. And so declaring, N'Zursa had sent guards to seize 'Greftus, had him ejected from an air lock into the void, in the manner of execution long favored by Ussan kaidons wishing to make an example of someone.

As punishment for your Failure of Clan Integrity, we submit you to the outer emptiness . . .

And so 'Greftus had died, flailing for air as he floated away, in sight of all Ussans who chose to witness.

Now it might be that he, Bal'Tol, must himself submit someone into the outer emptiness. He had ordered imprisonment before; he had ordered assaults on a band of criminals. But he had never ordered a public execution via air lock. It wasn't an honorable way to die.

Passing through the plaza outside the Hall of Strategy, Bal'Tol came upon the Homage to Enduring Bias. The remains of the machine, also called the Flying Voice, had been secured in a sphere of glass, where they floated, unlit, evincing no intelligence. It had remained thus for centuries. The glass was reverently cleaned every cycle, and the repairers peered at the remains of Enduring Bias, hoping that perhaps there might be a sign of life. Because Ussa 'Xellus, in his writings, had declared, *Though the Forerunner construct Enduring Bias has fallen silent, never assume that it will not speak again. It was damaged when the Primary Section was struck by a comet fragment, but it may be that it is slowly repairing itself inwardly. It may someday come to life to give voice once more . . .*

"My Kaidon," said C'tenz, coming from the Hall of Strategy. Bal'Tol saw the tension in C'tenz's hands—he had a way of clasping them in front of him when he was concerned about something. But C'tenz was a strong, intellectually vital Sangheili who had more responsibility than a youngling normally did. He wore ancient leather battle armor nearly everywhere, and one of the still-functioning burnblades in a scabbard on his hip. Bal'Tol knew of the whisperings that C'tenz must be his own offspring, because of the young Sangheili's quick elevation to second-in-command, but in truth, it was not so.

C'tenz glanced about and spoke in a lowered voice. "I was reluctant to interrupt your meditation but . . . I was just coming to find you. A new group of the 'Greftus Faction has been confirmed. And some of its members seem to have passed recently into the second phase."

Bal'Tol grunted acknowledgment. The phases of the Blood Sickness were simple. First there was a period of disorientation and malaise, easily misdiagnosed. Then the Blood Sick became querulous, paranoid, and prone to long, wildly inarticulate speeches, punctuated by howls of fury. 'Greftus had been deep in the second phase when he had gathered a considerable following, and was just into the third, most violent phase when he was arrested—he had murdered two patrollers as he was taken prisoner.

"It's curious," C'tenz said. "The pattern these Blood Sick fall into, when they are near one another. With everyone else, they're either quarrelsome or imperious. But with one another they seem to silently choose a leader—there are five of them, at least, who have clustered around this 'Kinsa. That is the only name he gives, but our records suggest he is Oska 'Meln. He claims to be sharing his body with the spirit of 'Greftus, who advises him in all things."

"How a rational Sangheili can believe such a thing . . ."

"Superstition is rife on the colony. And you know what Tirk says."

"Indeed. All too well." Tirk 'Surb was the head of Refuge Security, a descendant of the legendary Ernicka the Scar-Maker. "He grows more conservative and backward-looking by each cycle. I suppose he asserts we have not enough religious fervor?"

"Essentially, that is his litany."

"We certainly have more than enough religion." All Ussans were summoned to Intonement once a section turn. "But nothing is enough for Tirk. Still, call him here and we'll investigate this 'Kinsa. And as for the Blood Sickness, we must prune away the infection wherever we find it."

He felt strange, as he said it.

Limtee.

"We will need to act quickly, Kaidon. We need to let people know that 'Kinsa is no visionary—he is just a glib victim of the Sickness. What do we do with all those who fall sick?"

"We have discussed a place of isolation for the Blood Sick," Bal'tol mused, thinking again of Limtee. "It should be attempted. Then we can redouble our efforts to find a cure."

C'tenz gave a snort of skepticism. "Probably a hopeless effort. I'm very much afraid that the five latest of the afflicted must be put to death . . . That might quiet this lunacy."

In his hearts, Bal'Tol knew it was not so simple. There were many who quietly sympathized with 'Greftusian ideas. He did not wish to provoke an uprising.

There was a swelling tide of discontent accompanying the gradual breakdown of the colony. Bal'Tol knew their murmuring: *Our colony is falling slowly apart. Where is our true home? Where is Sanghelios?*

He wished he had an answer for them.

High Charity, near Delta Halo
The Office of the Prophet of Exquisite Devotion
2552 CE
The Age of Reclamation

"I prefer you to stand in my presence, Prophet of Clarity." So declared the Prophet of Exquisite Devotion as Zo Resken glided into the office in his antigrav chair.

Zo was surprised. This was unusual protocol. "May I use my belt?"

"Yes."

Zo switched on his belt and turned off the field of his chair, which settled to the floor. He then stood, trying his best to look respectful.

"You seem a little put off by the rule," Exquisite said. His face reflected the usual false benevolence, but his voice betrayed his irritation. The High Councilor was sitting in his scaled-down throne, near the place where the wall-windows of his office cornered. Beyond the glass, mist from the Hanging Gardens separated rainbows from sunlight. Further out, seen filmily through the atmospheric shield, the glory of Delta Halo's ever-winding silver band wheeled in a slow rotation; a sun hung like an eternal golden lamp in the black distance. "But you see, Prophet of Clarity, I outrank you considerably. Soon I shall outrank you even more. Standing before me shows respect. If we sit together, we are equals."

"As you wish it, Your Eminence," Zo said, gesturing, *Obedience is my pleasure.*

"So . . . I am telling you something in confidence because you will accompany me to a meeting of the High Council tomorrow, as my assistant. And you will find things are different. It suits me that you should show no surprise—and if anyone speaks of it, you should remark on the improvement."

"How will things be different, High Councilor?" Gesturing *If I may be allowed to respectfully ask.*

"In the coming cycle, Tartarus will be made military chief of the Covenant. The Elites within the Honor Guard will be replaced by Jiralhanae. Don't look so startled, Clarity. You should have seen this coming. The Jiralhanae are loyal to the High Prophet of Truth—and to myself—and most important, they are loyal to the Journey. The Elites have left us no recourse. As you know, the High Prophet of Regret is dead because of their incompetence. As you saw with your own eyes, the Supreme Commander of the Fleet of Particular Justice and his forces lost Alpha Halo to the humans. Elite failure mounted upon failure by their kind—they cannot be trusted. And there is more, evidence of dissidence among their ranks and uncertainty with regard to their allegiance. The remaining Hierarchs feel this activity cannot go without some reciprocity. The Sangheili will be used on the front lines of war. But they will be demoted."

Very carefully modulating his voice, Zo said, "Do you not think there is a risk of a rebellion as a result?"

"There is no time for such a thing, when we are so close to the Path's end—the Great Journey is nigh. But you need no further disclosure. Just do as I tell you. Now, go into that room, where you will find my requirement on the holodisplay. I am ordering a variety of necessary items. See that they are sent to me from the comptroller."

"With pleasure, High Councilor."

Zo went into the adjoining room, shaken, feeling Exquisite's eyes on his back as he went. Why was he here? Just to make arrangements with a comptroller? Or was there another reason?

He had heard a rumor that very day, in the gravity lift. That Exquisite Devotion was, quite secretly, a kind of enforcer for the High Prophet of Truth—this was partly true, given what Truth had already disclosed to him.

Zo himself had no enforcers, no protection. Exquisite Devotion had two Brutes stationed outside the office—and even more allies, at least among San'Shyuum.

But he did have something that Exquisite didn't have . . . friends among the Sangheili.

They might help him if he needed it. And if he gave them something first.

A warning. And one he was risking his life to give.

CHAPTER 16

Zo Resken, the Prophet of Clarity, scarcely noticed the herbal vapors pervading the warm fog around him in the Chancel of Recovery. The hemispherical room was located within a majestic tower at the center of the Holy City. He was waiting for someone, and was nervous about meeting him here. Sangheili were generally never found near a San'Shyuum healing facility, and certainly not within it. It was frowned on by both species—and the herbs were not cultivated for Sangheili biology. The improbable meeting place meant few would suspect him of sharing information with a Sangheili here. Zo had made certain he had this small chamber reserved.

The herbs vaporized here were all gentle salves for San'Shyuum skin and lung tissues, nothing narcotic . . . though he'd almost wished he had some of that sort. Perhaps it was insane, appointing to meet G'torik 'Klemmee here, with the possibility of the Prophet of Exquisite Devotion learning of the encounter.

Zo squinted through the blue-and-green fog, peering toward the entrance, coughing slightly as he waited. He wore a light robe and under it an antigrav belt, and affixed to the belt was a plasma pistol. As the door opened, rather suddenly, Zo nearly drew the weapon.

But it was G'torik, arriving alone and carefully closing the door behind him. The burly Sangheili commander pushed through the fog toward Zo, arms extended as if the healing murk was something solid to be moved out of the way. He coughed and blinked, clashing his mandibles to express chagrin. "Your Eminence, O Prophet of Clarity, you called and I have obeyed, but I wonder, with all that has happened, if it is wise . . ."

"Come," Zo said. "If anyone approaches, you simply came in to check on my welfare. Say that I asked you to look in on me. We are at war, and the battle lines have never been so close to High Charity . . ."

Clarity took a deep breath of the fumes, focused his eyes on G'torik, and then continued.

"While we are alone, let us not be Your Eminence and Commander 'Klemmee. We are merely Zo and G'torik." He had just been reading his ancestor's writings—Mken 'Scre'ah'ben's *Untold History of the Rending*—and had been struck by the informal way that Mken had spoken to Ussa 'Xellus in their private negotiation just before the destruction of the Refuge.

So many centuries had passed that much of the story of Mken, famed for having brought the Needful Maidens to High Charity from Janjur Qom and thus ensuring the healthy propagation of San'Shyuum, was smirched by uncertainty; records had been damaged and much of what was recorded could easily have been colored by poetic license. It all could be myth and nothing more.

But wiser historians like Zo Resken knew that much of the tale was true. Zo had strong substantiation, for he alone had discovered Mken's writings placed in an environmentally protected chest hidden in the family storage vaults on High Charity, important writings lost for all those dusty millennia. There were ruminations from Mken that might be considered heretical, so Zo had worked hard to keep them a secret. As far as he knew, he was the only one aware of their lengthy and explosive disclosure.

"And it is as Zo to G'torik that I tell you," Zo went on, "for some time now, the High Prophet of Truth has been . . . how shall I say this? He has been sharpening his knives. One of those 'knives' is the Prophet of Exquisite Devotion, to whom I am now practically enslaved. And now I fear that with the death of Regret, Truth is ready to make his move."

G'torik made a growling sound in his throat. "What sort of move?"

"It is as I feared, but sooner than I had supposed. He plans to push the Elites aside. Starting with the Honor Guard. They will be completely replaced by the Brutes. He will take control of the Covenant's military by way of the Jiralhanae . . . with Tartarus at its head, the Elites to become subservient to the Brutes."

For a moment, G'torik was stunned to silence.

"How has he kept this quiet? The Jiralhanae are no hand at keeping secrets. They bristle with hostility, and are open about their hatred for the Elites . . . but this? How could the Hierarchs support such a move against the Sangheili? The Covenant would surely collapse!"

"Truth is blaming Regret's guard for the High Prophet's death—the Elites were tasked to protect him. Their failure to do so has cost the Covenant a Hierarch. The High Council is not taking it lightly, nor did they take the catastrophe at Alpha Halo well, which as you know was laid at the feet of the Sangheili. And I do not think the Elites on the Council will be listened to, were they to raise their voices in dispute."

"*What?*"

"That is just a guess. I am quite certain, however, about the Honor Guard, and a general demotion of the Sangheili. Exquisite Devotion told me so personally."

"The High Council Elites, silenced? Such a thing would be unprecedented. And this idea of pushing all Elites from their posts, demoting them . . ."

"There's more—I have gathered much information since we last met. Truth has apparently sent special orders to Brutes stationed around Earth. Why would he be giving such orders, from here? That task is below him. And orders only for the Jiralhanae? He's also sent another fleet to Earth—again, not a job for his high station. Why? And according to data I've acquired from comptroller files, he has already placed a large order with the Sacred Promissory—the weapons armory here on High Charity—but he has kept this quiet even now. The order, as I understand it, is the mass production of traditional Brute weaponry. It appears to me at least that he is arming the Brutes to a perilous degree. I personally believe that he is setting a trap for your people—and reaching for full control of the Covenant."

"What you speak of will not be taken lightly by the Sangheili."

"I am aware, hence our counsel."

"What I mean to say is: if Truth takes such action, it will most certainly lead to war. *Civil* war, Zo!"

"I suspect Truth may welcome a civil war with the Elites; that is likely his very trap. He can then eliminate them quickly—and consolidate his strength with the Brutes . . ."

"This validates my own news. Truth gave orders to assault the temple before any news of Regret's death became known. Our ships fired down onto the Sacred Ring after the Demon made his approach, but the Honor Guards within the temple had almost no chance to defend Regret—he was already marked, and all help that could have been afforded him was restrained. I have confirmed it—my uncle had word from a captain on one of the Phantoms. Truth did pull out the reinforcements."

"So it's true . . ." Zo now suspected that Truth had little interest in sharing power with the other Hierarchs. He wondered just how far Truth would go before the activation of Halo and the commencement of the Great Journey. Would he even strike at the High Prophet of Mercy?

"This is insanity. The High Council will not stand for this."

"Listen to me, G'torik—do not inform *everyone* of this. Choose specific Sangheili in the right positions, those who can keep their mandibles shut, lest your people lose the advantage of surprise if news gets back to the Hierarchs. Understand that you cannot trust the High Prophet of Truth any longer. And beware the Prophet of Exquisite Devotion. It will be only a short time now."

G'torik snorted. "The *High Prophet of Truth*. The *Prophet of Exquisite Devotion*. These titles they bestow upon themselves bring shame to the Covenant. They have no loyalty to the Writ."

"There is, of course, another complicating factor: the Flood."

The Flood—the startling, gruesome outpouring of ancient parasitical creatures accidentally liberated from the containment vaults in the first Sacred Ring, Alpha Halo. They'd spread quickly, infecting any within their grasp and incorporating whatever sentient life they came upon. The Flood seemed mindless as individuals yet guided by some mysterious, overarching intelligence. The Flood had been presumed to be obliterated when Alpha Halo was torn apart by the Demon, but recent reports from the surface of Delta Halo indicated that the parasite had already been released from its containment by the time Regret's forces had first arrived. Now it was causing havoc on the surface and had complicated all efforts to acquire Delta Halo's activation key, the fabled Sacred Icon.

G'torik scratched a mandible in puzzlement. "The Flood—the parasites were contained for a time."

"The Flood is a great disruption—at least now, Truth knows this. It may well aid him if he intends to replace the Elites, even at the risk of civil war. He'll no doubt use it to his advantage somehow."

G'torik waited before taking in his next breath, as the dark weight of realization took hold. Then at last he asked, "Zo—I must know. Do you have some . . . some agenda of your own in telling me all this?"

"Have you not learned to trust me?"

"Of all the San'Shyuum I have ever known, you were the only one who troubled to know my people, beyond what was necessary for the purposes of the Covenant. You do see us as we are, as a people. As *souls*. I believe that. But speaking of all this surely must be a great risk for you. Why do you take that risk?"

Zo was taken aback. It had not occurred to him to question his own motives. He supposed that on some level, his ambition did enter into this. If, as he suspected, the High Prophet of Truth was going to manipulate the Jiralhanae to seize control over the Covenant, then Zo might have a corresponding influence over the Elites. Who knew what that could lead to if the Elites were triumphant?

But perhaps more than anything else, his taking this risk was all about the inner revulsion he felt for Truth's schemes, and of course, for Tartarus.

Privately, the Prophet of Clarity had begun to question the Great Journey, though he had long practice at pretending to be a zealot. In truth, he respected the Forerunners and their astounding relics, but it did little for his faith when he saw the treachery of those who called themselves High Prophets, those who were tasked with protecting that ancient, superlative knowledge. If Truth was capable of such schemes in the very light of a Holy Ring, then what parts of the Covenant's own origin might also be false?

But the Covenant and High Charity—this was all he'd ever known, it was all *any* of its members had ever known.

And it seemed to him that Truth was putting them all in grave danger, with or without the consummation of the Great Journey. If civil war took hold, would such a thing even be possible?

"G'torik," Zo said at last, "I am risking myself telling you all this, because I do not think San'Shyuum can long survive without your people. None of us can survive the Flood and the humans without unity."

"So be it. Some of us will be on guard, and we will make the necessary contingency plans, as you advise."

Delta Halo
Control Room
2552 CE
The Age of Reclamation

Stepping off the Phantom's gravity lift with the others, G'torik gazed up in awe at the Chamber of Consecration—Delta Halo's immense control center. Fittingly, it was more like a temple in its shape, at least on the exterior, than some module used for controlling a mechanism. Ornate walls of silvery-gray alloy converged on an intricately configured dome from which sprang a tower . . . the focal point of the energies that would activate the Halo, beginning the purification that would open the doorway to the Great Journey itself.

He had already been awestruck several times on this visit to the Sacred Ring. First, arriving on the cruiser, G'torik had seen the Halo itself, or a portion of it, from space—it seemed impossible to witness the entire Sacred Ring with the naked eye. Its immense size held aloft in orbit around a blue gas giant, a perfect circle—and within its band, the surface of a world. Surely no ordinary mortal could have created such a thing. He had never been, inwardly, a particularly pious Sangheili, but just looking at the Halo in the viewport gave G'torik a shudder of religious wonder.

As they'd gotten closer, he could make out the clouds in filaments and broader strokes of white, over the land within the ring; the marbling clouds parted in places to reveal water, structures, hills and valleys—the handiwork of the gods. Astounding.

Then he had been summoned to the purpose that had brought him here, as guardian for High Councilor Torg 'Gransamee. It was not normal for an Elite of his stature to be called to protect a High Councilor—traditionally a ceremonial role reserved for the Honor Guards. But the Jiralhanae had now become Honor Guards, and these Elites chose not to employ them.

Things were anything but normal, for the original Sangheili Honor Guard was no more.

Since his alarming conversation with Zo, ominous clouds had gathered. Citing the death of Regret and the colossal failure that took place at the first Sacred Ring as evidence, the High Prophets of Truth and Mercy publicly handed the role of Honor Guard to the Jiralhanae, a unilateral move without the approval of the Council. In response, some Sangheili within the High Council threatened to resign, while others saw fit to come here to the Ring and prepare the Chamber of Consecration for the Sacred Icon. Still, there was a danger that the High Prophet of Truth might make the final move that Zo had foreseen, with civil war to erupt at any moment.

And there was the Flood.

G'torik had watched on remote viewscreen as the Flood had been encountered in the quarantine zone, the vast, frigid territory between the Ring's massive containment walls and the Sacred Icon's central housing—a location on this Halo the Covenant had designated as the Repository of Fate. The Icon was the key to activating Halo. Without it, the Ring could not achieve the purpose for which it was designed. Only hours ago, the Hierarchs had sent a small team to retrieve it, but there had been no reports since then. Did they perish in the sweeping depredation of the Flood?

G'torik knew that once the Sacred Icon was put into play, activating the Halo at the control room, all that was impure would be burned away—which would surely include the parasite—and faithful Covenant believers would be transported to the realm of the divine. This very act could stave off the potential war to come Zo had warned about.

For a moment, G'torik wondered what that meant—*faithful Covenant believers.*

Now, striding just behind Torg 'Gransamee, who in armored finery and towering headpiece led a column of Sangheili High Councilors and a handful of other Elites who had once served as Honor Guards, up to the Chamber of Consecration. G'torik felt a flush of shame as he thought of his own doubts—and, yes, they still troubled him. Was this impossible creation, the Halo, not proof of the reality of the Great Journey? So the Prophets insisted.

They trooped along a bridge arching over a large body of water near a series of canyons—the control center stood on a single giant parapet, with large doors opening to a narrow corridor, an antechamber, and eventually the central chamber of the control room, where more bridgelike structures converged on the control board itself. There, the Sacred Icon would be applied, activating the Halo, and the Great Journey would finally commence.

Torg 'Gransamee looked around in puzzlement. "Where are the San'Shyuum, G'torik?" he muttered. "They were to be here at the same time for the activation ceremony . . ."

G'torik had been wondering the same thing. "I had thought you might know."

"It is the San'Shyuum who have the key, the Sacred Icon— they claimed that Tartarus acquired it, and the others who went with him were lost to the Flood. They may have been delayed. We will wait—we have waited centuries, as a people, for this moment, after all . . ."

They waited a good deal longer, murmuring, stealing reverent looks at the control panel. G'torik all the while wondered if that tingling he felt at the back of his neck was the consequence of the regard of the gods. Would they not be here, however invisible— watching?

At last they heard the clomping of boots.

"Look. There are the Jiralhanae," said Torg, pointing at the large forcenumber of Brutes marching over yet another peripheral bridge.

G'torik didn't like this at all. The Brutes seemed overarmed for the occasion. "So many of them. Why? And where are the San'Shyuum Councilors . . ." His voice trailed off as he saw that some of the Jiralhanae were heavily armed with bulky ballistic weapons of their own kind, ones he'd only rarely seen before— might these be the weapons Zo spoke of? The new ones secretly ordered by the High Prophet of Truth? The Brutes were being led by a close associate of Tartarus, a captain called Melchus, the chieftain's thick-chested, brown-furred second-in-command, carrying an imposing gravity hammer somewhat smaller than the Fist of Rukt, though likely just as threatening.

And there were no San'Shyuum to be seen at all. There was no High Prophet of Mercy. No High Prophet of Truth.

"This must be treachery," G'torik said under his breath.

"Nonsense," Torg sputtered. "They would not conceive of such a thing in this holy place. The Prophets must be—"

But then Melchus roared—and charged the Elite Councilors.

The other Jiralhanae who accompanied him took this as a sign and flew forward in concert, converging on the outnumbered Sangheili.

The battle quickly came to a fever pitch. The two groups exchanged shots in the open before violently colliding at the center of the bridge, the Jiralhanae burning, blistering, smashing with shock waves—killing before the Councilors could reach them with their energy swords. Other Elites managed only light damage with plasma rifles and needlers, while the Brutes' double-bladed carbines fired spikes that breached the Sangheili's energy shielding and tore into exposed flesh. The Brutes had the element of surprise, forcing the Elites backward against the control mechanism near the sheer drop to the control room floor far below. The Sangheili had come here on a spiritual mission and were unprepared for this turn of events—with no cover and no place to turn.

Melchus reached two brave Elites who rushed to meet him, their crystalline-pink needler rounds glancing off the Brute's thick shoulder plates. Melchus slammed his powerful gravity hammer down on one guard, turning him to exploding flesh and bones; the other was knocked off his feet by the impact of the weapon on the walkway, the gravitational wave launching him off the bridge. Another Elite came at Melchus with an energy sword, swinging it viciously. The Jiralhanae captain sidestepped the blade with surprising speed for his bulk, and slammed his hammer into the attacker's midsection, throwing the broken body into the air. The guard was dead before he hit the ground.

"Get behind me, Uncle!" G'torik shouted. He sprinted toward Melchus, hoping that if he could take down the Brute captain, then the Jiralhanae, leaderless, might be confused enough to give the Sangheili Councilors a path through, and perhaps a sorely needed advantage. If he could get close enough, jam his rifle into the Brute captain's mouth, he might do it . . .

Melchus was howling with glee and bloodlust, dispatching another Sangheili guard who'd fallen, wounded, under a barrage of spikes. The guard was splashed into nothingness by the Jiralhanae as the air resounded with shouts of pain and fury and the sizzling, cracking sounds of the weapons, the echoing thunder of war hammers.

Maddened with fury, G'torik heard himself shout, "Melchus! Face me and die, traitor!"

He was almost upon the Jiralhanae captain. He poised the plasma rifle as Melchus started to turn toward him—

But almost as if swiping at some tiny flying pest, Melchus swung the hammer to swat the plasma rifle, and it shattered like a thing of thin glass in G'torik's hands. The smashed rifle exploded in an expanding bubble of blue plasma, which knocked G'torik backward so that he skidded over the smooth surface of the bridge, fetching up against the rail.

Stunned, G'torik fumbled around for another weapon. His hand closed on the dropped hilt of the energy sword; he then saw another, still in a dead Elite's hand. He got dizzily to his feet and snatched up that one, too, activating both swords, a plasma blade in each grip. Their translucent blue-white blades crackled into being, charged with electrons flowing through magnetically shaped streams of superheated plasma that narrowed into two razor-sharp cutting edges.

G'torik looked around and saw that nearly all the High Councilors were dead, many of them shattered, crushed unrecognizably. Some of the wounded Elites were still being shot up by the snarling Jiralhanae. Others were summarily tossed off the balcony onto the distant floor below. The Sangheili had fought valiantly and only about half the Brutes remained. But the trend of the fight was obvious.

Why didn't we bring more protection?

And where is my uncle?

"Torg 'Gransamee!" G'torik shouted. "Torg!" Then smoke from burning flesh wafted away and he saw it—Melchus standing over his unarmed uncle. The brute captain was crushing Torg 'Gransamee's throat under his enormous, hooflike two-toed boot.

And Melchus was laughing as G'torik's uncle gurgled and died.

"Traitor!" G'torik shrieked, rushing at Melchus. "Monster!"

This time he got close enough to slash the captain with both swords—the Brute's shoulder plates partly saved him, but G'torik managed to cut Melchus's ribs, slashing to the bone, making him roar in pain. The wound gave off smoke, and a spurt of the Jiralhanae's blood coursed past the blade—while the only other surviving Sangheili guard was coming at Melchus from another side, distracting him with an appropriated spike rifle.

Far from mortally wounded, Melchus leapt back from the energy blade and slammed his hammer down on the other, closer Elite. The Sangheili guardian flew to pieces.

Frustrated to the point of madness, G'torik rushed in, both his blades flashing, one after another slashing down at Melchus. The

Brute captain ably blocked the slashes with the handle of his hammer, snarling, "You will die like the others, weakling!" The energy swords spat sparks as G'torik struck again and again, looking for an opening.

Melchus jumped back, trying to get room to swing the hammer. G'torik braced to rush him, but Melchus was faster than G'torik expected. He swung the enormous hammer in a blur of speed, and G'torik just managed to duck it, a split second away from having his head disintegrate into a cloud of vaporized flesh and bone. G'torik threw himself aside, slashing at Melchus's booted ankle, drawing blood but not cutting deeply.

"Your death approaches! Beg for mercy, but it will not be granted!" Melchus bellowed, rushing at G'torik.

G'torik sidestepped and let Melchus by, slashing at the Brute as he thundered past. He drew blood again, cutting deeper into the Jiralhanae's side.

Melchus roared in pain and fury, and spun about.

G'torik readied himself to try the tactic again. He was, at least, faster than Melchus.

Melchus raised his hammer as if about to charge, but made a quick adjustment on it instead. Grinning nastily, Melchus slammed the gravity hammer down so hard that it blew debris from the battle into the air.

It was as if a giant invisible hand slapped at G'torik. He felt himself spinning through the air with an irresistible gravitational-force shock wave. The interior of the control room whirled and blurred—and he kept flying, strangely far . . .

He realized he'd been knocked off the bridge, his fall eventually broken by the heap of bodies beneath him.

G'torik lay injured and stunned, and darkness soon closed in. The last thing he heard was Melchus laughing.

High Charity
The Hanging Gardens, Pod of Esthetic Musing
2552 CE
The Age of Reclamation

"The Elites have failed to protect the Prophets!" So boomed the voice of the High Prophet of Truth from the announcement system. A couple of diminutive Unggoy, faces hidden in their methane breathing masks, stopped to listen to his words, as if in rapture.

Inspired by Mken 'Scre'ah'ben's example, Zo Resken had been attempting to walk through one of the Holy City's many Hanging Gardens without antigrav belt or chair. He had donned the belt, but it was dialed to almost no support, and though the gravity on High Charity was lower than what would have been considered normal on the homeworld of Janjur Qom, he was finding it hard going. Puffing, he stopped between two low, grassy hills, to listen to the High Prophet's announcement, feeling a chill at the booming voice, despite the heat of exertion.

"Let no warrior forget his oath. Thou, in faith shall keep us safe, whilst we find the Path! With my blessing, the Jiralhanae now lead our fleets! They ask for your allegiance, and you shall give it!"

The little Unggoy skipped excitedly. A passing Kig-Yar, who probably hadn't been paying much attention to the announcement, scuttled irritably onward, as if spurred by Truth's voice.

Let no warrior forget his oath. "So it has begun," Zo murmured, turning away from the happily scampering Unggoy. "And where will it go . . ."

Now what am I to do? Zo wondered, switching on his antigrav belt and hurrying toward the exit. It was clear now that the rebellion had already begun—word of skirmishes on High Charity and even the surface of Delta Halo had reached Clarity. The

Elites had at last left the Covenant. Even some Mgalekgolo were said to have sided with them, though others remained loyal to the Covenant. Zo suspected that the changing of the guard had been implemented and the Elites responded in force. It was just as he had discussed with G'torik.

The choice was now before him: Zo could either remain loyal to Truth and Exquisite, or openly turn against them. The High Prophet of Truth was a Hierarch, and he held what was left of the Covenant in his hand, but he knew the difference between obeisance to evil and noble devotion. Truth was not on the side of nobility.

It was rumored about Delta Halo that it would be activated soon—but that was before, when the Covenant wasn't tearing itself apart at the seams. Zo had received word that the Elite High Councilors had gone on before the Prophets to prepare the chamber for the consecration of the Sacred Icon, but according to the displays set about High Charity, Tartarus had already retrieved the Icon and given it to the High Prophet of Truth personally. What had remained of the Elite Councilors? Were they caught up in the carnage of this great schism?

A large, gray, metal-gloved hand slapped painfully down on Zo's shoulder. "Prophet of Clarity," rumbled the Jiralhanae. "You will come with me."

Zo turned around angrily, but all words of defiance died on his lips as he saw the Mgalekgolo bond brothers standing behind the Jiralhanae captain. The giant hulking Hunters, equipped with enormous weapons and shields, said nothing—they never needed to speak. They were all brooding antagonism, which communicated itself quite effectively. Clearly these were loyal to the High Prophet of Truth.

"Prophet of Clarity, the Prophet of Exquisite Devotion wishes to discuss certain matters with you immediately," declared the Brute. "This is all I know. However, if you don't come with me willingly, I am content to let the Hunters bring you by force. You know well enough of their kind: Hunters are not gentle."

Zo glanced at the Hunters.

"May I get my chair first?"

"If it is nearby."

Zo cleared his throat. "So, then. Let us go and see what I can do for his holiness the Prophet of Exquisite Devotion."

CHAPTER 17

The Refuge, the Ussan Colony
Section Five
2552 CE
The Age of Reclamation

Escorted by Tirk 'Surb, the priest Tup'Quk, and six heavily armed protectors, Bal'Tol and C'tenz were walking side by side through the sculpture garden in the plaza outside the Hall of the Godminds on Sublevel Four. They were looking for the Blood Sick who clustered about 'Kinsa. Tup'Quk, a Sangheili bent with age, bristling with the odd hairs the very old sometimes sprouted from various crevices, came shuffling slowly, the ceremonial jewelry jingling from his pierced mandibles. He wore a robe sewn of fragments of holy objects, shiny cloth, and the skin of *glebos*, a small furred animal that hopped about in the eco levels.

So far Bal'Tol and the others had seen only a few softly chanting pilgrims traipsing for the Hall of Godminds, wending in the sacred pattern between the statues. The sculpture garden included three-dimensional images of the legendary Ussa 'Xellus and Sooln; nearby were Tersa and his warrior mate, Lnur; there were portrayals of Sanghelios held in Ussa's protective arms; there was an image of the spherical form of the Refuge, bursting apart, its dividing sections, in the sculpture, held in place by transparent wires; sculptures of Ussa's son and grandson; there were mythologically posed renderings of the gods; sculptures of Ernicka the Scar-Maker and others slashing apart the slithering semisaurian rendering of Salus 'Crolon; images of popular Combat Section warriors grappling in floatfight.

They reached the far side of the sculpture garden and Bal'Tol looked through the entry to the wall, a high archway painted with figures from myth, where pilgrims sat, communing with the changing geometrical forms in the great chamber. They intoned the names of each figure, as given to them by the priests. *What would Ussa 'Xellus think of all this? Bal'Tol wondered.*

Within that hall, three-dimensional translucent forms quivered, sometimes chimed, and seemed to whisper without words. Ussa's records suggested the Hall was in fact a device for observation and communication within the original shield world. It required the Flying Voice to fully activate it, and Enduring Bias was still silent and perhaps defunct. The Hall of Godminds was held in reverence; this name for it had been handed down for generations. Some went there to pray to the gods. It had its own priest, as did the Combat Section and the Place of Blessed Passing.

Privately, Bal'Tol regarded all this as just so much accreted superstition; he assumed a cosmic reality, a cosmic mind. He had glimpsed it, contemplating the dance of chaos in meditation. But it was no good talking of such things; the Clans needed to believe in their gods and priests. Even Ussa 'Xellus had believed, once upon a time, in the gods, the divinity of the Forerunners, and had believed the relics of the Forerunners sacred. But Bal'Tol was his own Sangheili; he believed what he chose, at least privately. Publicly, he believed in all the gods who'd come to haunt the minds of the colony since Ussa's death: the Flying Voice; Ziggur, who had been a nearly forgotten nature spirit from old Sanghelios, and was said to inhabit the gardens of the eco level; Moraphant, who carried spirits of the dead from the colony to the Sacred Ring, where they would await the bridge of light that would take them someday to the primal paradise that was Sanghelios; the lower spirits who animated the machinery of the colony and inspired the repairers' guild; Forerunner Sun and his consort, Forerunner Moon, who governed the other gods . . .

Forerunner Sun and Moon were the primary focal point of worship now in the Refuge. It had not been so for the Sangheili ancients—they had primarily worshipped the sacred artifacts and those who made them.

Bal'Tol turned to Tup'Quk as the old priest hissed, "Look. There are your defilers!" He pointed.

In the corner of the statue garden, where the wall that housed the entry to the Hall of the Godminds cornered with the plaza's wall, eight Sangheili were sitting cross-legged on the floor, listening to 'Kinsa. One of the rapt listeners, Bal'Tol saw, was a floatfight hero, Norzessa.

"Do you see who that is, there on the right?" C'tenz whispered.

"Yes," Bal'Tol muttered. "Most disturbing."

Norzessa was quite possibly the most adored of the floatfight heroes. Bal'Tol had himself given Norzessa the Relic Medal to wear for one swing about the sun; he had been impressed by Norzessa's energy and resourcefulness in the zero-gravity arena.

The entire Combat Section possessed no gravity—several centuries earlier, its artificial gravity nodes had collapsed on themselves, and the section, at the time mostly a storage area, became a chaos of floating crates, machines, and frightened workers. On every visit to Combat Section, Bal'Tol had wondered what would happen to the colony if all the artificial gravity failed in the other sections. How long would they survive in zero gravity? Many of the machines would stop working, their mechanics no longer meaningful. Hysteria and mass panic would be the result. And then would come clan fighting, always something ready to break out, and much bloodshed . . .

But so far no other gravitational node panels had failed, and the Combat Section alone was gravity-free. It had become a place where Ussans could exercise their thirst for combat, without butchering one another—it was their site for athletic competition. A violent competition to be sure, but slaughter was usually avoided.

As a childling and then a youngling, Bal'Tol had gone there, between scheduled floatfight combat competition and practiced free-fall acrobatics. He'd broken his left arm that way once, damaging nerves, and that had ended his dreams of becoming a floatfight competitive hero; his arm had lost some of its responsiveness with the injury.

"Come, Tup'Quk, we'll see what is being spoken, and how much defilement is at hand," said the kaidon.

The patrollers closed around Bal'Tol as he approached 'Kinsa and his group, but Bal'Tol gestured for them to move aside. Close by him was C'tenz, who had a hand on the hilt of his sheathed burnblade; he could hear old Tup'Quk huffing along behind him, taking tiny steps, breathing hard. A good many of the colony's medical resources had been used up, and not enough new medicaments were being made. The art had been partly lost. The elderly suffered for it, and the young were too few.

"The corrosion is everywhere," 'Kinsa was saying. "It is the wrath of the Forgotten Gods!" He was a brutish Sangheili with wide-set mandibles and a heavy forehead. There were cryptic symbols inscribed into the skin of his bare arms. He wore a homemade cuirass of sewn-together pieces of metal from old broken machinery—countless connective bits from the Disassembly floated around the sections, held for centuries by gravitation. Sometimes small fragments of it were scavenged by shuttle pilots and bartered as keepsakes of the Forerunners.

On 'Kinsa's head was an old, dented copper-colored helmet. He jabbed his hands, right and left, with stabbing motions to emphasize the words as he spoke. "The corrosion spreads from our souls into the very walls! The drinkfluid generators are failing, one by one; the atmosphere cleansers will be next. Why did it all work for centuries and suddenly came this cascade of failure? Why? I'll tell you! Because of Sangheili like him!"

He jabbed an accusing finger directly at the kaidon. 'Kinsa's listeners turned, startled, and saw Bal'Tol and his retinue. Two of them quickly rose and edged away.

Norzessa, however, stayed where he was, glaring at the priest, if that was his intent—his face was so scarred by floatfight battle it was difficult to tell.

"The true spirits of this place are displeased with us," 'Kinsa snarled. "Punishing us for losing the ancient way back to Sanghelios!"

Bal'Tol saw it then—the webs of scarlet pulsing on 'Kinsa's face and hands. It showed up when the third-phase excitement came upon the Blood Sick.

"You are defilers of this sacred place!" Tup'Quk quavered from behind two heavily armed protectors. "Defilers!" As he spoke, the ornaments on his jawbones jingled furiously. "Go to your homes and pray for forgiveness!"

"Defilers, you say?" 'Kinsa spat. "Of what is already *hopelessly* defiled? The Forgotten Gods refuse to be erased! They have told me the way; we shall take the vessels you hide away in Primary! We shall take them and all our people to Sanghelios."

"First of all," said C'tenz, "the way to Sanghelios is lost to us. We no longer have that data. The way was erased from the memory devices in the vessels—perhaps Ussa 'Xellus did that on purpose, after the betrayal of Salus 'Crolon. Second, there is not enough room on those ships for everyone. And third, we are not sure they will fly. In fact—I'm sure they wouldn't, since like so much else, they've had many parts cannibalized—"

"Cannibals!" raved 'Kinsa. "You are the cannibals! You are like the Blue Mandibles of Section Two!"

It was long since Bal'Tol had thought about the Blue Mandibles, perhaps because it was a profoundly unpleasant memory. The dark blue blood of Sangheili had stained the mandibles of a savage group that had overrun parts of Section Two cycles before, during a food shortage. There had been a failure of irrigation systems on the eco level, a die-off of some of the flora, simultaneous with a breakdown of the protein synthesizer. A band led by a Blood Sick marauder had commenced feeding on "lesser" Ussans. Bal'Tol had himself led troops against them, and the Blue Mandibles had been overrun and slaughtered.

"We are none of us cannibals," said Bal'Tol. He was speaking more to the followers of 'Kinsa than to the Sangheili himself. "We eat the same foodstuff you do, Oska 'Meln."

"*What did you call me?*" 'Kinsa's hands balled into shaking fists. "Liar! *I am 'Kinsa!* I am the voice of 'Greftus! And through 'Greftus, the voice of Forerunner Sun! His solar radiance will burn this place clean!"

"I am allowing you an opportunity to surrender, whoever you may think you are," Bal'Tol said. "I plan a special place of isolation for people with your sickness. I am inclined to offer it, until such time as a cure can be found."

"Sickness? It is *you* who have the sickness!"

"Careful, you fool!" C'tenz shouted. "You have been offered a chance for life!"

Now Norzessa sprang to his feet, facing the deputation, and then half squatted as if about to spring. He, too, wore a scrap metal cuirass across his chest. "You will not touch 'Kinsa! He alone knows the way to Sanghelios! Death to anyone who approaches him!" One of his hands went to the handle of a long curving knife in his belt—a floatfighter's "quartermoon" blade, not very different from the ancient curveblade of Sanghelios.

Tirk 'Surb then stepped in front of the kaidon, a burnblade suddenly in one hand and a plasma pistol in the other. "Stay back! You are *all* under arrest! I have heard seditious talk here! Talk of burning the colony? That is enough for me!"

The patrollers had their weapons at the ready now, lined up in front of 'Kinsa's followers.

There were frightened faces, along with those savagely defiant. But Norzessa knew no fear. "'Kinsa is the voice of the gods!" he shouted. He drew his quartermoon blade and spun it in his hand so fast it looked like a whirling ball of edges.

What really alarmed Bal'Tol, however, was the appearance of cold confidence now on 'Kinsa's face. And the fact that 'Kinsa was looking behind the deputation.

Bal'Tol turned and saw fifteen Sangheili coming through the door from the corridor, lined up, all wearing similar scrap cuirasses that seemed the badge of 'Kinsa's followers. Some had pierced mandibles shining with spurlike adornments, the backs of their hands bristling with metal spikes. They carried homemade weapons known as mec-missilers—crossbowlike constructions that fired short, razor-sharp bolts, or spears. Each weapon had a rack of four bolts, made of hammered light metal and wood from the eco level, set to fall into firing position.

Unexpected. There are far more of them than we surmised, Bal'Tol thought gloomily.

Tirk 'Surb and the others were turning about now as well, seeing they were caught between enemies. "What is this treachery?" Tirk sputtered.

"And did you suppose," grated 'Kinsa, "that we do not know who arrives in a shuttle from Primary Section? We were informed, and we have prepared! The only prisoners here will be you."

"Dishonorable cowards!" roared Tirk, and he charged at this new group of fighters, the other patrollers right behind him. And forgetting, perhaps, about Norzessa, who took his cue to rush Bal'Tol and C'tenz.

The Sangheili with the mec-missilers were surprised by the suddenness and boldness of Tirk's attack, and hesitantly stepped back, only one of them loosing a bolt that flashed over Tirk's shoulder.

Tirk was already firing his pistol, almost point-blank into the face of one of the enemies. His target shrieked and staggered, dropping his weapon, as Tirk slashed into the one beside him with his burnblade. One of the patrollers bellowed in pain, going down with a mec-missile bolt in his abdomen; the others were then among the enemy fighters, furiously battering, slashing, firing sidearms.

A mec-missile caught the elderly Tup'Quk in his mouth as he opened it to shout, the imprecation never to be voiced. He fell back, dead, the shaft jutting from the back of his head.

Bal'Tol spoke into a communicator on his wrist, sending it out wide. "This is the kaidon, outside the Hall of Godminds, we're under attack—" There was no time for more, and he spun around, his hearts feeling as if they were banging against each other as he witnessed C'tenz grappling with Norzessa, his friend struggling to keep the quartermoon blade away—even as C'tenz's burnblade was carving its way into Norzessa's side. The floatfighter seemed to ignore the searing blade, snapping at C'tenz now with his mandibles.

Acting instinctively, Bal'Tol drew his own sword, the weapon for the most part ceremonial, and drove it at Norzessa's side.

The floatfighter broke loose from the clinch as the second blade came at him and shoved C'tenz away. C'tenz stumbled into Bal'Tol—inadvertently saving his life. A mec-missiler's bolt hissed by Bal'Tol's head so close he felt the friction of its passing.

One of the patrollers had rushed to protect Bal'Tol and put himself between the kaidon and the floatfighter. It was an act of courage and a tragic one, given Norzessa's reputation. Almost instantly the protector's head flew from his shoulders, trailing dark blue blood, as Norzessa used his quartermoon blade with masterly skill.

Bal'Tol rushed in, furious now, and struck at Norzessa before he quite had the quartermoon blade back in play, and drove his long light ceremonial sword through the floatfighter's throat, twisting it to make sure he took his enemy down.

To his amazement, Norzessa kept fighting, slashing with his curved blade, barely missing as C'tenz pulled Bal'Tol out of the weapon's way. Bal'Tol lost his grip on the bloodstained sword and Norzessa came, gargling lifeblood, but his eyes alight, with the kaidon's blade still stuck to the hilt through his throat.

C'tenz struck hard at Norzessa's blade arm and cut through his wrist, just above the armor. The sword and severed hand fell, and Norzessa, spitting thick blue-purplish blood, went to his knees. C'tenz stabbed him twice more, cursing him, and Norzessa fell, convulsing, as Bal'Tol turned and saw that Tirk 'Surb was also down . . . two razor-sharp bolts in him, one just above the breastbone, one in the groin. The old warrior was dying. Bal'Tol instinctively sidestepped as a bolt came his way . . . but not quite far enough, as the mec-missile caught him, low on the right side, penetrating and passing through.

Wrenched with pain, Bal'Tol searched for a weapon—and looked for 'Kinsa. Where was he? Where had he gone? If they could kill 'Kinsa . . .

He threw himself flat as another short spear zipped at him, flying over his head. He saw a patroller slashing at the mec-missiler—

A shrill trilling cut through the battle shouts and cries of pain—it came from the hallway entrance of the sculpture garden.

Bal'Tol looked up to see 'Kinsa standing at the entrance, blowing in a long whistle of some kind, made from scrap tubing. He lowered the whistle and shouted, "Troops are arriving!"

There was a contingent of patrollers at the shuttle bay. That must be them—it would take time to get others from the other sections.

There were eight of 'Kinsa's fighters left alive, along with 'Kinsa himself, calling orders to them. Launching a few more of their kinetic bolts, they then rushed out, under fire from the two surviving patrollers. They made it to 'Kinsa, and followed him, running into the hall.

"My Kaidon!" C'tenz said, his voice choking, helping Bal'Tol to his feet. "Are you badly hurt? You bleed!"

Bal'Tol clutched the injury, felt blood pumping between his fingers. "It is not a mortal wound. It passed right through, just under the skin—I'll surely survive. But we've lost Tirk and these others. A fine battle was fought. Honor shone brightly here, C'tenz. But make no mistake. This was also a tragedy. More than you could possibly realize."

High Charity
Trial Court for Tools of Conquest
Gravitational Refinement
2552 CE
The Age of Reclamation

Zo Resken, the Prophet of Clarity, had been fairly certain he could handle this little interlocution with the Prophet of Exquisite Devotion. It was odd, though, that he had been brought here to the Trial Court, a weapon-testing facility, where he'd never been before. Few were permitted.

Now that two Brutes squatted to either side of him, disabling his weaponry, ripping out wires with the blades attached to their spike rifles, he wished he hadn't asked for the damned chair. Within it, he had stored Mken 'Scre'ah'ben's own records, treasures from his ancestor. In his most recent study of them, Zo had noticed hints of something he'd never before seen in prior observation, indications that some within the Ussan Refuge might have survived. He hoped the records were unmolested by the Brutes' violence, but right now he had little certainty.

"Really, isn't that quite enough damage to my chair?" he asked sharply. "I must protest. You'll interfere with its modulator."

"Yes, yes, quite enough, he is disarmed now," said Exquisite Devotion, approaching in his own antigrav throne. They were in a hallway lit by a harsh overbright light from the viewing window. Light reflected from the golden fluting of his collar. The holograph of the Sacred Ring over his headpiece seemed to dim, as if ashamed.

Zo Resken and Exquisite Devotion were not alone—they were under the watchful eyes of two bobbing surveillance drones drifting about overhead; guarding Exquisite were four Jiralhanae, including the one who'd brought him, and the two accompanying Mgalekgolo who stood at times either inert or twitching in the background, patiently awaiting an order to spring violently forward.

To Zo's left was a broad, high pane of glass in a metal frame, and beyond it a large white room, not quite a cube. Several Sangheili waited sullenly in the white room. At the room's farther wall was a heavily reinforced blue-metal door. In the white room's floor, at short regular intervals, were patterns of red dots, which looked to Zo's inexperienced eye like gravitational nodes. "Look now, upon the chamber of Gravitational Refinement," said Exquisite silkily, gesturing at the window into the white-walled room, as the door in the back of it opened. "Do you recognize any of those Sangheili?"

Zo knew them all. There was Duru 'Scoahamee, an Elite High Councilor—or formerly, before the recent Jiralhanae takeover—a tall Sangheili with a noble brow and, typically, clasped mandibles. He wore armor but no helmet, and was unarmed. Behind him were two others, K'hurk 'Bornisamee and Tilik 'Bornisamee. K'hurk and Duru were, until that very day, Elite High Councilors.

Tilik had always been high-spirited. Now he looked despairing and haunted.

"I know them," said the Prophet of Clarity with a creeping feeling of dread.

Melchus, the chief captain of Tartarus's own Brutes, came into the chamber behind the Elites, carrying a very large unrecognizable weapon. Was that the one being tested here?

As it happened, the entire room holding the Sangheili was part of the test.

"Much has happened," Exquisite said, "that, I would assume, you do not know about. Or we wouldn't have spotted you strolling about in the gardens. A large group of Elite High Councilors, particularly those who opposed the replacement of the Honor Guards with Jiralhanae, have been, let us say . . . executed."

Zo blinked at him. "Executed?"

"They did not find what they hoped to on the Sacred Ring. They found their deaths instead."

"You . . . killed them?"

"We did. Mutiny is best put down before it gathers strength, and these were the tip of that spear. Do you know who was among them? Why, your friends Torg and G'torik who shambled about with you, no doubt babbling treason, in the Hanging Gardens!"

"G'torik . . ."

"We haven't recovered his body. But I'm confident he's dead, somewhere nearby. He could not have gotten very far."

"But . . . I . . . why am I here?"

"For several purposes," Exquisite purred. "First—look through the glass. Witness what happens to your friend Duru 'Scoahamee."

Melchus directed the other two Sangheili to stand back—Duru was sent close to the window. Then the red nodes on the floor lit up, and suddenly Duru was slammed hard onto his back by an invisible force.

"Look!" said Exquisite. His long bony two fingers and thumb hovered over the holocontrols of the throne. "I can hold him down. Just enough to keep him still."

Duru was spread-eagle on his back, on the floor, gasping.

"What are you doing?" Zo asked, the dread taking command of him.

"Why, I am controlling local gravitation," Exquisite cackled. "And you would respond that is nothing new. But think of it. We have artificial gravity in our habitats. We have gravity-based weaponry and vehicles that use boosted-gravity drives. And yet how little we have explored the possibilities of gravitational refinement. What possibilities it has as a tool of influence and ascertainment. The problem, of course, is that it takes a good deal of energy to focus it. Our purposes in this chamber today are for"—he looked at Zo significantly—"interrogation."

Zo spoke, just to keep his mind busy, to stall the Prophet of Exquisite Devotion. "I have never heard of such a use in the Covenant . . ."

"Oh, it is new. Very new, very experimental—perhaps it will not be practical for our needs with the humans, given their time is almost at an end. But for dissidents? For rebels clawing at us as we make our final steps on the Path?"

Exquisite's long slender fingers flutteringly adjusted a recently installed holocontrol over the arm of his throne.

Duru's right hand immediately flattened out to micro-width, blood and bone powder and marrow jetting out to the sides.

Duru's scream was muffled by the window, scarcely audible. But somehow Zo heard it echo loudly in his mind.

"You see?" Exquisite asked, breathing hard with a sadistic joy. "I made his hand collapse under localized gravitational amplification. Gravity increasing—in just that spot! Discretely and separately. Imagine what can be done with such a device in the process of interrogation."

"Yes . . ." Zo's throat seemed so suddenly dry, like the soil of a desert planet. "O Prophet, I was told you wanted to discuss something with me?"

"There are indications that you have a relationship with the Sangheili that is something more than what might be appropriate for your official capacity. In fact, you were witnessed with these

Sangheili in the Hanging Gardens, and they are now numbered among the heretics. It seemed, to my eyes, that you were having an intimate conversation with them." He gestured to the whirring globes overhead—the drones watching them. "These probes were stationed outside the Hanging Gardens. Just close enough to catch a glimpse of those you talked to, those now guilty of sedition. Torg 'Gransamee is dead—and G'torik will soon be confirmed dead as well. And for good reason. When I summoned you to my chambers, I imparted some troubling information to you about the Elites. I revealed facts I knew you might pass on, and I did it quite intentionally. It didn't matter if that information leaked out; in fact, we wanted it to. And when we sent probes to watch G'Torik, later, we heard him repeat much of what I told you. Just as I supposed he would. And here you are. We knew, then, you are all too closely allied with these dissidents."

"Really . . . a misunderstanding, merely, Your Eminence."

"Don't take me for a fool. Oh, and there are other rumors coming from the Ring. You are aware of the Supreme Commander of the Fleet of Particular Justice, now shamed for his loss of Alpha Halo?"

"I am. It is Thel 'Vadamee," Zo replied. "But that is all I know."

"You must know, then, that he was given the mantle of the Arbiter by the High Prophets of Truth and Mercy, tasked with the acquisition of the Sacred Icon. Early reports indicated that his life was claimed at the Repository of Fate, the site the Forerunners referred to as the Library. That he died battling the parasite deep in the Ring's quarantine zone and failed at retrieving the Icon."

"What does this have to do with me?" Zo asked.

"Some reports from the surface of Delta Halo indicate that the

Arbiter has . . . reappeared. That he's somehow come back from the dead."

Zo didn't know what to make of this. What was Exquisite suggesting? "Back from the dead? Hard to believe, Your Eminence."

"The Arbiter was seen leading a resurgence of Elites on the Ring, making war against our Brutes as they faithfully shored up our plans to activate Halo. So, you see my chain of thought and my concern? It may very well be that you are privy to information about the actions of the Arbiter, given that you fraternize with those who oppose us. We wish to know his whereabouts, what his forces are, and where your friend G'torik might be, if he lives."

Zo Resken looked through the window, where Duru was quivering in pain. "I don't know anything about the . . . the Arbiter."

"You are lying to me. There is much you know that you keep concealed."

"I am telling the truth, I know nothing of his return or this resurgence you speak of! I know only that he was believed dead . . ."

"Really? Watch."

Exquisite's fingers flickered over the controls, and Duru's right leg, from the knee down, was crushed by the sudden influx of high gravity. Sangheili blood spurted out a remarkably long distance, forced by the high pressure. The gravitational force went back up Duru's leg to just above the knee, so that a bubble of blood appeared in his thigh, and then burst.

Zo turned away, sickened. "My Prophet . . . I am loyal to the Covenant . . ."

"Are you, now? Watch again." When Zo hesitated, Exquisite shouted, "I said *watch*!"

Zo made himself look . . . and saw that the gravitational refinement device was now crushing Duru's lower half . . . from the knees, upward, inch by inch. Slowly.

Duru's scream now penetrated the window quite clearly.

"For the sake of the High Ones, please . . ." Zo breathed. "Enough of this. End his life!"

But Exquisite took his time, using the gravitational force of a giant planet, focused on a small area, and crushed Duru bit by bit until his innards spewed out his mouth and . . .

Zo, retching, could not continue to watch this savagery. The remaining Sangheili in the gravitation room with Duru tried to keep an honorable level of dignity. But when their eyes strayed to what was left of Duru, the horror contracted their faces, made their eyes bulge, their mouths drop.

"Now," Exquisite said. "That is what happens to traitors. Traitors to the Covenant, and to the Writ of Union. You should feel no pity for those who would sacrifice our ways at this late hour, when we're on the very edge of the Great Journey's consummation. Now . . . Melchus—push that young one, Tilik 'Bornisamee, forward . . ."

Melchus forced Tilik 'Bornisamee toward the unrecognizable remains of Duru. Tilik's relation cried out, begging to be taken instead—Zo could tell by his gestures, his face.

Tilik's uncle snarled in rage and turned to Melchus, crouching to lunge at him—and was knocked flat on his back with a stunwave from the hammer Melchus carried.

Tilik stepped defiantly forward, closed his eyes, and waited for death with as much dignity as he could muster.

"Now, Clarity," said Exquisite. "I would like to believe your loyalty, but the company you keep leaves much to be desired. Still . . . perhaps you can change my mind. Come, stand beside me and activate the device yourself. Prove yourself loyal to me—and then I will consider if you can perhaps be trusted."

Zo gaped at him. "Me?"

"Yes, you."

"I cannot. That is . . . not . . . my . . ." Zo couldn't think clearly. Couldn't come up with an argument. "You can't expect me to do so."

"You, Prophet of Clarity. You *will* do as I request."

Zo moved his antigrav chair closer, closer, feeling that Tilik was watching him through the window.

"You see? The magenta key? Press there. There is no alternative for you, Clarity. Or you will surely be the next one in that room. Do you understand?"

"Yes," said Zo, almost whispering.

Zo's hand hovered over the controls. He thought, *It's a cruel universe. Just go along with it. He'll kill them anyway. Survive. You don't want to die that way. Exquisite Devotion will take extra time killing you . . .*

But after a long moment Zo said, "I . . . cannot. I am sorry, Prophet. It is unjust. It is not what the Great Ones would want of us. These Sangheili were faithful servants of the Covenant and . . . I simply cannot."

"Then you will follow them. You will perish in agony just as they have."

Zo's own voice already sounded dead to his ears. "Yes. I understand."

"Do you indeed?" Exquisite seemed genuinely surprised. "You are reconciled to your fate and would accept death now, along with the traitors?"

Reconciled? Hardly. But resigned. "I accept it."

"Very well, then." Exquisite tapped the controls himself, and, taking his time, proceeded to murder Tilik.

Zo felt dizzy, as if he might fall out of his chair. Then, after what seemed an eternity, he heard, quite distantly, Exquisite say, "Guards, take this *former* Prophet of Clarity, while I finish with these Councilors. We will not only then see what he knows, but witness how a treacherous Prophet faces such a death—I daresay it will almost be a privilege for him."

CHAPTER 18

rying not to think of the unspeakable death that awaited
him, Zo Resken, escorted by guards, propelled his antigrav
chair down the corridor that led to the rear entry of the gravity refinement chamber. Before him strode a helmeted Jiralhanae,
contemptuously walking with his back to Zo—who was now
without a weapon. Behind him, close enough to breathe down
Zo's neck, was another Jiralhanae; he could smell the rank odor of
the Brute, hear his armor clanking. Just two to escort him to his
death—a measure of how little the Prophet of Exquisite Devotion
now respected Zo Resken.

With a kind of rueful despair, Zo decided that Exquisite was
correct. Zo was as physically weak as most modern San'Shyuum—
he had no hope of breaking free from these two powerful guards.
His chair was weak, too; at other times he might have attempted
to use its antigrav fields to wrest a weapon free, or to lift him over
the thugs. But the ceiling was too low here, and the gravitational
fields of the chair had already been compromised by the damage

done to it. He had just enough mobile power to keep up with the Jiralhanae.

The blue metal door was but a little way up ahead. Another locked door stood to its right—perhaps an entrance to another cell, where some other grotesque killing machine could be tested. But no—he saw a holosign on it that read, in San'Shyuum lettering, Energy Conduit Access.

Zo forced himself to consider the records hidden in his chair. Could he use them, perhaps, to bargain with the Prophet of Exquisite Devotion? In his most recent study of Mken 'Scre'ah'ben's writings, it appeared that the Refuge, the Forerunner world taken hold of by Ussa 'Xellus's forces long ago, did not simply detonate and vanish as the histories told, but evidence of its survival remained. Could the site still be there, with all its many relics? And perhaps the descendants of the ancient Ussans as well? The prospect, Zo thought, might entice Exquisite Devotion, and ultimately the High Prophet of Truth. Would they see value in such a record now as they began to finalize their efforts of consummating the Great Journey? Perhaps not, but there might be just enough that Exquisite would see fit to spare his life.

But why should Exquisite Devotion bargain for what he could simply take?

Something must be done to save the records, which should have been left with someone trustworthy. Mken 'Scre'ah'ben's writings, and his own . . . they were his treasures, his legacy, whether or not they had value to bargain . . .

Soon they would wrench him from the chair, strip him of his antigrav belt, force him into the gore-splashed room . . . and it would begin.

He could almost feel the crushing hand of extreme artificial gravitation on him now as they approached the door. He could imagine his lower half flattening, bone and blood forced into his upper half. His skin rupturing, bursting. Exquisite would take his time and then . . .

The door to the right banged open, and Zo saw G'torik and two other Sangheili half crouched in the open doorway, beyond them a room clustered with pipes and glowing energy concentration cubes.

G'torik had an activated energy sword, and the other two were armed with plasma rifles. He knew one of the others—Crun 'Brinsmee, an experienced commander. The Jiralhanae instantly reacted, the one in front swinging his spike rifle toward the ambushing Sangheili.

"Get down, Zo!" shouted Crun.

Zo threw himself onto the floor. His chair bobbled up a bit and he glimpsed, from the corner of his eye, something being thrown by Crun. A plasma grenade.

G'torik blocked the rounds from the spike rifle with his energy sword, and then struck hard at the Jiralhanae's throat, driving the charged blade deep, even as the other Sangheili fired at the rear Jiralhanae to keep him off balance.

There was a thud and a flash of light. A shock wave slapped Zo and he staggered, seeing G'torik stumble back, struck indirectly by the blast from the grenade. Something thick and purplish-red splattered over Zo. It took him a moment to realize it was Jiralhanae blood.

Zo got to his feet, switching on his antigrav belt, and looked around. The two Jiralhanae were dead on the floor of the narrow passageway, and he was relieved to see that G'torik was getting up. "Are you hurt, G'torik?"

"Nothing significant."

"There was a battle—Exquisite told me . . . at the control center."

"We exploited the signal being captured by his drones . . . and saw your little exchange with Exquisite. Yes—a battle, though it would be more accurate to call it an ambush. I was knocked off the balcony and . . . when I could, I stowed away aboard a Phantom and found my way here."

"Enough chatter!" Crun growled. "Come with us! You will have to leave that chair, San'Shyuum—it won't fit where we need to go and we cannot linger. The Prophet will realize something has gone wrong soon enough!"

"They could have us under surveillance right now," said the smaller Sangheili nervously. He peered down the hallway. Though he carried a rifle, he was dressed as an engineering officer, not a warrior. G'torik, meanwhile, had found new armor, Zo saw, and was recovering from his injuries. Crun wore the classic heavy armor, shiny silver and blue, of a commander.

"You, I do not know," said Zo to the engineering officer.

Zo knelt by his antigrav chair and opened a panel on the back. He took a small black satchel from the niche hidden under the seat.

"My name is Tul 'Imjanamee," said the small Sangheili. "I hope you are worth all this risk."

"I promise you he is worth it," G'torik said. "He is one of our only true San'Shyuum allies."

"I will do anything I can for you," Zo said, feeling giddy at this wrenching turn of events. "You have risked all for me. I now have more loyalty to the Sangheili than to any so-called Prophet on High Charity."

Although I'll be sorry to leave the chair, Zo thought, slipping through the door after the others. *It has served me well.* He slung the satchel over one shoulder. If he lost it, he'd never again have access to the writings of his ancestor.

Zo could immediately see the reason for leaving the chair behind, though. Fat, daunting pipes and energy conduits flowed in mazelike confusion around the room, criss-crossing the scuffed metal floor. He would have never gotten his chair through those spaces and over those obstacles. A Hierarch's antigrav throne could lift over most anything; some could even teleport in close quarters, and fire powerful energy projectiles. Zo's chair was third rate in comparison.

The only light here in the energy conduit chamber was from places where the conduits were interrupted by energy transmutation cubes, which throbbed with a yellow illumination. The light didn't reach the dim corners of the big room; the high ceiling was in shadows.

Crun paused, went back, and locked the door behind them. "That won't hold them long."

They followed G'torik across the open space, Zo moving as quickly as he could, adjusting his antigrav belt to a higher mode. They came to a series of waist-high pipes that blocked the way; Zo tried to climb over on his own, but finally had to accept help from G'torik. Staying well clear of the glowing cubes that the pipes passed through, they crossed two sets of contiguous conduits and then spied two more sets ahead. They'd gotten most of the way across the room before they saw, beyond the pipes, a closed door lit with a red light.

"That is the way out," said Tul. "It leads to a ramp that will take us to a maintenance ship. We can use it to get away from High Charity . . . if they do not realize we're aboard."

"Tul!" Crun called. "Run up ahead and open the door so we can get through it as quickly as possible—and scout outside!"

Zo knew this order came about because he was slower in clambering over the large pipes than the Sangheili. Crun wanted that door open and ready when Zo finally got there.

Tul ran ahead, while Zo looked back at the door they'd come through—no one seemed to be trying to break it down. That was good. It—

The door was suddenly blasted inward.

"By the Great Ones!" Zo swore, as they all paused, startled and unsure, seeing smoke and flame rise from the blackened, punched-through entrance. He could see a Mgalekgolo hunkering down, trying to force its way through the opening, which was not quite big enough for it.

"Tul!" said G'torik, "this chamber—what does it do, precisely?"

"It serves the laboratories," Tul said, rubbing nervously at his mandibles as he watched the Mgalekgolo forcing its way inside. "The experiments with gravitational projection take fantastic amounts of power and this room controls the output of that energy. It is highly unstable, not to be trifled with."

The Hunter was now through the door . . . and now its bond brother was making its way into the high-ceilinged conduit room.

"You should simply run," Zo said. "I will be close behind. I can evade those worm-bellied oafs, I hope."

G'torik gave a clack of his mandibles accompanied by a growl—a Sangheili way of signifying angry refusal. "No—we came to rescue you from the Prophet of Exquisite Devotion. And rescue you we will!"

Then Tul came huffing back to them. "The exit door—it is locked from outside."

"By now you must realize you're trapped in here!" called someone from behind the Hunters.

Zo looked, and saw the Prophet of Exquisite Devotion gliding his throne across the floor behind the Mgalekgolo, still a good distance off at the far end of the room.

"Hold, Hunters," commanded Exquisite. "I would speak to these fools!"

The Mgalekgolo lowered their cannon-fitted arms, but kept their shields up, as Exquisite paused beside them. "I am fitted with a rather good force field," he said. "Don't waste my time by firing upon me. Now, surrender, and I may let some of you live. Just hand over this former Prophet and depart. Leave him to me and I will forgive your sins."

"That we will not do!" G'torik shouted. In a low aside to Zo, he asked, "*Does* he have so strong a force field around that chair?"

"Not as good as a Hierarch's. But your rifle or sword won't get through it. It'll need some powerful energy to do it."

G'torik grunted at this news, deactivated his energy sword, and tucked the hilt away. "Tul—give me your rifle!"

Tul handed it over, but said, "What use will it be?"

"Go," G'torik whispered. "See if you can get that exit door open. I'll be there quick as I can. Go. All of you. I have a plan . . ."

"What is your answer?" shouted the Prophet of Exquisite Devotion.

"I have an offer for you, Exquisite," G'torik replied. "Leave this room—or die here with the worm-guts!" Just to make his point, he fired the rifle at Exquisite. The plasma bolts splashed harmlessly on the globular force field.

"So be it—destroy them," Exquisite commanded. "All of them."

"We're not leaving you here, G'torik!" Crun said, raising his weapon.

The Mgalekgolo opened fire with their assault cannons, the weapons making a sound that was like the bellowing of some gigantic primordial beast.

In the strobing green light of the plasma energy projectiles fired from the cannon weapons built into the creatures' right forearms, Zo saw the titans with a momentary photographic clarity. Heavily armored in blue-gray and silver metal, their weapons tipped with green crystals, massive, scythelike spikes projecting over their backs, their helmets only partly disguising the writhing mass of Lekgolo worms functioning as a gestalt mind to control each Hunter's conglomerate body. The Mgalekgolo carried shields that were themselves bigger than most ordinary bipedal creatures. They had no real faces. He had always found the Hunters especially repellent.

And then the plasma projectiles struck, hitting thick alloy collars holding the conduit pipes to the floor, not far from Zo. He ducked, but not before the shock wave knocked him off his feet, sending him skidding backward.

Trying to get up, Zo felt a searing pain on the right side of his face—he'd been burned in the blast from the assault cannons. He wondered blearily if he was now disfigured. But it didn't matter—the Mgalekgolo would kill him soon enough. Zo felt Crun helping him to stand. The collars over the pipes were blackened and warped, one of them twisted apart—charged gas was pluming up, roaring, from the breached conduit. About thirty strides beyond the blast mark, the Mgalekgolo were climbing clumsily but inexorably over another set of pipes. On either side of the Hunters were the glowing energy transmutation cubes. Exquisite Devotion was levitating his chair over the same pipes—and firing a blast from his chair's weapons system, which hissed overhead.

G'torik fired his rifle repeatedly and shouted, "Crun—hit the transmutation cubes!"

Crun, too, fired, and they hit the cubes together. There was no immediate effect. Another blast of green plasma energy flashed by. G'torik and Crun kept firing at the transmuters built into the pipes—

And then the cubes exploded, releasing their concentrated power in a double detonation that ripped through other pipes nearby; a series of conduits erupted, and flak from shattered metal ricocheted from the distant ceiling, making temporary stars out of sparks. Exquisite Devotion shrieked, vanishing in a sudden fireball.

Something else was flying asunder—the Mgalekgolo bond brothers, fountains of orange blood flecked with hot metal shrapnel, both blown to pieces, gone in an instant. The room reeked with a thick, nauseating wormlike odor.

"Ho!" shouted Crun triumphantly. "Two Hunters exterminated!"

"And—where is Exquisite?" Zo asked, coughing from the fumes of pipes and blasted Hunters.

"There!" Crun said, pointing.

Zo saw him then. Exquisite had been thrown from his chair, which lay spitting sparks behind him. He was crawling across the floor.

Tul said, "You have started a chain reaction—we must get away from here!"

"One moment!" G'torik shouted. "The Prophet's vaunted energy shield is down!" He vaulted over a pipe, then another, drawing his energy sword. He skidded to a stop in front of Exquisite Devotion, activated the sword—and Exquisite screamed as G'torik quickly sliced him into three parts.

"That is for those who died for your pleasure, false Prophet!" G'torik cried.

The deck vibrated and hummed under their feet as G'torik rushed back to Zo. They stumbled to the next set of pipes, scrambling over in frenzied haste, Crun and G'torik helping Zo, and then to the door . . .

But what was the point? The door was frozen shut. Locked.

And yet—not quite. It had started to swing aside, and then stopped, open just a hand's width. What had moved it?

Then Zo saw the tentacles feeling their way through the opening—a Huragok.

"That would be Sluggish Drifter," said Tul, pleased. "We've worked together many a time." He thrust his hand into the open space and made a series of hand-signing gestures designed for the Huragok. The alien Engineer slipped its wispy tentacle tips into small openings in the doorframe, overriding the order the door had been given, and it swung out of the way.

Zo thought as they all hurried through, *They'll be waiting for us out there. The High Prophet of Truth and a legion of Jiralhanae.*

But when they stepped into the corridor, they saw that emergency vacuum-sealant doors had closed off this part of the corridor. There was a vibrant slamming at the sealant door on their right—no doubt Exquisite's Jiralhanae trying to break through.

"The Huragok's locked them out for now," Tul said. "But we have to move like a *skorken* with its tail afire!"

The door they'd just come through sealed behind them—and not a moment too soon. An angry *thoom!* shook the corridor, and the force of the chain reactive explosion in the conduit room dented the door, making it crumple partway inward, as if some vengeful god had throttled it from the other side.

"That was too close," Tul said. "But at least now it won't open for them. Come."

He led the way down the ramp ahead, and Zo, driven by raw fear, had no difficulty keeping up.

Tul waved them through another door and across the deck of

a small hangar. They climbed into an oval metal-and-glass vessel, just big enough for the four of them and the Huragok. No sooner had Zo followed the others than the hatch in the maintenance vessel sealed.

"Get to your seats, get to your stations!" Tul shouted, rushing to the controls. The Huragok trilled a question to him, and Tul hastily gestured and answered before activating the maintenance vessel.

Moments later the small hangar had depressurized and the air lock had opened, the little craft sailing out of the upper levels of High Charity. As they passed through the murky clouds within the Holy City's massive dome interior, Zo used one of the ship's viewscreens to take in the destruction below.

It had begun. Already the city was in complete chaos, wracked by all-out civil war. Then, in the corner of the screen, Zo saw something he could not believe. His Sangheili companions came and stood near, gazing in shock at what the viewscreen conveyed.

The immense Forerunner Dreadnought at the center of High Charity, which had for so long served as a reminder of the Writ of Union between San'Shyuum and Sangheili, had suddenly rent free from its moorings and begun to climb, a burning sun beaming from where its long-since-decommissioned engines were. The noble and ancient vessel shook the entire city, concussively reverberating through the air, and rumbling through the supply ship as it rose skyward to the upper parts of the dome. Zo gazed in horror at what he saw—the entire city began to dim and darken with the Dreadnought departing upward, having lost the source of much of its power. This truly was a sign of the times.

"By the gods," Zo said, covering his face in shame. The Dreadnought had been the skeletal core of High Charity for century after century. He could not conceive of High Charity without it, or the Dreadnought without High Charity. The sum of the two was the last homeworld of the San'Shyuum, the only world left to them. But it appeared the Dreadnought was abandoning them all.

"It is Truth in that ship, Zo," G'torik said solemnly. "He has taken what is left of the Covenant fleets and is heading for the human world, Earth. He is seeking the Ark."

"What about Delta Halo?" Zo wondered. "Why would he abandon it?"

"He has given Tartarus the Icon and sent him to activate the Ring," G'torik explained. "The Arbiter and our allies there have planned to stop him; they claim to have new insight about the Ring's purpose, which leads them to believe that activating Halo could bring an end to everything and everyone we know. I would like to join my brothers and avenge those we have lost, but the space between Halo and High Charity is now perilous—far too dangerous to pass through. Not only is it filled with Brute ships warring with our own vessels, but there is rumor of the Flood as well. That is a risk we cannot afford. Our best chance is escape to a remote system, and then reassess what options we have."

"I have a code to get through the inner wall," Tul called as Zo buckled himself into a seat behind him. "Let us hope they haven't . . ."

The little vessel approached and the inner wall opened, allowing it to pass neatly through an atmospheric barrier. They were through, and still alive.

"But now what?" Zo asked.

"We have some allies . . . who by now have heard about the treacherous massacre of our Councilors," G'torik said. "They are waiting for us. But we must leave this area quickly. Despite everything, it won't be long before Truth finds out that Exquisite Devotion is dead—and realizes what we've done."

Up ahead, a vessel loomed. Was it High Charity security? Zo's mouth went dry at the thought.

But he saw it was a moderately small fleet supply ship, not a warship, and an air lock was opening for them. Tul slid them cleanly through its air lock entry.

Only seconds after the air lock closed, the supply ship was on its way through slipspace, heading to a little-known, half-forgotten corner of the galaxy.

CHAPTER 19

The Refuge, the Ussan Colony
Primary Refuge
2552 CE
The Age of Reclamation

al'Tol was standing in the doorway of the Blood Sickness Isolation Ward, inspecting the empty facility, depressed by how much it looked like a jail, and thinking of his beloved Limtee. As his mate, she would have produced eggs and childlings, and she would have been at his side, wisely counseling him. But she had died alone in her quarters, even as he'd badgered the bio repairers and pored through the old medical records, trying to find a cure. She'd locked herself away so that she wouldn't have to go through the final stage of the disease where anyone could see it. And when it had become unbearable, she had used a sharp edge on her neck, taking her own life. But it wasn't true suicide; that was dishonorable. It was the Blood Sickness that had driven her to it, Bal'Tol knew—it was the Blood Sickness that had killed her.

The colony had rounded the sun thirteen times since the day he'd found Limtee's decaying body on her cot, her tender flesh glued to the surface by dried purple-blue blood.

He closed his eyes and let out a long sigh. Then he forced

himself to look once more at the crude metal cages they'd built around beds and a few small amenities, down the long room.

"Great Kaidon . . ."

Bal'Tol turned to see Qerspa 'Tel, the biological repairer. Truly an overblown title for such a dusty, ineffective windbag. Qerspa wore the blue uniform of a biorep, its color symbolizing the blood of Sangheili.

"You should be resting," Qerspa said. "Your wound is not yet healed."

"I feel better, moving about. Is this facility the best we can do, Qerspa? If we could give them individual rooms . . . these are like cages for animals."

"We had little time for anything better—and no room, Great Kaidon. You asked for it to be produced quickly and . . . this is the best we could do. But in time, we will have better facilities."

Bal'Tol growled to himself. Then he said, "Start bringing the sick ones from the lockups to this facility. It will be somewhat better." He walked into the hallway and Qerspa hurried to catch up with him. "Qerspa, are you certain this disease is not communicable? That it doesn't spread by infection, one to the next?"

"We have done many experiments. We cannot locate an antigen. We are certain of this, Great Kaidon."

"So, then, it is genetic. Or poison of some kind. Or both."

"Both? We have supposed the Blood Sickness to be an inherited trait. Some mutation. How could it be both?"

"I don't know—we understand it so little. Some could have a genetic sensitivity to a toxin in the environs, some unknown agent. C'tenz has surmised as much."

"*Phh!* That young one's guessing, with no knowledge to back it up."

"Perhaps. But he's surprisingly learned, and you should let him tell you his theory . . ." Thinking of C'tenz, Bal'Tol realized it was time to meet his young second-in-command on the eco level.

He hurried on. Four patrollers, bristling with extra weapons since the war with 'Kinsa's followers had begun, met him as he and Qerspa emerged from the hallway and onto the main promenade. Bal'Tol turned to Qerspa. "Back to work with you. We might end this war once we end this disease. Order what resources you need—of those we have."

"My Kaidon, many of the resources we need are in Section Five. The chemicals processor is there. And that is under control of 'Kinsa."

"Yes." Bal'Tol's Sangheili controlled Primary, Sections Six through Fifteen. Two, Three, Four, and Five had been taken over by 'Kinsa. But that included the prized Hall of Godminds, and much needed equipment and supplies storage. "Do what you can with what you have—and we will get Section Five back soon. Fairly soon."

He turned away and led his protectors to the lift that would take him to the eco level and his meeting with C'tenz. He was fairly sure of what C'tenz would tell him. More breakdowns in the agricultural supply pipes. And the equipment to keep agricultural supply in good repair would be found in the 'Kinsa-controlled sections.

The deterioration, the general entropic breakdown of the Refuge, was being accelerated by this war . . .

War? Nothing but skirmishes, and only a few of those. It was difficult to enter the air lock of any section that didn't permit one's vessel there.

What a pitiful war it had been so far. But it would have to be joined, and fully—or the whole colony would perish. He was simply waiting for the best strategy.

At the moment, Bal'Tol had come up with only one possibility.

He could destroy the sections that housed the rebels from the outside. He had more ships, more firepower, more men than 'Kinsa. But besides the loss of vital equipment, there were many hundreds of innocents in those sections to consider. Massacring them was no real solution.

Was it?

The *Journey's Sustenance*, a Supply Ship for the Fleet of Blessed Veneration
Ussan System
2552 CE
The Age of Reclamation

The *Journey's Sustenance* emerged from slipspace into a system unknown to Zo Resken—that is, at least to his personal experience. But he would find soon enough that he had in fact heard of it.

The hijacked supply ship had been intended to deliver a load of foodstuff and other goods to the Fleet of Blessed Veneration. The shipmaster was D'ero 'S'budmee, a scowling, peevish, slightly bow-legged Elite who seemed to resent his own decision to defect, although he knew it was irrevocable. D'ero had been horrified and enraged by the reports of the Jiralhanae massacre of the High Councilors.

Everyone aboard, except perhaps the Huragok, was bereft of their old ranks and titles. Indeed, D'ero was now 'S'bud, not 'S'budmee, for he relieved himself of the honorific suffix now that he had abandoned the Covenant.

All who were aboard the *Journey's Sustenance* were adrift, a handful of Sangheili and one San'Shyuum in orbit around a gas giant, pondering their next move.

Zo gazed out the viewport at the sun of the system rising beyond the planet's horizon. They were adrift from all they'd known,
all former attachments. The Covenant was all that most of these
Sangheili had ever experienced. It was true that one or two of
those onboard had come to their fleet directly from Sanghelios.
They had known their homeworld, they had keeps and clans
there. But even those Elites from Sanghelios had been caught in
the unforgiving coils of the Covenant. Some even wondered what
kind of convincing it would take for those still on Sanghelios to
believe the treachery committed by Zo's own people.

Now they were all in this together . . .

"Well, Prophet?" said D'ero, approaching with Tul. "Do you
have any ideas as to where we go from here?"

"Why do you ask me?" Zo muttered. He could see a faint re-
flection of his face in the transparent port. The burn he'd gotten
in the energy conduit room had marked him, but not horribly, and
the pain was now slight. "You ask me where we go because I am
a 'Prophet'? I have no authority over you now. I am a Prophet no
more. I am but Zo Resken."

"And have you no advice at all?" Tul asked. "You were closer
to the heart of the Covenant than us."

Zo tugged fretfully at a wattle. "I can only advise that since we
have a ship full of delivered supplies, we can survive for a time—
but I doubt that Elites like yourselves would simply want to flee
while your brothers are still at war. With Truth headed to the Ark
and the Icon being brought to Delta Halo, it is likely that we are at
a tipping point. If they initiate the Great Journey, we will find out
firsthand whether or not the Rings do what the prophecies seemed
to have foretold. Still, I would have liked to speak with the Arbiter
myself."

"We have some information already," said Tul. "Before we left,

I received notice from Commander Rtas 'Vadum, who is fighting alongside the Arbiter. Tartarus was stopped, he and his Brutes were slain, but the battle continues around Delta Halo."

"This is the third vector of chaos," Zo said with a sigh.

"What do you mean?" Tul asked.

"Something that the fabled Prophet of Inner Conviction wrote at the end of his life. He said that every civilization fights a perpetually losing battle with chaos; every society is always under siege, even when it seems at peace. And he said that there are vectors, fronts of chaos that penetrate a social order here and there. One comes, then two. And when there are *three* at once . . . then a society will crumble. The first two vectors of chaos afflicting the Covenant were the humans and the Flood. Now civil war is the third vector. The Prophet of Inner Conviction was correct in his theory: the Covenant will not survive."

"Treacherous scum, the Covenant," declared D'ero. "They do not *deserve* to survive! Those who have sided with the High Prophet of Truth, and with the Brutes—they deserve to crumble into dust and be forgotten."

Zo winced. He knew there were many worthy San'Shyuum and Sangheili still on High Charity, though their fates were unknown. But he was not in a position to argue with the captain of the vessel that was at present his only salvation.

"This system," Zo said, changing the subject. He waved a hand to encompass the sun in the distance, the planetary field. "What do you know about it?"

"Precious little," growled D'ero. "I chose it because on the charts the system is a scarlet border. Not much is known about it. It is listed only as the Ussan system in our records. Named after some forgotten Sangheili."

Zo knew what the scarlet border meant. Forbidden. "I wonder

why it's off-limits. Something embarrassing, no doubt, to the Prophets, or the . . ." His voice trailed off as it struck him. "Captain, did you say this was the *Ussan* system?"

"Yes. So it is."

Could it be the one? Named after Ussa? Not so strange, then, that it would be forbidden—and it was sensible for D'ero to go to a system marked as such to elude the Covenant. They did well to hide out, for now, in a forbidden system. And what else was hidden here?

"Yes. This is *destiny*," said Zo, one hand on the glass of the port as if trying to touch the solar system itself. Some of the gloom that had wrapped him since his arrest was at last lifting. "This is . . . a rare opportunity."

"What?" Tul asked. "Why?"

"Because if I am right . . . and we must yet confirm it . . . this is the system to which the ancient Sangheili rebel Ussa 'Xellus brought his people. D'ero is correct: this place is forgotten, by most. But as I've said, I have read Mken 'Scre'ah'ben's writings. I have the tale he told of coming here . . . and the extraordinary thing that happened, perhaps in this very system."

"What happened?" D'ero asked irritably. "Tell us, for the Ring's sake."

"I will tell you what I know—but first you may as well know what I think our intention should be. We wait and listen, yes. But more than that. We will explore."

"Here?" Tul said. "There can't be much in this system of value, or it would already have been exploited by the Covenant . . ."

"*Forbidden* carries a heavy weight. The Covenant prefers to forget this system. But in fact, here could be thousands of Forerunner relics. Many will have been destroyed, in the wreckage of the extraordinary world that, if I am right, once orbited that sun you see, beyond the gas giant. And there might be something else . . . vestiges of the people who once resided here. Sangheili who long ago held the Prophets in disdain and might provide help in this time of need."

Tul double-clacked mandibles to express doubt. "Should we not return to Delta Halo and aid the Arbiter?"

"Not every fight can be won," Zo said, walking away from the port. "That is something Ussa 'Xellus learned. And it is a painful lesson, I can assure you."

CHAPTER 20

The Refuge, the Ussan Colony
Primary Refuge, Command Center
2553 CE
The Age of Reclamation

ow long has it been?" C'tenz asked. He asked it rhetorically, because he knew full well.

"Half a solar orbit, at least," Bal'Tol said gloomily.

How many days was that? Hundreds. It made Bal'Tol sick to contemplate the situation.

And he was also sickened by the break in the outer hull of Section Seven. He could see it on the monitors in the command center of Primary Section. Only two of the scout-eyes worked anymore. And one of them had found a breach in Seven—luckily the meteor had struck only an air-compression module, which was itself locked off from the other modules. A little atmosphere had been lost. But that meteor shouldn't have been able to break through the hull at all. There were repellent fields around the colony's hulls, only switched off when maintenance was done.

Now repellent fields were beginning to fail on some sections because they couldn't access generator repair parts in Section

Two. "We should have moved everything vital to Primary many cycles ago," Bal'Tol said. "N'Zursa wanted to do it. But the other Section captains complained that it would leave them vulnerable, that it discounted them . . . it was all politics, really."

"Those fields have to be repaired," C'tenz said. "We'll have to raid Two."

"They'll see us coming. Their air lock surveillance is perfectly intact there."

"There are other ways to get in, Great Kaidon. It's possible to locally cancel the repellent field. We could cut our way in, without serious depressurization inside."

Bal'Tol turned dejectedly from the screens. "If we knew for a certainty what was going on inside Section Two . . . perhaps. But suppose we cut into an area where they've moved some of our people, the innocents? We could kill them all."

"I have a system I think will reveal what's in any section area, if I can get close enough. It is an adaptation of the old scancam system, with increased output. I have it ready for testing."

"Have you? We must attempt it, then. C'tenz, we need to know what conditions are like for everyone in those sections. Are they sick? Have they resorted to cannibalism? Does 'Kinsa torture those who resist him? We know nothing for certain."

C'tenz made a rueful snorting sound. "You have been subsidizing them! They are not starving."

"We have exchanged food for supplies—but suppose that 'Kinsa and his followers are keeping the food for themselves?"

"They do have a protein synthesizer, which could feed everyone."

"It requires a base to synthesize from. They must have come close to running out of the base materials." Bal'Tol rubbed his eyes wearily. "I wonder how many Sangheili in those sections actually support 'Kinsa. I would have expected someone to fight back against him."

"There have been some bodies jettisoned from Five—you were informed of this."

Bal'Tol grimaced. "Yes. Do you think they took up arms against 'Kinsa?"

"It's possible."

"And . . . we had attempted defections. They're short one vessel now." Bal'Tol had been watching on these same monitors when the shuttle had been hit by the projectile. A silent explosion in space—and sixteen Ussans had been killed as the vessel turned inside out from the puncture. 'Kinsa's arms craftsmen had made crude, space-ready missiles that had done the job. And that made invasion from Bal'Tol's sections all the more difficult. "If only I knew, C'tenz—I should try again to transmit a message to 'Kinsa's sections. Encourage our people to fight him." There was a public address system he had used, before all this started, that transmitted from Primary Section to the others.

"I do not think there is any doubt that he has deactivated the transmission system—at least from outside signals. And, respectfully, Kaidon, words alone avail little."

Ten cycles after 'Kinsa took over, six Ussans had successfully escaped 'Kinsa's contingent. They reported harsh privation, worsening air quality, food rations cut to minimum, martial law, enforced worship of 'Greftus, and 'Kinsa himself. And there were more outbreaks of savagery from Blood Sickness.

It would be much worse by now.

"We will go, C'tenz. Organize a raiding party, and find the proper penetration point."

"Respectfully, my Kaidon, you cannot go along. You are too vital to the well-being of the Refuge. It simply cannot be contemplated."

"I want to see for myself how things are there."

"You can trust me to report to you."

If you survive, Bal'Tol thought. But aloud he only made a discontented grunt of dissent.

He turned again to look at the rows of monitors—and saw something a sentry had been watching to amuse himself and forgotten to take down. It was footage of a floatfight tournament. There were several great floatfighters competing, whirling, hurtling, hurling themselves through space, pitching headlong through zero gravity in the Combat Section.

Combat initiated not by order of the kaidon was never legal in the colony. But Sangheili needed conflict—the necessity of some form of combat to maintain their sanity, their identity. So over time the floatfights had evolved, a sport that could be deadly, one that was always dangerous . . . and which gave a Sangheili, watching or taking part, a chance to satisfy that innate hunger for battle.

The atmosphere in the big hemispherical zero-gravity room was already splotched with floating, warping billows of gore. It was striped with stretch-lines—taut, flexible vertical bands that were used by fighters to realign their trajectory, to rebound, to swing about for an attack.

The judges usually removed a fighter before he met his end—if a judge decided a competitor was too torn up from the throwing blades, the quartermoons, and the spiked gloves, then a beam of intense red light was projected onto the wounded Sangheili and he was forced, by the rules, to "curl up," to take a fetal position, which then made him extraneous to the fight. Referees would fly out, mildly propelled by jetpacks, and take him out of the competition. If he was pulled out, the audience, lined up in the straps along the walls, would hoot derisively at the fighter, or groan with sympathy if he happened to be a favorite.

There: V'urm 'Kerdeck, the greatest surviving floatfighter, was rocketing through the middle of the echoing arena, slamming spiked gloves as he passed through, knocking adversaries spinning. Then he did a tuck and roll in midair so that his feet could propel off the netting that protected the audience, sending him back in for another fly-by.

It was a vicious sport—but it had been found that over the centuries, it provided the outlet that kept relative peace on the colony. At least, most of the time it did. Sometimes fights broke out between sections. And now, with 'Kinsa, social unrest had become hostage taking, blockades, exploding shuttles, shrieks unheard in the insulation of the Primary Refuge.

Bal'Tol watched the match unfold, every fighter against every other. They grabbed the stretch-lines and swung about like some primeval tree beasts, coming back at their enemies; they rounded from the stretch-lines and the nets, they collided, they shouted in fury and pain. On and on it went. First one and then a second and third eliminated. Until only two were left . . .

The floatfight commission tried to prevent deaths—sometimes unsuccessfully. And it was not unheard of that the last two competitors might kill each other.

Bal'Tol felt a shiver down his spine. This recorded unfolding of a floatfight might be a foreshadowing, with its trembling globules of blood in the air . . . a dire omen of what was to come to every part of the colony.

**The *Journey's Sustenance*, a Supply Ship for
the Fleet of Blessed Veneration
Ussan System
2553 CE
The Age of Reclamation**

Zo Resken kept them at it, but it was becoming difficult. Somewhere, their enemies were still fighting their allies. And they were here, endlessly searching a forbidden solar system. Their vessel was not equipped with long-range scan equipment. It had not been devised for surveying. So commenced the traveling and scouring of this large system . . . looking for the forgotten.

They were on a treasure hunt that encompassed millions of miles. Seeking out the relics that Zo insisted would lead them to a stunningly rich reliquary, they prospected rocky moons, planets where the skies screamed with methane winds; they searched through the asteroid belt; they flew close to comets and examined them, looking for clues . . . finding all too much and yet all too little.

Their food supplies were close to exhaustion; so, too, was their patience. Arguments broke out over trivial matters.

Only surface exploration of the moons, the planetoids, the asteroids, alleviated their restlessness. Time wore on; time slipped away.

But the asteroid belt was as large as the orbit of a planet halfway to the farthest reaches of this system. There was much to see, and much that was difficult to see.

And chance had kept them in the wrong part of the asteroid belt . . . the opposite end, with the sun between them, on the plane of the elliptic, and the Ussan colony.

But then the day came . . .

Zo Resken irritably glanced up as the hatchway hissed open and G'torik came into the pressure-suit storage hold that doubled as a laboratory. "I came to look at the latest harvest from the asteroid belt," G'torik said. They called it the harvest—they were now using a weak gravitation field to scoop in anything they found in the asteroid belt that looked artificial.

"Here," Zo muttered, taking another fragment from the scratched and dirty metal table and putting it under the down-pointing cone of the analyzer. The three-dimensional image of the twisted metal fragment expanded, slowly rotated in holographic representation over the table. There was part of an ancient yet familiar ideogram on it. "You see that? Forerunner."

"Yes. But . . . it is the same problem: small fragments." G'torik nodded at the relics on the table—a pile of rubble, really. "Is it not possible that there is nothing else out there? That the explosion destroyed the construct utterly—and even if it survived a while, in two thousand solar cycles it might well be gone . . ."

"It has been *more* than two thousand solar cycles, in fact, by quite a bit, since its purported end," Zo said, looking at another fragment of alloy. "Odd how this material is so metallic and yet is not mere metal. We have reproduced some Forerunner materials, but *this* may be one of their final innovations."

"You are holding it with your bare hands," G'torik noted. "You did run this harvest through the radiation cleanser?"

"Yes. It takes two cleansings. It is as if someone wanted to create a great deal of toxicity around these fragments—to deliberately give the impression that there is nothing to find here but deadly rubble." He looked at G'torik. "You and the others want to give up the search?"

After a moment's hesitation, G'torik admitted, "It might be best—especially in light of news that is perhaps more exciting to a Sangheili than to a San'Shyuum."

"And what news is that?" Zo asked, trying to decipher the ideogram.

"Tul decoded another set of subspace communications. We have had confirmation of what came to us only as inference, before. The Covenant is . . ." He pointed to the rubble. "Like that. In fragments. Shattered. The Flood destroyed what remained of High Charity . . . the Prophet of Mercy killed . . . the Ark shut down and the Halos silenced by the Demon . . . and the Prophet of Truth dead at the hands of Thel 'Vadamee, may the Great Ones bless him for it."

Zo set a fragment aside and selected another. "So, Mken 'Scre'ah'ben's prophecy was correct. At last, the Covenant has met its end. Earlier reports indicated that the Elites had actually joined the humans?"

"It is true," G'torik mused. "The humans claimed that the Rings were not a means to achieve the Great Journey, but instead weapons of mass destruction, used by the Forerunners to purge the galaxy of all sentient life, cutting off the Flood from any source of continuation."

Zo sighed, wrestling with the paradigm shift, but feeling the weight of its truth. "My ancestor theorized as much—in secret, of course—based on evidence he had gathered from his time on Janjur Qom. Whether they were gods or not . . . it appears that the Forerunners were victims of their own design, committing themselves to self-annihilation for the sake of preserving sentient life throughout the galaxy." His thoughts lightly nudged the intriguing parallel between the Forerunners and the Ussans. Both committed themselves to an end, rather than surrender to their enemies. Both appeared to have vanished from the face of the galaxy.

"There is more. The Sangheili who once served the Covenant in the fleets are now beginning to return to Sanghelios and its colonies. It is a mixing of blood, however. Many still regard the Forerunners as holy and hold to some form of the Path; others believe they were only just another race, brilliant beyond measure but merely mortal. The Arbiter is being held by his people as the newly fledged leader of those who have truly abandoned the Covenant. They hope to lay claim to the spirit of Sanghelios keep by keep."

"Indeed?" Zo looked over at G'torik. He could see exultation in his friend's body language and the sparkle of his eyes. "So—you and the others here have a homeworld to return to. I am glad of that, G'torik."

And, he thought, *I'm a bit envious.*

"Why not come with us to Sanghelios? High Charity is gone. There is no place left for you now. We do not even know where the surviving Prophets went, if any survived to begin with."

"Ah. To be the only one of my kind on a planet with countless natives who now thoroughly hate the San'Shyuum? It doesn't seem wise. No new Writ of Union in my future, I'm afraid." Zo felt as if the room's gravitation was increasing. "Is there anything amiss with the grav fields?"

"No. I feel nothing out of the ordinary."

"I just . . ." He let out a long breath and slumped back into a chair. It was not an antigrav chair. He had only his belt now. "When I think of the other San'Shyuum, I feel heavy, as if . . ." He grimaced, remembering the Sangheili captives flattened, crushed by Exquisite Devotion in the gravitational refinement chamber. The horrifying memory never left him for long. He felt somehow that it had aged him before his time. He revisited that place in his nightmares.

"Your people are out there somewhere, Zo," said G'torik, as gently as a Sangheili knew how. "Some *must* have survived. I am sure of it. But until you find them, you should come with us to Sanghelios."

"I will consider it. Perhaps. But I have not given up here yet."

"We have been searching for much of a solar cycle . . . We've found nothing but space trash."

"But you have forgotten the accounts D'ero turned up—the logs of other captains who had spoken to Kig-Yar pirates. They came upon larger artifacts in this system. One of them claimed that something in this asteroid belt had actually fired upon them . . ."

"The Kig-Yar!" G'torik sniffed. "Who can trust their word?"

"Mken 'Scre'ah'ben suspected that the colony may have survived—may have used the explosion from long ago as camouflage. Put that together with the Kig-Yar tales . . ."

Tul came in then, with the Huragok, Sluggish Drifter, trailing after him. The Huragok was like some weightless *nelosh*, an aquatic animal from his ancestor's records of Janjur Qom, floating through the air, its long neck twitching, its coils whipping out, tendrils seeking here and there. It signaled to Tul, who said, "Sluggish asks if it can repair some of these items." He pointed at the wreckage on the table.

"These, I fear, are beyond repair, even by a Huragok," Zo observed sadly. He sat back in the chair, and adjusted his antigrav belt to remove a point or two of his weight. But it didn't help much; the pressure was all in his mind. "Maybe I should journey with you to Sanghelios . . . if you really believe I will not be summarily executed there upon our arrival."

"You will be under our protection," Tul said. "When we tell them our story, you may even be revered there!"

Zo grunted skeptically. "If the rest of you do not wish to continue the search . . . then I cannot insist. I have no authority here. And Sanghelios would be one of my very few options." He looked at the twisted, blackened bits of machinery piled on the table. "I had hoped to find something else among asteroids and debris. Something that might connect me with my ancestor, the Prophet of Inner Conviction. He often lamented about the failings of his own people, as have I, and it seemed that we were brought here by sheer fate." He refused to admit to himself that he might well be the last living San'Shyuum.

D'ero's voice crackled from a comm grid on the wall. "Zo Resken! There is something up here you will want to see. Come to the bridge."

Suddenly the excess weight lifted away from Zo and he sprang to his feet, moved quickly past Tul and G'torik, and almost collided with the Huragok, which just managed to jet out of his way.

Soon he was entering the bridge of the *Journey's Sustenance.* "D'ero, you called and I have come . . ."

Tul, G'torik, and the Huragok had followed, arriving a few moments later, as Zo sat down in the copilot's seat beside D'ero.

"There!" grumbled the captain.

He pointed at the holoscope, which showed a three-dimensional view of a crowded section of the asteroid belt. Great whirling stones, some rimed with ice, tumbled past one another; the light was stark, coming from the sun on one side; the dark sides of each asteroid were inky black.

"What am I to see here?" Zo asked, puzzled.

D'ero tapped at the scope's controls, and the image magnified, zooming in. Still Zo saw nothing—until two gigantic ragged-edged chunks of rock rolled out of the way, revealing a sharp-edged silvery object. Clearly it was artificial, its shape odd and yet organized; it was forged material, at a glance, like the fragments piled on the table. But it was much larger than any artificial object they had encountered in the asteroid belt, and even the *Journey's Sustenance*.

The object remained relatively stable, not spinning like those around it. And along its surface was a shimmering coat of force.

"Incredible," Zo said breathlessly. "We were here all this time, and it still managed to avoid detection."

"It is *operational*, judging from the force field," Tul said, looking over his shoulder. "And someone has kept it that way. Zo—we may have just stumbled upon the Ussan colony."

"Are we truly going there?" D'ero asked. "Because chances are, they will not be friendly to intruders. If we reveal ourselves, we may not receive a warm reception. We may have to fight for our lives."

CHAPTER 21

Bal'Tol was pacing back and forth in front of the monitors. "Are they through the hull yet?" he asked, again, as Xelq 'Tylk, the scout-eye operator, moved the surveillance bot in for a closer view.

"They are now removing the plate, Kaidon." Xelq was squat, stocky, powerful of arm. He had mandibles with a number of small metallic studs punctured into them—studs made from metal he'd found in the debris field. He had once been an up-and-coming floatfighter, but had given it up to work in Colony External Maintenance. His preference was being out in space, going on several expeditions to tug dangerously close asteroids to higher orbits, and was one of the few Bal'Tol trusted in the small maintenance vehicles.

Bal'Tol looked at the monitor, could see the eight-legged maintenance vehicle, like an arachnoid of metal, clinging to the hull of Section Two. On either side of it were metal-and-crystal cylinders, field interruption stations, each producing a transmission wavelength that had allowed them to be magnetically fixed to Section Two's outer hull. Expanded to interlace, the fields had provided entry for the external maintenance vehicle by breaking up the repellent field in that discrete area. It also extended a containment field over the gap opened in the hull, to keep the air pressure in. There was an internal air lock, as well, a pressurization fail-safe.

Bal'Tol could just make out the rough square where C'tenz and the others had cut through the hull, using Forerunner technology no one quite understood, beams of light that seemed to move narrow lines of materials apart, as if the hull material was simply persuaded on a molecular level to move out of the way. But if a Sangheili chanced to put his bare hand in the beam of light, perchance, no harm was done.

Bal'Tol could see half of each of the three Sangheili on the mission—C'tenz, Torren, and V'ornik—on the mission, each one limned on the left side by the sun, the other half invisible in pitch-black shadow.

"Cannot you move the scout-eye in a little closer?" he asked.

"If I do, at that range, there is risk. It is one more anomaly to be spotted by 'Kinsa's followers," Xelq said.

"Very well . . ." Bal'Tol muttered. He had a dark foreboding about this mission. "I wish I had gone along."

"You, Kaidon? It is I who should have gone. But C'tenz said I would be needed here. Torren and V'ornik have almost no experience in pressure suits."

"How you *do* reassure me," Bal'Tol said acidly as he resumed pacing. He had never admitted to himself, before now, how very much C'tenz meant to him. Truly, he felt that C'tenz was like a son to him. And yet he had sent him on a suicide mission.

Bal'Tol stopped in front of another monitor that showed an internal view of the new isolation ward in the Primary Section.

He could see Qerspa 'Tel, the biorep, calmly noting symptoms in a voice recorder as he stood over one of the snarling third-phase patients strapped to a cot. His heart sank at the sight. Was there any hope for his people?

Sometimes Bal'Tol thought he could feel the desperation of all the Ussan Sangheili like a tightening cable—each strand in the cable another Ussan—keening as it readied to snap.

"We are entering the hull," said C'tenz softly.

The transmission spurred Bal'Tol to hurry back to the drone monitor. He couldn't see any of them now. They'd slipped through the gap.

"Shall I activate his helmet transmitter?" Xelq asked.

"Not unless they are discovered. The enemy might detect the signal."

"We have located the air lock to the . . ." There was a moment of static. Then, *"The air lock is opening from the other side. Torren! Back, get back to the . . . they are here, they—"*

"Xelq! Switch on the visual!" Bal'Tol commanded.

A moment, and then the image flickered to life in another monitor, the feed from Torren's helmet. "I am receiving only Torren so far!"

Bal'Tol stared and saw, from the point of view of the visual recorder on Torren's helmet, a glass-helmeted face grimacing in hatred, a face with the red webmarks of the Blood Sickness. One of 'Kinsa's, wearing a pressure suit. "They must have been aware of the intrusion for a while now," Bal'Tol said, his pulse thumping. And then there was a blurred motion, and an ax smashed into Torren's faceplate, Sangheili blue blood splashing on it, covering the gleeful face of the attacker, the sound of Torren screaming in pain.

"I have C'tenz," Xelq muttered.

And the monitor image changed. It was the visual on C'tenz's helmet as he looked at the Blood Sick adherent who'd murdered Torren, straightening up with the bloody ax, turning, lunging, the weapon raised, howling at C'tenz.

Five flashes as C'tenz quickly fired his plasma rifle . . . there might have been a sixth, but there was a clicking that informed Bal'Tol the rifle had malfunctioned after the final shot. Many of the colony's weapons were breaking down.

He saw the enemy still staggering at C'tenz, then C'tenz's rifle smashing the damaged lunatic's helmet, as he swung like a hammer—his foe collapsed, but then five more rushed at C'tenz, dragging him down, their faces crowding the monitor . . .

Which quickly went black.

"What—where is he?" Bal'Tol asked breathlessly.

"I—they damaged his recorder—"

"Try switching to V'ornik!" Bal'Tol shouted.

"I can't pick up his transmission."

"Then use the scout-eye, Xelq!"

A flicker and the monitor switched to the view of the scout-eye, maintaining the orb's position near the arachnoid maintenance craft. There, V'ornik in his pressure suit was jumping, in the area of low gravity, out through the gap cut in the hull. A spurt of energy or a projectile—it went by too fast for Bal-Tol to be sure—zipped up past V'ornik as he scrambled to the hatch of the small vessel. He vanished inside, and the hatch closed.

The vehicle quickly lifted off—but one enemy, in a pressure suit, was emerging from the hull gap, and then another, the two of them firing sidearms at the eight-legged maintenance vehicle, scoring its sides with black marks, one shot finding its way into the repulsor tube.

A blue-white flare vented from the repulsor tube, and the vehicle went spinning off into the void, its engine damaged.

Bal'Tol stared, feeling weak from grief in one instant and

energized with fury the next. "I will call every soldier, every able Sangheili we have! If they have murdered C'tenz, I will do whatever I must to extinguish this blight from the colony."

There was a crackling from a monitor—and then suddenly it showed the face of 'Kinsa himself, up close. He was using the helmet taken from C'tenz.

"Bal'Tol—are you there?" 'Kinsa demanded, leering.

"Transmit my voice, Xelq!" Bal'Tol said hoarsely. " 'Kinsa—can you hear me?"

"Ah, there is the kaidon! But *I* am the kaidon now—you are the false kaidon! The Forgotten Gods call to you. Submit yourself to the outer emptiness, Bal'Tol. Do that within, and your precious C'tenz will not die!" 'Kinsa's face was marked with the red mesh of the Blood Sickness, but there was a trembling insistent control in him. He seemed to be right on the edge of losing control—yet always in cunning command. "He is well known to be your favorite—will you keep him alive, Bal'Tol? Then surrender to me!"

Bal'Tol's eyes had swung to another monitor. Something was there—and an idea formed . . .

"Suppose that we let the Forgotten Gods decide, 'Kinsa? Any gods you like. Let them decide. Your people against mine in the Combat Section. Floatfight, 'Kinsa! I will be there—as will you. Ten against ten! That will be the way of it! All surveillance nodes will be trained on the fight; everyone will see. What do you say? If we lose—all of our fates are in your hands."

"The Combat Section . . . ?" 'Kinsa drew back. Behind him were several figures, two carrying weapons. C'tenz was there, bound with wires, lying on the floor. The figure moved—C'tenz was still alive. "The floatfight has never before been used in that way. Why should we do it?"

"You can demonstrate for all to see that the gods are truly on your side. And it will all be over shortly. If you are afraid of me . . . if you have not the honor to meet me in Combat Section . . . everyone will soon know of it."

A priestly figure armored with a patchy cuirass stepped into view. "We should speak of this. I hear the Forgotten Gods sing of it. Forerunner Sun and Forerunner Moon would make you the conqueror, 'Kinsa!"

"I will . . . consider the offer," 'Kinsa said reluctantly, and switched off the monitor.

Xelq stared at Bal'Tol as if he were the one gone insane with Blood Sickness. "But what if it goes against you, Kaidon?"

"I cannot attack the sections directly without killing everyone in them, including the innocent. All that we need to repair the colony would be lost in the battle. And C'tenz would die. This way . . . we bring 'Kinsa out in the open. And we'll finally have a chance to finish him."

"The Blood Sickness might prompt them to accept . . . it makes them yearn for confrontation."

"Yes—such a challenge is innate to their madness," Bal'Tol said. "I believe he will accept. It is the only way to save C'tenz and end this conflict once and for all."

**The _Journey's Sustenance_, a Supply Ship for
the Fleet of Blessed Veneration
Ussan System
2553 CE
The Age of Reclamation**

"You are correct," D'ero declared. "There _is_ a battle raging there— and a damaged craft. Something for exterior hull work."

D'ero, Tul, G'torik, and Zo Resken were on the bridge of the *Journey's Sustenance*, gazing raptly at their holographic imaging tracker. They could see the slowly spinning eight-legged maintenance vehicle, moving away from the enormous, geometrically odd artifact. Possibly some form of colony.

"This could be an opportunity," Zo said. "D'ero, will you be guided by me?"

"I do not know what else to do, in the face of all this, other than be guided by you."

"Then get as close as you safely can to that small vessel. Keep out of probable firing range from the colony there, if that's truly what it is . . ."

"It will be done."

The small, tumbling vehicle, like an arachnid blown on the wind, spun slowly through the void—closer and closer as D'ero approached.

"Will the tugfield have enough power to stop it?" Zo asked.

"Possibly. You wish to bring it into the freight hold?"

"I do, if there are no signs that it is near destruction."

"I will scan it, but cannot offer surety that the object is stable."

They took the risk and tugged it into the freight air lock. A *clunk* was felt all through *Journey's Sustenance* as the artificial gravity and pressurization were returned to the freight hold and the small vehicle banged down onto the deck. They could see it on the ship's internal monitors; it had landed on its leglike struts, but one of them was badly damaged and the vessel was tilted askew, giving off smoke.

Great Ones, if you are the gods I once believed you to be, please don't let my actions kill us all, Zo thought as he and G'torik and Tul armed themselves with carbines and rushed to the ramp that would take them down to the freight hold hatchway.

Zo took a long breath and then opened the hatch, stepping through. The air was acrid with a metallic burning smell. Smoke was coiled near the ceiling.

Zo took the lead, calling out, "Is anyone alive in there?"

"They might not be able to hear you through the hull," Tul remarked.

Zo ducked under the vehicle's fuselage, feeling heat pouring off it, and came to the hatchway. He reached out to it—

But the hatch opened on its own; a ladder extruded, and a coughing Sangheili half climbed, half fell down onto the deck, followed by a wisp of smoke. He was armed with a blade of a sort Zo had never seen. He wore a pressure suit—a rather antique one, more cumbersome than anything Zo knew, but he'd taken off his helmet.

The stranger turned, wiping his eyes, and then stared at Zo as if he weren't sure he was seeing correctly.

"Ah, yes, I suspect you may never have seen a San'Shyuum in person," said Zo. He lowered his weapon. "I am Zo Resken, once called the Prophet of Clarity. We mean you no harm, if you in turn mean us none."

The Sangheili gaped—then looked, blinking, at Tul and G'torik. The stranger spoke, but Zo couldn't quite decipher the dialect. Something about the gods . . . ?

"Did you understand that?" Zo asked, looking at G'torik and Tul.

"Somewhat," said Tul ruefully. "It sounds like Old Sangheili. Words I don't know, strange accents. But I think he was asking if you were one of the gods."

"Speak slowly to him, as well as you can, and tell him I am merely a friend to the Sangheili. Tell him we mean him no harm."

Tul conveyed the message, and the stranger signified understanding.

"Prophet!" called D'ero, on the comm system.

Zo didn't bother to correct him on such a point anymore; could he be a prophet if the prophecies he once held sacred were proven false? "What is it?"

"That craft—get away from it! The ship says it's highly unstable. Get out of there! I must eject it from the air lock—now!"

"Everyone out!" Zo called, hurrying toward the door.

Tul spoke to the newcomer, and they all rushed toward the hatch. In moments they were through it and G'torik slammed it shut. "Decompress and eject, D'ero!" he shouted.

Zo rushed up the ramp to the corridor and the bridge. He felt the ship shiver as the small craft was released, and hurried to the holomonitor that tracked it out into space. He saw the vessel, in miniature in the holo, spinning away in the void before it exploded. The flames were there only a split second, snuffed out by the vacuum. A few seconds later the hull clattered, some of the fragments striking it.

"Any breach in the hull?" Zo asked.

"Nothing broke through," D'ero reported, looking at his instruments. He turned to take a long suspicious look at the stranger, who was gawking around the bridge. "Prophet . . . you think he could have deliberately caused that craft to explode? Perhaps it was a trap."

"I do not think so," Zo said. "I think he is but a dazed, lost Sangheili. We will attach translators; give one to him, and with those and the language we have in common, we can hope to understand one another."

The translator devices were small disks that affixed to the skin above hearing membranes. Once they were affixed, with the ship providing cybernetic input, Tul introduced everyone on the bridge to the stranger. He replied, speaking slowly. "My name . . . that by which you call me . . . it is V'ornik 'Gred. I am living there—" He pointed at the colony section visible in a holoviewer. "This. The Refuge."

"Ussa 'Xellus—this is his colony?" Zo asked, speaking slowly.

"Yes. Ussa colony. You? Where are you from?"

Zo sighed. Where indeed was he from? Nowhere, now. "I grew up in High Charity. You likely don't know what I'm talking about. D'ero 'S'bud—he is from Sanghelios itself."

V'ornik's eyes widened. "Not possible."

"Oh, but it is," said D'ero. "I grew up in Zolam, a state in the southern parts of the continent of Qivro. I ranged the hills hunting *maegophet* and *doarmir*—and I have even killed a *helioskrill* with a spear, in the ancient way."

V'ornik stepped a little closer to D'ero, reached out a trembling hand . . . and D'ero suffered his shoulder to be touched.

"Yes," said D'ero. "I am real; a mortal being . . . from Sanghelios."

"You will . . . take us there? Sanghelios?"

"Now, that I suppose is a larger question. We have to know we can trust you first."

Zo turned to D'ero. "You are captain of this vessel. I wish for us to move closer to the colony—and I wish to take our own maintenance craft there. Will you permit this? And stay nearby, as long as you can wait for me?"

"You are thinking this one here can get you into the colony safely?"

"I am going to attempt just that. If he is willing. I have to make contact with these people. This discovery . . . you don't realize what this means to me. I must go to the colony."

"You are not going alone, Prophet." D'ero looked at G'torik. "You must go with this fool, if he is so insistent."

"Then you think me such a fool, too?" G'torik asked. "Your supposition is right. So I *am*."

"Here is one more fool, then," said Tul, tapping his own chest.

Then the Huragok came in, drifting over the floor, snaking its head curiously toward the stranger. It stretched tentacles out to him, signaling a desire to repair his pressure suit.

V'ornik scrambled backward from Sluggish Drifter, snarling, snapping mandibles, raising his weapon.

"No!" Tul said, stepping between them. "He serves us. Repairs what is broken."

V'ornik seemed repelled by the Huragok. He clearly had never seen one.

"Yes," said Zo, struck by a thought. "Sluggish Drifter repairs things, V'ornik. Is there much that needs repairing on your colony?"

V'ornik looked at him. "Yes. Very much. So very much. That . . . thing can repair our world?"

"Much of it. Yes. Things you cannot repair, often the Huragok can."

"Then . . . we will go. All of us."

The Refuge, the Ussan Colony
Primary Refuge
2553 CE
The Age of Reclamation

"What?" Xelq blurted. *"Me?"*

"Yes. He chose you to wear this."

Xelq had stepped into the hallway from the colony control center, looking for the kaidon. Qerspa 'Tel meanwhile had just arrived, looking for Xelq. Qerspa put the necklace of rank around Xelq 'Tylk's neck. It signified that he spoke for the kaidon in Bal'Tol's absence. "He seemed to think that if the vessel that has approached is a danger to us, you are the best one to deal with it in his absence. Your experience with zero gravity, I presume. You are 'acting kaidon.' But do not excite yourself—I am sure Bal'Tol will return and you will be a mere technology supervisor once more."

"He is not really going to the Combat Section now, is he? Already? He believes this nonsense about the gods judging the contest?"

"He must. 'Kinsa has been pressured by his followers to accept the challenge. He is there with his chosen ten already. But this is no floatfight—not truly. It is a chance for each side to kill the other's leaders. That's the truth of it."

"And the kaidon's orders for me?"

"You are to communicate with the aliens in the vessel, if it is possible. If they seem dangerous, use what weaponry we have to keep them at bay until he returns. If they can give us aid, then use your own judgment."

Xelq groaned. "I should be there with him! I am good in zero gravity. And I was once a good floatfighter—"

"Who is there? Kaidon?" The voice came from behind Xelq. He turned and realized it was coming from the near-space receiver. *"This is V'ornik!"*

Xelq recognized the voice and hurried to the transmitter. "It's Xelq here, V'ornik. Where are you? We thought you dead!"

"I am alive, and I am on a ship with a Sangheili. He has come here from Sanghelios! And stranger things yet! Adjust the repellent field—we are coming in another maintenance craft. Let us in!"

"Are you Blood Sick? You are speaking madness! We are already under attack!"

"They are mostly Sangheili—from Sanghelios itself!"

"What? And you believe this?"

"I do. And they can repair things we cannot, Xelq! Let me speak to the kaidon—let *them* speak to him!"

"He is not here . . . I am in charge for the moment but . . . I cannot allow such a thing!"

"You have always thought me a fool, Xelq, but this time you must trust me! They are here to help us! Just this once—trust me!"

**The Refuge, the Ussan Colony
Combat Section
2553 CE
The Age of Reclamation**

Bal'Tol was fitted with the chest armor and helmet allowed to floatfighters; he had a quartermoon blade in one hand and a spiked cudgel in the other. He floated close to the push boards, beside the cables of the netting. With him was Z'nick 'Berda, the best available floatfighter, and eight other Sangheili with some experience at it, most of them patrollers—colony security—with some experience in combat.

V'urm 'Kerdeck, the one-eyed hero of floatfighting, was poised across the zero-gravity arena, floating in place, tugging on a spiked glove. Even half blind, he was the most dangerous opponent here. There were nine others beside him, 'Kinsa adherents readying themselves. But it was V'urm who held Bal'Tol's gaze.

"Z'nick," Bal'Tol said. "Beware—there is no protective grid for the helmets." He added dryly, "V'urm 'Kerdeck himself is here."

"Just stay behind me, my Kaidon—I will deal with V'urm. He is even older than I am."

The priest—in truth a pseudopriest, since he represented a false faith—was harnessed to a wall bracket behind the net. He had a burnblade in his hand, and held it near C'tenz, who was bound, head to foot, himself tied to a bracket.

Bal'Tol watched and saw C'tenz squirm in his bonds. "Where is 'Kinsa?"

"There!" Z'nick said, pointing.

'Kinsa was coming through the open metal doors in the curved metal wall behind his fighters, lined up raggedly as they bobbed in the gravity-free arena.

'Kinsa had a mec-missile launcher in his hand.

"'Kinsa makes eleven," Z'nick observed. "It is supposed to be ten on ten. And he has a weapon that is not traditional here. Quite dangerous."

"Perhaps that was why he pushed for doing this so quickly. We have no choice. And we have a chance, despite that there are no rules here—his adherents may buckle if he dies."

The champion was the first to leap into space, but the others followed almost immediately, pushing off and twisting, angling, swinging one another about in practiced moves that would get them where they wanted. The stretch-lines pulled taut between floor and ceiling, passed through the space of the room here and there, to be used as additional propellant bases.

I'll have to take on 'Kinsa's champion, Bal'Tol thought, *because he is coming right for me. Kill him. Then get to C'tenz and free him. And kill 'Kinsa if I get the chance . . .*

Bal'Tol positioned himself to push off from the wall, but Z'nick had already launched himself on a trajectory to intersect V'urm.

Cursing under his breath, Bal'Tol pushed off, his stomach whirling as he rocketed through zero gravity, thinking he would end up overshooting V'urm. But V'urm was already engaging with

Z'nick, slashing with one hand, crunching with the spiked fist of the other, cracking Z'nick in the helmet so that he spun in the air. Z'nick tumbled and rolled to slide out of reach, avoiding the slash that would have disemboweled him if it had connected.

Then Bal'Tol was there, but awkwardly positioned, and could only passingly clout V'urm with his cudgel, making the floatfight hero's helmet ring and knocking him out of reach.

Flying past, Bal'Tol glimpsed V'urm grabbing a stretch-line, spinning on it, coming back.

Bal'Tol suddenly felt an instinctive warning, and turned to see a mec-missile coming at him. He twisted left, so the arrowlike bolt of metal slashed by, scraping along his neck.

He saw 'Kinsa in the distance cranking another mec-missile into place. So the bolt that nearly skewered his throat had come from 'Kinsa.

Bal'Tol grabbed a stretch-line and spun, so that the next bolt missed as well. One of 'Kinsa's followers was there, suddenly, roaring as he flew at Bal'Tol, slashing with a burnblade. Bal'Tol blocked it hard with his own blade, and the impact knocked his adversary askew, giving Bal'Tol a chance to bring the cudgel into play. He smashed it underhand into his enemy's knee and felt bone shatter. Shrieking and bent double with pain, he was within reach of Bal'Tol, who then stabbed his blade into his mouth.

Another bolt flashed past Bal'Tol, reminding him that 'Kinsa was somewhere on the perimeters. If he could find 'Kinsa and kill him, then this savage fight for the colony might come to some resolution.

His view of 'Kinsa was blocked by a cluster of three Sangheili—two of Bal'Tol's patrollers and a very large adherent, all tangled up with one another as they struggled.

Airborne puddles of purplish Sangheili blood were spreading

in the zero-grav environment. Three patrollers floated by limply, clearly dead. One was almost decapitated, his head just hanging on to his neck by a strip of skin.

Bal'Tol pushed off from a stretch-line, and rocketed over the cluster of three fighters. One of his own was dead and the other was being choked in the spiked grip of the large follower, who was luridly webbed with the marks of Blood Sickness. Bal'Tol was well positioned above the strangler, and stabbed down hard on the back of the enemy's exposed neck, severing the spine. The impact stopped Bal'Tol, making him wrench about in space as he tried to hold on to his weapon, so that he was swung through a floating cloud of Sangheili blood. He had to spit some from his mouth, and lost his grip on the wet, slick sword hilt.

He came out of the blood cloud, straightening up in midair, still floating with momentum.

Perhaps now is the time to get to C'tenz, set him free . . .

Blood and struggling fighters blocked his view of C'tenz. *Find him!*

Then Bal'tol saw V'urm coming toward him, one mandible half broken off, fresh wounds making his face almost unrecognizable. Bal'Tol could only see that one eye glaring out of a mask of purple gore.

Beyond him floated the body of Z'nick.

V'urm was flying at Bal'Tol head-on, body stretched out behind him, quartermoon blade sweeping up, roaring out a battle cry: "Death to the false kaidon! Long live 'Kinsa!"

Bal'Tol swam in the air to one side, brought his knees up, and kicked at V'urm.

V'urm grabbed at the kicking foot and used it to pull Bal'Tol close. "An amateur's move!" he sneered. He swung his blade at Bal'Tol's neck. The kaidon writhed back, so the quartermoon struck a glancing blow but rang resoundingly on Bal'Tol's helmet. A spike of pain lanced through his skull. Anomalous lights danced in Bal'Tol's eyes, nausea swept through him, and his hearing seemed to twist itself in a knot of unintelligibility. He struggled to get into a fighting position, to strike his enemy with his cudgel, but V'urm was positioned over Bal'Tol, quartermoon blade set to rip through the kaidon's neck. V'urm leered in triumph.

A bolt of red light from somewhere behind Bal'Tol seared into V'urm's face, and instantly charred it to a crisp.

CHAPTER 22

A hole as large as Bal'Tol's hand was burned through V'urm's face—a tunnel of blackened flesh, right through the middle of his head and out the other side.

The dead floatfighter then drifted by, entering a cloud of blood, and seemed to turn languidly in it, as if bathing.

I'm having strange thoughts. And then Bal'Tol considered, more to the point: *Who killed V'urm, and how did they do it?*

"Greetings, Kaidon of the Refuge," said a lilting voice, vaguely male in tone.

He felt himself grasped by invisible hands—a tugfield of some kind, turning him around. He saw that the other surviving fighters were all pushed back against the walls. Gawking, staring at the thing that held Bal'Tol in place.

The legendary Enduring Bias was hovering before Bal'Tol, almost in reach, glass lenses glowing, whirring with machine health. The AI was in perfect control of its position, seeming at ease in zero gravity.

"Am I dreaming?" Bal'Tol wondered aloud.

"As to that, I cannot testify," said Enduring Bias. "You were struck a good blow on the head. Your helmet was damaged. Thus you could be concussed, and subject to hallucinations from brain injury. However, I can attest that I am quite objectively real."

"You are truly here?"

"Yes. I am restored and fully functional. More than once I requested that Sooln acquire a Huragok. But she was never successful. Then I suffered damage when we were struck by the comet fragment, and for centuries, I was quiescent. I was sometimes able to listen, as much time passed. Now the Huragok has come at last, and I can proceed with my duties once more. I am frankly grateful to the visitors from Sanghelios and High Charity."

"Sanghelios . . . It exists? It is real?" Bal'Tol felt queasy, and not quite himself. The whirling blood, the bodies, all seemed to blur together.

"Yes. I have never been to Sanghelios, but I think we can reasonably infer that it is objectively real. High Charity is real, or at least was real according to their testimony."

"High Charity? I don't know . . . that place . . ." The room was swirling around him. He blinked hard and tried to focus. The swirling receded. And then he heard a shout of warning. Was that Xelq's voice? Bal'Tol looked around—and saw that 'Kinsa was aiming his mec-missiler, and from not far away. He was aiming it not at the kaidon, but at Enduring Bias.

"No!" Bal'Tol shouted. " 'Kinsa, don't! He is from the gods! It is—"

The bolt flew directly at Enduring Bias, and deflected in midair. The crude missile snapped, and its pieces spun away.

Then a bolt of burning red light jetted out from Enduring Bias, and struck 'Kinsa in the chest, burning its way through his hearts.

'Kinsa went limp and drifted off, trailing smoke and blood.

He looked for C'tenz, and the priest who'd guarded him. The priest had fled—but someone was with C'tenz. *Hard to see . . . V'ornik!*

Yes. V'ornik was there, floating over to C'tenz, cutting him loose.

"C'tenz . . ." Bal'Tol muttered.

"My scan suggests the one identified as C'tenz will need medical attention," Enduring Bias remarked. "He must be attended to immediately. And so must you. Please come with me." Bal'Tol found himself towed gently through the air. "You have two very capable clanfellows in Xelq and V'ornik, Kaidon," Enduring Bias went on as he flew ahead, Bal'Tol behind him with a tug field. "They cooperated when there was no logical alternative. That is precisely when one should engage in such a risk. Xelq, on V'ornik's advice, allowed the San'Shyuum to enter—so interesting to meet him!—and three Sangheili, and the Huragok, from the outworld vessel, and it has been delightful to engage the services of the Huragok. So very talented. A beautifully bioengineered creature. It quickly restored me to working order. I knew Ussa 'Xellus quite well, you know, and I am fairly certain of what he would want me to do now . . ."

"Ussa 'Xellus . . ."

"Yes. I understand he is your ancestor. I am quite interested in learning the niceties of culture here. I have listened and heard a great deal, but I have many questions."

They had reached the hatch to exit the floatfight chamber, and Bal'Tol saw someone blocking the way. 'Kinsa's priest.

But the priest abruptly stripped off his cuirass, threw it aside, and knelt—that is, he formed his body in a kneeling position, floating that way in zero gravity. "O messenger of Forerunner Sun and Moon! O Flying Voice! How many times did I walk beside your preserved form, supposing it an empty shell, not knowing you were but biding your time! I doubted and followed 'Kinsa! Forgive me, O messenger of the gods! I cry out in contrition!"

"Certainly," said Enduring Bias blithely. "You are quite forgiven, and you are thoroughly redeemed, if the kaidon wills it. Now, please move aside. I wish to get the kaidon to a place of medical assistance."

The Refuge, the Ussan Colony
Section Five
2553 CE
The Age of Reclamation

They were in a decrepit but operational section-to-section shuttle, Zo Resken gazing out the front windows, as the craft silently approached the air lock. G'torik and Tul were back on the passenger deck with their armed escort, the Huragok, and amazingly, an Oracle, hailed as Enduring Bias.

Xelq was piloting, his motions smooth, in the seat to Zo's left. He glanced at Zo—his eyes lingered on what was, to him, an alien form. "Zo Resken, I'm concerned that even Enduring Bias cannot find a way into Section Five."

Infected by Xelq's skepticism, Zo, too, doubted that the Oracle could relax the repellent shield and open the air lock to Section Five.

But gliding up to join them, Enduring Bias said, "I am integrated into the programming of this colony, even in its present form. Every system has a connected workaround, which I myself designed, that I can now implement. For example . . ."

The flickering shield over the air lock vanished; the doors unsealed and opened.

Muttering unintelligibly, but with a tone of wonder, Xelq flew the small craft neatly into its hangar. The doors closed behind them; the hangar repressurized.

"So what now?" Zo asked. "Isn't it likely there are still these rebels you speak of, even with their leader dead? That some won't want to give up the territory they've seized? I can assure you, there will be resistance."

"Yes, that is likely," said Xelq. "And there is some danger from the Blood Sick. But . . . we will send our patrollers out first, and the god messenger. We shall keep the Huragok in the shuttle until needed—why expose something so valuable to enemy fire?"

Something so valuable. What an understatement, Zo thought.

Enduring Bias was priceless—a living relic of the Forerunners. Who knew what secrets it nursed within its memory banks?

And the colony itself! Each section was a magnificent Forerunner artifact. Yes, it was timeworn, and blotted by use. The air was musky and coarse. The walls were often dingy. But within those scarred and smudged walls lay the intact submolecular machinations of the Forerunners. Doubtless there were numerous functions the Ussans knew nothing about—power and entelechy, energy and possibility secreted away, unused but intact, within those panels.

In many places, Zo thought, the Sangheili's own innovations were a kind of technological crust over the Forerunners' design—the control center with its monitors, the pressure suits, the eco-level agricultural systems, were all added on by the Ussans. But even the Ussans' humble innovation was fascinating, tantalizing to Zo's historian soul. This new, peculiar Sangheili subculture could generate a hundred scholarly treatises.

What would Zo's ancestor, the Prophet of Inner Conviction,

think, if he could have seen all this? He would likely rejoice—there were lifetimes of study to be had here. And Zo Resken had only one lifetime.

If only he had another San'Shyuum to share it with, children to pass it all on to. But he was alone.

The thought sent a pang through him, and he forced himself to focus on the problem at hand. They had to enter this section safely, put down any remaining resistance . . . and try to save this dying colony any way they could.

Minutes later—led by eight heavily armed patrollers, and Enduring Bias—Zo, G'torik, Tul, and Xelq crossed the open space of the small hangar and passed through two doors. There were only four rocket launchers still working in the entire colony. They were normally kept locked in a small armory, rarely ever opened. Bal'Tol had given permission for two launchers to be passed out, with nine rounds each. There were only known to be thirty shells left in all of the Refuge. Most Ussans had never seen these weapons.

The two armed Sangheili patrollers then entered the main corridor ahead of the Ussan column, and brought the launchers into play as mec-missiler bolts flew at them from recessed doorways—the missiles were burned away in midair by Enduring Bias.

Several irregular pulses missed the Ussans, fired from a rickety, antiquated plasma rifle.

The patrollers, eager to use their newfound weapons, fired back at the doorways with rocket launchers. Twin fireballs suddenly appeared and expanded, startling the patrollers themselves. The enemy was flung burning through the air, dead before falling to the deck.

The column, with Zo, G'torik, and Tul at the rear, continued down the corridor, picking their way over smoking corpses.

Living history, Zo thought. *I am a vector of history here, large and small. It is unsettling, exhilarating, horrifying all at once.*

"Are we making a record of what is happening here?" Zo asked, looking up at Enduring Bias.

"Yes, I am recording all that happens here," said Enduring Bias. "As per instructions, I am transmitting it via the devices the colonists refer to as 'godminds,' sending the visual feed to all the colony spaces where living beings are found. They are now witnessing what happens as we proceed, so that they may modify their behavior accordingly."

They reached the plaza outside the Hall of Godminds and entered the sculpture garden. Zo, for his part, was noticing the smell. The colony's air had seemed rank to him, from the moment he'd set foot in it. It was particularly bad here. The reek of unwashed clothing and even raw sewage came from the clotted corners of the room. Scrawled on the walls were writings, which Zo could not read. The florid red lettering suggested angry denunciation.

Some of the sculptures had been knocked down, too, he saw. A pity—he would have enjoyed assessing their cultural history.

"What has happened here?" asked Enduring Bias. It hovered over a pile of rubble, on which there were two broken heads shaped from some dark synthetic material. The heads had taken a beating, but the Bias recognized them. "Why, that was an image of Ussa 'Xellus, and his spouse, Sooln 'Xellus. Someone has vandalized their images! Why, I wonder . . ."

"Ussa 'Xellus was a symbol of the 'Xellus clan," Zo said. "Bal'Tol is of that clan. So Ussa's images were purged by the enemies of his clan. That, anyway, is my surmise."

The advance patrollers stepped cautiously, the group going to the doorway of the Hall of Godminds—and were promptly met by weapons fire. Projectiles and burning, handmade grenades, steel bolts, and energy blasts all came their way.

Zo and his companions took cover behind the sculptures. An image of a floatfighter hero took several sizzling charges for Zo, and then the rocket launchers fired twice in response, with coughing sounds. The shells detonated to screams and cries of agonized rage.

"Cease fire here!" commanded Enduring Bias, in a voice suddenly taking on an unprecedented deep-toned authority. "You will damage the machinery! Leave this resolution to me!"

The intelligence construct glided through the door, its repellent field turning several missiles in midflight. Then it began its own offense, the heat beam choosing targets with exact analytical precision, so as not to damage the mechanisms underlying the forms of colored light that hummed in the Hall of Godminds.

There were short, abortive shrieks, then several voices pleading for mercy. "We did not know you!"

"Forgive me . . . forgive us!"

"Lay down your arms and surrender, and perhaps Bal'Tol will give you amnesty," said Enduring Bias. "I shall recommend it. The decision, however, is solely his."

But two unrepentants rushed out, howling, their faces riddled with pulsing networks of scarlet.

Enduring Bias exterminated them in less than a second.

"Now," Enduring Bias said, as those who had surrendered filed out. "I suspect there will be little resistance hereafter. We must proceed to the protein synthesizer. I know what must be done there. Tul, I request that you go back to the shuttle, with appropriate protectors, and fetch the Huragok. It should be safe for the Engineer now. We will need its full assistance."

**The Refuge, the Ussan Colony
Primary Section
2553 CE
The Age of Reclamation**

Some time had passed since the sections had been systematically cleared of the few remaining followers of 'Kinsa. Not much resistance had been found after Section Five. The holographic blow-by-blow from the messenger of the gods had made the outcome clear for any who resisted.

Bal'Tol now stood at the dais, where Enduring Bias had silently lain dormant for centuries. The transparent case had been taken away and the intelligence now floated at Bal'Tol's right, as if in benediction. To Bal'Tol's left stood Xelq, V'ornik, and C'tenz. V'ornik had never looked so proud.

Bal'Tol glanced around, saw that the plaza held as many Sangheili as could crowd in. Others watched via remote access. Virtually the entire colony was watching, listening.

Also present was the San'Shyuum, Zo Resken, who stood a little apart with those Sangheili who claimed to have once been a part of the Covenant, and who had brought the San'Shyuum here. And there was also D'ero 'S'bud, watching from the *Journey's Sustenance* by way of a transmission from Enduring Bias.

"Clansfolk of the Refuge!" Bal'Tol called out. "Heed me!" He could hear his own voice echoing to other chambers through remote address grids. "A new era has dawned for us all! A time of revelation and epiphany approaches . . . and has come upon us this very day! We have all heard the news—how the dishonorable regime of the Covenant has fallen. How those who believed as we did have triumphed at last!"

There was a mass clicking of mandibles and a chorus of cheers at this.

Bal'Tol raised his hands for silence, and went on. "Earlier, I sat in meditation, and saw again order emerging from chaos. So it will always be: the endless dance between the two. I witnessed something more in that vision: a unity, a closing of the circle. I have been told that we are known as a lost tribe of Sanghelios. That some on Sanghelios still remember the people of Ussa 'Xellus, who traveled away and hid among the stars rather than surrender to the will of the Covenant. But at long last, it is time for us to reunite with our people on Sanghelios! Some of us may choose to remain, others will choose to travel to the homeworld. I assure you that a place is being made there for us. A new home, safe under an open sky!"

There were gasps and the shuffling of feet at that. Fearful murmurs.

"No one will be forced to go to Sanghelios. If you are not ready, you may remain here. And we are in the process of making this a safer colony to live in than ever before. The rumors are true—thanks to Enduring Bias and the Forerunners' Engineer, we have found a cure for the Blood Sickness. It was the protein synthesizer all along, which has been subtly malfunctioning for many cycles now. We have supplemented all meats and eco-level foods with synthetic protein for some time. Enduring Bias, working with the Engineer, located the source of the toxin—a viral subprotoid in the synthesis tubes. Once ingested, the toxin spawned the Blood Sickness. Some were more susceptible than others."

He paused, thinking of Limtee. *A cure. Too late for her. Too late . . .*

His voice ragged, Bal'Tol went on. "Now those we have isolated have begun to recover. The protein synthesizer has been repaired, and is safe. And under Enduring Bias's guidance, Qerspa 'Tel is even now refining an antitoxin that should cure the Blood Sick among us for all time."

Another rousing series of cheers.

Once more he held up his hands for silence. "And now . . . everyone proceed to your assigned stability stations. Enduring Bias will show you something miraculous. The colony is about to be transformed—exactly what Forerunner Sun and Forerunner Moon intended. Watch and wonder—we live in glorious times!"

Seats had extruded from the floor, unfolding, with straps, in the Primary Section's control room. Bal'Tol sat in the center of the small room; to his right and left were Zo Resken and C'tenz. V'ornik was there, behind him, beside Qerspa 'Tel, Xelq, G'torik, and Tul. Above them floated Enduring Bias.

"I am almost ready," said the construct. "Completing calculations."

"Zo—what will you do?" G'torik asked. "I mean, after this is completed?"

Bal'Tol glanced over his shoulder, curious. He had almost grown used to this strange, alien creature—this San'Shyuum.

"Ah," said Zo Resken. "What will I do? I have no real home. But what do I have here? A treasure trove, a glorious repository of scarcely understood Forerunner history. Who knows what other secrets wait here to be unfolded? If it is permitted to me, I will remain. I submit to the will of the kaidon."

"It is permitted," said Bal'Tol. "You brought our salvation to us. It would be an honor to have you remain here."

"What are we hoping to see, Kaidon?" asked C'tenz. He had mostly recovered from the severe punishment at the hands of 'Kinsa, but still appeared a bit bleary.

"Observe," Bal'Tol said.

A hologram appeared above them, projected by Enduring Bias. It showed the Primary Section of the colony moving through space. The image was broadcast from a scout-eye viewpoint, sent some distance out from the colony.

A jolt went through the room around them, the colony section itself seeming to creak and grumble. A great rumbling sound emanated from the walls . . . and the hologram showed the Primary Section moving, with repulsors glowing on one end.

Another section appeared, evading asteroids, yet coming inexorably toward Primary.

"Kaidon!" V'ornik blurted. "They're going to collide!"

"Have faith in the messenger of the gods," Bal'Tol said. But he had some private anxiety himself. Would this truly work, after so much time had passed?

This could all be a terrible mistake, a catastrophe in the making . . .

Then they saw Section Seven connect itself with Primary Section—it seemed to lock on with a precise wrist action from some giant invisible hand, and the colony around them vibrated, reverberating with the interface.

Bal'Tol remembered to breathe again.

Another section came into view . . .

Each one was a risk. If one of them was askew, disaster would follow. Why hadn't he left well enough alone?

He'd been clouded by success, by the promises of the new era. But now . . .

Another section clicked neatly home.

It happened again, and again. And an overall shape was emerging. A curve, a segment of a circle.

It took time. Bal'Tol's head injury, not fully healed, was beginning to throb by the time the final section connected.

But it was all there, as the Forerunners had intended.

It was a complete circle, the various sections united into one circular structure. The parts that had made it into a full sphere were long gone, shattered.

But the broken circle was whole once more. Ussans could move easily from one section to another, through a stabilized colony, one more alive in its unity.

"By the Great Ones," Zo Resken muttered, gazing at the holographic image of the united sections. "It looks like . . ."

"It does," said G'torik.

"It's smaller," said Zo. "It's not the same but . . . now, with the parts connected . . . it looks almost like one of the Sacred Rings."

Bal'Tol was both exuberant and saddened. All this time, he had been assuming he would be returning to the homeworld as well, that he would be going back to Sanghelios. He had dreamed that he, too, could complete that circle, a descendant of the legendary Ussa 'Xellus, returning to Sanghelios in triumph.

But he was the kaidon. If his people chose to remain—and a good many would—he must remain here, for their sakes. After all, sacrifice was expected of a leader.

Sacrifice was honorable.

Perhaps one day he would visit Sanghelios. But for now, he would stay in the place of his father and forefathers.

He could almost hear Ussa 'Xellus's voice. *Take care of my people, Bal'Tol. You are my blood. You, too, are 'Xellus.*

Bal'Tol sighed. Here, in the unbroken circle of the Refuge, he would remain, probably forever.

EPILOGUE

D'ero 'S'bud, for once, looked almost cheerful.

"And there, Xerq—do you see that? That is the Temple of the Sundered Sky. One of many Forerunner structures still standing in Zolam."

In truth, Xerq could see only the faintest gleam in the distance, below the mountains. But he had heard of Zolam, many times, from D'ero, who hailed from its outskirts. "Will you show me Zolam sometime, D'ero?"

"Yes. If . . ." He spread his mandibles in a Sangheili version of a scowl. "I should say—*when*. When it is safe for us to visit. There is still tension there, and danger of war. There are those still arguing for their madness, muttering of the glorious Great Journey. Foolishness still seems to be in abundance here. But then again, fools are found in every species on every world."

G'torik and C'tenz joined them on the ancient cupola built out upon the cliff side. In silence they gazed for a long moment at what they could see of Sanghelios. It was so unthinkably vast to

Xerq. It had never occurred to him before coming here how small the Refuge truly was.

But then he had always turned his thoughts outward, to space, the stars. The endless possibilities. And one had come to fruition— to be here, on the homeworld.

He stretched his arms, luxuriating in the sublime blend of strangeness and familiarity. He had at last adjusted to the gravity, the air sweeter than anything he had ever breathed.

And there was something about the sky—hints of yellow and blue with roseate touches, red at the horizon—that spoke to his very soul. He recognized this place, though he had never been here.

Ussa 'Xellus had led his ancestors away from this blessed place—and now, at last, millennia later, their descendants had returned. And to Xerq, it felt as if his forebears were here, too, along with Ussa 'Xellus, invisible but present, at his side, gazing out at the mountains, the plains, the golden sky, the distant cities . . .

Of Sanghelios itself.

And it was good, it was right to be here. As Bal'Tol had stated: order hidden within chaos, eventually emerging to reaffirm itself.

Another circle was completed with this return to the homeworld. A broken circle reconnected, just as the orbit of Sanghelios after a cycle's travel around the sun; as its two moons, Suban and Qikost, revolved around the planet, confirming, always, that this was the true homeworld of Sangheili.

"We have returned, Ussa 'Xellus . . ." C'tenz murmured, as if he'd been reading Xerq's thoughts. "Just as you had once said we would. We have returned at long last."

ACKNOWLEDGMENTS

JOHN SHIRLEY

Special thanks to Ed Schlesinger at Gallery Books, Jeremy Patenaude and everyone at 343 Industries, and my wife, Micky.

343 INDUSTRIES

343 Industries would like to thank Kendall Boyd, Scott Dell'Osso, John Liberto, Bonnie Ross-Ziegler, Ed Schlesinger, Rob Semsey, John Shirley, Matt Skelton, Phil Spencer, Kiki Wolfkill, and Carla Woo.

None of this would have been possible without the amazing efforts of the Halo Franchise Team, the Halo Consumer Products team, Nicolas Bouvier, Tiffany O'Brien, and Kenneth Peters, with special thanks to Jeremy Patenaude.

ABOUT THE AUTHOR

John Shirley is the author of numerous novels and books of short stories. His cyberpunk trilogy, *A Song Called Youth*, was recently rereleased in an omnibus edition from Prime Books. His story collection *Black Butterflies* won the Bram Stoker Award. His tie-in novels include those for *Bioshock*, *Borderlands*, and *Grimm*. He was co-screenwriter of *The Crow* and wrote for *Star Trek: Deep Space Nine* and other acclaimed television series. He lives in California.